He went to the kitchen and started the kettle. A wake-up vodka would do him the world of good, he decided, get the blood flowing, still the nerves a bit, sharpen the disorientation from the nightmare. Today's the day, must be decisive: I *will* have a vodka. This new Dutch refrigerator was very efficient, and the bottle of pepper vodka lay frozen solidly in its bed of ice. Chertkov began to chip away at the ice.

Then stopped. And listened.

The door knocker *was* clattering.

Not the "neighbors," Chertkov calculated, they'd bash the thing down. Throwing the ice pick into the sink, he crept down the hallway as the door knocker tapped away endlessly, holding his breath.

The dry snick of a key. Chertkov stopped, his hand suspended over the scarred porcelain doorknob. The concierge's key, the KGB had the concierge's key . . . the door began to move and Chertkov numbly awaited his fate. . . .

# THE STALKING HORSE

## Brendan Howley

FAWCETT CREST · TORONTO

A Fawcett Crest Book
Published by Random House of Canada Limited
Copyright © 1988 by Brendan Howley

ISBN: 0-449-21768-x

Printed in Canada

First Fawcett Crest Edition: November 1989

For all at Number Seven,
Miss M. above all

Special thanks
to John Wood

"Their conscience is merely a stalking horse, moved by their interest to conceal. . . ."

Sir William Hamilton
*The Edinburgh Review*
1852

# Prologue

Chertkov dreamt of the lilies.

He had seen a color plate of the painting only once, in a broken-backed art book, at the university in Kiev where his uncle worked; Chertkov couldn't have been more than seven or eight. They were lilies, beautiful French water lilies, floating on blue-green light. The lilies were the first clue the nearsighted Chertkov badly needed spectacles, for all of life appeared as the glorious blur of the pond flowers to his weak eyes. Young Chertkov told the librarian at the desk his problem and the man had laughingly lent him his spectacles. Seeing properly was a revelation, a new world. Months would pass before Chertkov could have his own, for this was the Soviet Union in the seventh year of Josef Stalin's dictatorship. Shortages at the factory, Madame Khabarovska, the village doctor, had said.

Thirteen years later, in the early summer of 1944, here in the temporary refuge of these beautiful French Alps, the image of the lilies was still Nikolai's talisman, an image resurrected in all its calm luminosity to stay the other dream haunting him. That nightmare was always the same: amid the screaming lathes of the Lyon factory, cap in hand, Chertkov stood as straight as he could next to the giant metal-press he'd accidentally jammed, waiting for the blow. The German kapo, a convicted killer from Essen known as the Conductor for his way with a stick, knocked an ear piece of Chertkov's spectacles off his ear with one professional lash of his truncheon and then bounced the other ear piece free with a lazy backhander. Pleased with this show of dexterity, the Conductor batted the smashed spectacles onto the scrap heap. "Alloy for the war effort," he cackled in pidgin

1

French, his grin all the more terrible in the blue-white light of the underground aircraft works. "Teach you to keep those Bolshevik eyes on your work"—a blinding crack across Chertkov's nose sent him bouncing off the workbench and his cap spinning into the grease bucket. Then the final indignity, the tears.

The lilies receded and Chertkov, lying on his rough monk's cot in his monk's stone cubicle, rubbed his eyes awake. Next to the cot stood a tiny table, a porcelain bowl, and a handmade crucifix; a single casement window looked out over the waves of Lac du Bourget, and, across the alpine waters, over the lakeside vineyards that broke and ran to the north-east, toward Lac Leman and the haven of Switzerland. The French monk had closed the shutters to let him sleep, but now Chertkov suddenly craved light despite his fatigue. He noticed these sudden lunges of his psyche more and more and wondered if it was a good sign; perhaps it was better not to notice the urges for cream, for an hour on Grandfather's boat, gliding along the brown Dneiper, its carefully patched sail a folded napkin of white against the sky, for the fragrant oasis at the back of a willing girl's neck, for light.

There was a candle stub on the side table and Chertkov lit it, using the same flame to start a Gauloise. The old shirt the monk had given him the night before was sodden. Chertkov sat up and plucked the thin cloth away from his back. He had lost thirty pounds since his eighteenth birthday and his body was still a stranger to him, an alien vehicle for his rubbed-raw senses. Tucking his shirt in, he touched the promontories of his sore ribs and wondered. Life in the year 1944 was all in the fall of the cards, he decided, shivering as he shook off the recollection of the SS factory at Lyon. There was no other way to explain the phenomenon of his luck: almost everyone he had known in the fourteen months since his capture by the Germans at Kirovograd was dead.

Chance: my number tomorrow, yours next week. Chertkov's fatalism made him stand when the camp commandant asked for "technicians to serve the Reich." Chertkov rose and fancifully described himself as *"ein Blecharbeiter"*—a sheet-metal worker. Sometimes the Germans shot those who volunteered; sometimes they took them away. Chertkov was lucky that morning; in a week's time, his body was in the Lyon factory of his nightmares, rented by his Vichy French employers on the first of February 1944 from the Reich's Head Economic Office for eight Reichsmarks a day. There, in the south of France, Nikolai

Chertkov was a slave, property of the SS, stamping out gearbox housings fourteen hours a day. Chertkov let the nicotine pry his mind from the memory—the hot tang of milled metal, the washed-out light from the light bulbs, the penetrating subterranean chill . . . his heart tipped against his breast with each pulse, and with each heartbeat Chertkov willed himself closer to home.

Before the war, Chertkov had been a gifted student of languages at Shevchenko University in Kiev. Unlike their Ukrainian neighbors, his parents were both Russians, of Polish and Czech extraction. Grandfather spoke Romanian and a strange Cockney English cadged from an expatriate British railwayman, fruit of Grandpa's pre-Revolutionary days as train-man; at home, young Nikolai was exposed to three languages. By the time he was fourteen, the boy could also speak fluent Polish, passable Czech and German, and a smattering of English as well. When Chertkov was conscripted at age eighteen, the Red Army signals corps taught him Morse and (quite sensibly, he thought at the time) put him in a tank. The tank was knocked out by a mine and Chertkov was captured by the Germans on New Year's Day 1943. After a week's captivity, he escaped for four days but was recaptured, hiding in a burnt-out barn. Somehow he avoided being shot out of hand; the Germans sent him to a POW camp near Plaszow in southern Poland instead. In Plaszow, Chertkov discovered the honorable trade of metalworking and was shipped by rail through a disintegrating Reich to the plant at Lyon in south-central France. Ever since his spectacles met their end on the factory scrap heap, Chertkov had lived in a world of dangerously soft blurs and hazy faces.

Chertkov struggled with the debris of his dream, the memory of the factory and the Conductor and Jacques, the ironic French Jew, the secret Marxist, the only man courageous enough to speak to Chertkov in his native Russian. After that, Chertkov allowed he had other languages and Jacques had tested him, adding to Chertkov's now-fluent French Jacques' own guttural Marseillais accent. The two became friends, sharing a battered cigarette or a swede in their thin soup; Jacques seemed to Chertkov the epitome of Gallicism, with his mordant wit and his hatred of the Boche. But Jacques did much more than teach Chertkov his harsh patois. Jacques was the first link in an escape chain run by the French Communist Resistance, the FTP; the next to last link in the chain ending at the Swiss frontier was this ancient abbey. Here, Jacques and his compatriots secreted hunted Jews—and foreign Communists thought useful to the

FTP, for Jacques had infiltrated the Lyon plant to locate and smuggle technicians of whatever nationality to the relative safety of the Alps of the Haute-Savoie for the D-day offensive. First Chertkov heard the Spanish demolition engineer, Fernandes, a Sephardic Jew, had disappeared from the factory one morning in the back of a cement truck. Then the Pole, little Rowecki, a Communist who had worked for Radio Warsaw, decamped, sewn inside a mattress destined for the delousing plant. The guards caught Jacques' next candidate, a Czech chemist hidden in an oil barrel bound for the Lyon generating station, and shot him, but the resourceful Jacques simply saw that Chertkov was transferred to the Czech's work station, closer to him. ''Two weeks,'' Jacques had whispered to him in Russian one morning. ''Courage, comrade. We have men, good Party men, valuable *résistants*, in our group who cannot speak to us for themselves: we need your skill.'' Chertkov could only nod in mute amazement—they were going to try to get him out. . . .

A fortnight later, the morning before the bombers came—just as Jacques had promised they would—the SS kapos beat Jacques to death for sleeping at his drill press. He made not a sound as the gun butts fell, taking his secrets with him to the limed pit behind the water tower where the SS disposed of the men they had worked to death.

Chertkov's memory of the following day was as sharp as a photograph: the two trusties, Carbonneau and Augert, slipping Chertkov into the above-ground working party that morning, the sudden diving scream of the American fighter-bombers, the ground trembling and exploding, the old flatbed truck scattering the working party, and unknown hands throwing him bodily into the back of the truck. Then the truck driving full-tilt through the shattered factory gate, leaving Lyon behind, the rolling ride into the mountains . . . and the mysterious Frenchman who drove the relic of an old Ford.

This FTP man was an odd one, his bespectacled eyes fervent, civilized and ruthless all at once, a man with gentleman's fingers who swore like a sailor when he slapped at the old truck's reluctant gearshift lever. He would not give his name but shared all his bread and wine with Chertkov without hesitation. And his insistence about things Soviet! He seemed to need to know as much about the Soviet Union as any Russian—it was an obsession with him. He had never been to Russia, the FTP man admitted shyly; was it true there were to be new industrial towns planted in the emptiest reaches of Siberia? How many? And the new hydroelectric dams, what of them? Were they the biggest? And the workers—how many were working on these projects? Chertkov answered these and the FTP man's other questions as best he could but his knowledge was no match for the Frenchman's arithmetic curiosity, his need for numbers on numbers. "How many?" The phrase eventually carried Chertkov, already made drowsy by the wine and the spring sun and the exhilaration of freedom, to sleep. He slept through the foothills and over the bridges and through the villages along the Alpine streams and might well have slept to the monastery gate itself, so great was his exhaustion.

Chertkov would never be certain what woke him first, the mad bucking of the speeding truck or the Frenchman's shouted warning as the old Ford's overheated brakes disappeared in a cloud of hot asbestos smoke. Chertkov woke to see the truck's hood diving and then leaping ahead as the brakes held one last time and then gave way. The truck rocketed down a steep curve at nearly sixty miles an hour, gravity and the truck's downhill momentum burning the last of the brake shoes to ash.

"Jump! Jump, comrade! I can't hold her!" The Frenchman, half-standing in the cab, his full weight on the unresponding brake pedal, pushed the wide-eyed Chertkov against the creaking door. But he was too late.

Out of control, the truck bounded over the pavement edge and was thrown upward by the ramp of the canted curve. The 1927 Ford hung airborne for a long second and then plowed into the base of a hillock. That was all Chertkov remembered, until he woke in this monastery cell, his chest aching, relatively unharmed. Chertkov had been thrown clear, but his friend, badly burnt, had fought his way out of the blazing truck. A charcoal-burner had found them, the abbot had said, put them on his cart, and brought them the last few miles to the Abbaye de St-Etienne du Mont.

You're bloody lucky, Nikolai, Chertkov said to himself, to have made it this far. The thin Russian let a stream of cigarette smoke rise luxuriously to the ceiling and strained to hear the monks. Chertkov now understood a half-dozen languages, but Latin was not one of them. Lying on his cot, Chertkov gave up trying to understand the Gregorian chant of the monks' compline. To Chertkov, the distant chanting of the men in their chapel stalls was like a fountain, a steady current of sound questioning and answering itself as men had done within these walls for centuries. He let the mysterious sound massage his brain and listened, straining to tease a new sound from the singing of the monks and the pulse of his own heart.

There.

Again.

And again: a faint coughing, then a whistle. A man, to be sure; no women were allowed this far within the monastery walls. Chertkov knew the tune: *The Internationale*.

The Frenchman who drove the truck.

The whistlings paused for a moment against the drone of the Latin and then the coughs began, reminding Chertkov of snatches of sleep in the underground factory barracks, the sighs and groans of men breaking in the night. Chertkov wondered if the monks would come. Perhaps they could not hear: Chertkov rose, slipped off his prison clogs, and opened the door.

Another quavering rendition of the Soviet national anthem echoed from the four-bed infirmary at the far end of the hallway. Chertkov walked deliberately to the infirmary door and pushed it open. The room was as dark as his own and a sharp fan of light crept across the smooth cobbles of the floor and up the bed frame to the wall. Chertkov felt farsightedly for the candle on the table top and something fell, a familiar something clacking to rest on the stone.

A pair of glasses, one tortoiseshell ear piece badly bent or burnt out of shape . . . one lens was whole, undamaged. Chertkov closed his right eye: he could see again.

He struck a match.

It was the Frenchman.

He was sitting up on his cot, shivering, his coat around his shoulders. Chertkov touched the flame to the candle wick and looked more closely. The Frenchman's hands were swathed in bandages and there was a burnt smell about him—his hair stank of smoke and his face, singed and red, was partially masked by the gauze over his eyes.

"Who is it?" The Frenchman's voice was hoarse and weak.

"It's me, the Russian," Chertkov said.

"So you heard me. You've come. We must be brief: the monk looking after me has gone to get my meal. Are you all right?"

"Yes. My ribs are banged up but I'm all right. You?"

"You were born lucky, comrade. I've burnt my eyes and there's blood in my lungs from the smoke and the coughing. Listen," the Frenchman said, motioning with a bandaged hand. "This is very important. Find my knapsack. The monk put it under the bed."

Chertkov did as he was told.

"Now find the canister inside. Is it still there?"

"Yes." Chertkov turned it in his hands: the straight-sided metal canister was quite light, of military manufacture, the diameter of a saucer but deep as an Army canteen.

"Listen, listen carefully to me, comrade. They will come to get you, my colleagues. If anything happens to me, there is only one of them you can trust. My coat pocket. Find my wallet. Hurry, they will be here soon!"

Chertkov turned the coat pockets inside out and the wallet fell into his hand. "Find the photograph. Have you got it? I wish to God I could see. . . ."

In his anxiety to please, Chertkov dropped the wallet. But he caught the photograph. Its emulsion was cracked and worn from repeated foldings and greasy with fingerprints. The photograph had been taken inside a stone chalet, its thick-walled fireplace framing four men who had forsaken their playing cards for the snapshot, glasses in hand and wine bottles ranged like ninepins on the table, cheerfully toasting the camera. The men were paired off each side of the table, an empty chair between them. The left-most drinker was a tall dark fellow, French by the look of him. Chertkov guessed him rich despite his climber's clothes, a leader—and then glanced again at him: the line of the jaw, the very glasses through which Chertkov now stared—*this was the Frenchman*. Chertkov's gaze returned to the Frenchman's colleague, a hard-looking, fair-haired Slav with a big pistol stuck in his belt and the blank, shallow eyes of a fanatic. The taller of the right-hand pair was the youngest of the quartet, with a beard that did not hide the smooth features of his unformed face. His companion was the oldest, a slight, gray-haired priest, his soutane crossed with the leather strap of a binocular pouch. Chertkov turned the photo over and pressed his new glasses up the bridge of his nose.

"Have you found it? Did the monks take the wallet?"

"No, no, it's all here. This is you in the photograph?"

The Frenchman lifted a bandaged hand and found Chertkov's arm with it. "Yes. In better times. Now there are enemies all around us. The Gestapo, traitors, men unfaithful to the Party. You must be extremely careful. The men who will meet you will take you to our headquarters in Petit-Egremont. Look at the photograph. Trust only the man with the gun, the one called Igor, do you hear? He is your countryman. He will get you

home. You must trust only him, understand? The way you trusted
Jacques and trusted me.''

"Trust only Igor.''

"Good," the Frenchman said, relaxing a little. "Very good.
Now take the canister and hide it. Not in your room, away from
the monastery. No one must know where it is but us. Then come
back and tell me. But hurry! No one must catch you!''

Chertkov stood and moved to the door.

"Comrade!'' The Frenchman's voice was breaking. "I saved
your life. I trust you, the Party trusts you. Go!''

There. Somewhere in the stone corridor a pair of sandals
slapped.

Chertkov held his breath.

*God, help me.*

He blew out the candle.

The sandal-slaps floated down the stone floor outside the cell
and then turned away, their sound disappearing behind the great
doors to the courtyard.

"Go! Go now!''

Chertkov hesitated for a moment, then, holding the canister
in one hand and the Frenchman's photograph in the other, he
ran madly in his stockinged feet to his own cell, sliding the last
yards along the smooth stones. He shut his door without a sound.
Stumbling in the half-dark, Chertkov peeled off his socks, threw
the shutters open to the setting sun, and lowered himself carefully the six feet to the terra-cotta roof below, retrieving the
canister from the window ledge.

He turned. And froze.

Across the courtyard, not ten feet below Chertkov's perch,
two columns of monks, cowled in their rough white Benedictine
habits, stood with their backs to him, surrounding an open grave.
The monks were burying one of their own. Chertkov shifted his
haunches; the tiled roof was still warm from the afternoon sun.
He looked down: the courtyard wall opposite him was an arcade
of archways with relief sculptures of saints set in its side. To his
right, the monastery's outer wall was pierced by a single wrought
iron gate; to his left was the main entrance.

A hymn began. The coffin had already disappeared and the
monks, one by one, tossed a handful of earth into the grave. *I'm
not going anywhere until they're done,* Chertkov reassured himself. *I'd kill for a smoke now.* He made himself take a deep
breath.

He reached for the canister, his curiosity freshening. He noticed the canister was not tin—the round shape was milled metal, light, like aluminum. Chertkov felt the smooth surface again. It *was* aluminum. He turned the canister over: the maker's markings had been scratched away. The lid was tight; he had to brace himself against the roofing tiles to really twist properly. He watched the monks as he strained; they might have been in another world.

There was a hiss and the lid came free from its seal. Chertkov's heart jumped: a wad of notes nested against the curved metal. Perhaps this . . . he pulled the folded notes from their nesting place and let the wind open one.

Chertkov held the top document to his face, then moved the glasses from his nose, seeking the right focus. But . . . they weren't Vichy francs or any currency he had seen. He tried to sound out the letters: *OBLIGATIONS*, he read, *TITRE À PORTEUR*. There was a yellow blob, a clamshell insignia atop each sheet; Chertkov held dozens of the strange documents in his hand.

Chertkov's head rose. The monks had stopped singing. Several of them began to shovel the earth from the grave side into the hole. Chertkov looked at the photograph in his other hand. Igor? A Russian in France? That was a mystery. A worried aristocratic partisan who trusts only Russians—another mystery. Folding and curling the papers to fit, Chertkov pushed the stack of odd notes back into the canister and cocked his ear, watching the monks begin to disperse. Only two men were shovelling now, young ones; two others had a headstone in a wheelbarrow.

In the distance, a truck rumbled.

The monks had no trucks . . . only horse carts. The Gestapo! Looking for him! Or the Frenchman's secret enemies, looking for him and his secret canister? Holding the Frenchman's glasses to his side, Chertkov strained his eyes to his right, along the valley road before it switchbacked up the abbey hill to the entrance. A single truck swayed haltingly up the gravel track, a cloud of dust rising behind its wheels. Chertkov looked down: the gravediggers were helping the other two with the headstone, quietly unconcerned.

The two monks shouldered their tools and began to walk to the potting shed just outside the abbey walls. One of the headstone monks was on his knees, patting the earth at the foot of the big stone. Go, get on with it, Chertkov prayed. The standing monk said something and they too left the grave after a moment of silence, the wheelbarrow's bearings twittering as they walked away.

Chertkov lowered himself to the roof edge and then dropped, bounding slightly on the rich turf. Setting off like a man possessed across the courtyard, Chertkov headed for the arcade, half-jumping the last few steps, the canister shoved under his arm. Thirty feet outside the abbey walls, just visible through an archway, stood the potting shed, a row of rubber workboots lined against its side for mealtime. Downhill from the shed, past a line of poplars, Chertkov could see the valley road. He made his way along the arcade, pausing behind a pillar, making sure there were no monks near the shed.

Someone was ringing the abbey bell.

*The truck, they've seen the truck.*

Chertkov ran from the arcade-end, out the small gate, to the potting shed door and scraped it open. The shed smelled of damp and old earth; a single window allowed a rectangle of light to form against a workbench, where, through the single lens of his friend's glasses, Chertkov found a useful-looking knife amid the pruning tools and seed packets. A roll of chicken-wire snow fence lay at his feet.

Gingerly, knife in hand, Chertkov moved the snow fence back. He peered out the window browned with grit, over the shoulder of the hill, down the curving road to the lake below. On the hill track, no more than fifty feet away through the row of leafless poplars, the truck geysered steam from its hood; two men at its side talked, one angrily, the other philosophically, then the philosopher waved his angry comrade up the hill. A third fellow jumped from the truck, a machine pistol at his side. He and the angry man began to climb the monastery road, past the open main gate, making for the central doorway of the abbey itself, walking in profile as they passed through Chertkov's view.

Chertkov compared each man in his turn to the men drinking in the Frenchman's photograph. . . .

No Igor.

But what to do with the photograph? *Trust only Igor.* Chertkov unscrewed the canister lid and pressed the photograph into the center of the ring of folded documents. He closed the canister as tightly as he could and then used the knife to pry away one of the loose ceiling boards. Standing his full five-foot-five, Chertkov thrust the canister into the cleft of a joist in the shed roof, deep under the eaves.

Checking the window, Chertkov waited for the Frenchman's

three compatriots to enter the main door of the monastery, then he slipped out the shed door.

He sprinted through the small iron gateway, back to the shadows of the monastery arcade. The staircase door was unlocked and Chertkov swung it open, cursing its rusty whine.

Then he stole up the stairs as fast as his short legs and thief's adrenaline could carry him. Slipping from doorway to doorway in the dark cool halls, his heart pounding, Chertkov picked his way back to the infirmary and listened.

Nothing.

He opened the door.

The poor Frenchman had hemorrhaged; there was blood all over his shirt front and a gurgling pink foam overflowed his lips. Chertkov tore the Frenchman's shirt open and tried to pull the bloody clothes away. There was a tricolor tattooed on the fellow's chest and an enormous bruise stood out against the tattoo, from the steering wheel, Chertkov guessed. The tattoo contorted as a single violent spasm gripped the man's chest. Chertkov felt for the thready pulse at the Frenchman's neck.

He's going.

"Bless me, Father . . . I have sinned . . . Father?"

Dear God, he can still speak. "Yes," Chertkov said, as calmly as he could.

"I have killed, Father. . . ." Chertkov thought he was saying. "I killed . . . Boches . . . I killed them. . . ." The Frenchman had grasped Chertkov's forearm in a wild grip, his next words lost—one sounded like Lenin. The fellow fought for another breath, his chest trying to rise, but a terrible snoring gurgle was all his will could force. Then his eyes rolled back and the body slowly twisted down.

Chertkov was six inches shorter and a good twenty-five pounds lighter than the man he tried to keep from sliding to the humiliation of the cold floor. He pulled the dead Frenchman's arm away from the body, trying to straighten his collapsed torso, anything to dignify the last moments of the nameless man who had saved his life.

A door creaked in the distance and a pair of monk's sandals scuffed down the hall, followed by the gritty metallic crunch of the Resistance men's hob-nailed boots. Chertkov took a fearful half-glance at the hallway. He counted the seconds into silence. And waited.

# PART I

## FRIDAY–WEDNESDAY

"May you live on one salary."
*Russian curse*

# Chapter One

A sort of *delerium tremens* overcomes Washington in an election year. The capital's nerves crackle with excess voltage, tapped straight off microphone wire and minicam cable; the city's circulation, overrich with traffic at the best of times, swells to the point of aneurysm with provincial journalists and ad salesmen and all the flotsam and jetsam the media tide sweeps before it. True, there was a meat-grinder of a stagnating war on and whispered rumors of great scandal, but Washington this particular election year was no different from Washington in any other fall—you had only to look at the sky: summer was coming apart at the seams.

After a sizzling September, the District of Columbia uneasily resigned herself to the rains of October. TV weathermen ran footage of slickered housewives and sodden Senate aides peering windward for the next bus and of ponchoed sanitation workers philosophically prodding leaf-clogged sewer grates with rakes. The October raindrops peeled away the brutal humidity and leached the chlorophyll from the trees of Rock Creek, bouncing and flicking off Georgetown's umbrellas and Cinzano awnings and McGovern posters and benignly dissolving the Indian summer of 1972.

One of those Georgetown umbrellas stood next to Morley Walsh's office door in a pool of rainwater. Just below the brass plaque designed to mislead the curious, its etched letters reading "National Archives and Records Service Office," Walsh had nine umbrellas standing in a real elephant's foot in the office entryway. The splashily coloured one he'd used this morning was his favorite; it gave his football lineman's bulk a debonair

air and nicely set off his robin's-egg-blue on gold tie. But then, as he himself was fond of saying, two hundred and forty hypertensive pounds gave him a lot to be vain about behind his expense-account smile. Save the flag in the corner, Walsh's office could have passed for an Ivy League professor's, with warm white walls, oak shelves filled by a books-by-the-yard service, and casement windows overlooking a small quadrangle. This forsythia- and rosebush-ringed square where Walsh strolled through his secret conferences was the most conspiratorial corner of a backdoor regime known as the Group. Since January 1969, Walsh had fed and watered this Group office and its operations from his special fund hidden in the undergrowth of the already lush General Services budget.

Just now, in a conspiratorial posture that typified the man, Walsh fondled his telephone, nestling it on his shoulder as he watched the quadrangle's foliage cringe in the downpour. First thing upon shedding his coat and umbrella five minutes ago, Walsh had placed his weekly call to a remote Virginia township, to the house of his eighty-six-year-old mother, Elizabeth, a formidable horsewoman who had outlived a pair of moderately well-off husbands, and whose sharp business sense had gained her several lucrative properties to boot. Living alone in an eccentric Georgian pile called Downrew House, Bessie Walsh Powell wore her pearls to bed, dusted the oils herself, kept faith with her accountant, and lived quietly, in keeping with her advancing deafness, a failing Bessie cursed and compensated for with a special telephone.

"My dear," Bessie was shouting to her son, "that doctor, the one with the Spanish name you arranged for me, was an absolute disaster." Walsh could picture Bessie complaining, propped up amid the mounded pillows at her Queen Anne desk, flaking face powder on the blotter, the inevitable financial papers, and the set of alarm bells that raucously summoned her to door, phone, and stable.

"Dr. Sanchez de Ferrares is a very well-respected urologist, Bess, dear. Didn't you hit it off?"

"The State Department may not be able to pee straight, dear, but there's nothing wrong with my kidneys. And the quack was too solicitous for my taste. Can't stand being patronized, especially by Latins." In fact, Bessie hated all doctors impartially: they had, she would often assure anyone within earshot, killed both her husbands. "So I have dismissed him. Without regret, I might add. You know what today is, Morley dear?"

Bessie dominated phone calls the way she overpowered and fascinated her husbands and Morley's boyhood friends, and repelled all but the strongest of her female acquaintances—through sheer force of personality.

"The sixteenth of October."

"And?" Bessie asked sharply.

Walsh bent and opened the valve on the radiator, for, despite his bulk, he felt the cold. "I've forgotten, Bess. Sorry."

"Don't apologize to me. Hang up this instant and call your daughter Robin at Vassar. The dear thing's a freshman just writing the first of her exams. You," Bess added meaningly, "are no better a father than Harry was." The dead Harry Walsh, Morley's father and Bessie's first husband, had been a journalist, a quietly reasonable man of no known opinions who covered everything from the Treaty of Versailles to the Berlin Airlift before dying of blood poisoning in Cairo in 1952.

"I'll call Robin, Bess. Thanks for reminding me. Anything else?"

"Tell that man in the White House I'm watching him. I read the papers. I may be lousy with real estate, but the do-re-mi comes as hard to me as to him. And I didn't give my money to see it frittered away on a clumsy break-in."

Walsh had his hand over the warming fins of the radiator. "Yes, Bess, I'll do what I can." Bess Walsh Powell's world was at once smaller and broader than her son's—her second husband, acquired while Morley worked his passage in the New York legal jungle, had been a lawyer with stratospheric political connections—and she had never accepted the passing of that world nor its privilege.

"And call that Enright woman." There was a weighty pause: this was Noelle Enright, Morley Walsh's ex-wife, an admitted mistake whom he had divorced in 1963. "Got a letter here, in the morning mail: her lawyer's whining about alimony. She married you for your money, Morley, and that she's got. You *are* paying the woman off, aren't you?" Bess had decried the match since first meeting Noelle, rightly suspecting a long financial wrangle would ensue.

"Always, Bess, always." He reckoned he was six months in arrears—at last count, that was.

"See you do. I'll have no more letters from her lawyers, thank you very much." Then, more gently: "Thanks for calling, dear."

"Get your beauty sleep, Bess."

He hung up. Pulling a drape over his view of the rain-drenched quadrangle, Walsh called to the office next door, "Jane, Group shuttle late or what?"

"Our faithful courier has just completed his appointed rounds," said a brisk voice with a deep Virginia accent. "How's Bessie keeping?"

"Never a virtue of mine, patience," Walsh called back. "And mother's fine—probably immortal." Walsh, a self-indulgent man, fiddled with the business end of a panatella while watching as the television camera panned to the jetliner's passenger ladder crowded with men in expensive suits, their ties flying in the wind. He turned up the television's volume dial. ". . . and behind the Secretary of State is—" a blast of turbojet drowned out the newsman's voice-over "—one of the senior National Security Council officials accompanying the Secretary to Geneva for the new round of bilateral arms talks with the Soviets . . ."

Walsh didn't need a voice-over to recognize the tall figure and the averted head of Ted Rappaport, Intelligence Security Adviser to the NSC, now halfway up the Pan Am stairs. Walsh grunted: the television reporter could match no more than a name to the aquiline face at the Secretary's side. What fifteen years ago had been an ad hoc intelligence team in a back-room office with a single desk and a tired photocopier (a tale Rappaport, there himself on day one, was fond of relating), was now the multimillion-dollar Group. Walsh shook his head, bemused by what television networks dispensed as information; their cameras bobbing above the fray, the photographers gathered on the runway at the foot of the stairs.

Walsh could well afford to smile. Despite his impressive Records letterhead and the beige IBM terminal in the side office (patched into nothing more secret than the Library of Congress), Morley Walsh was a lawyer, Rappaport's legal counsel, a phone call away from walk-in privileges at Rappaport's basement lair at the White House.

"He carries Rappaport's black bag," the NSC staff assured one another, their voices envious, for not one of them would ever see the contents of Group's legendary luggage. Close-lipped, brutal when he had to be, Walsh was Rappaport's perfect conduit. Like a transistor, Walsh never operated on impulse: he reacted precisely to changes in Rappaport's field. "Another Bormann," belched an inebriated journalist once, a big soft man from one of the liberal Maryland dailies, unfortunately within Walsh's hearing. A phone call later and suddenly the

Maryland stringer's sources unaccountably dried up for anything resembling intelligence: the poor fellow was reduced to rewriting the more polite boys and girls.

Message received, said the astute pressmen following NSC affairs. They shook their heads over their drinks, and several were moved to salve their consciences with a vague story or two, but nobody had much inclination to nose around unbidden behind Rappaport's throne after that. But they talked among themselves: one fine day, Rappaport will be looking over his shoulder, ran the prophecy. And that large shape in the rearview mirror will be his face-man, Morley Walsh.

"Pouch," announced Walsh's secretary, Jane Carey, a thirtyish, sharp-minded Southerner temporarily stalled in the civil service shuffle. Jane carried a worn gray canvas pouch bearing now-illegible stencillings—dire warnings to prying eyes, for the most part—and a thick thread Walsh tore off on his first try.

The telex machine woke and hammered a burst of letters. Walsh peered over the top and dismissed the transmission. "Slow news day," he said. "Why haven't we got a lid for the telex? Makes a terrible noise. Look, Rappaport's wearing your Christmas tie." The Secretary of State turned to wave to the photographers, trapping Rappaport between him and the Boeing's bulkhead. The taller man turned his face inward, away from the cameras, then dove into the aircraft's open doorway.

"Nine ninety-five at Schwartz's." Jane waved the pouch impatiently. "The soundproof telex lid's back-ordered. Treasury has priority."

Walsh switched off the television and cleared a space on his desk. "Figures. Thanks." Walsh lit his cigar while Jane removed the plate bearing Walsh's morning corn muffin.

"All classified material on-premises for the weekend present and accounted for?"

"You really ought to check the receipt book every morning; you'll find Mr. Rappaport's materials in the safe."

Walsh growled and brushed the crumbs to the carpet. "Speaking of every morning, Monday let's have one of those real buttery rolls from the French place. I'm sure these other . . . *things* are some sort of mistake."

Jane stopped, holding the plate in midair. "Eight hundred calories, you said, that's your limit. Courier's coming back at eleven, so you have an hour." The plate resumed its path and accompanied the severe Jane back to the outer office.

For a moment, Walsh watched her go; his interest was purely

professional reflex—he preferred the company of a moderately expensive call girl named Valerie; he wasn't due for a visit to Valerie's Silver Springs town house until next weekend. This last consideration decided him: he would string Noelle's alimony out until Christmas and send Robin's end-of-semester cheque at the last moment. Things were a little tight just now. Walsh twisted his key in the courier bag's lock and began to scan the contents.

Yes, yes: here was the hectoring circular from the archive library on returning twenty-four-hour materials promptly, then summaries of *Pravda* editorials, a pair of NATO extracts, odds and ends from Tel Aviv and London on expected terrorist strategies for the fall . . . Walsh impatiently signed off and returned the whole batch unread. Why do they bother, he thought, opening the last item, the Group's diplomatic bag from Vienna Station, an oversize leather wallet bigger and flatter than a bank night-deposit bag, but with the same locked zipper.

Walsh fitted his key and opened the bag. Every Thursday afternoon, Vienna Station, clearing-house for Group's European operations on both sides of the Iron Curtain, collated the week's raw intelligence and air-expressed the diplomatic bag to Washington; London, Paris, and Madrid would report separately over the weekend. Tipping the bag's contents onto his blotter, Walsh separated east from west: Bonn, Athens, and the other friendlies to the right; Moscow, Warsaw, and the other satellites to the left.

Walsh always did the Eastern bloc first and this Friday Hungary was on top. Pearson of Budapest Station, a blunt Yale man rumored to be distantly related to Rappaport, had a pair of turned Hungarian army colonels atop the CONFUCIUS network; both ticking over nicely, thanks, reported Pearson, who had slowly been reeling the two colonels in since spring. And ticking they should be, Walsh reckoned, for the three thousand a month they cost us. Walsh scrawled, "Audit?" and his initials in the margin of Pearson's communiqué and shuffled the Budapest file farther to the left—Rappaport himself could crack the whip when he returned. Warsaw Station next, where Lavoie ran two nets, one military, PUNCH, the other trade union, JUDY. JUDY reported expecting a rail shipment of twenty Soviet tractor-trailers, possibly for missile transport, by month end; PUNCH, embarrassed, could neither confirm nor deny this tidbit. Walsh marked the new JUDY material "Cross-reference GDR, CZ: transport?" and slid it aside to photocopy for Rappaport: of such bargaining chips are arms talks made, Walsh knew.

And now for the meat and potatoes, Walsh thought, as he reached for the Moscow Station file. Walsh tapped his name on the distribution list, just below Rappaport's, whose signature panel was of course blank. Walsh bet himself: six months, eight months at the outside, Rappaport's out and I'm in. I might even get lucky and be home free right after the election.

After that, Walsh mused, who knew how far Rappaport's Moscow network could take me? The network was precarious, true, and its product ranging from the tantalizing to the useless, but the danger added spice: if I had a nickel for every time Rappaport used his Moscow gossip as a pretext to call the White House, Walsh figured wryly, I'd be making my alimony payments like clockwork. Walsh brightened at the prospect of delivering that same gossip himself. All things considered, if the rain holds off, maybe get in a little golf, then Saturday dinner at the Bistro Français—this might be a good weekend after all.

He skimmed the usual appendices, flipping the green-flagged sheets to one side. The co-signature panels held his attention for a moment, but there was nothing new there—all present and accounted for. The dossier had left Group archives two hours ago, fresh from the textured beige cubicles and the fluorescents. Archives would have done their updating overnight and shoved the file onto the next available shuttle van downtown.

The next item might prove interesting; Walsh had a congratulatory pull at his cigar. One of Archive's Red Army specialists had included a formal group portrait taken at last year's Moscow Warsaw Pact conference for distribution to the bloc army magazines. The photo had been taken in the big Stalinist baroque room, all red drapes and chandeliers, which housed the ongoing Warsaw Pact intelligence conference. A bevy of army intelligence brass from all the Pact countries stood like choirboys in front of the dais, some sixty officers in total. The diligent Group archivist had highlighted the notables, standing rigidly on the risers in their formal uniforms, and had drawn numbered arrows above their heads. Walsh checked the key clipped to the wire photo—fourteen was Efremov, Red Army intelligence/ Australia, seventeen was Mysak, head of Polish military intelligence . . . and at the end of the first row, number twenty-two, was Moldov, number ten in Red Army Intelligence, head of the GRU's American directorate. Cheerless, ambitious, utterly professional, that was the book on Moldov: Moldov owned a half-pound of paper in his Group file, everything known about his life, from his travel habits to a hearsay report about his ex-mistress's favorite perfume. You could tell from the thin line of his mouth—Moldov was a very tough nut.

Walsh grunted and returned the group portrait to the dossier. A Kodak transparency lay atop the next page.

Walsh held the slide up to his desk light; the image was a pool of grays and blacks. He rummaged through his bottom desk drawer, retrieving an old hand-held light-box he had last used to sort through one of Rappaport's patented audiovisual shows last spring. Chile, Walsh seemed to remember; felt like a sales seminar, sitting there in the dark with the talking head beeping the slide carousel along. Nestling his glasses in his hairline, Walsh fitted the slide into the light-box, then stopped.

A weepy ballpoint had scribbled last Wednesday's date on the slide frame—the photo had been taken at the Warsaw Pact meetings thirty-six hours ago. There was no indication of source. Rubbing his thumb against his forefinger, Walsh fitted the transparency into the light-box, curious.

The black and white image was grainy and overblown, tipped slightly, as if the photographer had drunk lunch. The camera was briefcase mounted, Walsh decided, judging from the perspective of the chairs and tables and the portraits of Brezhnev just visible between the pillars. The Warsaw Pact intelligence council by the look of things, squat men in a variety of uniforms, sitting around a U-shaped table in the chandeliered room from the Archive group portrait. Walsh nodded; the photographer had rested the briefcase on the table top before the timer tripped the shutter. What the hell was this thing doing in the pouch? And why hasn't Rappaport told me about the source who took the photo itself? He checked the signature panel again—McKiernan in Archives was going to have a mail slot full of memos from Security, that was for damn sure.

The flattened Slavic features of Moldov, the walleyed GRU colonel, the rows of medals on his chest half-hidden by the braided sleeves of an orderly serving mineral water, scowled directly into the lens, the side of his mouth pursed open, his hand over the bulbous microphone in front of him, as he lectured the officer to his right.

Walsh turned the light-box slightly to backlight the right-hand side of the slide better.

There. Next to Moldov. On the right, listening raptly to the GRU boss's every word.

"Merciful . . . mother mine," Walsh breathed, his pulse suddenly rocketing into the hundreds. The little slide projector

trembled as Walsh took a deep breath. *It can't be. Not him.*
"Merciful mother," Walsh repeated, as he slid the light-box
onto his lap.

There was a polite feminine cough. "I *said*, the *Times* has a
piece on declining Soviet oil production. Copy for the econo-
metrics file?" Jane was standing in the doorway, wearing her
firm camp counsellor face and waving the clipping.

Walsh cleared his throat and steadied his reading glasses on
his forehead; he reminded Jane of a large, puzzled crustacean.
"Certainly, certainly." And then, after a beat, as the inspiration
struck: "Bring me the NOAH file, would you? And run out for
some lozenges? Please? Appreciate it. That sore throat's back."
For a finishing touch, Walsh guiltily butted his cigar in the
chrome ashtray Rappaport had given him in '68.

There was a muffled thump as Jane opened a drawer in the
double-locked file cabinet set in the wall between her office and
Walsh's. The only network the West had in the Soviet hierarchy,
a patchwork of amateurs and dissidents Rappaport himself had
handcrafted since the President's first visit to Moscow—that was
NOAH, its product all marked "Station Chief DC Station/Eyes
Only."

Jane returned, the zebra-striped NOAH file in her hand. Jane
clicked her tongue reprovingly. "Give up the fat cigars, Mr.
Walsh," she threw over her shoulder. "Be the best thing in the
world for that throat." Walsh sat quite still, waiting and listening
for the flutter of the coats in the hallway and the slam of the
burglarproof front door.

Walsh hesitated. Perhaps I should call Rappaport, he thought.
Perhaps I should try to get him off the hook. But Walsh knew
the litany all too well: Rappaport would simply bob and weave,
let the problem slide inevitably to Walsh's desk, and cheerfully
call it delegation.

Walsh opened the dossier.

He lowered his glasses again and exhaled from the depths of
his lungs, the air currents riffling the edges of the papers lying
atop the open dossier. The telex machine began to rattle and
bump again, but Walsh ignored the noise, for he had bigger fish
to fry. He turned the dossier pages quickly until he found the
NOAH photo directory. Fifteen photographs ranging from clear
passport images to hurried street snapshots captured the faces
of the principal NOAH agents, identified by their animal code
names: only Rappaport knew their true names.

Walsh moved the light-box next to the photo directory.

There was no doubt about it.

The rounded officer with the dark eyebrows and thick glasses sitting next to Moldov was Rappaport's pride and joy, his ticket to heaven, code name CATALYST. And there CATALYST—whoever he was—sat, cool as you like, right next to Moldov. It's tea time and pass the sugar, Walsh thought.

I'm his main man, his babysitter, but Rappaport's cut me out of the CATALYST loop for two years. The old guy's cracking up. "See next week's thrilling installment, when Morley picks up Rappaport's pieces one more time," Walsh said to himself.

What was that saying my old case officer had? "If you want to catch a moth, light a candle." That was it. Walsh spun his chair to face the wall. The safe's installer had had a sense of humor; the small safe containing Walsh's NOAH emergency procedures was hidden behind a fat brass barometer with no back—"for when the pressure's on," he'd said.

Laying his cigar to rest, Walsh weighed opening the safe and the NOAH instructions, sealed by Rappaport personally. Forty-one left, forty-one right, eight left, and the Chubb would unburden its dark belly. Walsh weighed the urgencies and the cautions and the politics. . . . Damn typical of Rappaport, he thought, to leave me holding the bag while he soaks up the Geneva ambiance, not to mention that nice little side trip to Paris Station on his way back.

Walsh closed the NOAH dossier. He stood, drew his casement window drapes open, and considered the secret garden. In the quad, the rosebushes trembled in a gust of wind: rain again soon. Morley Walsh stood very still, his shoulders slightly hunched, like a big cat coiling for the leap. Nothing like a spy scandal three weeks before an election, Walsh reminded himself, to nail a few hides to the wall. One thing's sure: play this one right and Ted Rappaport'll be clearing out that office in the White House basement in a hurry. And the new tenant'll be me.

*Wait.*

# Chapter Two

The Bolshevik revolution would be fifty-five years old in a fort-night.

There were few banners or posters in this, one of the best preserved quarters of turn-of-the-century Moscow; a few flags hung listlessly from the Central Post Office, the red fabric trans-parent in the dusk sleet, the pennants five-year-old leftovers from the jubilee year of 1967—the workers had grown tired of the sleet and left the job for tomorrow. But TASS's television cameras would hardly pan higher than the flags; they would require better backdrops than the badly stained concrete of the apart-ment towers rising above the beautiful old buildings, cruel tow-ers hived off a single cindery loaf. The dripping tram wires netted the Saturday pedestrians below like so many tired fish, their breath trailing overhead as if ideas drawn by a cartoonist's hand. Above the wires, the October sky was stagnant as ditch water, the early evening clouds frozen in place by the first cold. Winter had not struck, but the damp-laundry smell of snow was in the air.

Chertkov braved the sleet and diligently timed his route through the evening crowds to the minute, as he had done every second Saturday since that spring day two years ago when it all began: the twenty-third of April, 1970, Lenin's hundredth birth-day. A number forty-one tram swung across the intersection before him, yawing like a sway-backed mule, its single light throbbing along the cobbles. There were faces in the steamy windows, blankly curious, eyeing with flickers of envy his tai-lored officer's coat, the plump circlets of his indeterminate middle-aged face, and the gilt trim of his oversize Army dress hat;

an angular boy thumbed his nose at the smartly uniformed Chertkov, who ironically nodded, returning the greeting.

Chertkov owed his tailored uniform, his important briefcase, and his two-bedroom flat on Boshaya Pirogovskaya, an exceptional luxury by Soviet standards, first to his wife's connections—Olga Pavelskaya's grandfather was an Old Bolshevik, her uncle a panjandrum in the Moscow housing ministry—and second, to his flawless Polish, German, and Rumanian, for N.G. Chertkov, major in the Red Army's Central Intelligence Directorate, the GRU, interpreted for Eastern bloc military maneuvers, certain Warsaw Pact summits, and the "fraternal" security meetings among the Poles, Czechs, the East Germans, Red Army Intelligence, and the KGB.

As was his custom, Chertkov had ended the outward leg of his habitual Saturday route at the Boulevard Ring, near the entrance to the Kirovskaya Metro, where Stalin had had his underground communications center built during the war. Chertkov stepped into the street and, crossing the train tracks, watched the girl walking ahead of him, carrying her bag full of newspaper-wrapped provisions. Her hair reminded Chertkov of Ludmilla's, pin-straight and thick despite the hours his latest lover spent in the swimming pool. Ludmilla was at work at the pool now, the little vixen. As she supervised the other lifeguards, she might even steal a glance at one of the *Vogue*s in her handbag, more forbidden decadence from Chertkov's cousin Andrei at the Berne consulate. Ludmilla dreamt of modeling someday, and Chertkov had first seduced her at her parents' flat with a dog-eared copy of *Vogue*, with its wondrous advertisements of unimagined chic. Chertkov still glowed at the memory of this first tryst with Ludmilla, when she had promised all manner of delights, flirtatiously trying to pry the magazine loose from her teasing Nikki. Chertkov sighed as he made his way across the street. Once Olga is parceled off to Leningrad, Ludmilla and I will steal a day in bed. It will be wonderful. He chewed his lip, anticipating.

Chertkov boarded the Metro at the Kirovskaya station and alighted at Kropotinskaya, across the river from Gorky Park. From the Metro's archway entrance, he walked across the square to the huge cloud of slowly rising steam above Moscow's circular open-air swimming pool, its high diving boards appearing and disappearing into the vapor. He searched the faces in the crowd at the iron fence and the changing room tunnels but did not find the one he wanted. There was an informal diving contest going on and the crowd was milling, watching, shouting encouragement to their favorite, and knocking back the vodka. A dark, smooth-muscled fellow, an Armenian perhaps, was at the board now and several of the men had a betting pool going.

"Presents for me?"

Ludmilla Petrovna wore a mock frown, fresh from her after-work swim, and toed the bag with a well-made boot. Chertkov reached for her but she skipped away, her wet hair flying under her hat. Her cheeks were still red from the heat of the pool and, free of make-up, she looked even younger than the twenty-three she claimed, which fueled Chertkov's masculine vanity more.

Masking his surprise, Chertkov said with mock seriousness: "You know who they're for, Ludmilla." She was circling him now, having hooked the string tie of his *avioshka* with her boot toe, pulling the shopping bag away, to the full reach of Chertkov's short arms.

"I think they're for me, that's what I think." She stopped the game and then, her leg still in midair, she hoisted the skirt of her coat, showing off her lithe thigh. "Best in the pool, better than wifey's, I'm sure." She laughed, knowing her teasing hit home.

"Not so loud, Ludmilla." Chertkov bent to straighten the bag and she followed him down, pulling out the big book on Dégas.

"Plunder then, if not presents. Teach you to be late." Then she kissed him, on tiptoe, leaning and knowing all the right buttons to push. I'm out of my depth with this one, Chertkov thought. Absurdly, there was a round of applause. Chertkov opened his eyes. The Armenian had done something spectacular in the meantime and half the betting pool looked crestfallen.

Ludmilla had moved away and was looking at the book. "How do you get this stuff, Nikki? Who else do you screw?"

"Don't talk like that, you know it bothers me."

"Not half as much as wifey bothers me." They were walking now, away from the pool. He put his arm around her and was rewarded with a wriggle of her hips.

"Can't you be discreet, Ludmilla?" Chertkov stepped away from her as they strolled. "Look, we have to change things. About Sunday. Something's come up."

Ludmilla stopped. "*What's* come up?" She looked at his face, searching his eyes. "Are you all right?"

The excuses tumbled over themselves as he spoke: "I'm all right, it's just it's Olga's birthday tomorrow. I have to go to her father's *dacha* Sunday. We can't get together until Thursday and I'm on duty Wednesday night. Olga's going to Leningrad. She'll be gone until Saturday. We can be together. . . .''

"Tickets and art books, you must be screwing somebody." Ludmilla hit him with the book, a bit harder than playfulness would allow. Then she smiled. "Thursday for sure?"

He nodded and she kissed him, harder this time.

Then Chertkov was kissing thin air. He looked and saw her sauntering away, swinging the big Dégas book. She waved at him over her shoulder.

"Thanks for the book," she laughed, cutting away into the crowd, her freewheeling hips rocking her coattails.

Chertkov walked in the other direction. A spoiled child, a professor's only brat, he thought, but there were physical compensations for Ludmilla's arch selfishness—these he could not sample for another five days. He forced himself to think of other things.

The swimming pool was on the return leg of his Saturday circuit: Chertkov recrossed the square. Making his way around a family of Uzbek tourists solemnly photographing one another, Chertkov noticed the small woman in the bottle-green coat on the steps of the Kirovskaya Metro entrance. He knew her: Marta her name was, she was a typist in a backwater State Security office outside the Ring Road. Chertkov remembered her face from the photo log of runners when crash meetings were called. Their eyes met and then fell, slipping away to scan the street for other eyes, hostile ones.

Tell me everything's safe, Chertkov said to himself. As if on cue, the woman lifted her copy of *Pravda* and revealed the pair of white gloves tucked in her belt, the "most urgent" signal, crash meeting four stops down the line—the Park Kultury stop. "All crash meetings at seven past the hour, even hours only," Chertkov recited to himself. He glanced at his watch: it was quarter to six. The woman walked past him, four or five paces toward the Metro doors, then dropped a small paper packet. Chertkov stepped behind her, retrieved the packet, and called to the woman.

"Comrade! Your parcel!"

The woman turned, checking her coat, and then did a creditable blush. "Kind of you, comrade. Thank you." She disappeared for a moment, moving away from a clot of passersby, a path which took her behind a newspaper hoarding. Chertkov joined her, holding out the parcel. The woman was prettier than her photo, younger as well, really barely more than a girl, thought Chertkov as he looked at her.

"The meet is with Leon." She was pushing the paper packet into her coat.

Chertkov was nodding and smiling; he spoke through his teeth: "Where is he?"

"He'll be on the platform. Black armband, look for the armband."

"What's up?" They bowed and moved apart, playing the crowd.

"Talk to him. He thinks he's being followed. Leon is a brave man, but he's worried, he needs your courage," she begged, nodding. "Leon respects you so much." The thought crossed Chertkov's mind that the two might be lovers. The girl stepped into the crowd and was gone. Is this the best they can do for me? Chertkov thought. A neurotic girl and a fanatic Baptist as runners for Paris's star operative? He let the crowd carry him to the head of the escalator and down to the southbound platform.

Chertkov did what any professional would do: he combed the Park Kultury station for unwanted company. He scanned the platform and stairwells from the Metro car, and then stayed on the Metro for two more stops, disembarking at Sportivnaya and buying some boiled sweets and cigarettes at the tobacconist's in the lobby of the high-rise Junostj Hotel. He returned to the Metro and allowed three northbound cars to pass before taking the one that would have him at Park Kultury precisely on time. He boarded the fourth northbound car and checked all the platform stops, keeping his face behind the CCCP decal on the sliding doors whenever he saw the militia.

The Park Kultury station was a madhouse. Dynamo had played Red Army that afternoon and the crowds were still feverish from the match. Chertkov fastened himself to three drunk fans, ripe with vodka and sweat. That was a good touch, escorting the drunks—Chertkov knew the militia would take that as a sign of good citizenship, especially in a privileged GRU officer.

Spilling onto the main concourse, singing at the top of their lungs, the four of them waltzed straight at Chertkov's contact, a ferret-faced student wearing a black mourning band on his thin coat sleeve, a boy barely out of his teens, pacing away like mad at the foot of the escalators. He hadn't shaved properly and his eyes were wild. A shouted order from above—bells rang and lights flashed: singing lustily, Chertkov swung the Stolichnaya quartet away, toward the up escalator, still leading them in song. Out of the corner of his eye, Chertkov watched the State Security "greens" come boiling off the down escalator and hoist one hundred and thirty pounds of struggling boy straight off the ground, like a pile of dirty clothes.

Not ten feet away, Chertkov felt his stomach turn somersaults as he sang, praying the boy would not call out or signal him. In the event, there was no time for heroics, for the KGB men had the boy off the escalator, heading toward the *voronok*, the paddy wagon, in less than twenty seconds; Chertkov had momentarily forgotten how fast the Metro escalators were.

Chertkov had his own problems now, the first of which was ridding himself of his three inebriated protectors. There were whispered conversations cascading down the escalator now, as the shoppers wondered at the boy's arrest. Chertkov said nothing; one of his new acquaintances was being sick below him.

Chertkov lost the hockey fans in the crush at the street doors. His pulse rang in his ears: those two, the girl and Leon the Baptist, were the first face-to-face contacts in his surreptitious trade with his umbilical cord to the West in two full years. What a way to lose your virginity, he thought, feeling his shirt cling to his armpits. But I feel strangely calm, he wondered. I must think.

On the street, the *voronok* was backing up, a "green" talking to the driver from the paddy wagon's running board, seemingly looking right at Chertkov, but then saluting another KGB man on the steps behind. Chertkov turned and moved closer to the doors, into the safety of the throng.

As he stepped sideways through the pressing crowd, something tugged at his elbow. "How was he? Did you calm him?" It was the girl, Marta, her admiring face pressed to Chertkov's shoulder.

Chertkov pulled her away from the crowd, very hard, lifting her off her feet. He stepped behind a door and jammed the girl between the open door and the wall. For a few seconds they were alone. "He's just been arrested, d'you hear? Didn't you see the *voronok*? You must be mad, following me after a meet." Chertkov looked over his shoulder. The paddy wagon was pulling away in a cloud of blue smoke, the KGB man still riding the running board.

The girl's grip brought him back. "What? Leon arrested?"

"Bring me the papers. Thursday, understand? The papers. Thursday."

Too frightened or too brave to cry, the girl stood, her shoulders wedged against the masonry, struck dumb. She simply nodded and Chertkov left her there.

Pushing his bag in front of him, Chertkov crossed the entering stream of Metro passengers at the doors, checked his back against the flow of the Saturday night crush, then dove into the herd at the head of the escalator. At the foot of the moving staircase, he strode off purposefully, following the signs to the northbound trains. Surely the "greens" would have pounced by now, he reassured himself; surely they would have grabbed me at Park Kultury. And that bloody girl . . . imagine hanging about after a meet like that! The train pulled into the station.

The Metro car was nearly empty, the second of a pair of trains working the same route. He took a seat near the door and sat down, watching the faces. Nothing. The usual stone faces, staring stonily at the black walls of the tunnels, at the lights, at the other stone faces. A woman with a dark mole on her cheek was staring at his books. Let her look, he thought. Let her look, the old cow: I have the connections. Connections to die for. He nearly smiled but thought better of it; the cow might mistake his smile for what *Pravda* was decrying as consumerist pride and tell him off. *Anonymity*, they had always told him, *that's the trick*.

His eyelid was twitching. Close, too bloody close, I feel like one of those knife jugglers in the State Circus. "We will get you out," they had promised; it ran around his head like a fugue: "We will get you out—at all costs. You mean that much to us, Nikolai." His eyelid flickered again. He needed to be alone. Chertkov had had enough of crowds. He needed space. To think. To breathe.

# Chapter Three

The slow chop of the Chesapeake lolled the sloop closer to the point. The suburban sailors had long since headed home to Baltimore and points west, for this was a chill Saturday night in October. The autumn sunset spread like egg yolk across the water, paving a dancing road to the west, up the Patuxent estuary, toward the Elysian fields of Washington. Two men, one a diminutive sort in a windbreaker, Topsiders, and a battered tennis hat, the other a sprawling beer keg of a fellow wrapped in a hooded hunting jacket with no nautical pretense whatsoever, sat comfortably on the sloop's deck in the glow of a Coleman lantern. Their murmured after-dinner conversation barely carried over the rhythmic slap of the tidewater.

The man wearing the tennis hat examined the tension of his anchor line and then peered into the dark shadow within the hunting jacket hood. Morley Walsh, who inhabited the jacket's ursine bulk, sought, coffee mug in hand, a more comfortable posture and the sloop swung for a moment. Ever attuned to his own wants, Walsh was reminded of his cold cigar. The spark of his lighter revealed his round, unlined face to his companion. The diminutive fellow, Charlie Kemper, whose sloop it was, was saying: "That's what I hear Rappaport thinks. What do you think?"

Walsh, aboard the sloop on sufferance—despite his Boston birth, he hated the sea—took his time in replying. His companion, Walsh noted as he exhaled, was a bit of a climber. You're too much the parrot and too little the hawk, Charlie, Walsh aphorized, filing the "little hawk" *mot* away for future reference and dropping his lighter into one of his jacket's dozen pockets.

"What do *I* think, Charlie? Tough times, tough times ahead. I think there's ten senators who'd give up sex for the chance to nail the Group's hide to the floor. I think all three networks, the *Post*, the *Times*, even the goddam *Podunk Evening Herald* would bet their circulations on this one. Sunday supplements, full color." Walsh, his gimlet eye pausing to skewer Kemper, twisted his cigar between his strong fingers.

"Not only do I think the whole thing's bound to blow, but it's my considered opinion we'll see a pogrom, worse than Bay of Pigs. You watch. Those Cubans waltzing around the Watergate make us fair game. From Rappaport on down. Cub reporters and the FBI with their noses up your kilt, Charlie, breakfast, lunch, dinner, and drinks."

Walsh found the deck chair let in a draft and pulled the jacket down over the small of his ample backside. "That's what I think, Charlie. You're a rational man, you've been with Group for ten years now. Hunker down and check your bank balance, m'boy. It's an ill wind. And an election year." There, that should sweat him, Walsh thought. That morning Walsh had scanned Kemper's personal file, with a crafty eye for his banking records; he even knew Kemper's docking fees for this rather pretentious boat. Walsh watched Kemper, waiting for the reaction to set in.

Kemper remembered the fallout after the Bay of Pigs and felt his résumé pass before his eyes. He knew his was the class Rappaport would turn to when the sacrificial lambs came to be culled; the troops below were anonymous and the generals above had long since totted up their political credits and debits. But his renewed career was just barely underway: as an old field hand, he had no power base in the corridors, little leverage yet at the round table. Kemper, who had waited nearly a year for Walsh to grant him a small network, felt a draft of his own while he sourly considered a future in real estate. Or worse. He zipped his windbreaker up to his neck and stared at the black water.

Walsh, with his lawyer's sense of silence, waited. First the stick and then the carrot, Walsh thought. Kemper was ideal for the job, a former field operative Walsh had brought home as a reward. Kemper knew the back-alley world of legmen and landlines, but he was a novice in the more dangerous world of memo and committee. Walsh canted his cigar upward and let his breath propel a wisp of smoke over the rail.

"With all due respect, Rappaport isn't the quickest man on the uptake but he sees we should be cleaning house, Charlie. By the time we finish the chore, he wants Joe Taxpayer to be able to eat off Group's floors. I'm talking *clean*, Charlie. Sanitized for your protection, the dead well and truly buried." Walsh topped the ash off his cigar and replaced it between his teeth. "No surprises. Rappaport was most specific about that. He wants no surprises, Charlie."

Walsh wasn't Rappaport's right arm for nothing, Kemper reflected: the secret world thrived on doom, and Walsh's voice suited the occasion. Walsh's face had returned to the shadows of his hood. Kemper looked down at the water, watching the mobile fretwork of the waves.

"What about BROKEN ARROW? What's Rappaport make of that?"

Walsh's eyes glowed fractionally within his hood. "We've never talked about that particular rumor." He drew on his cigar, his hands on his thighs and his elbows out, rocking on his broad backside.

The rhythm of the waves broke as the wind rose. Kemper shoved his hands in his pockets. "Know what I think? BROKEN ARROW's a Russian invention. Make us chase our tails, raise our blood pressure, set committees at each other's throats. Crap." Kemper threw a matchstick to the waves and returned his hands to the warmth of his pockets. "Crap," he repeated, "BROKEN ARROW's a mathematical impossibility. Aren't enough Marxists in Berkeley and Manhattan put together to amount to much. So who can the Russians recruit these days? Who's going to buy the socialist worker's paradise? BROKEN ARROW is sick think."

Walsh pursed his lips. "Exactly. In my mad moments, I think Group and CIA supergrades reinvent BROKEN ARROW when things get slow. Keeps the underlings on their toes."

There followed a silence broken only by the licking water.

Kemper spoke first. "So what's in a houseclean for me? Zero: nobody loves a hatchet man. Give me a network, let me show you what I can do."

Walsh threw back his head and laughed. His laughter bounced off the water and echoed back from the point, slow and rich, like fresh cream. "What *are* you doing these days?"

"Going slowly crazy. This week, editing a memo on Third World religions from Rangoon Station. Last month I filmed a Canadian aerospace engineer making a fool of himself with a Czech swallow."

"Small time. How about something real? How about *survival*? How about a whole ass and a decent pension?"

Walsh tipped the jacket hood off his head and his hair rose in stiff fingers in the wind. He dabbed his cigar at Kemper. "We have a man in Moscow Rappaport wants out. Detente is the flavor of the month and Rappaport doesn't want his man blown. Bad for election-year image, he says. Especially when the body in question is Rappaport's baby—solo heroics usually rate you a very small office in Weights and Measures when the whistle blows."

"If you're lucky," Charlie Kemper replied. "Rappaport's broken his own rule, running his own network: let him take the heat. We'll still be here if he takes a fall."

"Don't count on it," Walsh said and sniffed.

The sun was long down now, and the warmish breeze from the west blended the cool salt sea air with the faint smell of diesel exhaust from the crab boats. Kemper stood and stretched his legs.

"Might as well write myself off right now, if that's what you have in mind. Errand boy on a defector run. Hell. Brother-in-law Bob says I can gross eighty a year in real estate. Get a Maryland license, he says eighty easy, the suburbs are really taking off. I don't have to tell you my wife says the same thing damn near every night."

Walsh squinted at him for a moment; Kemper was deceptive, a counterpuncher; not a hawk, Walsh revised—more the porcupine.

"Why me? What's security up to?" Kemper had his back to the rail, leaning on his elbows. "Why not call in CIA? They can handle it, right? Let them earn their dough. Besides, Rappaport has five better men for the job than me. There's Calder and Russell for starters. I mean, I'm no slouch, but those two have twice the Eastern European experience I do."

"Your modesty does you credit, Charlie, but it's not a matter of the talent on hand within the organization, you see." Walsh twirled his cigar and flicked a disc of ash away with his ring finger. He pulled a fragment of tobacco from his lip before continuing.

"You haven't quite got it, Charlie, grasped the principle."

"What d'you want to do, go outside the Group? Who you going to use?"

Walsh paused. Then he gave Kemper a slow grin. "Yes. Let's go outside. You never saw this. I got it this morning." Kemper took the yellow telex paper and held it up to the light: "DC

STATION EXECUTIVE EYES ONLY STOP SOURCE GIRAFFE REPORTS
ARREST NOAH LINKMAN LEON APPROX 1400 LOCAL TIME . . .''

"Jesus, I'm not cleared for NOAH!" Kemper looked up at
the stars and wrinkled his brows beneath his floppy hat. He
lowered his gaze to the telex flimsy and regarded the big man
in his best deck chair with disbelief.

"You are now," Walsh said evenly. "Question is, what are
you going to do about it?"

"Since when do we go outside? For a defector run? Besides,
we'd have to split the take if we use the Company. If we get him
out."

Walsh waggled a finger free. "NOAH's getting him out—
we're just going to hold his hand when he does. And we go
outside. This once. Because we have to. Remember, it's a
housecleaning. If the Moscow connection is blown, Rappaport
wants our fingers well away from the pie. Let CIA take the flak,
he says, anybody but us. So we use outside talent. Cosmetics,
that's the word Rappaport used. Better cosmetics if the Watergate thing blows."

Walsh's tone allowed no contradiction. Somewhere overhead
a gull screamed. Kemper looked past Walsh to the darkening
waves for a long minute and then asked, "Morley, why me?"

Walsh hated wasting the last inch of cigar and pulled hard
before he replied. "Rappaport figures Mr. Moscow ought to
come home. Next month, election's over, the front page
people'll be hot on the trail again. Imagine what the press would
make of Rappaport running his own empire, his own private
mole in Moscow, while the White House spouts detente? The
heavens would fall. Charlie, this break-in thing, the sharks are
circling," Walsh said, satisfied he'd had the best of his smoke.
"Why you? I need a cut-out to the outside and you're my man,
Charlie, it's that simple."

"I need a day to think it over. I'll get back to you about . . ."

Walsh waved him off with a grimace. "You don't exist if you
want the job. Leave of absence at the usual pay. Book yourself
into a drunk tank for all we care. I don't want to know, Rappaport doesn't want to know. Everything stays under your hat
and off paper, right? No memos, no new files, no need to know.
Oral only, personal to me. Fund it cash-and-carry—Quinn's
vouchered you twenty grand. You need more, we'll talk. Don't
cut any new contracts; those secretaries talk in their sleep. And
no access to Rappaport unless at his explicit request." Walsh

handed Kemper a plain card bearing a single phone number in ballpoint.

"If you decide to take it on, call here by tomorrow noon and I'll lay on the papers. No more until you're on board." Walsh, now things were progressing smoothly, was pleased to affect a nautical flavor. He had one last pull on his cigar.

"Thanks for the dinner and the chat. Think it over. Dream time for me; I've got my hands full now Rappaport's in Geneva." Disappearing again into his huge jacket, Walsh rose and tossed his cigar overboard. "Remember: talk to me first, Rappaport only at his explicit request. Understand?"

"Understand." Holding the Coleman, Kemper saw Walsh down the stairs to the cabin.

Kemper extinguished the lantern and leant at the rail. Rappaport'll have a goddam child if this one blows: there must be a way to cover my . . . Kemper stifled a nervous cough. He played the odds off for a moment and decided Rappaport would require his pound of flesh, win, lose, or draw. Then there was Morley Walsh. If Walsh, of all people, wants to go outside, Kemper rationalized, this job's got to be one of the great stinkers of my brilliant career. If it's outside he wants, outside he's going to get. Kemper had a short list ready of course, but he'd known five minutes ago the man he would go with. Above the swaying mast, a pair of marsh owls flew close and then dove for darkness. It was night, and their hunting time.

# Chapter Four

Outside Moscow stands a string of white *dachas*, sprinkled in the woods like so many mushrooms in the shade of the pines white-sheathed by the light overnight snow. They belong to the Soviet élite, the concert pianists, the computer scientists, to members of the Politburo and its satellites. One of these *dachas* sits froglike at the end of a freshly plowed road, a faceted pair of windows staring into the evergreen shadows, a Brothers Grimm miniature. A herd of Chaïka limousines grazes in the side yard, their well-waxed noses nudging a spindly hedgerow. Behind the hedgerow lies an all-weather porch enclosing an enormous table ringed with the decadent offspring of the politically anointed.

Boris Alexandrovitch Moldov, full colonel of the Red Army Intelligence Directorate and father, enjoying the second Sunday of his first week off in nearly four years, was serving ice cream and rum cake, his head still woozy from the GRU staff bash at the Hotel Rossiya Saturday night. His good humor kept a ridiculous party hat on his head and a creaky smile wreathing his face. He loved the kids; they made much more sense to him than their parents, most of whom had long since lost their animation in the GRU hothouse. The last of the cake went around the table, passed bucket-brigade fashion until Moldov's son Ilya, whose Young Pioneers party it was, received a mammoth piece, the center square with the big red icing-sugar star.

Forgoing the calories, Moldov led the children in a tuneless song, and then, throwing on a huge sweater, carried a glass of steaming tea to the tree stump down the snowy hill from the *dacha*. He ran a finger around his jaw and rubbed the spot that

38

relieved the pain in his bad eye, the walleye. On the worst days, Moldov wore an eye patch, but things had been better lately. Brushing the first snow of autumn from the stump, he sat and thoughtfully sipped his tea.

The aroma of Johnny Walker and duty-free American hair spray fought a losing battle in his memory with the rank smell of perspiration and boilerplate suits: the promotion party for Ferenko, one of Moldov's assistants, the night before had co-incided with the latest shipment of luxury items from New York. Moldov sipped his tea and smiled at the sound coming from the *dacha* of the children singing "It's a Small World" in excellent English and shouting the Russian part. Moldov liked everything about Walt Disney (he'd even seen a bootleg copy of *Mary Poppins* at a private Goskino screening) and had claimed the record from the effects of an Aeroflot pilot now in the GULAG for smuggling. Good party last night, Moldov thought to himself as the tea soothed his stomach. Too much caviar and shoptalk, but Moldov felt pleased about Ferenko's promotion; he had rec-ommended it personally.

Ferenko was a bland Georgian, a slim man of thirty-five with a pretty, hairless face and flat enameled eyes. Moldov had brighter men among his subordinates—Ferenko was cautious, with the imagination of a thick plank. But he was the best ad-ministrator Moldov had, an asset Moldov valued because, as the directorate joke ran, the comrade-colonel remembered every-thing but the details.

Moldov had settled his feet on a convenient rock when his young wife gave their special call for the ring of the secure phone linking Moldov's *dacha* with Moscow Center. Moldov sighed, and carrying the tea glass in one hand and juggling a small snowball in the other, he led his shambling body up the hill.

At the end of the *dacha*'s high-ceilinged central hallway was Moldov's study, a bright place lined with photographs of the Great Patriotic War, dominated by a print of a beardless officer, standing next to a burnt-out Tiger tank smoldering in the shadow of the Brandenburg Gate, its turret askew, like a chicken with a wrung neck. The *VéChé*, the high-frequency hookup to GRU headquarters, rested next to the regular phone on his desk under the big photo. Monday starts on Sunday in this business, he thought, as an electronic grunt burped down the circuitry and into his ear. A voice floated above the static.

". . . about it backwards. That takes time. Are you following me, comrade-colonel?"

"Are you following me": one of Ferenko's pet phrases. "You haven't told me anything yet. What the hell do you want?" Moldov pulled at his earlobe and breathed noisily. Ferenko was one of the new generation of Red Army intelligence officers; he had a pedant's overprecision and verbal tics, except when drunk, when he became a riotous extrovert. He had unnaturally small hands, like a child's, which habitually pressed his files to his asthmatic chest when his inferiority complex was stung. Moldov could hear Ferenko nervously licking his lips between answers while in the background metal ladders clanked under booted feet. Ferenko was calling from his underground cave.

"The computer is down, comrade-colonel. We have a week's worth of punch cards to process and Roskov's on medical leave. . . ."

"Medical leave? Balls! Roskov's as hung over as you are— put him on report. We'll see how his delicate health is after a week of double-shifts." Moldov cleared his throat violently, rumbling his smoker's phlegm. "Don't bore me with your housekeeping problems, Ferenko. The Army promoted you because you have a brain. Start thinking."

Ferenko was practically in tears; registry was going through hell, that was the way the job went when the big boys wanted to be fed. Ferenko's voice steadied as he replied. "Sir. Yes. We have a lead that ties in with RAYMOND's transmission last night."

"Go on."

"RAYMOND simply reported that his superiors were immediately informed of the Baptist boy's arrest last night in the Park Kultury Metro. I hope this doesn't mean an internal investigation, sir." There was a pause. "Sir?"

"RAYMOND's a state secret. Keep talking about him on a phone line, even a secure one, Ferenko, and next thing I'll be reading about him in the *Times* of New York." Moldov thought he heard a sniffle at the other end but that could have been static.

"Sir."

"And how the hell d'you know about RAYMOND, Ferenko?"

Ferenko began to cough, buying time. "RAYMOND's name is mentioned in the docket cross-reference." Pages turned. "Right here, comrade-colonel, direct from Center. Source RAYMOND is right there in black and white."

Moldov said nothing, listening.

There was a pause as pages turned even faster. "Sir. Yes.

Now about the boy, the one the 'neighbors' pulled in last night at Park Kultury. Turns out Mikhail—that's my assistant, Major Dubov, the soccer player, you remember—Mikhail's been keeping a file on the boy since we got that photograph of the Red Army officer standing with him outside the Bolshoi.''

Moldov licked his teeth before he replied. "Anything else?"

Ferenko was turning pages again. "Yes. Sir, if RAYMOND's right, we should be thinking about running an internal. That boy is a runner. He must be helping service someone, comrade-colonel. There is a possibility the Red Army has a 'pig.' Here. In Moscow."

"Are you quite finished? What's all this manure about an internal? I won't have my service turned inside out, hear me? A 'pig' in Moscow Center? Where is your proof? Where are the meets, the drops, the linkmen? I'm beginning to have doubts about you, Ferenko: your promotion's gone to your head, you're thinking too much. Stick to the job I gave you, do what I tell you, when I tell you, understand?"

"Yes, comrade-colonel."

"Be in my office first thing tomorrow."

Moldov threw the special telephone back into its rest and reached for his box of Cuban cigars. He lit one and rubbed his eye as he smoked. Moldov watched his hand stroke the contours of his cigar. When he was under the gun, his conditioned response was a dreamlike hibernation as the problem drifted past his mind's eye. He raised his gaze to the picture of his wife in her Italian summer dress under a birch, her smile focusing in the middle distance. Like a madonna: I wonder if the rumors about her and young Roskov are true. Lora Ivanova was Moldov's second wife, a lithe brunette eighteen years his junior, her body still firm even after her rocky pregnancy with Illya. Moldov rubbed the corner of his eye with a finger tip and rolled his cigar around his mouth. His bad eye had been dry lately. Best to see the GRU physician tomorrow. Probably the hormones again.

Ferenko. Internal. Moldov transferred his panatella to the other side of his mouth and slowly closed his eyes. If Ferenko was right, this one was going to ricochet around Moscow Center . . . He slowly tapped his fingers on the desk top. There are a few—what was the phrase the American in Berlin used?—there are a few curve balls in this one: Moldov, care, old man. Be careful.

Moldov's eye began to throb again. He let his eyelids fall for a moment. He was suddenly tired, tired of twenty-five years of fighting off his clever subordinates, fighting for power, fighting to keep RAYMOND to himself, to safeguard all his RAYMONDs, men whose failings and strengths he knew better than any lover's, men whose treachery had won Moldov this very *dacha*. All this without the good family and political connections Ferenko and his schoolchums had. Major Ferenko had grown rather big for his boots. Moldov rubbed his good eye, then gently closed it.

And Lora Ivanova in her beautiful dress smiled down at him from her photograph, watching over him with loving grace.

# PART II

## MONDAY–WEDNESDAY

"And clouds now gather over me
In secret silence, as before . . ."
*Pushkin*

# Chapter One

The entryway door slammed. "They should fix the hydraulics in the goddam closer," the postman thought to himself; the graystone was the oldest and worst maintained on this section of West 75th. A sneeze echoed: the rookie postman had a cold, but had been persuaded not to call in sick by his amorous roommate, an advertising copywriter who needed their apartment for an afternoon with Heather, his latest conquest from the typing pool. The postman stepped into the once elegant alcove, now littered with discarded flyers and unforwarded bills. Nothing for numbers one or two but the usual stuff. He reached into his pouch for number three's.

Unlike the aluminum replacements serving one and two, the last mailbox was an aging brass affair with a Bakelite button above its paint-spotted frame to summon the occupant of the third floor front. The autumn rains worsened the postman's sinus condition, but his memory was undeterred; there was something different about the envelope in his hand, something he couldn't quite remember. Today was Monday; the U.S. government checks for the week weren't due to drop into mailboxes throughout the five boroughs of New York until Friday. In the past, Apartment Three received one check monthly from a post-office box address somewhere in Maryland, and in a different make of buff envelope, but the government check visible through the address panel was the same as the others he delivered. Today the same buff envelope was in his bundle but with no check inside. And postmarked New Jersey, for some reason. Poor guy, the postman thought as he sniffled; Uncle Sam's screwed up again. The postman stuffed a post card, a brochure promising

45

Jamaica for less, and a coupon for the local dry cleaners into the box with the government envelope and slapped the brass box shut. Checking his watch—it was just past two—he kicked the recalcitrant door open with a gum-booted foot and wondered how his roommate was doing with the fabulous Heather.

Upstairs, in the kitchen of number three, an espresso pot bubbled and spewed steam on the gas stove top, mixing its vapor with a cloud of Camel smoke that rose to the ceiling in art nouveau swirls. A pair of restless feet in J.C. Penney work socks crossed the floor to answer the pot's burps. Turning down the gas flame with a practiced twist of his thick wrist, Marty Prevadello returned to his kitchen table. There a copy of Yashiroda's *Bonsai* text lay opened next to a tree Prevadello was dwarfing; the book had been a get-well present from his sister-in-law a couple of years ago. A steel rule, several sets of pliers, a spool of soft copper wire, and the litter of clipped tree limbs were the only disorder in the room. The rest of the kitchen was almost crisply neat, with disciplined bachelor places for the frying pans and knives; the definitive masculine touch was a Golden Gloves schedule tacked next to the wine rack. Here Prevadello for the time being took his contemplative lunches, in the third floor front of this perennially renovated graystone which stood between two upper-class cousins near Broadway and 75th. The scale of his meals was a bachelor's, and his honest bachelor fare, for three, say, consisted in a straight multiplication of his own dinner—three plates of linguine, three roast chickens, three zabaglione. His was a small, simple life, habitual, removed from the growing trendiness of the street below.

The 75th Street apartment had belonged to a painter before Prevadello's retirement and the place still smelt faintly of turpentine and earth pigments; Prevadello liked the bohemian flavor of the apartment's past and made no attempt to cleanse it. When the painter left for Oregon, Prevadello moved in to find his only closet stacked six-deep with old *New York Times* arts and leisure segments that age and a leaky roof had reduced to solid obelisks of pulp. He thriftily took his machete to the mess and had a lifetime supply of tinder for the fireplace. Next to the closet a flea-market oddity stood guard, an oak egg-crate hat display, refugee from a failed milliner's shop; Prevadello, for reasons he himself had long forgotten, collected hats: there were at least two dozen nestled in the egg-crating—Borsalinos, fedoras, six Panamas, an improbable Stetson given him as a retirement present—and yet more hats. Typically, Prevadello rarely wore any of them (certainly not the Stetson), preferring a gray beret from Woolworth's.

The hallway walls bore several hypnotic paintings of a modern sort and pencil drawings of attenuated nudes which might have been Matisses but weren't. Prevadello had drawn them himself at a figure drawing class at CCNY. The drawings were dominated by a framed charcoal by a different hand altogether—an ex-convict Prevadello had quietly set on his feet. Prevadello's bedroom was severe, with flat white walls and a narrow bed typical of rooming houses; a trio of bonsai trees stood on the windowsill. There were no carpets; Prevadello preferred the *tatami* mats he had bought during his hitch in Korea. Without exception, the remaining furniture was light-grained wood, without cushions, notable only for its simplicity. There were none of the usual concessions to the creature comfort middle age covets, no living room, no reclining chair. The front room was an enormous space split floor to ceiling by a rattan partition; this area alone was the size of most flats and the chief reason Prevadello loved the place. On one wall he kept his books, an impressive array running from a first edition set of *Das Kapital* bought at auction (that indulgence set him back a week's pay twenty years ago) to an autographed Tennessee Williams he'd found in a hotel in Cuernavaca. One of his colleagues had expressed an interest in Prevadello's book collection some years ago—the fellow was strictly a classics-by-mail man—and was astounded by the titles on Prevadello's wall. "You read these, I mean, *all* of them?" Prevadello politely poured him a drink and guided him toward a more convivial pursuit on the far side of the rattan.

Here Prevadello kept his one vice, a full-size snooker table. In his youth, too short for basketball, too slow for stickball, Prevadello had taken to snooker. Addicted in a matter of days, he practiced endlessly after school. His dedication soon impressed Prevadello senior, who bought young Martino the cue he still used. Prevadello relished the satisfying click of a well-struck ball and the uncanny control the hours of practice gave him over the breaks. Predictability, that was the thing; one could never be a money player without predictability, the foreknowledge that simple physics would see one through if only the nerves obeyed. Prevadello could while away solitary hours on stuns, screws, combinations, and all the arcana of the art.

And those hours taught Prevadello concentration, made him discover the true span of an hour, and now, decades later, after a lifetime of working to other men's schedules, its duration shocked him. The leisure his time in harness had won him grew precarious, an intimation of his own mortality. For the first time in his life, Prevadello visited a dentist regularly, an urgency inspired by the tutting noises the good Dr. Spiegelman made as he tinkered with Prevadello's antique bridgework. And though Prevadello had a nearly intact set of Italian peasant hair, he checked his hairbrush warily some mornings. More and more, Prevadello found himself browsing drugstores, a connoisseur of treatment shampoos.

Prevadello now spent his days cultivating a disengagement from his twilit past, a metaphysical process akin to peeling his conscience apart as botany students do onion tissue. His self-dissections, conducted on long rambles through Central Park and, of late, off-season walks on Cape Cod, were not the demonstrative stuff exotic therapies are made of; he was too private a man for that. In fact, his past employers had ensured that Prevadello had seen a psychiatrist for some months following the breakdown that led to his retirement; those records are sealed. Those who knew him doubt the shrink gleaned much, scoffing that Marty more than likely ended up interrogating *him*. There was a cloistered past to be harrowed, that much can be said for certain; the rest of Prevadello is eminently unremarkable.

Common-sense, durable clothes bought off the rack fitted an average body made unaverage by forearms and shoulders thickly padded with muscle developed by two years of serious middle-weight boxing in the army. Prevadello shunned the external marks of nonconformity, for his greatest pleasure (a noun he himself would never breathe in this context) lay in observing with himself unobserved: that was the perfect *gestalt*.

But as Prevadello's postman well knew, Manhattan is not without its share of bachelor ascetics. Prevadello's living arrangements, though austere, were not unlike those of his neighbors below, a pair of homosexual actors who vented their domestic frustrations with inexpensive flatware, for which ruckus they unfailingly apologized when Prevadello lay awash in his bath. The first floor occupants were known to Prevadello only by inference: reams of mail from Eastern Europe and an aroma of slivovitz that climbed the stairs in absolute silence. All this is most unremarkable for that quarter of New York in the fall of 1972.

But what is remarkable about Martino Saverio Prevadello, first son of Maria and the late Filippo, is his twenty-year stint as a New York City Police Department detective, an enigma to his colleagues from the start. Yet if his colleagues found him a mystery, he was also something of a legend to a generation of police academy graduates who heard him lecture on surveillance technique and interrogation, a dowdy fiftyish figure even in his thirties who left chalkboards covered in perfectly horizontal, perfectly illegible handwriting.

His Robert Hall suit bunched at the shoulders and swelling across his belly, eraser and chalk in one hand, a yellow mug of espresso regularly replenished from a battered thermos in the other, Prevadello would pause at either end of his circuit to stand and sip at the edge of the lecture stage, the toes of his sensible shoes reflecting the rows of stuttering fluorescents above. Annually, after his first teaching appearance, there were heated cafeteria conferences wherein wiser voices (those with relatives on the force) assured the doubtful that the homicide investigations Prevadello related were not figments of his imagination but cases he had supervised and solved. The wise ones cited chapter and verse in the archives downtown and told the doubters to see for themselves. The skeptics were found, converted, in the front row for Prevadello's next class. If Prevadello ever noticed these realignments, he gave no sign. And the reluctant legend grew.

There is far more of Prevadello's life not on file, except in certain sealed records in Washington unavailable even to his police superiors. So there were rumors. There were rumors of a broken marriage (false), a spell—or two—with an obscure subsidiary of American intelligence (vague but true), and rumors of a time apart—variously in a fishing shack on a Long Island beach (a poor guess), at a rich uncle's villa near Venice (uncles near Venice, yes; villas, no), or, after his Korean stint, an unhappy spell in the monastery of a particularly strict order, location unspecified (true, though as yet unconfirmed in the cops' bars where Prevadello was still a topic several drinks into the evening). Prevadello commuted not in the oversize cars his suburban coworkers preferred, but on a used Vespa motor scooter he carefully maintained himself, for he hated the subway with a passion and his native frugality forbade him the use of an automobile. The scooter was easy to park, cheap to run, and the wire panniers Prevadello had fitted to the frame were ideal for transporting the simple foods he bought at well-chosen shops in Little Italy.

When the downstairs door slammed and heralded the arrival of his mail, Prevadello was smoking a second after-lunch Camel (enjoyed through a cheap plastic filter) and twining a short length of wire about a reluctant bonsai tree limb; on the far side of the table, a set of pliers was a place-mark in *Time*'s melancholy account of the latest corruption scandal in the ranks of New York's finest. Prevadello paused, examining the symmetries of the plant, and sipped his espresso. He set his espresso down to attend to the daily mail. Pulling his keys from the depths of the silver boxing trophy (stuffed with old receipts and half-pencils, sure signs of thrift), Prevadello descended the chilly stairs in his shirt-sleeves and customary woolen vest, which he embarrassedly hoped hid the bounce of his round belly with each stair step.

He opened his box: travel flyer, two shirts laundered and pressed for the price of one at King Wah's, and a hurried thank-you post card from Roberta Fields, a divorcée Prevadello occasionally took to dinner, nothing serious; Roberta was a fortyish buyer for Gimbels, witty and eligibly attractive, and with plenty of men in tow, but with a soft spot for Prevadello's conversation—Roberta's ex-husband was a homicide cop in Queens. The harried Roberta had flown to San Francisco and Prevadello had not only escorted her to LaGuardia, but fed her cat, Waldo, a thick brute, for the weekend as well.

Prevadello had to look twice to be sure. Then he tore the buff envelope open. Prevadello could read what his postman could not, the slip of paper informing him that his Federal pension' account was closed. Clipped to the slip was an incomprehensible form letter with a scrawled signature and a phone number in Silver Springs.

"Bastards," he breathed. The expletives that followed grew in inventive filth as Prevadello climbed the stairs. He knew the scenario well enough; he'd played this one out, including the Silver Springs phone number, with variations, to burn an Air Force officer suspected in a Bangkok smuggling case. As he opened his door, Prevadello was already mentally reciting a different phone number, one that would ring the phone on Charlie Kemper's desk. He slammed his door, trod very heavily to the kitchen, and dialed. There followed half a minute of low comedy as Kemper's secretary tried to fend Prevadello off.

"No, you *can't* have my name," Prevadello replied savagely, swinging around his small kitchen to reach into a jumbled drawer. He retrieved a small blue sheet-metal box with a pair of switches on its back, closing the box's jaws like a clamshell around the phone lead. "Tell him it's the Korean Veterans' Association calling. The New York branch. He'll know me." *Hope the blue box's batteries are still good,* said a voice in Prevadello's head.

There was a series of clicks as Kemper shunted the call off the main switchboard and through the scrambled circuits. At the first roar of scrambled noise, Prevadello flicked both switches on his blue box and Kemper's Boston accents came filtering down the line.

". . . you there, Marty? Hello?"

Prevadello reached for the pack of Camels and tapped the plastic mouthpiece on the counter in a single arc.

"Charlie, they've cut off my pension. Know anything about it?"

Forgetting his mouthpiece, Prevadello drew heavily on an unfiltered Camel and imagined he could hear index cards riffling between Kemper's ears. "Don't bother with the rehearsed stuff, Charlie. The truth will be hilarious enough."

There was a pause.

"What *are* you talking about, Marty?"

Prevadello let the silence work its way back to Washington.

"Marty? Hello?"

Prevadello exhaled, hard, and switched the phone to his other ear.

"I said, they cut off my pension. You know why because you told them."

"I don't run the pension accounts, Marty. I'm a busy man. Call them."

Outside, the brawling traffic punctuated a human argument with horns and slamming doors. Prevadello leaned against the windowpane and saw two men pointing at their fenders in the rain.

"Charlie, you have a short memory. One of our better schemes: McCann, William Ronald, remember Willie McCann, retired Air Force maintenance officer we played games with in sixty-four? Smuggling dope from Bangkok in spare parts crates as I remember. We did the same thing to his pension when he wouldn't sleep with the girl from Ipanema or whatever other bright trap we'd set for him. You and me, Charlie. Remember?"

"Haven't a clue what you're talking about, Marty. Can I call you back?"

"*No.* I want you to conference-call Pensions and tell them with me on the line you didn't authorize revoking my pension. Go ahead, Charlie, call—"

"—I've got better—"

"—no, you haven't. You'll find the truth a singular experience, Charlie, I promise you. I *quit:* past tense, quit repeat quit, get it? Give me my dough and leave me alone."

Kemper said nothing.

"Charlie, my pal Duncan's still at the *Daily News.* This'd make a nice fat cover story, don't you think? 'Pension Rip-Off: Spooks Robbed Me, Ex-Cop Says'."

"Well, Marty, my pal Mullen's still in P.R., and he did us up a snappy little press release. Got it right here. Says you never worked for us—not never, no how, no way. Know why, Marty? Because you've been inside some pretty ritzy rubber rooms in your day, and we submit this whole thing's a figment of Mr. Prevadello's shaky imagination. Got the picture?"

"The checks've gone through my account for four years."

"Your account. *Our* bank."

"What the hell d'you mean, *your* bank?"

"I wouldn't go waving your pass book around, know what I mean? If I were you. A man in your delicate condition."

"Partner," Prevadello said slowly, "what the hell do you want? You know I'm out the fifteen thou I loaned my brother. Give me a break."

"So I heard. A man should conserve his capital. Don't you remember the retirement seminar?"

"You're a regular laugh riot, Charlie. You going to tell me what's going on?"

"I want a package delivered."

"You mean *Rappaport* wants a package delivered."

"Nice distinction. No, me, not Rappaport."

"Hire a courier. That's their thing."

"Think of it as vocational training, Marty."

"Drop dead. And you can shove your pension, too. I don't care if I have to live on beans."

Kemper, who had been paid for fifteen years to defuse just such temperaments as Prevadello's, replied softly: "Beans it is, Marty, because NYPD's not getting your offset money either."

Prevadello slammed the phone down and shut his eyes so hard his retinae refused to register for several moments. He rubbed the center of his forehead with the back of his fist and let his sight return.

*I have to go out again:* Prevadello repeated the incantation and then drew on the shrunken Camel. *Four years away*, the inner voice said. ''The door is never closed,'' the pension officer with the face like warm Spam had told Prevadello in the drab Foggy Bottom office. ''We hold the contract, you know. If we need you, you'll know.'' Prevadello had told the pension officer what he thought of him in a few short words and let it go at that. *Four years: that's a lifetime's peace and quiet in this trade.* Prevadello laughed to himself at the thought: I'm like that old tart in *Zorba*; every face on the street knows the magic words to get me on my back.

A murmured thought came to him then, a benison from the past, pitched in the voice of one of the old boys in the Hudson Valley monastery who'd once lived in Morocco. They had been talking of fear in the northern Sahara, fear of one's insignificance in all that sand. After a moment, the old boy suggested the most dangerous thing about the desert wasn't the heat, nor the miles between oases, but the risk one ran of confronting God. Prevadello didn't comprehend the idea then, but as his past appeared and disappeared like a haunted star, he began to get the old boy's drift. Then the mountains of Morocco dribbled away in his memory and the hot breath of a South Bronx hallway rose again: twenty years after and I still can't fight off the memory of her. The Camel was still burning; Prevadello felt the heat between his fingers.

And then a more distant heat crossed his mind, the dreamed heat of gasped breaths as Prevadello bent over the child's desperate face, something breaking in his chest as he watched.

Prevadello butted the Camel. The downstairs buzzer rang once, paused, and then rang again. Prevadello gave the Camel a final twist and headed for the door. He opened his door noiselessly and leant over the stair railing into the entryway alcove. A broad-shouldered figure turned a fair unshaven face upwards. ''Alpha Couriers. Delivery for Premmadello. Sign for it?''

''Open it, will you? I'm not expecting a package.''

The fair face looked at his clipboard and then up again.

''Can't open it, mister. Rules. Government property, says here. Sign for it now?'' The fair face smiled hopefully. The rain had slicked his hair down; the courier looked like a genial rube.

''Down in a moment. Hang on.'' Prevadello climbed down, wishing he hadn't answered.

"You Premma—ah, dello? Korean Veterans Association? That you?" The courier, a boy no more than eighteen, was fiddling with the wet carbons and trying to prolong his respite from the rain. *Nice touch, that,* Prevadello thought, misspelling the name. *I'll have to congratulate Charlie on his wit.*

"My dad was in Korea," said the boy. "Tanker. Shermans. Know any tankers?"

"No, I'm afraid not. We're mostly infantry."

The courier was new to the job, for he couldn't separate the invoice copies properly and Prevadello had to help him. The boy dripped on Prevadello's stocking feet before he muddled off to his next stop. Prevadello watched him board a double-parked van with "Alpha—you bet!" cheerily lettered on its rusty side, then splash the truck into the Broadway circus, with wipers whining and its transmission making a noise like knives sharpening. Prevadello, his breath growing a disc of condensation on the door glass, saw none of this: he was staring at the envelope.

Prevadello poured himself a fresh espresso and a largish tot of *grappa* before opening the package. He settled into the armchair next to the tiny fireplace and tore open the envelope with a single pass of his penknife.

An 8 x 10 photograph fell into his lap, and with it a single sheet of typescript; a pair of Yale keys, one marked "safe-room," was taped to the top of the typescript. The photograph was an enlargement, showing only the head. The face was Slavic, with a single bristly eyebrow running behind thick-framed spectacles, a young face for a fifty-year-old, full of baby fat and calm. *Spoiled, too, if I guess right,* thought Prevadello. The typescript, littered with capitalized acronyms and worknames, meant nothing to Prevadello.

*So. We have a face and story.* Prevadello turned the photograph over but the back of the print was blank except for a rubber-stamp clearance panel with Kemper's countersignature. After clearing off the table from his bonsai labors, Prevadello pulled the cord of the still-scrambled phone to its limit and, swearing off another Camel, picked up his copy of *Time* for diversion and settled in to wait.

Half an hour later, at five past three, the phone rang at his elbow. Prevadello flicked the scrambler on.

". . . Hello? I said, have you got the material there, Marty?"

Prevadello set the envelope on his lap and said nothing. Kemper's country club chuckle echoed in the ear piece. "Marty, you're getting like those Italian opera singers you listen to, the ones who won't sing the encore until their adoring public shouts itself hoarse begging. You're a prima donna, Marty. You listening to me?''

"Prima donnas are the females. And the ones I listen to never have to worry about the state of their retirement finances. Who's your new friend, Charlie, the one with the glasses?''

"You don't need to know anything except he's coming out from behind the Curtain. Nurse him home to Group, that's the job. Do that and I'm off your back.''

Prevadello allowed himself an ironic laugh. "I've known you for damn near twenty years, Charlie, and you've never been off my back. It's your favorite stepladder. What's this job net you? That condo in Hilton Head?''

Kemper clicked his tongue reprovingly. "Not on what they pay me. Let's get down to business; this is costing money. Accountability, that's the word these days. Count thy shekels, lest they be counted against thee.'' They had had a Biblical dialect thing once, Prevadello remembered, an invention born of stake-out boredom. Kemper paused to draw breath; there was a rustle of paper as he found his place. "Now, you're to meet CATALYST—that's him with the eyebrows—and when the Curtain parts—''

"Shut up, Charlie. And spare me the oil on troubled waters shtick, especially when you're the one doing the troubling. Whose idea's this? I'm no European field man—you've got the wrong guy. I don't know Moscow from Massapequa. Scraping the bottom of the barrel, aren't you, calling me in on a defector run? Phone your clever CIA friends. Or is Rappaport still trying to change the course of world history? That it?''

A pause. "Tell your Italian heritage to shut up,'' Kemper replied easily. "He's coming out—you're not going in. It's a milk run, but you lose him, you *will* be eating beans, I guarantee you that. I'm the contractor: you're the mule I want.''

"I see Rappaport's paws all over this. Still play bridge with him? Or hasn't the old villain retired yet? Or has somebody signed him into the nut-house like he did me?''

"Look, we've been through this dozens of times: Rappaport just did what the shrinks told him.''

"That's Rappaport all right, doing what he's told.''

"Keep going, Marty. Do the whole speech.''

"Very funny. Rappaport kept me inside to even things up, get back for all the grief I gave him. I could have been out in three months and you know it.'' Even before Rappaport extended Prevadello's commitment to a plush Group "rest home," as the euphemism ran, the two had cordially disliked one another for years. Before his 1968 breakdown—Prevadello called it "burning out," the Group psychiatrists called it "acute anxiety syndrome"—Prevadello had never really tried to pinpoint the nature of the antipathy; Prevadello was an ex-boxer from Queens and a Democrat by birth, while Rappaport was real-estate Republican, Southern California tennis courts, and martinis in sterling shakers. That was part of it, but there was more, an unspoken competition they stoked in one another's egos, like phosphorus under a fingernail. Prevadello had never trusted Rappaport. He had seen him play tennis once at a party; Rappaport had been deceptively fast, playing deft spinning volleys at unexpected angles, his lanky reach as dangerous as his long stride—Rappaport, Prevadello reminded himself, covered a lot of ground.

Kemper sighed. "No. Look, Marty, believe it or not, I've come up in the world. This is my operation."

"I thought by now you'd be farmed out to personnel, or writing nice, obscure staff assessments for Madrid Station, free-floating. What the hell are you trying to do an honest day's work for? Buy another boat?"

There was a guilty pause.

"Charlie, you sick son of a bitch. You bought another goddam boat and I'm expected to provide the wonderful defector reports to polish your file." With a sudden glow, Prevadello realized he was enjoying himself, really enjoying himself.

There was another silence.

"Well, why don't you just ask?" Prevadello inquired, dead-pan. "Would I let my beloved partner, a fellow cold warrior, have his yacht repossessed for the sake of an expenses-paid free trip to . . ."

"Frankfurt."

"I should be grateful it's not Vienna."

"Give yourself a break, Marty. Losing a defector's an occupational hazard, happens to the best of us. Frankfurt's a new town, new operation. A clean slate. Ease up."

"That's what Rappaport said when he put me out to pasture. A clean slate."

There was a pause. "Well, this *is* a clean slate. It's Frankfurt."

"Very nice, Frankfurt. All airport, as I recall. Jesus, Charlie, you've got balls, sending me to Frankfurt to nurse some Russian home to get yourself kicked upstairs." Prevadello was smiling now, but kept his voice dry.

"As your former partner, I reckoned you wouldn't be dragged back to the trenches without a little leverage."

"As your former partner, I agree completely. I want an interest-free loan of three thousand bucks before I lift a finger."

Kemper had turned his mouth from the phone but Prevadello heard the nervous cough anyway. "That's right, three thousand. My Vespa needs an overhaul and I could do with a spell in Italy after the show. Three big ones, up front, open term. No damn deductions at source while I can't check my contracted pay, either. You *can* get me the three, can't you, Charlie? Wouldn't like to think I was doing business with a go-between."

"Two."

Prevadello said nothing.

Kempler exhaled. "Twenty-three."

"Like pulling teeth, partner, like pulling teeth. Twenty-eight."

"Twenty-five."

"Twenty-seven five. Cabled into my account at Chase Manhattan. Tomorrow. Deal?"

Kemper sighed again. "Deal. The Group giveth and the *paisan* taketh away."

"Never do business with a Venetian, Charlie. You WASPs aren't up to it. So how the hell are you?"

"Oh, I'm all right. Two kids in college, wife on the warpath, the whole ball of wax. Aside from that, I'm healthy. Give up smoking yet? Marg bet you had, said you'd be a changed man."

"Absolutely. Never felt better. And I'm married with three kids, two cars, and a pooch. I'm a changed man all right." Prevadello broke open a fresh pack of Camels and uncapped a Bic ballpoint. With a schoolboy lick of the pen, Prevadello wrote a careful "One" on the back of the typescript. His good humor spent, he grunted, "When do I leave?"

"Your passport doesn't come through until Thursday. Backlog at the shoemakers. I'll have it for you in New York Wednesday. Very special, done to order, delivered by me. We'll meet at the Village safehouse. You've got the safehouse keys there."

"Back door, through the mews?"

"Don't want the world to know, do we? Stick to the back door—and take the subway, check out the garment district, the whole show. Spotting a cab in that neighborhood is a piece of cake. You writing this down?"

"Every blessed word," Prevadello said. "Start talking."

"Right. CATALYST, find that? NOAH's the network servicing CATALYST. Found it?" With that, Kemper began the Socratic process of priming the fuse.

# Chapter Two

A serpentine of idling cars and trucks congested the Brooklyn off-ramp just across the bridge; three men in green jumpsuits were pushing an Allied Movers van across the intersection of Fulton and the expressway on-ramp and half the borough was waiting behind them. Dodging around the traffic jam, Prevadello had the Vespa doing thirty as the twin arches of the bridge tower disappeared in his shaking mirror. Brooklyn is a labyrinth of cross-streets where sometimes even the cabbies plead with St. Christopher, but Prevadello knew Brooklyn from Greenpoint to Sheepshead Bay like a native after his Brooklyn South stint in the mid-fifties. The traffic on Flatbush was really rolling now; Prevadello weaved through the potholes in leafless Prospect Park, dodged between a trio of number forty-seven buses, then banked the Vespa right on Parkside Avenue, taking the long, scenic route.

Demons: Pat Geraghty, then his desk sergeant, shrewdly told Prevadello he'd make a good detective " 'cos you're so easily bored, bud; copping's a matter of keeping your Machiavellian wop brainbox entertained." The rest of the precinct locker room laughed at the time (it was a notoriously Irish station house) but the remark was as accurate as it was glib. That night Sergeant Pat Geraghty stood Patrolman Prevadello a beer, quietly lecturing him at the bar, and a mystified Prevadello was made to understand he was now the sergeant's protégé.

The mercurial Geraghty earned the nickname The Old Man for his efforts with the young ones. Prevadello needed a faith in those days; his head full of overthought doubts, he had left the monastery on the banks of the Hudson with his logic intact and

59

his certainties in tatters—a renegade. Geraghty, high-strung himself, nursed the youngster along, giving him the best of the veterans for patrol partners, feeding Prevadello a strange brand of mother's milk and police lore, and channeling his intellectual ruthlessness toward the trade, sensing the obsession in him. Once his protégé made detective, Geraghty kept his eye on the quiet Prevadello, watching him nurture and play his informant nets like a virtuoso. Prevadello ran his nets the way touts run the horses, dropping a small bet here for the big payoff later. And when Prevadello's net caught him a Polish fish trying to recruit émigré merchant sailors, Geraghty had seen enough.

Geraghty sent Prevadello to an interview at one of the back tables of an Irish bar on Third Avenue with the hard-faced gentleman in the Jaeger suit. That round of drinks and Prevadello's intelligence days in Korea led to what sounded like a job offer; Prevadello wasn't quite sure what the fellow meant by "the Group." Geraghty did; he had bought all the drinks and opened the door to the Group for Prevadello. "A flesh-peddler," Geraghty called himself: Sergeant Pat Geraghty, NYPD, Prevadello's sponsor that humid night, was the best recruiter the Group ever had. And half the men he had pointed in the Group's direction were still in the game.

Prevadello swung the Vespa into the sleepy back streets of Brighton Beach. You could smell the sea from here; the gulls wailed like cats from the roof tops and flew holding patterns around the dead smokestacks. Prevadello parked the scooter behind a two-story brick warehouse with a big painted sign reading "Ocean View Sports Club." The back door opened on a rank of pool tables, vintage 1920, under a leaky tin ceiling; a quartet of Jewish kids was practicing and Prevadello watched for several shots before nodding to the silent desk clerk, who shuffled the classified section of his *Times*.

"You want a cue, Mr. P.?" the gap-toothed clerk asked, as if Prevadello still came in daily. "Been a while, huh? Still got the touch?"

"Yeah, it's been a while." They looked at one another, Prevadello and the elderly clerk with the slicked-back dyed hair, then slowly shook hands.

Manny never stood on ceremony. "Tell me what you think of this, Mr. P: 'Active Pet Store in Dutchess County. Fifteen thou. Owner retiring.' Sounds O.K., huh? What say we go partners, Mr. P.?"

"Not much on pets, Manny. I like trees. They're quiet, you

rake, they grow, you know what I mean?'' Manny nodded and searched his paper again. Prevadello watched as one of the boys playing pool pulled off a nice bank shot. "His nibs in?'' Prevadello asked, still watching.

"He's in back, Mr. P.''

"Drunk or sober?''

"Well, you know, Mr. P.,'' said Manny, ducking his head once again deep in the classifieds.

A magnificent carved arch overhung the main hall and Prevadello remembered that the place had been a fur shop and cold storage business when Teddy Roosevelt was president. A mingled must of old wood and chlorine from the swimming pool crept along the corridor to the gym, and the thud of leather and canvas and flesh echoed.

The double doors sighed as Prevadello passed through. Geraghty, a little more shrunken, bent a little more below his former six-three since the last time Prevadello had seen him, was as flushed as ever. His office was a Victorian cubicle two steps up in the center of the gym, overseeing a dozen fighters working out at the weights and the bags or chasing one another around the two rings. Prevadello shuffled into a slow combination and Geraghty, a smile breaking over his flat mandarin's face, jerked a thumb at his trainer, a beer-bellied man in a Police Athletic League sweat shirt. The trainer threw a towel over his shoulder and jumped down the steps to the gym floor, yelling, "Keep your weight back and Anderson's gonna beat your brains in, Lefkowitz, I keep tellin' ya'' to a tallish fighter wearing sweat pants in the near ring. Prevadello nodded in agreement; the kid *was* winding up, rocking back on his heels when he started his counters—Anderson, the black fellow, was knocking him silly waiting on Lefkowitz's weight shift.

Geraghty didn't get up from his gleamingly anachronistic Swedish chair; a new surgical supply cane leaned against his desk. Hundreds of copies of *Ring*, some dating from before the war, stood like ordnance crates in neatly squared-off piles around the peeling wainscoting. Half a dozen PAL award medallions, stacked like saucers, rested atop a box with "Liniment" scrawled on its side. Geraghty had a notebook with handwritten rankings in front of him. His heavy tortoiseshell spectacles hung around his thick neck from a bright red Kresge's thong and Prevadello noticed Geraghty still wore his old beige cardigan, now mottled with coffee and the mid-afternoon Jameson's. He still looks like a character actor's idea of the mick boxing trainer, Prevadello thought.

"There he is, how about that. How the hell are you, you old pasta sucker? It's been months," Geraghty said, offering a meaty hand, his voice hollow, more fragile than Prevadello remembered.

"How are you, Pat?"

"You know me, Marty . . . never better." Geraghty tightened his grip and winked.

Prevadello gripped the hand just as fiercely and observed, "Nice to see you enthroned, your grace," and then both of them turned as the fat trainer in the Police Athletic League sweat top yelled a particularly vile epithet at the flat-footed Lefkowitz.

They watched for a moment.

"You should get in there, Marty, see what Lefkowitz has." Lefkowitz was getting whiplash from his sparring partner's upper cuts. Ozzie shouted again, cracking his towel in annoyance, bending his knees and motioning angrily.

Prevadello sensed Geraghty's eyes on him. "You don't give up, do you, Pat?"

"Look who's talking. C'mon, let's see some action."

Prevadello grinned and began to take off his shoes. "All right, I'll give him a couple of my best."

"Hey, Ozzie, got a live one for your guy Lefkowitz," Geraghty yelled.

"Give Gramps your gloves," Ozzie called to Anderson, who slipped out of the ring between the ropes. Prevadello had his coat and cardigan vest off and Geraghty was holding the headgear and mouthpiece as Prevadello worked his hands into Anderson's sweaty gloves.

"Sure you know what you're doin'?" Anderson asked, still breathing hard. "He got a pretty good jab, man."

"Mine's not too shabby either," Prevadello replied gently, trying to freeze the silly grin off his face.

"Hey, man, put me in yer will, huh?" Anderson said, stepping back to watch.

Prevadello climbed between the ropes, his socks sliding slightly on the canvas. Lefkowitz, puzzled, was looking at Ozzie. "I gotta do this?" he called. "Guy's older'n my dad."

"So am I, sonny," Ozzie barked, "and I'd whip you too, the way you're fighting these days. O.K., Pat, I got the bell and the watch. Say the word."

Geraghty, leaning on the edge of the ring in Prevadello's corner, looked up at Prevadello, deadpan. "One three-minute round. Keep it clean. Try not to kill him, Marty. Ozzie, whenever you're ready."

Prevadello stepped into his corner, trying to seat the mouthpiece. He had barely time to get it in place before Ozzie hit the bell.

Lefkowitz, thinking it was a put-on, stepped up and did a little shuffle, muttering, "Hit me, pops." Prevadello obliged with a sharp pair of jabs that backed Lefkowitz up, then he waited for Lefkowitz to shift his weight and uppercut him, snapping the boy's head back satisfyingly. Prevadello called to Geraghty as he circled: "Pat, the kid's winding up and getting caught."

"I think you're right. Hey, Oz, he's winding up, for Chrissakes," Geraghty shouted.

Ozzie nodded and shouted at Lefkowitz, "Up, up, up on those toes. Get your weight forward, dammit." Lefkowitz kept circling, trying a tentative hook Prevadello easily parried. Prevadello jabbed Lefkowitz again, waited for him to commit himself, then caught Lefkowitz on the weight change again with a jab, this time knocking him back a step.

"Got no wind," Prevadello shouted around his mouthpiece.

"You or him," Geraghty called out, laughing.

"Me, dammit," Prevadello said, beginning to breathe hard as he feinted to his right.

"Teach you to show off," Geraghty shouted. "Lefkowitz, *hit him*. He won't break. Use your speed."

Lefkowitz got off a quick flurry of punches, landing one to Prevadello's temple that made his head sing. "Better," he growled at Lefkowitz. "That's better."

"*That's* more like it, Lefky," Ozzie shouted. "Get over them punches!"

Prevadello stepped aside and Lefkowitz battered thin air for a moment before Prevadello worked over his exposed ribs. Lefkowitz *was* fast, faster than he looked, and the hooks came back, accurate and hard, and suddenly it wasn't funny anymore.

Prevadello feinted as if to close, bobbed, and caught Lefkowitz with a nice uppercut as Lefkowitz dropped his head. The gym went silent after that. It was a fight now. "No more advice, pal," Prevadello muttered, closing for real now, trying to corner Lefkowitz, who skipped away with a clever bounce off the ropes.

"C'mon, Lefky, fight 'im, don' dance wi' him," Anderson was yelling. They circled again, as Prevadello realized he was giving away a good four inches in the reach department when Lefkowitz simply fended him off and then spun a series of punches at his head.

There was a fire in Prevadello's chest and his calves were aching, but he kept jabbing at the swarthy face in front of him and once broke through with a clean shot to the jaw. Lefkowitz came barreling back in, this time his weight just perfect.

Prevadello knocked the first punch aside and twisted the second away with the back of his glove but Lefkowitz's third effort, a fine left, caught Prevadello right on the chin.

Prevadello's knees buckled and he genuflected, his head spinning. The bell was clanging away madly as the room slowly came back into focus, dominated by Lefkowitz's worried face peering down at him.

"Pops? Pops, you O.K.?"

"Nice hit, kid. Now help me out of here." Be nice to breathe again, Prevadello thought. Geraghty and Ozzie helped him from the ring and took the gloves and mouthpiece.

"Not bad, you know, you really taught the kid something. Lefkowitz had his weight just right when he bopped you," Geraghty said.

Lefkowitz was pacing behind them, worried, his gloves off and his headgear tipped back on his head.

"Hey, kid, nice punch. You're learning." Prevadello stuck out his hand and the boy shook it. "You used to work here, huh?" he asked Prevadello shyly.

"Yeah. In the dark ages. Thanks, kid. You'll be all right if you keep that weight right."

Leaving Lefkowitz's higher education to Ozzie, Prevadello and Geraghty walked slowly to the office. "Ozzie's O.K., but he's not nearly as good with the young ones as you were, Marty," Geraghty said, motioning Prevadello to a Salvation Army chair whose back bore a crescent of sweat salt. "Nice job. I thought Lefkowitz'd never learn," Geraghty said with certainty, throwing the freely sweating Prevadello a clean towel, then sat down.

"Gatorade's in the cooler under the chair. Help yourself. I've got to get the paperwork in shape." Geraghty considered his ranking chart and then stroked out a clause in the photocopied contract on his blotter. "Got a good-looking junior featherweight from Kew Gardens named Robinson who's six and oh, great jab. Not much else this fall. Remember Willie the Worm Getty, the black southpaw? Got him as far as a ten-rounder in West Philly with the Mexican who's number five in the world this year. . . ." Geraghty's voice trailed off and he put down his pen. "You here on business or what?"

"Kemper's leaning on me," Prevadello said, sipping his drink and trying to slow his breathing.

Geraghty sucked his teeth ruefully and spun his pen cap on his blotter. "Ah, your beloved partner. Shortish, a clotheshorse, tight with a dollar when there were drinks to be bought—" a mortal sin in Geraghty's world "—that the guy?"

"One and the same."

"What's Kemper want?" Geraghty asked, returning to his work. He lowered his glasses to the bridge of his nose and then crossed out another clause in the fight contract on his desk, his ballpoint rolling slowly down a ruler. Geraghty looked up when Prevadello didn't answer.

"Surely to God you know what the bastard wants. As I recall, Kemper"—Geraghty raised his eyebrows for emphasis—"ain't no genius."

"Hey, easy. We're talking about my old partner here. He's no genius but he was smart enough to save my ass a couple of times."

"O.K., O.K. I'm out of order."

"I'll say." Prevadello took off his beret, warmed by the rise in his blood pressure. You're still a moody bastard, Geraghty, he thought, remembering Geraghty's pet boxing ploy—needle, dance, needle, dance, until your victim blows his stack and, off-balance, he's yours. "Charlie Kemper," Prevadello said, "can't afford another screw up. Especially . . ."

". . . when it's your ass. My point, exactly." Geraghty smiled sardonically.

And so was peace made. Prevadello took a breath. "Group personnel cut my pension off. I called Kemper. He danced around and confessed to needing a defector picked up in Frankfurt. Milk run, he said."

"If I asked you this morning, you'd have told me Frankfurt's the tube steaks you buy from Nathan's."

"That's what I said. I mean, Germany? Why me, I asked Charlie. He was," Prevadello said carefully, "not too responsive."

Geraghty put his ruler down, looking balefully over the top of his glasses. "I got a great lawyer for you. Jewish guy, goes for the jugular—"

"You kidding, Pat? The fees'd kill me. I'd go bankrupt the day after Rappaport settled out of court."

Geraghty's rejoinder was pitched a fraction too high, his voice breaking from the years of boilermakers and ringside shouting: "Group's got guys all over Germany. What the hell's Kemper want with a geriatric like you?" He cleared his throat with a noise like old drains.

A rheumy tear rolled from Geraghty's eye and Prevadello caught a whiff of Jameson's punctuating the old boy's challenge. Prevadello wondered what was in the teapot at Geraghty's elbow. He's on the lush side of noon, Prevadello thought as he fitted a Camel to his filter. Geraghty's question slipped off him like rainwater. "I need a software man. Inside Group, Pat, nobody who knows me. Not here. In D.C." Cooling, Prevadello tucked himself into his coat and lit the cigarette, watching the fighters in the far ring through the smoke; Lefkowitz had learned something—a series of rights had Anderson snapping off the ropes. "Who's my man?"

Geraghty wiped the tear away with the back of his finger. Something broke in him then and he blushed. "Let's not talk shop, Marty," Geraghty whispered, his voice gristled, his Corkman's features suddenly weak. "Run me down to the pub. Let's have a jar for the old times, let's watch a bit of the Series. . . ." Geraghty was looking at the cane.

"No, thanks. I haven't the time to peel you off a bar stool, Pat." Prevadello moved to the desk and shook Geraghty by the shoulder. "I've got to be in Frankfurt on Thursday." Prevadello tightened his grip and pressed bone; depressingly, because Geraghty had once had deltoids hard as hawthorn. Holding Geraghty back, Prevadello reached for the drawer handle at the foot of Geraghty's desk and pulled it open. A half-filled fifth of Jameson's sloshed and Prevadello lifted it to the desk top. "Let's have a bit of the holy water here, shall we?" Geraghty sighed and pointed to a disreputable pair of Duralex tumblers on the ledge. "I don't get around much anymore, Marty. Not since the knee gave out. I sit in here and ride the oak and watch Ozzie shout, so. . . ." He shrugged and wiped his eye again.

Prevadello filled each tumbler above the filmy line of fingerprints and sat on the desk, tucking his coat under his haunches so as not to disturb Geraghty's neat bookkeeping. "You're drinking too much, Pat. Don't do it alone." He picked up the teapot and lifted the lid: more Jameson's. Geraghty looked embarrassed. "Think they don't know?" Prevadello asked, dropping the lid and inclining his head to the fighters outside.

"I don't give a shit. Bottoms up." Geraghty drank half the

tumbler without drawing breath. He put the tumbler down and reached for the contract. He wrote his signature in the same firm hand Prevadello had known twenty years ago and then folded it. "I do O.K., Marty. Pension, this joint and all, I do O.K. It's just I get lonely. Sonofabitch, I get lonely. You don't come around anymore, I got BO or what?" Geraghty licked the envelope without looking up, his pride edging back. Prevadello waited for him to finish.

"I don't come around because I miss it too much, Pat. I miss you, I miss the kids and the jokes and giving a kid some pride."

Geraghty eyed him for a moment and then dropped the envelope into a wooden tray crowded with circulars and sports page clippings. "I know what you mean. Ozzie's my reason for opening the doors every morning, rain or shine. He's a real bastard, but the kids respect him. Keeps me going. Poor guy lost his wife last spring. Cancer." There was a silence broken only by the grunts of the fighters.

Geraghty tapped Prevadello on the knee. "I gave you a lot of advice once. Here's one last piece. If you want to live forever, don't listen to a word the doctors tell you. I'd still be walking around if I followed my own goddam advice." He finished his whiskey, sipping carefully as they watched Ozzie circle the ropes, shouting encouragement. The fat little trainer had actually begun to get Lefkowitz into his punches more. Then Ozzie yelled once in triumph as Lefkowitz really got the hang of it and Anderson had to yell, "Time." Prevadello said not bad and Geraghty glowed.

"Well, maybe, just maybe the kid has a chance, huh?" He waved a clenched fist at Ozzie and the ungainly Lefkowitz, whose mouthguard grinned back. "Now," said Geraghty, brightened by the kid's progress as much as the whiskey, "what was all this crap about Kemper?" He was still looking out the glass partition, his big shoulders twitching sympathetically as he fought Lefkowitz's battle.

Prevadello turned his tumbler in his palm. "The pension isn't the half of it. He's up to something, empire building. I'll bet blood he's jerking me around on this Frankfurt thing."

"It's your blood," Geraghty said noncommittally. "Why come to me?"

Prevadello took a sip; perhaps Geraghty wasn't as sober as he looked. "I need a software man. Fast."

Geraghty spoke slowly, as if to a child. "I hear you. Why?" He sniffed and blew his nose.

Prevadello started, recognizing the old barrackroom-lawyer tone of Geraghty's voice. "I don't . . ."

Geraghty interrupted, tapping his spectacle frames with the Bic. "Do I have to draw you a picture? I've heard tell from your own lovely lips that Kemper's never had an original idea in his life. He's a technician, running to somebody else's timetable." Geraghty cleared his throat again. "Who's his boss?"

"Not Rappaport, he'd have Charlie on a very short leash. Beyond that, I don't know; I'm four years out of date. After I left I heard Doremus and Kemper did the bloc scientific and trade delegations. After that I lost track."

"Not going to the class reunions, are we?" Geraghty had forgotten Lefkowitz; he was doodling triangles on his blotter now.

"Hate them. Besides, I'm ancient history."

"That's rich. What do I look like, the fountain of youth?" Geraghty rummaged through his hoard of names, the effort wrinkling his forehead. "Software. It's a problem, it's a problem all right." Geraghty began to hum to himself. "Have to be someone young. Not one of the old hands, somebody who'll play ball. Young and with access to the archives. Plus maybe the phone logs. There's Campbell and Blair but they know you. And that," Geraghty said, squinting behind the glasses, "will never do." He began to connect the triangles with dotted lines. "So who else has the Old Man wet-nursed?" Geraghty asked himself.

Watching him, Prevadello had a morbid moment, picturing Geraghty's funeral; they'd have to shut down half the spook-holes in Washington if everybody came.

"Lift off: still got a few brain cells left that ain't pickled yet, Marty."

Geraghty had rocked forward in his chair as he spoke, moving so suddenly Prevadello thought the old Irishman was in the throes of a stroke. "Old Man's getting forgetful in his dotage." Geraghty craned his head and the rubbery muscles on the side of his broad neck stood out. "Goddam knee. Can't see the goddam clock in this chair—what time is it, Marty?" Geraghty wore a triumphant grin, as if he'd just found gold among the mill-ends. Geraghty knew his desk top like the back of his hand; he reached for an orange Ace writing tablet while still looking at Prevadello.

"Five thirty-five."

"Five thirty-five, four thirty-five," he sang, writing for a moment, big Roman numerals. "Catch the D.C. shuttle. Call this number when you get in; it's a motel in the 'burbs—there'll be a message waiting for you there when you check in. And don't say thanks, you'll break my heart.''

"What stories are you going to tell this guy in D.C.?"

Geraghty made a soft shushing sound, then raised a finger to his lips. "I'll do what I always do, Marty: feed 'em what they eat.'' Geraghty waved the paper slowly and Prevadello took it.

"Marty," Geraghty said, "come see me when you get back. The dough's not much better than unemployment, it's true, but I never bounced a check in my life. Anytime, Marty. You know me.'' Geraghty began his low laugh again, winking over the rim of his tea-mug.

Prevadello said nothing as he put his beret on.

Geraghty had the grace to laugh. "Go on. Hit the road, Marty. Brush your teeth and take all your vitamins. And watch your back, always watch your back.'' Geraghty reached for the phone. He was speaking softly into the receiver by the time Prevadello looked back through the blurred glass of the double doors. Geraghty cupped a hand over the mouthpiece and yelled: "Call me when you get back, hear?''

And what do I do to say thanks, Prevadello thought as he started the Vespa in the wind-blown parking lot, send Geraghty a bottle? He let in the clutch and the scooter carried him back across the East River, the sweat of his match with Lefkowitz cooling on his back as he headed home.

Upon his return, Prevadello booked a seat on the D.C. shuttle and, forgoing his solitary dinner, took one of his contemplative walks, to be in the evening crowds, with people. Outside, the rain had stopped and a helicopter, its lights winking, rose above Fifth Avenue, wrapping itself in the twilight cloud like a shy bird. Rush hour had disappeared into the tunnels and bridges leading off Manhattan by the time Prevadello's evening walk took him to the lee of Rockefeller Center. Prevadello wondered what time it was in Moscow and if his man was even now pacing the floor waiting for the boot against the door as the green vans fanned out and rolled up NOAH.

A cab pulled close to the curb and Prevadello instinctively stepped back to the barricaded storefronts. A couple leapt out, a leggy overdressed woman and a pudgy man, suburbanites on a spree, smiling self-consciously at one another and pretending not to notice the mobile audience on the sidewalk. Theatergoers, Prevadello calculated absently; normal people on a normal

Monday night. He felt a sudden spur of loneliness as he began to walk again, edging away from a mob of giggling kids talking over the fleshpots of Times Square. Like an uncertain swimmer, Prevadello made for the isosceles island of Father Duffy Square, now harboring a stalled M104 bus.

Who the hell am I kidding? Prevadello thought. I'm past it.

The vacuum of West 47th drew Prevadello in. As he looked sightlessly into the shop windows, his mind perversely flitted from CATALYST to the image of a mock Federalist building, its tea-colored brick staining the granite trim, set in a quadrangle of mesh fence, a pair of trees slowly dying on either side of the main stairs.

A schoolteacher's face slid behind CATALYST's, the masculine frames of her glasses replacing his. Mrs. Moore taught eighth-grade geometry in a tall room with cool slate blackboards and a clock that metered the hours with crisp clicks of the pendulum. Mrs. Moore was stooped and thin, with a star-shaped cataract on her right eye. Her dresses were tubes of smooth pastel fabric that disguised her gender entirely; for as long as anyone cared to remember, Mrs. Moore had borne all the symptoms of careworn widowhood. Except, of course, when she spoke, enraptured, of perpendiculars and chords: for Mrs. Moore, these things were articles of faith, and she sent a generation of her Jewish and Italian graduates into the world fired with her belief. And none more so than Marty Prevadello, whose appetite for geometry had a practical side—geometry won snooker games.

The commercial practicalities of snooker satisfied by Mrs. Moore's cracked voice urging "side-angle-side," there then remained the abstract logic of it all. And so Prevadello's mind was marked as deeply by Mrs. Moore's pronouncements as was his snooker strategy, and the rigor of her proofs gave his own thought order. The Jesuit fathers who taught Prevadello in high school made much of his reason, but to him their distinctions were a poor second to the pragmatic clarity of thought Mrs. Moore showed him. And, later still, in the crisis of the Army boxing ring, a straight line was still very much the shortest distance between glove and jaw.

Prevadello found himself staring through the antitheft grillework at the display window of a bookshop, watching the play of the Broadway neons on the fading dust-jackets. A patrol car slowed behind his back and then moved on and for a moment Prevadello knew again the fear of the man on the run, when there was but one way out and it wasn't yours. Prevadello turned and stepped into a pool of streetlight to start a Camel for the walk home.

At Broadway, a small crowd turned as one to eye him, their alcoholic blather falling and then rising as one of them, a long-haired girl, let loose a laugh, chanting a broken nursery rhyme to the moon. One of the men flung his arm around her and joined in, then the voices died away at the sight of the blocky fellow staring at them from the lamplight. Someone said, ''Day pass from Bellevue,'' and there was a nervous laugh. They moved away across Broadway, to a different world.

Prevadello shouldn't even have been there. That's what the cops said that night in any of their hangouts you'd care to mention in the five boroughs; he shouldn't have been there.

If Prevadello had called in sick—he had a fever of 102—it wouldn't have happened.

If he and Velazquez had gone for the coffee they'd promised themselves, it wouldn't have happened.

There were dozens of other ''ifs'' invented, traded, and discarded that night in the summer of 1950. When the ambulance came they couldn't separate the girl from the policeman. That's what the papers said, and though Prevadello had never had the courage to read the old clippings, he remembered that much. His captain took him to the precinct's local, a place called Eddie's on 23rd, and kept both the conversation and the brandy moving. Prevadello remembered that too, and the newsmen at the funeral and the mother's anguish, but most of all he remembered the child.

The front-page photos the next day showed the Ramirez child was effortlessly pretty in the way Hispanic girls often are, with splendid eyes and even teeth and hair as dark as the South Bronx corridor she died in, in a walk-up at Melrose and 151st, near the A & P. In the summer of 1950, this was a neighborhood teetering on the edge of the decline that twenty years later would see the South Bronx a wasting war zone. Strictly speaking, Prevadello and Velazquez had no business being on the Four-Two's turf, but Velazquez swore afterwards the face he'd just seen in the A & P parking lot was a narcotics suspect whose name by now has been lost.

They shouldn't even have been there. But they were.

And when the call came through, theirs was the closest car by five minutes; their response was reported as ''prompt and professional'' in the ensuing report. The substance of the dispatcher's radio call was simple: there had been a hostage-taking in the apartment building.

Later, the court of inquiry reconstructed how the two sixteen-year-old junkies had broken into the apartment of one Ira Grossman, seventy-four, but they hadn't checked things out. He was in and stayed in because the two junkies had three knives and a Saturday night special between them. The junkies ransacked the place, first locking Grossman in the bathroom: a mistake, for the old man had a terrible fear of breaking his hip in the bath and had a phone there. Grossman dialed forty-two division while the junkies trashed his home. Prevadello and his partner Bobby Velazquez arrived within two minutes, backed up by two other cars within three minutes. The accounts differ from here on in, mainly because there was only one light for the three flights of stairs, and not even Velazquez, famous for his bravery, dared use a flashlight.

So he and Prevadello crawled up the stairs while the other four officers worked their way across the roof to the fire escape. The third floor hallway was so dim neither Prevadello nor Velazquez could see the numbers of the apartments. By this time, old Grossman had reached the fire escape, fragile hip and all, calm as you please. He left the window open for Officers Rutherford and Fitzpatrick, who proceeded to surprise the two junkies in the midst of piling Mr. Grossman's furniture against his front door.

The junkie with the gun fired three rounds from his mail-order .25 cal Beretta at the window.

Shots were exchanged and at that moment, the doorway to Prevadello's left fell open. Velazquez later argued that at least one of Fitzpatrick's rounds must somehow have found its way along the apartment hallway through the closed door and clipped the gypsum over his head; ballistics never did account for all the Rutherford-Fitzpatrick rounds. Suffice to say, huddled in the pitch-black stairwell, both Prevadello and Velazquez thought they were on the receiving end of a first-class fusillade. Echoes are by no means an accurate way of locating a pistol shot at close range, but Prevadello fired by reflex.

The distance separating the Grossman and Ramirez apartment doors is approximately eighteen inches.

And Carlotta Ramirez chose the moment Fitzpatrick fired to cross the hallway with her cat. Prevadello was a far better shot than Velazquez (ballistics found three of Velazquez's rounds around the Ramirez door frame) and Martino Saverio Prevadello shot Carlotta, aged eight, twice in the chest.

Carlotta, alone in the apartment at the time, was a deaf-mute.

The junkies got three years each, plea-bargained on the attempted kidnap, and were all out in time for their nineteenth birthdays. Fitzpatrick was cited for bravery; both Rutherford and Velazquez left the force that Christmas. The boys at the precinct house raised nearly a thousand dollars for the Ramirez scholarship fund; Prevadello, devastated, gave his life savings. By the time Prevadello visited the Ramirez family, they had heard of his action and, with great dignity, gave him Carlotta's rosary.

The court of inquiry cleared Prevadello and Velazquez entirely.

Prevadello turned in his badge, signed up with the Army and went to Korea, did his bit for two years behind a trestle table in Army Intelligence, returned, and tried the monastic life. After that fiasco, Prevadello rejoined the Department and was assigned to Brooklyn South in September 1952 and so distinguished himself there that he had his gold shield in record time.

Despite once having a North Korean pepper the hillside over his head with an automatic weapon and three times having a fellow resident of New York City try to kill him at short range, Marty Prevadello had fired but two warning shots since that summer morning on Melrose Avenue. Twenty-two years ago.

It was just past ten when Prevadello turned the corner for home. He had walked from the West Forties to the West Seventies past Carnegie Hall and through Central Park, navigating by feel, thinking.

Someone had wrapped yards of McGovern-Shriver bunting around the bare limbs of the solitary sapling in the tiny front yard of Prevadello's graystone. The Eastern European gentleman from the first floor paced around the tree in ever bigger circles as he angrily pulled the paper free of the branches. Prevadello strode past him without a word.

Upstairs, Prevadello pulled an old paint can from his closet. The dried paint sealing the lid fought him for a moment but Prevadello opened the Ziploc bag inside the can without trouble; the bag contained a legitimate U.S. passport in the name of Phillip Silvestri, featuring a Brylcreemed Prevadello in bifocals, two paper-clipped bundles of crumpled twenty-dollar bills, a set of NYPD issue handcuffs and key, a shaving kit complete with a change of Fruit of the Loom socks and undershorts, and a Model 1903 .32 Colt in a clean orange cloth, a pair of eight-round clips taped to the Colt's handle. The handle itself was double-wrapped in rubber bands to fit Prevadello's grip, a trade secret gleaned from the perfectionist Geraghty. Prevadello worked the semiautomatic's mechanism, satisfied himself, and then fitted one of the clips to the gun. He folded the cloth, tucked it into the bag, and then returned the bag to the can.

He was back in the game.

In Washington that night, well after midnight, the dream woke Prevadello, sweating and tumbling the sheets. The usual inventory of horrors: hungry hawks wheeling and grotesque vehicles with great lights moving on the peripheries of his brain like reptiles. Velazquez's eyes in the dark. And the gunshots. He blamed the six strong coffees, but caffeine was not the culprit. Duty, a voice said, as he searched for a pattern in the shadowed ceiling plaster of the anonymous airport motel. Prevadello knew the truth of his sleeplessness—he was back in the game. He was a hireling again.

# Chapter Three

The weather stripping had not been fitted properly when the Zil limousine left the factory; that was the problem. Nikolai Georgievitch Chertkov, his physique drawn snug and round by the good cloth of his best uniform, peeled off a doeskin glove and felt along the ceiling seam. A jet of frozen Moscow air shot between his fingers. Chertkov sighed and made a mental note of the license plate—the Party General-Secretary's well-known passion for deluxe automobiles did not brook such flaws.

Sunday had been dreadful: two huge afternoon rows with Olga (and on her birthday, he thought guiltily), a stilted dinner, and a final boozy free-for-all, salvoes counterpoised by Chertkov's moody silences as he weighed his future. Each phone call, each of Olga's reprimands made him start, each corridor noise caught his breath as he alternately loafed and prowled; not until a weeping Olga departed to a cold bed did Chertkov relax enough to think. I have survived the first day, he reminded himself. I can survive two.

The call from the GRU translation pool came at six this Monday morning, as Chertkov plotted his options in the dark. He picked up the phone as casually as he could and was relieved to hear the familiar voice of the GRU sergeant who ran the pool. The assigned translator was stranded at the Alma-Ata airport and Chertkov was to be picked up by limousine and sit at the General-Secretary's side during this morning's military session of the Warsaw Pact summit. Chertkov slipped his papers into the slim French briefcase sent him by his cousin in the Berne embassy and then dropped the soft bag into the brittle Russian-made attaché case he always carried. This Monday marked the summit's opening: the Party photographers would be about and one ought to observe such details as carrying his frugal and patriotic Red Army case.

For a moment, he considered reading *Vestnik*, the TASS news summary, but put it back. For the remainder of the trip to the Kremlin gates, Chertkov skimmed yesterday's Sunday *France-Soir*, which, like his Saturday strolls, was part and parcel of his NOAH trade-craft. Chertkov browsed slowly through the personals. Long habit had accustomed him to this task, which he performed religiously every Monday. He ran a finger down the columns and had actually passed the microscopic ad when the message hit him.

Slamming the paper closed, Chertkov sat bolt upright. The little translator, nerveless when closeted in the General-Secretary's Politburo holy of holies, tried to compose himself. He reached for the glove he had dropped to the floor in his anxiety. Surely the chauffeur would notice, surely he would begin the detour, just as surely as the GULAG gates would open instead of the Kremlin's. . . .

Chertkov's eyes were closed. Far away in the warm dark, the edge of the newspaper was damp, corrugated by Chertkov's fingers. Willing his eyelids to rise, Chertkov opened the newspaper slowly, as if the pulp and ink might swallow him whole. He had not been dreaming.

The translator forced himself to exhale. He smoothed the paper across his lap, murmuring the procedure to himself as the Zil crossed Red Square. Chertkov looked at his watch and tried to think: nine twenty-five. He caught his face in the rearview mirror.

It was a surprisingly calm face, though buttons of perspiration blossomed on his forehead. He could feel every hair on his head. Chertkov forced himself to recall the mnemonics they used on their clever cassettes. They had told him repeatedly they would save him before the *voronoks* were out the garage door.

Crash meeting sites, fall-back timetables, dead-drops—Chertkov's life-rope began to twine itself together in his memory. It had better, for the moment he saw the innocuous plea in the lost articles section of the Paris paper, Chertkov had his weekend's uncertainties resolved for him: NOAH was falling to pieces. Chertkov's vision became an escape-waltz, a blur of fir trees, red shoulder tabs on green cloth, rubber stamps on wire merry-go-rounds, and a yellow and black border barrier pole. The Zil rumbled over the paving stones and swung slowly through the Kremlin gates. Chertkov folded the newspaper and pushed it down between the seat cushions. The limousine in line ahead of his slowed to a stop and for long horrible seconds Chertkov thought this was the end. But a shaven-headed Polish Party functionary emerged from the car instead of the green uniforms of the KGB, a smile plastered on his face for the photographers. As he emerged from the GRU limousine, Chertkov grasped the handle of his attaché case tightly as he scanned the rows of faces on the steps, their faces pink in the wind.

The TASS cameras began to flash, recording the ersatz enthusiasm for posterity as the Pole climbed the stairs. Chertkov followed, swept toward the protocol men mouthing their "fraternal best wishes" and "spirits of socialist comradeships." Thrust up the stairs by the crowding of lesser lights in the entourage, Chertkov ducked away, sliding along the far side of the column pressing toward the doors. A pair of KGB men stepped forward, moving like a matched pair of mannequins toward Chertkov.

Should I call out something inspirational as they drag me away? The KGB men kept moving, straight at him, and then nodded at the last minute at Chertkov's rank. I am an orphan, Chertkov thought as the door to the great hall opened before him and the crowd of diplomats and aides dissolved toward the cloakrooms. The hornet-striped barrier pole in his mind smashed down as the stony-faced security officer examined Chertkov's case.

They let him through.

He moved to his place diagonally behind the General-Secretary's chair, a place sterile and mineral-watered, next to a bust of Lenin in a silver dish, ringed by poppies.

Chertkov was the first on the dais of the great room, except for the technicians fussing with the headsets and the switching booths and the coils of microphone leads. Several hundred bloc delegates, the gilt of their military uniforms flickering in the chandelier light, grazed in the crowded aisles of the auditorium. Not until he sat down fifteen minutes later did Chertkov begin to think; he sipped his water with all the restraint he could muster. Old grandpa Chertkov had sayings for all occasions; his sweating grandson thought of an old one as the aging GenSec stilled the mechanical applause and the spray of flash bulbs which greeted his arrival. Yes: the devil looks after his own, that's what he'd say. He sipped his mineral water again and waited for the meeting to begin.

* * *

The combined Pact security services session had gone well. The lowly Poles and Romanians would have been dismissed by now and the rest of them seated in their assigned places around the table in one of the small conference rooms, Chertkov reckoned, digesting their Central Committee lunches, brought up from the CC canteen in special deep aluminum trays. The translator, no longer required, walked across Red Square and boarded a southbound number twenty-five trolley bus. Not far now, he reassured himself.

Emergency only, they had told him during the ride in the back of a truck that smelled of bleach and cleaning chemicals, a lurching ride into the featureless proletarian district south of the river. The truck stopped at a dismal café, where plywood tables wearing plastic mats knocked into one another as the clientele, all workers from the district, came and went. The first and only meeting had been there, and the cut-out, an efficient-looking fellow, fortyish, wore a big sweater made of real wool, Chertkov remembered, and seated himself at Chertkov's table.

He wouldn't touch the vodka Chertkov offered him. Instead, he drank endless glasses of orangeade and lisped Ukrainian, talking nonsense and biting the words back with nervous lips; he found, he said, he could whisper better without his false teeth. Chertkov looked at him uncertainly and the Ukrainian laughed, his crow's-feet puckering like a film star's, showing off his gums. It was a splendid ruse, for all heads, including Chertkov's, turned away at the height of his hollow grin. At that moment the cut-out pressed a rectangle of paper the size of a postage stamp into Chertkov's hand. Chertkov tapped a cigarette end against his open palm and read the note: "Emergency only," it read. "Shykofsky at Central Laundry Number Three, Transport office. Days. 8-4. Mention Nekrasov. Emergency only." The last phrase was underlined three times.

Chertkov had dropped the slip into the ashtray and the cut-out lit his cigarette, sliding the still-burning match beneath the paper after lighting the cigarette. The slip burned instantly and Chertkov guessed the paper was treated. The cut-out laughed again and sharply patted Chertkov's cheek in mock affection, then, still laughing and chatting nonsense, he stopped the swing of Chertkov's head with a rigid thumb: Chertkov's realigned vision caught sight of a pale man in a peaked cap seated next to the door. The man touched the side of his nose and left the café.

"Got the picture?" the cut-out whispered out the side of his flaccid mouth, beaming at the bored waiter. "Memorize. Good friend, O.K.?" Then shouting: ". . . and that's all I know about Siberian girls!" He punched Chertkov's arm; his filthy laugh still rang in Chertkov's memory.

The trolley bus ground its way south after depositing Chertkov at the edge of an industrial enclave just outside the Ring Road. It was all concrete and slush hereabouts, bunkerlike warehouses and prewar brick smokestacks pouring steam; big trucks were the only traffic. You've taken some chances, Nikolai, Chertkov said to himself. And Tuesday night, you'll take some more, when the time comes to translate the Washington *rezindentura* cable to Moscow Center for Moldov. Thinking of Moldov, Chertkov nodded to the sour, bespectacled girl in the tiny office off the entrance; she looked like a cameo set in the wall, so small was her work space.

In reply, the girl took in Chertkov's uniform and jabbed a pencil down the hall. In the strip of pebbled glass running across the doorway ahead of him, Chertkov could see the steam rising off the great vats. It was five to three and the afternoon shift was in full swing, boiling and bleaching and ironing in tropical clouds of mist that rose to the wire-glass roof and rained from the rafters. A rough signpost hung from a chain on the wall; Chertkov turned left.

The transport section was a narrow office painted a watery green with a Party calendar on the door featuring the smiling tractor drivers of Omsk. A pair of slate chalkboards were covered in delivery routes and three burly drivers were shouting at one another cheerfully and playing cards on an upturned garbage can, slapping the cards down and making sounds like tympani. Shykofsky was talking on the telephone, ignoring the shouting men. He looked up, his wet eyes widening as Chertkov stepped in front of his desk, the envelope containing the *France-Soir* ad in his hand. Shykofsky set his face resignedly.

"You're from the quartermaster," he said, as if this were bad news. Shykofsky took the envelope.

"Where's our stuff?"

"If you want the whites for the officers' mess, you're going to have to wait just like everybody else. My girls are going to be unpicking their uniforms to repair the linens if Nekrasov don't get me some thread. That was the deal for you lot: thread first, napkins second." Eyes downcast, Shykofsky shook his head, taking the envelope. "How's that asshole Nekrasov doing? He never comes for cards anymore." Chertkov shrugged and said, "He has a new kid," which inspired one of the drivers to remark rudely on Nekrasov's masculinity. Nekrasov actually *was* Chertkov's mess steward—Nekrasov's kid, Chertkov remembered: that was the all-clear.

Reading, Shykofsky growled, "Tuesday, am I right? Nekrasov's getting the stuff Tuesday?" Without looking at Chertkov, Shykofsky had returned to his invoices, carefully rolling the newspaper ad into a pulpy ball as he wrote.

"Tuesday," Chertkov barked, "that's no bloody good. You've got two months' worth of our laundry and we've got a hundred East Germans coming to dinner Friday," Chertkov said as he slapped the desk top. "What do I look like, a camel? Get the laundry on a bloody truck. I haven't all day for this."

Shykofsky looked up, his eyes far away. A whoop rumbled around the room. One of the drivers, a fat fellow in a peaked hat, had won a hand and was counting his roubles.

"You don't believe me? Come here," Shykofsky said, "and I'll show you how many serviceable trucks I have today." Chertkov followed his gaze and saw the open door to the truck park. "Vassily, deal me in the next hand. Back in a minute," Shykofsky said.

"Sure, chief," the man called Vassily replied. The others didn't look up, their eyes on the cards flicking onto the garbage can.

The indoor truck park looked like a wrecking yard; disassembled engines lay like sleeping livestock on the floor, surrounded by scrounged paint cans harboring what few parts the mechanics had to work with. Three of the mechanics were sitting smoking in the cab of a stripped-down truck while one of their colleagues disconsolately beat a fender back into shape. There were half a dozen trucks, hoods up or propped on jack stands, idle.

Shykofsky, satisfied, took Chertkov by the arm and, still manufacturing a covering chatter about the linens, guided him inside a chain-link cage where the tools were stored under lock and key. The dispatcher sat down on an old tire carcass, his back to dozens of boxes of fan belts from Hungary, Five Year Plan leftovers. He offered Chertkov a cigarette; they smoked in silence for a moment.

"What a day to choose! This is damn dangerous for me," Shykofsky said *sotto voce*. "The militia are coming today. Somebody's syphoning off petrol again and it's my arse. Here." Shykofsky took a flip-top spectacle case from his pocket and handed it to Chertkov. "This is what you came for." Then loudly: "You can tell the Central Committee for all I care—I haven't got the trucks."

"If you had the trucks, you'd have no petrol. You're useless!" Chertkov shouted back, turning his back to the truck repair area. "Inside," he whispered, "inside the spectacle case? All in there, concealed?"

"We can do the delivery. Tuesday. Maybe." Shykofsky nodded, speaking very clearly, not looking at Chertkov, and tapped the tire behind him: "None of these fit the rims of our delivery trucks; soon we'll be down to four. Four tires. This plant is supposed to deliver to half the hospitals in Moscow, with four spare tires. I'll tell you a story. My wife spent a week in Hospital Number Eight last September. Gallbladder: they never changed her sheets once." Chertkov waited, surprised to have mined so rich a vein of rancor in a total stranger. "We're four blocks away and can't get them clean sheets for the sick and the old. Madness." Shykofsky shook his head, his spleen nicely vented.

"I need to make contact, comrade. *Today*," Chertkov said, his voice low.

Shykofsky stood, his wire body tense. "I told them it wasn't foolproof. But they wouldn't listen." A thin, wheedling smile crossed his narrow face as he raised his voice again. "I have one truck this week, comrade. One. It's been on the streets for the last eight hours. The other six haven't got a set of sound tires among them. Not to mention a carburetor. Nobody ever thinks the whole show might come to a grinding halt for the sake of a spare tire." Shykofsky ran a hand down his face, like an old man, but pointed subtly at a mechanic bashing a fender. *Plant stoolie*, Chertkov registered, and raised his eyebrows fractionally in reply. "Fact is, we can't deliver for another two days. That's the way it is. I have to fulfill the hospital quotas first or I have the militia knocking on my door. I can't risk it. I got a wife and kids." Shykofsky took a hard pull at his cigarette and said out of the corner of his mouth: "You're too hot. Cool off."

"Wednesday, it's got to be Wednesday." Then, softly: "Are they watching the plant?"

"The militia? No," Shykofsky said, "God, no. They called this morning. We're on report because of the hospital screw-up; there's bugger all I can do about it." A new look came over Shykofsky's face—fear. He stared at Chertkov. "It's coming apart, isn't it?"

There was no point lying. "I saw the greens take Leon, the Baptist. I was there." Chertkov looked over Shykofsky's shoulder; the big mechanic bashing the fender had stopped and was looking at Chertkov's Army uniform.

Shykofsky took a puff and shook his head. His hand was shaking. "I hope to God the boy kills himself before they take him to the cellars. I hope to God."

"God has nothing to do with it, friend." Chertkov had had his fill of theology; the whole lot of them made him ill, waiting and praying for their lousy deaths. He ground out his cigarette. "I'm not going to lie in bed waiting for the greens to come through my door. And you can tell NOAH they can . . ."

Chertkov stopped speaking. Through the closed truck-park doors, he could see the doors of a green Volga opening. There were four men, moving. . . . Chertkov grabbed Shykofsky by his shirt: "Is there a side exit out of here?"

"Left at the canteen."

"Keep talking. Walk slowly. Go."

Shykofsky led him back into the main building and every step of the way, Chertkov could feel the fender-basher's eyes singeing the back of his neck. In the office, the slamming of the garbage can continued, the drivers ignoring Chertkov as before. Those boys are in for a surprise when the militia sit in for a hand, Chertkov decided.

"Stall," Chertkov said as they left the transport office and walked past the canteen. "I need five minutes."

Shykofsky shrugged. "The militia want petrol, not you." He reached into a bin and handed Chertkov a filthy old coat. "Here. Take this. For cover. It's all I can do for you."

Chertkov did not stop, shrugging the coat on and tucking his uniform hat into the coat front, saying nothing. The two of them turned down a short hallway and Shykofsky pointed to a door. Their eyes met for a moment.

"One last thing: don't try to fly. They watch the airport far too carefully. Helsinki, Frankfurt, they might as well be the moon. Take the train." Shykofsky opened the door, his small eyes unwavering.

"The train has worked for us in the past. Try for the Jewish train to Vienna. The KGB are," Shykofsky said slowly, "rather happy to see the back end of us." He smiled wanly. "I will try to get word out you're heading for Vienna. No promises, understand? But I will try." Shykofsky offered his hand and they shook hands quickly.

"Thanks. You've been damn kind." Chertkov stepped outside.

You're next, Chertkov thought, as the door clanged shut.

They could hear that across the river in Dzerzhinsky Square, Chertkov cursed. He found himself in an alley covered with corrugated tin sheeting, his feet suddenly trapped; a child's bell tinkled somewhere. The door's opening had toppled a pair of rusted bicycles into the shadows—Chertkov's ankles were caught between their jangling frames. He reached down and, catching his fingers in the spokes, felt his way out of the fallen bicycles.

They had told him never to do it.

What the hell choice do I have? His head bent against the whipping wind, the rank smell of the coat rising, Chertkov crossed the street, jogging now. To his left, the lights on the great netted Shukhov television tower glowed dimly through the curtain of snow above the silhouetted roofs. Just beyond the tower was the Shabolovskaya Metro stop.

Never, they had said.

"Never is for the dead," Chertkov muttered, heading to his right, away from the laundry's truck path, toward the street. He needed to run, to feel the wind slip past his face as he pelted down the street; he knew the need was panic. Chertkov took a deep breath, opened the gate, and stepped through into the falling snow. He walked as slowly as he could, measuring his stride, his eyes fixed. *Slowly.* He made himself move his shoulders; to free his eyes, he watched the arcs his breath made before it disappeared.

A bus roared past, belching smoke, then melted into the falling snow. A bureaucrat's instinct came to him then and Chertkov looked at his watch: quarter to four.

He could hear the train as he descended the Metro stairs.

*I will go alone.*

# Chapter Four

Prevadello met him in the dark outside the isolated suburban Washington motel, a flake aged twenty-five or -six tops, with a broad New York accent, a street bounce in his sneakered walk, and an impatience in his handshake. Now they sat in a VW Beetle with peeling flower decals and no muffler, parked on a side street at first light. Danny Hayes was doing the talking; Hayes had done all the talking when Prevadello called him after midnight and since picking Prevadello up at the motel this morning. He was relentlessly cheerful, which was even worse.

"My old man works at the Felt Forum," Hayes rapped, "at Madison Square. Golden Gloves, you know? I got to know the guys who set up the ticket computer. Got interested, went to Hofstra, computer science. Got the gold medal senior year, my folks thrilled, job offers coming in. Then my roommate had this brainstorm of making a skin flick. Great way to meet chicks, except we got busted. Mr. Geraghty got me off with a clean record. I did some special stuff for him after that, custom software. For the department he said. Which I doubt; cops won't have the stuff I was working on for another five years." Hayes stopped to see if Prevadello was paying attention. Shrugging, he continued: "Mr. Geraghty got me on the Group payroll after I hit the streets. Fifteen thou a year, expenses, and all the programming time I need. I make a little on the side from guys keeping track of the NFL stats now and again but I keep my nose clean otherwise." He waited for Prevadello to be impressed.

Hayes watched him for a moment and then prodded Prevadello's shoulder with a gloved hand. "Look, I'm the best in the biz when it comes to software, no ifs, ands, or buts. No brag, just fact. What was your security clearance when you were twenty-two?''

"Sorry. I just expected someone . . .''

"Surprise.''

There was a silence broken only by the dopplered sound of a passing siren. Then Prevadello smiled and stuck out his hand and Hayes shook it, this time slowly, his mouth in a crooked grin. "Apology accepted.''

"Smoke?'' Prevadello tipped out a Camel. Hayes nodded.

Prevadello opened the vent window all the way; the windows were misting over. "I've been asked . . . *told* to do a job. I've got a day before the job starts to ask my favorite questions. Bring the directory?''

Hayes handed him a slim envelope. Prevadello pulled out the contents, columns of dot-matrix names, addresses, and phone numbers. Prevadello scanned the first page: all the department names had changed. Special Projects was now Tactical Services and Campbell's surveillance team bore an acronym Prevadello could only guess at—what the hell was *DPM*? But the amazing thing was the numbers: the staff had doubled. Kemper had an empire of eight called Security Services/Liaison (P). "It's a photocopy,'' Hayes warned. "I recommend you burn it ASAP.'' He's like a wine steward, Prevadello thought, pushing the house red. "I also recommend you use pay phones only. Trace you down pronto.''

And I owe you a jar of Jameson's for this kid, Pat Geraghty, Prevadello thought. "Thanks for the advice. Can you pull files if we get a make?''

Hayes cracked a grin. "Mr. Geraghty said you'd ask that. All the personnel stuff, straight out of the data base, baby.''

Prevadello opened the door and got out. "I don't need Mrs. Brezhnev's hat size. I want to follow some money. Can you find out who recommended Charlie Kemper's last promotion?''

Hayes nodded his head yes, impressed. "You want hard copy?''

"No. Just the name. Worknames, too, if you can get 'em. Can you do it by this afternoon?''

"Sure. Got a directory in my safe at home.''

"Fine. You going to Group now?''

"I'm troubleshooting a data link. Take me till lunch time. Why, what's up?''

"Meet me at the Georgetown post office at three-thirty. Any

expenses, use this—'' Prevadello handed Hayes a credit card
''—and check your answering serviee for messages. Plans can
change. O.K.?''

"Fine and dandy." The kid was still smiling. "Want the
camera now?''

"Sure. Save the lecture." Prevadello put his finger to his lips
as he took the Nikon bag. "These I know, thanks." Prevadello
fitted his beret on and then bent back into the car. "Group still
run cabs?''

Hayes, puzzled for a moment, nodded. "Capitol Central
Cabs. 337-3000. Ask for Jimmy or Marcus.''

"Group have an account name?''

"Platt-Mitchell and Associates." He beamed: "We're a film
production company. Funny, huh?''

"Good luck with the data link. And check your answering
service, in case. Every hour.''

The VW door slammed. Prevadello, Hayes' Nikon bag jogging at his side, was lost in the early morning shadows of the
little park across the street before Hayes could reply.

An hour later, Prevadello stared out at the gentle curves of the
suburban landscape filling the van's windshield. No: not him.
The car was a big Chrysler and Prevadello guessed lawyer—the
driver was talking into a mini-cassette machine, watching himself speak in the mirror. Prevadello had parked the van Hayes
had arranged for him next to a telephone pole with a big trans-
former on its cross-struts; painter or utility company, he didn't
care what people thought, as long as he could park out here
unmolested for another half an hour. Prevadello dunked his
doughnut in the black coffee and looked down the cul-de-sac
again in his side mirror.

Kemper lived in Weyanoke, one of the Fairfax County suburbs inside the Beltway. The house was at the foot of the cul-
de-sac—there was only one way out. And Kemper was home;
Prevadello had done the wrong-number bit from a pay phone
five minutes ago at the doughnut shop. Prevadello sipped the
coffee. It was now nearly eight. Kemper would be leaving.

Prevadello rolled the wax-paper doughnut wrapper into a ball
and lobbed it into the unheated back space of the van; there was
still frost on the floor's scratched paintwork. He checked the
mirror again. A gray Chevrolet was backing out from behind a
flat-topped hedge, a plume of vapor rising behind the bumper.
Prevadello put the rented hard hat on and slumped in his seat.

The Chevy stopped, turned, and headed for him. The Chevy with the government plates ran the stop sign. That had to be Kemper. Prevadello gave Kemper thirty seconds, time enough to make the four-lane west of the housing estate, then dropped the gear lever into first, and let in the clutch.

Kemper had always driven like a maniac, which would make tailing him obvious, but Kemper had never been one for rear-view mirrors. He was already at the lights four hundred yards ahead. Prevadello floored the van, keeping well to the right, in Kemper's blind spot—Kemper would never leave the fast lane. The light stayed red and Prevadello could see the Chevy, some ten cars ahead. Some of the old pros liked vans for tailing, but nobody more than Prevadello; you could see for blocks above the traffic. Or, out here, for a good half-mile. On the golf course to Prevadello's right, the first sweater-clad foursomes were already out, moving slowly in the last of the chilly morning fog.

Five minutes later, they were on the Columbia Pike, heading northwest. Kemper weaved in and out of the buses and trucks but Prevadello had little trouble keeping the Chevy in sight as the traffic began to congeal on the Parkway south of the Pentagon. They crossed the Potomac over the Key Bridge and Prevadello felt a twinge of nostalgia. In the old days, Kemper would have crossed at the Arlington Memorial. Prevadello wondered what had become of Kemper's old midtown office above the travel agency on Rhode Island Avenue. Prevadello had haunted the trattoria around the corner with him, spending good Group money on untold numbers of slow lunches. In the old days.

Kemper was parking, backing into a space on the 3300 block on M Street. Georgetown: he's come up in the world, Prevadello thought as he turned up the slight rise of Wisconsin Avenue, around the corner from Kemper's parking space.

He recognized the man's back. Kemper had sprung from his car and was chatting with a woman in an Aquascutum coat. The building behind them was red-brick Victorian, set into the hillside one block north. Kemper wore his hair longer now, Prevadello observed, and expensively razor-cut. His tie was fatter and a glossy Madison Avenue paisley instead of the frayed Black Watch he'd worn since before the flood; the tent-peg gymnast's body and the parade-ground gait were still the same.

Kemper was a miniature, Prevadello judged, a Brooks Brothers model viewed through the wrong end of the lens. The woman laughed and tossed her hair as Kemper, still talking, opened the door to his Wisconsin Avenue office. Nothing's changed, Prevadello sighed, he's still the life of the party. Prevadello looked down the street, searching. There wasn't another parking place for miles. Prevadello pulled into an alleyway next to a gourmet shop and slipped onto the dash the District of Columbia Bell Service Call placard Hayes had thoughtfully supplied.

Waiting for a tribe of office workers to pass the mouth of the alley, Prevadello left the van, Nikon bag in hand, and walked quickly to the corner of M and Wisconsin. He saw an old metal pay-phone sign sticking out of the doorway of a Chinese variety store and stepped across the intersection.

The pay phone was just inside the door. Prevadello's elbow rubbed against a stack of November *Time*; the unsmiling proprietor was smoking a cigarette and reading a paperback about horoscopes. He did not look up as Prevadello pulled the photocopy of the Group directory from the bottom of the Nikon bag and found Kemper's extension.

"Platt-Mitchell Associates . . . g'morning." Female voice, sexless, absolutely cool. There was a door slam in the background and the buzz of a security lock: Prevadello guessed the operator was somewhere at the central switchboard in the Executive Office Building. Hayes had told him last night the Group now had offices all over the capital district, some fifteen of them.

"Extension 362." There was a click on the line and Prevadello held his breath. Then reason returned: that couldn't be the tape banks, never hear them in a month of Sundays. He shook the phone gently and the mouthpiece clicked again. Bad phone.

"362 liaison." Another female, this one probably older, overweight by the sound of things. Jolly.

"Mr. Perkins, please." A pause: that was an ancient Kemper workname but Prevadello didn't care; she'd either have a crossfile or a damn good memory. So did Kemper but Prevadello figured the gambit would work: half the FBI knew Kemper as Perkins from the UN days.

"Ah, yes, Mr., ah,"—you could hear her brain working—"Perkins is in a meeting until eleven-thirty. Who may I say . . ." Prevadello hung up, then dialed Hayes' number.

"Hayes, Data Center."

"It's your hitchhiker from this morning, O.K.? Call our mutual friend at extension 362. If he's out, call me right back at

325-7834. Four rings, then hang up. If he's in, two rings. If he's in and booked for lunch at eleven-thirty, six rings. Got it?''

Hayes had already hung up.

A minute later the pay phone rang.

Six times.

Satisfied, Prevadello dialed a Manhattan number, leaving a message for Roberta, asking her to mind the bonsai for the next week.

Prevadello wandered the two aisles of the variety store, thinking. He bought a Redskins cap, a map of the District of Columbia, a pair of Ray-Ban sunglasses, and a cheap transistor radio with an ear plug. Might as well take in the sights, he thought to himself. He tuned the radio to the all-news station and began to stroll, the happy tourist.

He orbited the neighborhood for the next two hours, until the Nikon bag felt like a cinder block hanging from his shoulder, practicing every surveillance technique he'd ever known to fight off the boredom. At eleven-twenty, Prevadello stopped after the fourth pass-by of Kemper's car and fitted the telephoto, taking a series of shots of the Potomac to entertain himself, thinking to fit them together like Matthew Brady's panoramic plates. Through the lens, the offices were beginning to empty as the half-hour-lunch shifts headed for the sandwich spots. It's an election year, Prevadello thought morosely at quarter to twelve, an image of Kemper with his water glass and note pad before him. He moved several paces to the west, mingling with the crowd at the bus stop. The tension was rising in him. What if Kemper takes a cab to lunch—or doesn't leave at all?

Prevadello calmed himself. Charlie'll be out: he'll have news to tell his godfather, the man who pulls the strings.

Prevadello picked up a discarded *Post* to hide the camera and telephoto, his eyes moving over the top of the columns to the brass-plated door thirty yards away. The brass'll catch the sun when it opens, he thought, raising the Nikon. Charlie Kemper's face came into the view finder, blinking into the midday sun. Prevadello's luck held, if only because Kemper had never missed a lunch in his life. Prevadello took another shot for cover's sake, dropped the *Post* in a trash barrel and began to walk east, twenty paces behind Kemper on the opposite side of Wisconsin.

He's walking, it's close, Prevadello thought, relishing his knowledge of the habitual Kemper. And it was. Kemper turned south on Wisconsin and entered a converted warehouse, now a trendy shopping and office arcade. Prevadello watched as Kemper crossed the courtyard and opened the door to a small French restaurant. A deli with a good view of the restaurant stood across the courtyard and Prevadello pressed his way through the lunch time throng to the counter. He ordered a ham and cheese on an onion bun and a black coffee and took up his post at a stand-up rail at the window.

Prevadello looked between the heads in the crowd milling in the courtyard. Kemper was chatting up the waitress, smiling away, shrugging. Prevadello put down his coffee. He's not ordering, he's sending her away. Better. He finished his sandwich and asked the counterman what was upstairs.

"Art gallery. Modern stuff," the man said without smiling as he wrestled a side of corned beef onto the slicing machine.

"Not your cup of tea?" Prevadello asked as he paid the fellow.

"Not my cup of Chivas, you mean," the counterman said, showing his twisted teeth.

Prevadello laughed. "I got a cold, pal. Can I get up there inside the mall?"

"Sure. There's a door at the back. Just follow the hallway to the stairwell."

Prevadello said thanks and left an extra two bucks in the change tray. The office doors along the hall were all closed save one; a shirt-sleeved fat man wearing a toupee was writing "sales motivation" on a chalkboard. Overheard an anemic "Greensleeves" piped into the hallway. Prevadello took the stairs two at a time; he loathed Muzak with a passion. A milled plastic sign on the second-floor landing read Danska Studio. Stuffing the Redskins cap and the sunglasses into his coat pocket, Prevadello stepped into the hallway. One wall was clear; a row of ferns hung like green spaghetti against the smooth glass.

There were three other customers in the gallery, an airy track-lit space overseen by a sullen blonde in a pantsuit. Prevadello nodded to her as the door hissed closed behind him. He took a brochure and walked slowly to the courtyard side of the gallery. A black couple, clearly wealthy, were admiring what appeared to be a stainless steel dolphin slowly revolving on a gray pedestal, their voices properly hushed.

Prevadello looked down into the courtyard. *Christ*. A jolt of adrenalin jumped in Prevadello's chest: it's lunch time with Charlie. A man big enough to fill the restaurant window was sitting down with Kemper. It wasn't the meaty face itself that impressed Prevadello; it was the silhouette, the way his face fitted into the broad blue pinstriped wash of the shoulders, ear-deep. Prevadello nearly dropped the Nikon as he tore at the bag flap. Focusing quickly, he squeezed three shots off. The waitress made the last photo, her white apron outlining Kemper's dining companion perfectly.

"Sirexcusemesir?" It was the girl in the pantsuit. "Photographing the art is strictly against gallery rules."

"Understand, miss. I'm a bird watcher, actually. Just caught a rare thrush, I'm pleased to say." Rocking on his heels, Prevadello beamed at everyone in the room, flashing his best hundred-watt addled smile. Uncertain, the black couple stood open-mouthed. "Sorry, sir." The girl's predatory face fell abruptly.

Lord, a *thrush*, Prevadello: still, it's the little victories that make life worthwhile, he thought fleetingly, dropping the Nikon into the bag and moving over to inspect several amorphous bronze shapes welded atop one another. Down below, Kemper and friend were laying into the soup.

"And the lines. I've always loved Brancusi's lines." The girl nodded her thanks as Prevadello lit her cigarette. It was past one and the black couple had left without buying anything. Prevadello had been making conversation with the salesgirl for the last twenty minutes.

"Can't beat him. Nobody comes close," Prevadello agreed lamely, glancing over her shoulder; this girl had enough pretensions for a dozen art galleries. Kemper was obviously *not* going to pay for the lunch. The big man was waving his pen about and making a fuss about signing for the bill while Kemper sat back, pleased.

"Next time you're in New York, we'll do the Metropolitan together. I'm in the book. Lambrusco, like the wine. On 57th." Prevadello put on his beret.

"Have a nice day. And good luck with the birds." She batted her eyelashes and was still smiling as he left. Prevadello marked the Danska Studio down as a dead loss and stepped onto the balcony. He walked around the courtyard mezzanine, stopping directly above the entrance to the French restaurant, and took out the Nikon. There was a good crowd still in the courtyard. He leaned over the brick balcony and waited.

They left together, the big man chewing a cigar, a walking hat on his head. A schmoozer, Prevadello said to himself, a corporate fixer, as he got a good close-up. The pair stopped. Kemper was being worked over pretty well: the big man was waving a reproving finger and turning on the charm. Kemper was looking at his feet and then up toward the wide blue sky. A bus roared and as the last of its noise trailed away in the courtyard's quiet, Prevadello felt rather than heard the word Frankfurt drift over the rail.

"Mother of God." Prevadello fought the camera back into the bag as he began to run around the balcony perimeter. He stole a look over the rail—the big man left first, moving far faster than Prevadello expected. The arcade had staircases at the four corners and Prevadello took the nearest, hoping and praying he could avoid the courtyard.

"Luck of the Irish," he murmured as he found himself in a passageway leading to a parking lot crammed with cars and delivery trucks. Prevadello began to run, backtracking around the arcade's exterior, dodging the overhanging bumpers of the parked cars. He caught sight of the big man's wool walking hat bobbing above the crowd. Kemper was nowhere in sight. I'm rusty, he admitted to himself, I'm rusty and clumsy and despite it all I've got a live one. Prevadello looked back across the street—the big man was examining the Harris tweeds in a display window not forty feet away. *He's made me.* "Where's the goddam sun," Prevadello muttered, but it was all right: he stopped in the shadows. Then a prosperous face came into the display window among the suit coats and scarves and mouthed something; the big man laughed, pointing at the merchandise, a hooting belch of laughter that startled the pigeons above.

You've nothing to do, you're killing time before heading back to the office. Act like it, for God's sake. Prevadello clasped his hands behind his back with a proprietary air and began to breathe again. The big man had resumed his beat, bent forward, a study in velocity. Instinctively, Prevadello liked the man's style, larger than life and energetic—he'd tie Kemper up in knots.

In the first of the little ghetto of old shops, a black newsboy chewed his gum as Big Man entered his store. Prevadello figured the sweeping was done and the stale copies of the *Post* and the *Times* were stacked and bundled next to the doorway for the morning trucks to pick up when the fresh papers came; the kid was lounging, watching the faces. Leaving the shelter of the doorway, the newsboy stepped back into the store. Prevadello crossed the street and had a glimpse of a pair of kids, edging toward the stacks of *Playboy*. The newsboy froze them with a practiced stare in the dish mirror over their heads, his gaze swinging from them to the doorway as Prevadello entered the store.

"You two. Make with the Spidermans and leave the girls for the real men. G'wan." He laughed as the pair blushed and moved back to the comics. Prevadello checked the mirror himself; Big Man was browsing in the back corner, his back to the mirror, his big neck levering up and down as he bent to see the titles.

"Hey, you two, I *told* you t'get outta there. Now beat it." The two boys left sheepishly, slamming the door and giggling as they ran off.

"Slow afternoon?" Big Man was talking over his shoulder as he scanned the piles of papers in the stand across from the till.

"Sorta. Sunshine brings in the weirdos. No offense," the boy said.

The large man laughed, a big, round laugh. "No offense. I'm going to Europe this weekend and I'd like to catch up on the news over there. This where I look?"

Prevadello watched as the newsboy came around the counter and pointed to the foreign newspapers clipped to the wire racks at the back of the store, near the cooking magazines. "There. Some of 'em are weekend, some are last week's, some of the dailies don't come out 'til tomorrow." He rattled out the words by rote, an echo of the owner's instructions.

"Ah, I see. The dailies, they're not delivered until tomorrow?"

"No. They're in the back 'cos they're air-freighted. Customs an' all. My dad says he's the one to price 'em though. Only him."

The large man bent down to examine the newsboy's face before he spoke. "Well, I'll give you, say, three bucks for your most recent *France-Soir*. You can pocket what I don't owe your dad. How's about that for a deal?"

Prevadello turned the page of the *Ring* he had in his hand, his ears suddenly live antennae. The newsboy grinned and loped past the paperbacks and the sunglass display to the back of the store, his knife in hand to cut open the bundles. "Thanks," said Big Man. Prevadello could feel Big Man's eyes scan his back, then move away: uncanny, Prevadello thought, that tactile sense of intimacy between watcher and quarry.

All Prevadello's instincts told him to leave first. Prevadello left enough change on the counter for the *Ring*, rolled the magazine, and thrust it into his coat as he left the store. His practice, in the old scheme of things, would have been to roll friend Big Man between two teams, one car, one sidewalk, crossing over every few blocks.

But those were the luxuries of another age. Prevadello recrossed M Street and planted himself at a bus stop, his beret newly squashed over his head, anything to change the image. He checked the bus stop sign; the next bus, pulling away from the stop some hundred yards to the east, might do the trick. Still no sign of Big Man. Prevadello stepped back from the curb, half-hiding himself behind a big Hispanic woman in curlers.

*Bingo.* The newsstand door opened just as the bus hove to a halt. The crowd at the bus stop pressed forward, pushing Prevadello into the Hispanic woman's soft behind. He stepped sideways, cut across the head of the line, and jumped aboard the bus via its open rear door.

At the head of the rear stairs, Prevadello turned and saw Big Man was back in action, heading west. Prevadello dove off the bus even before the driver realized he had a stowaway.

Big Man resumed his stroll, his newspaper under his arm, his body naturally clearing his path through the afternoon browsers. Prevadello kept to the shadows, allowing Big Man as much as half a block's lead before closing in. Prevadello took the next bus long enough to get two blocks ahead of Big Man, then doubled back on the other side of the street after alighting. His own back was clean, of that Prevadello was sure—and Big Man showed no sign of doing anything but enjoying his constitutional. The shop fronts became bureaucratic boxes; Prevadello's covering screen of pedestrians was disappearing.

The government was back at work.

Big Man slowed his pace, fishing for a key. Prevadello stepped into a side street and cut between two parked cars. Deep in the shadows, he watched over the tops of the cars.

A warm band of sunlight fell across M Street and a two-story Georgian house abandoned by an awning crew for the lunch hour. A tony place it was too, with an iron-gated archway leading to a small quadrangle within; surrounded by cones of gathered leaves, a gardener, his kneepads pressed into the carefully tilled soil, wrapped the rosebushes and the forsythia in burlap for the winter. Big Man stepped between the ladders and was gone. Prevadello peered across the street to the doorway. One of the ladders obscured a brass plaque. "National Archives and Records Service Office": you'd think the cover people could come up with something a little more creative, Prevadello reflected—"Records Service" in this neighborhood spells spook in any man's language. Prevadello turned and slipped into a cluster of lunch-time stragglers, heading south, the Nikon bumping against his belly like a newborn child.

A subdued Hayes led the way up the stairs; they had not shared a word since the boy had plucked a thoughtful Prevadello from the 31st Street steps of the Georgetown post office. Hayes' apartment was well to the northwest, in an anonymous tower girdled with acres of desolate parking and artificial hills like bunkers where no children played. The hallway smelt of patchouli and somewhere deep in the walls a solitary typewriter clacked. His apartment door was lit by a frosted glass fixture now a mausoleum for summer flies. Hayes produced a key from his leather jacket. "Watch out for Benny," he said, as he turned the door handle. "My German shepherd."

"You first." Prevadello shifted the bag from the photographic supply store higher on his chest. He had a mortal fear of large dogs; a school friend had been bitten once, decades ago, while Marty watched, rigid with fear. Benny began to bark but Hayes cuffed him affectionately and closed the kitchen door behind the dog, motioning Prevadello in.

"Benny's all right. C'mon, take the nickel tour."

Hayes' living room was sparse: a few posters stuck to the walls with browning tape and a row of records in milk crates running along one wall, punctuated by cases of beer empties. A stereo system occupied one corner and a computer terminal and handmade bookcase the other. The kitchen was around the corner; magazines with names like *Software Digest* and *Computer Sciences Journal* lay in heaps next to a tired couch. A film projector stood atop a coffee table scarred by cigarette ends, its lens aimed at a blank square of wall. "I'm big on foreign movies," Hayes said laconically. "Seen much Fellini?"

Grunting, Prevadello shook his head. Outside, in the distance to the south, the afternoon Potomac crept away through the reds and golds of the Virginia trees—Hayes' place had a view, if nothing else. Resigned to Prevadello's silence, Hayes flung his leather jacket onto the couch and disappeared down a short hallway, calling "bedroom" and "closet" like a tour guide, his sneakers squeaking on the bare floors. He opened the last door with a flourish: "Window's ready for action . . . chemicals are in the cupboard," Hayes said, teetering on a stool while unscrewing the bathroom's only light bulb. The window had been blacked-out with squares of aluminum foil held in place with masking tape.

The bathroom turned red as Hayes fitted the darkroom bulb. Prevadello stood the fat brown bottles of developer and fixative on the shaving ledge. The sink's finish was badly burnt by the chemicals and a smear of rust trailed down its side. Prevadello, who had an ex-military man's tyrannical fussiness, asked, "How long have you been developing in here?" He ran his finger over the battered porcelain; a scratched developing tray lay on the top of the cistern.

"I still do some 8 mm stuff, mostly for the hell of it." Hayes got off his stool and caught Prevadello's expression. Hayes' bemused eyes cooled behind the aviator glasses: "This ain't *Better Homes and Gardens*, pops, but it does the job. Where you live, Central Park South?"

"Come back in a quarter of an hour," Prevadello said brusquely, favoring Hayes with a Mona Lisa smile as he broke the Nikon out of its leather case, "and tell me who Big Man is." He twisted the tap open and switched off the light.

Hayes hesitated, then muttered, "Right, pops," and closed the door. The last crack of light disappeared as the boy stuffed a towel into the gap; his sneakers bounced down the corridor. Prevadello turned, bowed his shoulders, and began to extract the film. Hayes had offered a Group-controlled freelancer's darkroom on the way north, but Prevadello would have none of it—one set of these shots would be sufficient: the freelancer who would not be tempted to copy an interesting negative is not yet born. Prevadello dropped the coil of film into one of his new canisters. Lid on. Developer bath O.K. Into the bath . . . Prevadello watched the luminous dots on his wrist watch flicker beneath the sweep second hand. The darkroom reminded him of an all-nighter in Seoul, reading recon. photos of Chinese Communist tank depots. Prevadello tapped the canister again for air bubbles. Red light on. Then the hypo, double time . . . Kemper's decided to emulate Rappaport and take over the world, Prevadello decided as he waited. He's grown half a foot taller, had a second childhood or hormone shots. Or a mistress. Prevadello had to laugh at the last conjecture—the notion of the unromantic Kemper with a lover was too surreal. Which probably means he's got a girl, Prevadello reckoned grimly. Or two.

Five minutes later, the film hung gibbeted from Hayes' shower rail, dripping into the filthy tub. Prevadello flushed the chemicals away and groped for the photographic paper amid a pile of toilet paper and ancient copies of *American Cinematographer* in the cabinet beneath the sink. Ten minutes later, squatting on the floor over the enlarger, Prevadello had his contact prints. My kingdom for a name, Prevadello thought, as he opened the door.

"Danny, show time."

Opening the door, Hayes loped into the bathroom.

"Here, take the milk. Wow. D'you know who you've been tailing?" Leading the way to the living room, Hayes took the contact prints in his hands. He propped his feet on his battered coffee table. Prevadello, seated next to him, sipped a glass of milk carefully.

"You tell me."

Hayes shook his head. "That's Morley Walsh." Hayes shook his head again, disbelievingly.

"Means nothing to me." Prevadello had another sip of his milk.

"Rappaport's bagman. Walsh is Beelzebub himself. Jesus."

Prevadello stood and moved to the living-room window. A group of kids had appeared from nowhere after school and were playing tag in the parking lot below, sprinting happily between the rows of cars. "What's the line on Walsh, then?"

"Like I said." Hayes lit his cigarette. "You see him in the hall, somebody's getting the ax."

Prevadello grunted. "Kemper work for Walsh?" Prevadello's eyes fell on the computer terminal, then Hayes.

Hayes stretched his legs and slumped into the depths of the old couch. "Work? Couple of the Operations guys were bitching about how Kemper does square root of zip, blocking the promotion lane. Interior decoration." He blew a cloud of smoke straight up. "Kemper hasn't got the brains."

Which means Charlie's right where he wants to be, Prevadello calculated. Underestimated and ignored: perfect. "You have access to the Group data base?"

"Not the agent stuff. Housekeeping, like what I was doing this morning, the bread-and-butter stuff, yeah. I key most of it in. Except the cosmic files. Rappaport's office does that, babe named Carol. Mr. Software, at your service."

Prevadello had to smile. He motioned Hayes to the terminal. "Do your thing, son. Let's start with the disbursement accounts."

Hayes swung into his chair and his terminal came to life.

Prevadello had a thought. "Rappaport's office keep track of all log-ons?"

Hayes began to tap the keyboard. "Yeah, Carol handles that stuff. But the access protocols are pretty lame. If I want in on the sly, I just erase my log entries as soon as I'm out." He looked up at Prevadello and beamed. "Helps if you wrote the entry protocols."

"I'm sure." Prevadello pulled up a milk crate and sat down.

Hayes cracked his knuckles, shuffling in his seat like a nervous bantamweight. "What are you looking for?"

"Money, just like everybody else. Start the travel, D.C. to New York. Walsh first, then Kemper."

"What about worknames?"

Prevadello thought for a moment. "Skip 'em. What I'm after are straight business expenses."

Hayes rattled off a volley of keystrokes and they were rewarded with Morley Walsh's travel cash records.

"Not a hell of a lot there, is there?" Hayes leaned forward and ran his finger down a string of glowing numbers. There wasn't: perhaps three dozen entries for the last six months.

"Probably has his own slush fund. Or his own budget parked somewhere else. Try Kemper."

The screen rolled upwards and Walsh's paltry entries were replaced by a solid page of Kemper's travel expenses. And another. And yet a third.

"Wow."

"So much for interior decoration." Hayes turned expectantly, but Prevadello had turned his back to look out the window as he thought.

He turned back, massaging his eyes and forehead. "When's the last entry in Kemper's file?"

"A week ago."

"Any other break of more than seven days in the last six months?"

Hayes scrolled to the top of the file and read downwards for a good two minutes. "No. Looks like he was traveling to New York almost every other day until last week. Figure it means something?"

"Can you examine any petty cash floats with your access?"

"Sure. Whose d'you want?"

"Rappaport's."

"Shit, I can't do that, even if I wanted to. They spread this stuff around, it's all under different budgets. Rappaport's under

Defense, maybe even in a different data base altogether. You gotta stop thinking like that, you'll get somebody mad." Hayes shivered.

"That's my specialty, son. Try Walsh's cash floats, then, will you?"

"Budget category?"

Prevadello silently cursed his memory and closed his eyes: "Try 'Records Archive.' " He found his Camels and lit one, offering the pack to Hayes.

"Thanks, but I'd like some lungs left." Hayes tapped away. "Nothing there."

"Dammit." Prevadello exhaled heavily. "Look, I haven't much time for this. Have you a central directory? Try keyword 'Records.' "

"Yeah. Sure, I'll try that." Hayes began to whistle, badly.

"Don't do that. Gives me the creeps."

Hayes sighed and then tapped the glass screen. " 'Debit Records Service,' see also General Accounting Office, file blah-blah—there's been twenty grand vouchered, but what's it mean?"

"Nothing. Unless we know where the money went, it's just a debit. Try Kemper's travel accounts next." While Hayes worked, Prevadello chewed another nail, his mind replaying its history of Kemper's ways with a purloined dollar.

"Hey, the account's been inactivated. Look."

"Are you sure?" Prevadello peered over Hayes' shoulder. But there it was. "Hell. What date?"

"Wow. Same day—"

Prevadello finished the sentence: "—Walsh withdrew the twenty." He went back to the window, needing to give his mind the illusion of space. "Take five. Get us a couple of beers while I think."

"Could nail a cold one myself." Hayes jogged to the tiny kitchen and there was a creaky *chung* as he slammed the old refrigerator's door, followed by Benny's sleepy bark. Three minutes passed; Prevadello returned to the window and trolled his memory for Charlie's favorite tricks, the twists and turns of his old partner's secret footwork. Prevadello pressed himself to the window frame, idly pitching and catching his beret, watching the river traffic; a helicopter dipped to the tree line, then prowled away across the brilliant sky.

"Danny. What about personnel files? You said we could see those."

Hayes reappeared with two bottles of Heineken. "The unclassified stuff, yeah. No postings or anything, just the payroll deductions, advances . . . take the beers!"

"That's my boy, now you're catching on." Prevadello took the two bottles and watched Hayes excitedly call up Charles McKinley Kemper's personnel data.

"Ever see an advance fronted like that in all your days, Danny?"

"Never." The boy turned from the screen, thoroughly pleased, and took his beer. "There's more. Look at this." It was just like the old days: Kemper had given himself a leave of absence (there was a cross-reference to his confidential medical file) and Walsh had backhanded him a nest egg. Charlie, Prevadello thought, you're losing your creativity.

"Mud in your eye." Hayes drank his Heineken in a single swallow and then belched like a schoolboy.

"So where'd the money go?"

"Can't say." Hayes pressed several keys.

"Then we have nothing." Prevadello found himself looking at Hayes' reflected back, seated at his terminal, mirrored in the apartment window. "Have to be someone young," Geraghty had said, ". . . with access to the phone logs . . ." *Phone logs.*

"That data base have Group phone logs on line?"

Hayes swung his aviator glasses around. "Yes and no."

"Hell's that mean?"

"Means I can call up local calls, but anything through the overseas exchanges, like WAVE, shows up only as toll calls to region Group stations, like Cairo or Geneva, not final numbers. Supposed to protect agents-in-place, I guess."

"It's a start. What can you show me?"

"Well, the files come up like your phone bill, pops, that's all. It's an accounting thing. Day by day."

"Local calls too?"

"Every call from a Group desk. You order out for Chinese, this—" he slapped the terminal display "—remembers. Keeps all the boys and girls honest."

Prevadello chewed his thumbnail. "We could go blind. Walsh must make a thousand calls a month."

Hayes shrugged. "What are you after?"

"I'll know it when I see it. Look, what tricks can you play with the phone logs?"

"I can sort by exchange, by area code, by area code and *time*, do an F.S.R.—"

"Wait a minute. What's an F.S.R.?"

"Frequency subroutine. I use the data base software to sort the numbers called by frequency."

"Do all executive offices, D.C. Station. Start with Walsh."

Hayes rubbed his hands together. "Danny, my boy, welcome to the major leagues."

Prevadello walked to the sofa and gathered the negatives and the contact prints. In the kitchen, stepping carefully over the sleeping Benny, Prevadello took a pair of barbecue tongs from one of the drawers and carried the lot down the hall to the bathroom. There, the old fan clanking and whirring overhead, he held the strip of negatives in the tongs and set the contact print alight, letting its flame crumple the negative to gobbets of burning plastic, then flushed the charred blobs away.

At his terminal, Hayes was examining three neat columns of telephone numbers, the Group directory on his lap. Line by line, the two of them painfully worked through Morley Walsh's phone records. He placed one call daily to a village in Virginia. Aside from that, no numbers occurred in groups of more than six a month but one. They tried September next: same thing. And August, and July . . . going back two years.

"Can you match the two numbers to a name?"

"Sure. I got the program from my buddy Carl at FBI data processing. First one's Elizabeth Walsh Powell. I've heard of her—that's his mom. Loaded." Hayes pointed at the other number. There was a long silence while the terminal gestated. I smell smoke, Prevadello thought, big smoke: please God, let there be a great big fire at the other end. "No match here."

"O.K., what's that mean? Unlisted?"

"Either unlisted or one of an unlisted extension series. Sorry."

"Shut it off for today, Danny."

"Got to clear my log-ons first. Want another beer?" The computer specialist hit a pair of keys and his screen went dark.

"Danny, get me to Union station—I'm taking a train back to New York." Prevadello touched the boy on the shoulder, pinching the crown of the muscle, gently. "You're good, very good, Danny, but this isn't beanbag, understand? You just broke a basketful of Federal laws: wrongful entry, misuse of government property, fraud. Forget me, forget Morley Walsh. Everything. Unless you *like* the slammer and sex-starved roommates. Your mind's a blank, right?"

"What'd you say your name was?"

"Good boy." Prevadello smiled and drained his beer. "Go get your coat." In the kitchen, Benny began to bark again. Next to the parking lot below, the band of happily screaming children scurried among the hillocks, chasing a single boy who mocked his pursuers with his speed. Twenty grand, Prevadello thought as he watched, to buy one milk run.

# Chapter Five

The tradition had begun, as Russian traditions will, in a raucous drinking bout. On a blissful summer night four years ago, Moldov and a dozen or so of his subordinates, their pockets clanking with vodka bottles, had tumbled down Moldov's stairs and into the night, "to outflank the Americans", the now-forgotten instigator had urged. It is just as well the instigator's name had disappeared into a vodka-fog, for the escapade broke every security rule in the GRU's extensive book. The pack of them, singing and swigging, eventually made its way to the gates of the United States Embassy, where Ferenko, liberated from his usual reserve by the booze, made history by relieving himself against the tires of a parked Chrysler. Now only Moldov and Ferenko kept the fitful tradition alive for their private talks, away from the office, wandering the same route *in memoriam* this chilly mid-afternoon, buying a length of fresh Polish sausage at the Party commission store behind the planetarium in the heart of Moscow's embassy quarter. The afternoon meeting had taken them from their secret nest to downtown Moscow, to the U.S.-Canada Institute, where the two GRU men had met with Alekseev, the Institute's disinformation specialist. All very interesting, trying to "bend" these American peace committees, Ferenko thought, but his time might have been better spent on his beloved archives. Moldov, on the other hand, relished the chance to pick Alekseev's brains about future talent spotting; that was how you rose to Moldov's prominence, Ferenko reminded himself, by being thorough. As they left the carefully anonymous front doorway of the Party store, Ferenko adhered to the tradition of forgoing shoptalk, and pursued the deeply important topic of soccer, in particular Orlov, the controversial Moscow Dynamo winger, much given, rumor had it, to ballerinas.

Moldov tore the top off the paper wrap and chewed his sausage happily. "Lora hates it when I eat sausage, you know," Moldov observed as he stepped past the door Ferenko obsequiously held open. "Bad for the heart, she says." Ferenko wisely said nothing and peeled the paper away from the end of his own sausage. They turned together into the crowd bent sickle-backed into the rising winds, Ferenko pressing his big uniform hat down, and crossed Vosstaniya Place while Moldov pontificated: "What can I say? It is simple: Orlov lacks cunning. Ballerinas or not, he is a creature of habit, and a winger without imagination is useless. Like a poor intelligence officer, eh, Ferenko," Moldov lectured, waving his sausage in midair for emphasis.

"Imaginative order and orderly imagination," Ferenko repeated, this truism being one of Moldov's bywords.

"Trust your imagination more, and you may yet triumph over that square head of yours. There, Ferenko, there is the scene of your greatest triumph to date," Moldov continued, as they walked northward past the American embassy on Ulitsa Chaikovskogo.

"Inspired by your fine vodka, comrade-general," Ferenko replied, providing his superior with his ritual cue; Moldov had few vanities, but one was being known as a wit.

Pleased at this opportunity, Moldov grunted, "Ferenko, if you'd really liked the vodka, you wouldn't have leaked it all over the imperialist ambassador's tires. Waste of good vodka!" Moldov nudged Ferenko in the ribs and horse-laughed. "Come, Ferenko! Today we will look at the zoo. I want to visit my mother-in-law, eh? That is a joke, Ferenko."

"Yes, sir."

Moldov looked at his assistant for a moment, then shook his head. "Know any jokes?" Moldov began to walk again, considering Ferenko over his shoulder for a moment. "You should learn some jokes, Ferenko: you'd be better for it."

"I will learn some jokes, comrade-colonel."

"That's my boy. Make me laugh. Keep me company. It's lonely being God, Ferenko." Moldov laughed at his blasphemy as they rounded the corner of the embassy now, quite alone as they entered the zoo at the Bolshaya Gruzinskaya gate. The Moscow Zoo suffered gravity badly; that which fell tended to lie where it fell, though scabs of gray-black snow masked the more unsightly piles of rubbish, the leaves and dirt and dead branches of autumn. The broad concrete pathways wound between the naked trees and met the foot of the fence separating the zoo from the press of the encircling city—low whitewashed brick apartments surrounded the zoo compound on all sides.

"Here, Ferenko, here you can learn about the human animal. No place better. Learn, Ferenko, the directorate needs your brain."

Ferenko nodded obediently and decided to exploit this momentary opening. "Comrade-colonel, I have much to learn, I agree, but might the directorate consider computerizing the American archive?"

"Computerizing? So: the business starts. Just when I was beginning to philosophize." Moldov dropped the butt of his sausage into a receptacle.

"Comrade-colonel?"

"Believe that about Orlov, do you? The ballerina, I mean."

"My brother-in-law is the team trainer, comrade-colonel."

"Worth a rouble or two against Dynamo this Sunday, you think?"

Ferenko allowed a smirk to pass over his narrow face. "I'd bet my commission, comrade-colonel. The Kirov's got an opening Saturday night. He'll be neck deep in ballerinas."

"Really," Moldov inquired absently, seeming to see Ferenko in a new way now this information had changed hands. "Ferenko. Next walk, see you stick to soccer, eh?"

"Sir."

They continued to walk toward the center of the zoo. "You have persistence: you ask me this every year, Ferenko, and a no's a no. Yes, it needs to be done. But we'd need twice the manpower. If I requisition ten more men, one of them will be KGB, don't you see?"

"With respect, comrade-colonel, the boys have the IBM machine under control now. That will save us much labor. We need not take on more staff."

Moldov, wordless, gave Ferenko his bag to carry and wrapped his hands together behind his back, silent again. What does he think of now? Ferenko wondered: he is a tortoise, pulling his head in when there's bad weather about. They walked quietly for several minutes, until they came upon Moldov's favorite spot; he stepped up to the walrus cage and hung his hands on the fence railings, watching. "A walrus is like a good spy, Ferenko, know that? Look how ugly she is, that one lying there, but how beautiful in the water. Two lives in one body, Ferenko, that's the trick, separate. Beautiful. Come here, you beautiful slut! Ferenko, the bag!''

Moldov grabbed the bag impatiently and drew out a handful of raw herrings from the jar he'd bought at the commission store. One of the walruses bristled her whiskers, flirting with Moldov. Ferenko watched as the American directorate head of Red Army intelligence fed the snorting walrus with his bare hands.

"Ferenko—that's my girl, have another—Ferenko, what do we gain computerizing the archive? Simply, in plain Russian, none of your witch-talk.''

Ferenko sniffled and rubbed his shoulder on the railing, cat-like, watching. "These days, we have to think like the computer, comrade-general. The directorate wastes a great deal of time processing the old card-files. We could save hundreds of hours with the new computer files.''

Moldov said nothing, flipping the herrings between the bars, making affectionate noises as the walrus cow fed. Half a dozen Moscow hooded crows strolled the edge of the pad, eyeing the fish; Moldov slipped another herring to the walrus with one hand and palmed a stone in the other. He threw the stone and the crows danced away, screaming. The walrus kept eating contentedly. "Ferenko, you know me: I'm an old-timer, got my start recruiting Poles in 1936. Danzig was the glamor posting then, know that? Just doesn't feel right to me, having electrons running agents. I'm a document man, give me a card, something I can feel.'' Something changed in Moldov then, a shift of his big back muscles, an awakening. Moldov straightened, the herring jar dribbling on the sand as he stared at Ferenko, the dull gold of his overcoat's dress braid blending with the dun stone of the zoo's walls. "You want an investigation, don't you?''

"The American directorate's a good place to start looking for an American 'pig.' ''

Moldov backhanded another herring through the bars but his enthusiasm had faded. "Everybody's got a theory, but if there's a 'pig,' he's in the Navy, that's my bet, Ferenko. Best opportunities for recruitment, worst working conditions, boredom. One signalsman turned and the West would have our submarine locations, and that's that.'' The crows had returned, edging toward the herring bones. Moldov watched them for a moment. "If State Security gets wind of an internal investigation, we'll be their tea-boys inside a fortnight. Can we keep the lid on? Short of shooting people?''

"Like you said, comrade-colonel: I'm persistent. There's more than one way to do an internal. As we transfer the files, we work backwards, check for leaks, cross-reference with RAYMOND's product—"

"—work backwards. You're a clever bastard, Ferenko. It's an idea. A possibility. An internal without doing an internal." Moldov shot the rest of the preserved fish through the bars with a shake of the jar. "Come. Let's go look at the birds. I want to see how the steppe-eagle's making out." Moldov left the jar inside the railing and strode off, Ferenko trailing him.

"Bag," Moldov demanded abruptly. He took the leather pouch from Ferenko and held it behind his back as his boots scraped on the walkway grit. Moldov cut through a coppice of trees, stopping halfway across. Ferenko followed into the flat light between the trees; Moldov was standing amid a quartet of firs, shadowed from the few zoo-goers about. As Ferenko's steps scrunched the pine needles, the GRU general turned and spoke, slowly. "They are cowboys, the Americans. They waste much time. We have some time in hand, Ferenko. How long do you need?"

"Six months. Five if I can have another two keypunch operators."

"You can have your internal," Moldov agreed. He took his assistant's forearm in his strong grip. "Do the job with the men you have. Patience, Ferenko, always patience. Like the crows back there. Wait, and the fish will come to you."

"Yes, comrade-colonel."

"Come. And cheer up, Ferenko. You got your way." He left the safety of the trees and waited for his assistant. "No games with the computer, then, Ferenko. Keep it simple. Day to day. No drama. Put Roskov on it, don't tell him why. Simple?"

"No computer dramas, comrade-colonel, I give you my word. Just jokes."

Moldov laughed again as they strolled, gesturing. "See. There! You made a joke! Not a good one, mark you, but a joke nonetheless. This way. Try to keep up, Ferenko." The bird cages lay close to the zoo wall, wire-mesh houses enclosing stunted trees, open to the sky. The steppe-eagle cage was empty.

"Damn. I was looking forward to a look at the new eaglet. Well, I had no food anyway. You have the night off, then?"

"Yes, comrade-colonel."

"Pity—could have used you. There's the Washington signal

to come through tonight. Home to the wife and kids, Ferenko, then. Bright and early tomorrow?''

''Yes, comrade-colonel. My respects to Madame Moldova.'' Ferenko saluted and walked away, his thin frame swaying slightly as he turned the corner. Moldov shrugged his shoulders deeper into his greatcoat; the wind was picking up again, rattling the tree limbs like wooden sabers. Moldov walked slowly down the path between the cages, setting his jackboots down reflectively, pausing like a window-shopper between steps. That one, Moldov decided as the birds called him, is a machine himself: Ferenko bears watching now he's colonel. ''One wonders about machines,'' Moldov muttered. ''One prefers flesh and blood.'' Not that any flesh is completely trustworthy—but Moldov trusted a man who can laugh.

They're still at it, Moldov realized. It was nearly nine, but the tanks were practicing on Moscow Center's parade ground, crawling across the expanse of the old Khodinka airfield in full-dress cosmetics, rehearsing under floodlights for their one-minute drive across Red Square commemorating the 1917 Revolution. Moldov couldn't actually see the parade preparations from his second-floor office—the first and second story windows of Moscow Center's most secret building look directly into the inward-facing windows of the low structure encircling it—but the roar of the T-62 engines rumbled through the great masses of concrete to his desk.

Where the hell is Korilov with my tea? Moldov moistened his lips with a tongue tacky from too many American cigarettes and a thirteen-hour day. Lora's right, Moldov admitted; I'm a bloodhound with bad teeth, one eye, and flat feet. But I'm the best—they can't deny that.

Moldov tipped his desk lamp away from his sore eye and sat quietly in the semidarkness of his Center office. Between the two files open on his desk, Moldov had cleared a place for the overdue tea and chopped egg *pirozhki* which would comprise his late dinner. He touched his cheek. Yes: it was warmer to the touch where the ache was. That'll be three teeth gone in the last six months. I'll have to cook up an excuse to visit East Berlin soon and get some decent filings. These Moscow dentists deal off the silver and putty your teeth instead; *Pravda* had just run an article on two dentists sent to the GULAG as silver speculators.

The door to Moldov's office moved as Korilov's wide Byelorussian behind pushed the door open. Korilov turned, his face a deadpan mask.

"My apologies for the delay, sir. I waited for Chertkov to finish with the Washington transmission."

"Chertkov took his bloody time, eh?"

"He said he had to double-check the vocabulary, sir. First time, things didn't look right in the Chinese material, he said. And he's a bit under the weather."

Moldov grunted and reached under his fat orderly's arm to grasp the file as Korilov lowered the tray. "Get him on the phone."

"Some English biscuits, too, sir. I got them especially for you."

Korilov flicked a linen napkin onto his boss's lap and surreptitiously glanced at Moldov's good eye. Madame Moldov had called twice this week to beg Korilov to not let the old colonel strain his remaining eye. "He's working too hard, Korilov. He comes home at midnight and I have to bathe the eye for half an hour before he can sleep. Watch him for me, Korilov." Korilov was devoted to Moldov—they had served together in the GRU since 1943 and the old boy worked as hard today as ever. But Madame was right. It was too much: the eye was red rimmed and brimming with tears and his eyelid trembled as Moldov raised his teacup.

"Now get out of here, Korilov. You'll be wanting to wet nurse me next. You and the wife are a fine pair."

Korilov shrugged and made for the door. "The tea is your favorite blend, sir. Compliments of comrade-colonel Chuikov. He sent it over with the afternoon messenger. Said to wish you luck."

Moldov glowered as he chewed the egg and rice pie. "Good crust on the *pirozhki*, Korilov. You know, I'd wish *him* luck if I were you. His wife can't keep her knickers up."

Korilov, who knew the score without knowing Chuikov personally, nearly smiled, but stopped himself in time. "Yes, sir. Thank you, sir. I'll be back for the tray."

Moldov nodded, not looking up from RAYMOND's latest treasure trove. Korilov closed the door quietly. The old mule's still in control, Korilov thought as he returned to his desk in the anteroom of Moldov's office. Still a few kicks left in old Moldov yet.

Moldov underlined the phrase as he listened to Chertkov, speaking to him from the translators' carrels one floor below. "No, no, comrade-colonel," Chertkov was saying, " 'geopolitical tensions' is the literal translation. It appears to be a new, fashionable term in Washington."

"Geopolitical tensions. Marx couldn't have invented a better one, eh, Chertkov? And what about 'subelement'?"

"That's not so much a translation as an invention, the best I could do," Chertkov said, then he chuckled. "I've no idea what the word means." He sneezed.

"Leave that to the Kremlin, they're just as good at it. And watch your health. You're no good to me sick, Chertkov."

"Good night, comrade-colonel."

Moldov circled "subelement" and topped it with a question mark. The ambiguous translation was the only blemish—this was an even better product than usual. Moldov put his paperweight on the corner of the page before him; the page was curling as the adhesive that held the freshly decoded strips of the Washington signal dried. Better than usual? Perhaps the best yet! RAYMOND was reporting last month's National Security Council briefing, which featured a task force report, code name GUNPOINT, on possible Chinese reaction to a Soviet-American nuclear weapons deal; an interim cost-benefit analysis from the RAND Corporation of an additional aircraft carrier in the Indian Ocean; and a contrary paper on the same subject from the Joint Chiefs of Staff. All very useful, all names and titles carefully annotated, very professionally done.

And lastly, in his personal code, was the best news of all. Ferenko could devil away busily for months at his internal, Moldov thought, but I have the key. From RAYMOND.

This was what made all the backbiting and the long hours and the worrying worthwhile. Something formal was required to mark the occasion. Moldov opened his desk drawer and poured himself a glass of vodka to celebrate. "To RAYMOND," he toasted, his voice echoing in the thick-walled office. By tomorrow morning, the RAYMOND material would be at the Central Committee offices on the Boulevard, and there, over their agreeable breakfasts, eaten of course in a circumspect, Party-like manner, the recipients would marvel. "RAYMOND, my dear RAYMOND," Moldov said, "give me my pig, and you may yet find yourself on a Soviet postage stamp." For RAYMOND, a postage stamp . . . for me, the Order of Lenin. And, better still, that Black Sea *dacha* with the little stretch of beach front old General Vyshinsky used to have at his disposal. Was that too much to mark such a success? He had another drink.

\* \* \*

Long after the tanks had shut down for the night, Korilov, unnerved by the uncharacteristic silence inside Moldov's office,
knocked on the door. Receiving no reply and mindful of Madame Moldova's warning, he peered in. Moldov had fallen
asleep, his work for the night done. Quietly, Korilov removed
his own tunic and wrapped it around the sleeping form of his
superior. On his desk was Moldov's personal code pad. Next to
the code pad was a short list of names, no more than eight or
nine, marked with ticks and arrows, under RAYMOND, written
in bold capitals. As he bent close, Korilov thought he heard
Moldov mumble something about pigs and postage stamps.
There: he said it again. Pigs and postage stamps? Korilov
shrugged as he closed the door. The old man's off his chump.

# Chapter Six

The alarm cut through a terrible dream.

He had been translating, his voice counterpointing a Romanian's drone. Chertkov had looked around the table, to make sure everyone could hear him. A matter of professional courtesy, nothing more.

To his horror, each man Chertkov considered lost his head. One at a time, seven men around the table, seven different heads lolling off seven collars. First the fat, domed head of Kondrashin, the KGB liaison: his black gimballed eyes rolled back and then his neck popped upward, like a child's toy. *Pop*-thud. Very clean, Chertkov remembered thinking to himself: thank God there was no blood. Then the Romanian with the mustache, his lips still moving, his words continuing from the floor. Next Voyevodin, the Central Committee deskman, who reached for his mineral water nonetheless. Moldov's teetered a bit before it fell, Chertkov recalled, shaking his own head for a moment, then gingerly stopping for fear . . . Chertkov cleared his throat again, more gently this time. The heads made hollow, fleshy sounds as they bounced off the polished hardwood, rather like dropped cabbages. But the hands at the ends of the uniform sleeves continued to play with pens, to finger drinking glasses, to nudge writing pads across the baize blotters: the alarm bell forced Chertkov awake as Central Committeeman Voyevodin began to pour his mineral water down his open collar.

The mantelpiece clock read seven-forty.

Fifteen hours since he had clambered over the fallen bicycles and left Shykofsky to his fate; Chertkov probed the sleep from his eyes and considered his alarm clock again. The Center night-shift had gone well—Moldov had been almost gentlemanly, sending me home early, just late enough, however, to avoid seeing Olga off at the Finland Station. But it had been a rough night thereafter. Chertkov coughed himself awake, thinking. Good points first. There had been no battering-ram four A.M. knock, no shouted orders as switches were thrown and walls went blindingly white in the night. They had not come. Chertkov had been awake, waiting, listening, trying to separate the tinkings and sighs of the fashionable old apartment from the faraway grind of the elevator as the cage climbed its shaft. But there was only the silence Chertkov remembered from lying on the bottom of the swimming pool with his hands slowly playing over Ludmilla's lanky-smooth body: a silence deep, warm, distant, like the womb—the "greens" had not come.

But they would: of that Chertkov was certain.

He put on his glasses. The washed-out morning sun crept through the curtain lace, its light the color of tin. Below, the trolley buses rumbled, their bells harsh with cold. Chertkov stood in the center of his apartment, immobile; the paneled walls were heavy with shadow, as if after a rain. He stared over the wedding-cake rooftops to the north, looking westward to the snow-shawled towers pentangling the convent of the Novodevichye and the beautiful twin ponds atop the river bank where as newlyweds he and Olga used to walk in the spring. A cluster of rooks crept around the convent bell tower, then suddenly climbed like fighters. Rolling off the peak of their climbs, the black birds settled into the limbs of the spidery birches at the foot of the wall, dabs of mascara on the papery wood.

Fifteen hours head start—so far, so good. Chertkov closed the heavy curtains. He called his Moscow Center office, telling Korilov he would be at the Lenin Library for the morning, then, depending how rotten he felt, at the clinic downtown. Yes, Korilov said, he'd heard a virus was going around; besides, there was nothing much in Chertkov's in-tray today but a couple of circulars from Center's translation desk on the upcoming Spanish exams. Korilov made a cautious joke about sun tans in Cuba. Chertkov shared a gust of conspiratorial laughter, then rang off.

He went to the kitchen and started the kettle. A wake-up vodka would do him the world of good, he decided, get the blood flowing, still the nerves a bit, sharpen the disorientation from the nightmare. Today's the day, must be decisive: I *will* have a vodka. This new Dutch refrigerator (another present from cousin Andrei at the Berne embassy) was very efficient, and the bottle of pepper vodka lay frozen solidly in its bed of ice. Chertkov began to chip away at the ice.

Then stopped. And listened.

The door knocker *was* clattering.

Not the "neighbors," Chertkov calculated, they'd bash the thing down. Throwing the ice pick into the sink, he crept down the hallway as the door knocker tapped away endlessly, holding his breath.

The dry snick of a key. Chertkov stopped, his hand suspended over the scarred porcelain doorknob. The concierge's key, the KGB has the concierge's key . . . the door began to move and Chertkov numbly awaited his fate. He closed his eyes behind his glasses.

"I did knock, Nikki. I thought you weren't home," Ludmilla whispered, as she pressed him backwards, away from the open door and open ears. She held him for a moment, her swimmer's arms compressing his ribs. Chertkov bumped the door shut with a toe, balancing on his other foot. He slipped Ludmilla's hood back and nuzzled her neck—he could feel the arc of her cheekbones through her hair.

"I'm home." Chertkov fitted his thumbs under her jaw and tipped her face upward; he could sense her pulse flutter against his fingertips. "God, you're early. I—" *Calm*, said a voice in his head and Chertkov simply smiled. "I didn't expect you 'til nine. Rough night."

"I am a dutiful employee of the sports ministry. I'm always early." She gave him a sharp salute, deadpan.

Ludmilla eyed Chertkov for a moment. "Rough night? You look guilty. Got a girl in the broom closet, have you?" She moved past him in her sweat suit, shedding her overcoat and Adidas bag. "I have two hours," Ludmilla announced, rocking her haunches as she walked to the window. "I have to meet with one of the ministry people about the diving meet next weekend. He's a real creep."

"Profimov?"

"No, he's all right. Dubayev, his assistant, he's the creep. Always sniffling around me, like a dog with a cold. He's already got a girl, they say. A physical education instructor. In Gorki." She wheeled, kicking off her boots. "Why've you closed the curtains? It's like a tomb in here."

Chertkov laughed. "I've lost my love of winter mornings lately."

Ludmilla put her hands on her hips. "You're up to something, aren't you? You haven't knifed the wife and stuffed her under the bed?''

"No. I need the apartment," Chertkov replied, playing along. "Her uncle would toss me out and move her idiot sister in if I touched a hair on Olga's head." Chertkov laughed again and made as if to chase her, but Ludmilla skipped away.

"*Nasty* this morning, aren't we? Hey, not so fast," Ludmilla warned, twisting a chair away from the wall and wobbling it at him. "Down, boy. You've got that 'I'm-not-up-to-anything' look on your face, you do."

She likes this bit, Chertkov thought, circling. "I'm *not* up to anything—"

"—*honest*. I had a colonel say that to me once. He had a way with a girl's knickers, that one. But *he's* in Paris now, unlike my latest lover, Field-Marshal Chertkov, who lurks in dark flats, afraid of the Moscow daylight!" Ludmilla giggled, reaching behind herself for the curtain-edge. She turned and threw the curtains apart. "There!"

As the feeble light drained into the room, part of Chertkov's brain registered an idea, an invention, a connection with Shykofsky's parting remark: "A colonel, eh? Did he ever give you a French coat, eh, did he?"

Ludmilla stopped her gambolings, open-mouthed. "From *Paris*?"

"Fresh from the shop, *mademoiselle*. Or, should I say . . . the warehouse?"

"I'd *love* a Saint-Laurent . . ." She had pressed herself against him, then realizing the implication, flung herself from him: "Art books and coats from Paris, eh? You're in the black market, aren't you? You've got a thing going, Nikolai, that's why you look so bloody guilty!"

"Shhhh." Chertkov prised his fingers over her lips and whispered, "Such coats!" He released his grip: "Not even the Foreign Ministry boys can get you these coats, first class they are . . ."

Ludmilla stepped away, pulling a stray strand of hair from her chin. The girl searched his face, turned her face away, then back, her eyes shining. "You don't know how I've dreamt of . . . of a real coat." She turned up an imaginary collar and crossed her hands over her chest like a model hugging her lapels. "What do you think?"

"Fits nicely in the waist," Chertkov said helpfully. He moved closer.

"*No.* You married men are all the same. All hands, no conversation. Talk to me," Ludmilla said firmly. "I'll make the tea." Ludmilla stopped in the kitchen doorway. "It's woman's work." She gave him a sardonic grin and turned up the stove. "I wear medium," she winked, "and my favorite color's royal blue."

It's working; I should have been an actor. Chertkov shook his head and looked at himself in the hallway mirror. I *am* an actor, he thought, pulling his soft chin; all these years—it's really quite remarkable. He was thinking again about Shykofsky's advice. In the kitchen, Ludmilla was humming a folk tune and slamming the pots and pans in a way she never did at her own flat.

Chertkov's kitchen was barely big enough for both of them to stand, for the bigger apartments in this section of the building had been split in two after the war. Ludmilla, her head topped with a bouffant of steam, was attacking the freezer.

"Water's boiled. Tea ready?" Chertkov purred as he moved next to her.

"Yes, Field-Marshal," Ludmilla sang, her head inside the freezer. "For tea-making, I get a matching pair of gloves . . ." She paused, then tried her French: *"N'est-ce pas?"*

"What the hell are you doing?"

Ludmilla turned, the boiling kettle in one hand and the bottle of pepper vodka in the other. "Melting, not chipping. Like a good wife."

"Matrimony and vodka, they're mutually exclusive, believe me. I'll get the glasses."

They toasted one another, linking arms, Chertkov having to rise on tiptoe to reach his lips with the tumbler. Then another, faster this time, Ludmilla blushing nicely as the vodka hit home.

The water pipes for both kitchens ran through the dividing wall—the pipes chimed whenever anyone turned a tap. Ludmilla mockingly toasted the ringing pipes. "Nikolai, darling, you've got the connections—you should get wifey's uncle to fix the pipes." Her diction gave her away: Ludmilla had no capacity for vodka. "Pour me another vodka, Nikki. Then tell me your secret."

"Secret?"

"Where you get the coats. And the art books. And the theater tickets." Ludmilla began to blink her eyelids, working the tears. "And the pajamas, look at them. They're foreign, aren't they?"

"Olga got them. They're Czech, yes."

"Olga, Olga, you expect me to believe that? There's another

girl, isn't there? I'm your morning girl, she's the afternoon. You've got a girl in the Foreign Ministry, that's where the stuff comes from.''

"You're mad. You think a man can handle a wife and *two* lovers? There are limits, you know." Chertkov, watching her dispassionately as she let her tears fall in calculated streams, tried to feel a remorse, a pity for this clothing-mad girl with the perfect body who had been his lover the few weeks since they had met at the pool, weeks spent talking and walking Moscow's back streets and bridges, avoiding her flat and her three curious roommates, denied his flat except when Olga was gone . . . wandering. Once, their enforced celibacy tried beyond endurance, they had made love, as apprehensive as they were lustful, in an apartment stairwell, their greatcoats tossed over the banister. An agreeably mad affair, an agreeable memory—and now useful. As useful as Ludmilla's appetite for black market clothes . . . it was all coming together; so much now depended on speed.

Ludmilla was still weeping; something symbolic was needed. He touched her arm reassuringly. "The answer's no—I buy, I sell, I fiddle and trade. And there's only one girl: you."

She watched him. "Promise me something. Promise me?"

"Promise you what? You're into me for a coat and gloves . . . promise you what? Roubles? Dollars?" Chertkov drew his pajama pockets open, the vaudeville gesture hiding his surprise at her sudden seriousness.

"Promise me you'll take care of me." Drunker now, Ludmilla was playing melancholy, pulling at her hair, drawing it over her cheek. "I need taking care of."

"What, what? Why all these worries?"

"You wouldn't, would you? Fob me off with a coat, leave . . ." She sniffed. "Promise me you'll always bring me beautiful things."

"Ludmilla, Ludmilla, you want me, you've got me. You think I'm going to Siberia to sell Saint Laurent coats? The market's here. Have another vodka, there's a good girl."

"Promise. Please?"

"Promise." Chertkov tipped her face up and briefly kissed her, even then thinking *she must go*.

She let a victorious smile spread over her face. "Nikki, my new coat, I want to wear nothing under my new coat sometime. I hear this is the fashion in Paris between very special lovers. You'd like that, wouldn't you?"

"Be a bit drafty."

"You're not listening, Field-Marshal."

"I always listen. I have the sharpest ears in Moscow: how d'you think you're getting your coat?"

Ludmilla put down her tumbler. "Oh, that much I know." She reached for Chertkov's glasses.

The minuscule kitchen proved to have possibilities not envisioned by Moscow's municipal architects. Chertkov's neighbors, an elderly couple pensioned off from the agriculture ministry, threw a pot at the dividing wall at the height of the proceedings, but neither Ludmilla nor Chertkov was in any state to notice.

Down the hallway, he could see the clock hanging on the wall, its brass hands forming a broken wing: eight-thirty.

Sixteen hours. Going on seventeen.

Chertkov sat in his pajamas at the kitchen table, recovering from his acrobatic exertions, watching Ludmilla prepare the tea. She served him silently, ritually, as if the tea were champagne, appraising the depth of his satisfaction before she spoke. She was as competitive in love-making as in her swimming or her voracious need to know the latest fashion in Paris or Manhattan . . . even if she could only dream of real suède or real lingerie, her beloved West German sweat suit her only trophy.

"There," she said, brushing his arm as she poured. "Try that."

"Very good," Chertkov said shortly.

"Nikki? How—"

"Shhhh, Ludmilla. I've an idea for a deal."

"Coats, this time?" Her athlete's metabolism sobering as quickly as it fell drunk, Ludmilla cleared the last of the washed and dried dishes from the countertop, Olga's apron tied modestly around her sweat suit. "I'd like a new coat for the sports federation conference in Tallinn in December. I'm going, did I tell you?"

"So you said. I'm leaving Moscow for a while, myself. On business—if things come together, maybe tonight. Or tomorrow. It depends."

Ludmilla was stacking dishes, nesting, enjoying her dominance of Olga's turf. "That sick, are we?"

"What was that?"

My God.

"Stay here, Ludmilla. Don't bloody move."

A skirl of wet rubber pirouetting against the corridor floor preceded two quick knocks sounding at the door, almost as one, and then a single punch against the wood, louder than the first pair. Chertkov held his breath. *I can jump from the window— four stories and the ice will do the job.* Then the knocking pattern again: no, the militia would have driven the door from its hinges. *But they know the knock sequence. . . .*

"Who is it?"

"Marta. From the Metro."

Chertkov opened the door and stepped into the hall, linking his arm with Marta's. A finger to his lips, Chertkov pulled the girl to the end of the hallway, away from the echo chamber of the stairwell, away from the light. Number 12: old Rezinkov was in hospital, something about his lungs; Chertkov pushed Marta against Rezinkov's door.

"What the hell are you doing here?" he whispered fiercely. "What if I were KGB? Whatever happened to procedure?"

"We thought you'd been taken."

"Taken—what?"

"We checked here last night. It was Shykofsky's idea. There was no sign of you."

"I had night duty. My God, you simply walk in. This place could have been alive with KGB."

The girl Marta was looking at him, her eyes glowing in the darkness. "You forget: I *am* KGB." She plucked at her uniform sleeve.

Chertkov leant closer to her, whispering, "Were you followed?"

"No. Who follows the KGB?"

"What's your cover, coming here?"

"The usual. Checking residency papers with the concierge." The girl rubbed her upper arms and smiled. "Sorry. I'm a bit cold. The car heater's on the blink."

Liar: you're scared to death, Chertkov thought. She raised a pair of fingers in front of her face. "They've taken two more."

"Who?"

"This morning. Feodor, Leon's brother. And Yermolev."

"Who's Yermolev?"

"One of the laundry drivers."

"Jesus. Did Yermolev do the embassy run?"

"No. Jut the regular deliveries. He's a Jew. His uncle's a refusenik." She smiled again. "Anyway, that's the theory."

"Does Yermolev . . ."

"He knows enough. Yermolev's Shykofsky's brother-in-law."

Would she ever stop smiling? *I've gone mad*—Chertkov's brain was liquid, his thoughts too fast. He pulled his pajama collar up, for the hallway was cold, so cold the wallpaper was flaked with frost. Pipes've frozen again, he noted mechanically. It didn't seem to matter anymore. Nothing did, but getting out—this place was already foreign, a separate world.

"What are you going to do?"

"I don't want to be your hero," Chertkov snapped, "that's for damn sure." He lay his hand on Marta's canvas satchel. "Did you bring—"

At that moment, a frying pan skittered along the hallway, followed by a screaming Ludmilla, her coat and Adidas bag thrown over her shoulder, her hair swinging in the half-light. "Nikolai, you creep! Couldn't you at least wait until I'd gone?"

Chertkov had forgotten to close the apartment door; Ludmilla had heard everything.

"Nikolai, you bastard, you liar! Who's this, the cleaning lady? Go to hell!" In her other hand was a cast-iron pot lid and this she released, discus-fashion, at Chertkov's midsection, and, not waiting to see the result, sprinted down the stairs, still shrieking imprecations. Chertkov stepped aside and the lid clanged against the wall, showering plaster and lath on his pajamas.

"That's one way to say good-bye . . . come *on*, Marta," Chertkov muttered, his voice urgent, "let's go inside before she's got the whole building staring at us."

"Who was that?"

"Never mind," Chertkov said, picking up the utensils. "Get inside!"

Thankfully there were no curious heads peering at them down the hallway: Chertkov's fights with Olga were commonplace enough not to attract attention. Shutting the door, Chertkov motioned Marta to the settee. "How long do we have?"

"Ten minutes. Fifteen at the most. The concierge thinks I'm checking the Azerbaijanis down the hall. They've been in Moscow illegally for years."

"Give me the papers," Chertkov ordered. "There's tea in the kitchen. Bring me a vodka, will you? And stay away from the windows."

The girl began to ask a question but Chertkov's expression cut her short. She said nothing and strode with eerie calm to the kitchen.

Chertkov emptied the contents of Marta's satchel onto the

table. He untied the string holding the folder closed; between two residency file reports were three fresh pages of letterhead. Chertkov whistled soundlessly, felt the bond and looked at the watermark—right from KGB stores. From underneath his imported turntable, Chertkov retrieved a dusty envelope, ordinary GRU Center issue. This he split open. He extracted a pair of forged KGB identity books, made for him in New York, they'd said, and a quartet of retouched passport photos of himself.

Chertkov slid the first of Marta's stolen pages carefully into his Czech typewriter, a gift from a "younger brother," a colleague in the STB, the Czech military security service. The girl returned with the pepper vodka and a clean glass and seated herself at the far end of the settee. "Make sure you use capitals for all the names," Marta said, "that's a must. I brought you an extra page. For mistakes."

Chertkov grunted his thanks. Keep it short, Chertkov counseled himself. Thankfully he made no mistakes, tapping away slowly at the typewriter, concentrating. He pulled the four-line note from the machine. "I need a name, someone in your section who's done business with Passport Control on the phone, but never been there."

Marta thought for a moment. "Uritsky, Pavel Petrovich. He's the document man in our section. He's in Yaroslavl for the week." Chertkov added a squiggle of a signature in green ink above the name.

Chertkov looked at her over the tops of his spectacles, pressing his identity photos into place through a piece of cheesecloth, using his glue pot as a rolling pin. She watched him flattening the stiff curve of the photographic paper against the page. "What is it?" Chertkov asked. "You can speak."

"Let me see."

Chertkov peeled the cloth away and was pleased: the result was really quite professional. He handed her the KGB identity booklet.

The girl turned the pages and felt the paper. "It's very good. You won't have any problems with that." The girl was still looking at him, her eyes bright. "I have to go. I'm going to try to see Leon. I have a present for him."

"You're mad, they'll pull you in too. A KGB officer with a spy for a boyfriend? They'll have you singing in the cellars in ten minutes. You'll get the whole lot of us arrested."

"Then we'll be together. All of us."

Chertkov sat silently next to her on the settee, his arm around her shoulders, playing the father.

"I love him."

"I know you do. Wait a day. You owe me that much." Chertkov squeezed her hand. "Leon would want me to run."

"Yes. Yes, he would."

"Then help me. Requisition a car for this afternoon. Can you do that?"

"But I already have this car for the day."

"Good. Can you invent an errand to Passport Control?"

The girl thought for a minute. "The Azerbaijanis will do."

"Even better. Park at the Passport Control office on Ogaryova Street at two o'clock. Leave the keys with the car."

"You're not going to steal a KGB car, are you?"

"It's precisely a KGB car I need." Chertkov pressed her hand again encouragingly. "Can you manage that?"

"What about the militia? I'll have to make a report."

"The car will be found by nightfall, I promise you." He smiled at her as gently as he could. "Besides, who follows the KGB?"

"I must go now. The concierge will be suspicious." The girl put her tea down. "Here. Go with God." The girl thrust a matchbox into Chertkov's hand, kissed him fleetingly on the cheek, and strode quickly to the stairs. Her footsteps pattered down the marble risers. Chertkov shook the matchbox and a small glass vial clinked as it hit the matchbox carton before falling into his hand. A present for Leon: *it's a martyrdom they want.* Shaking his head, Chertkov rolled the vial about in his palm for a moment, then pocketed it. He locked his apartment door, emotionless.

He showered, shaved, put on his best civilian suit, and hid the KGB documents in his greatcoat lining, then left the apartment. As the elevator clanked to the ground floor, creaking as it fell, Chertkov wondered what he would feel if they stopped him in the street. He decided he would run. What if they shot him—what would he feel then? Release, probably. A spark of pain, but then nothing. Release: that would be all right. He dismissed the thought as the elevator stopped.

"Good morning, Ekaterina," he called to the concierge, an enormous woman in a blood-red sweater. She scowled and returned to her tatting—she had always hated him; she had a nephew in the GULAG. "*Au revoir,*" he muttered as he opened the big twin doors.

And then he was in the street, striding fast and swinging his arms for warmth, his glasses fogging a little from the exertion, but he was past caring. Chertkov ignored the freshets of snow from the growing storm as they burned his face. He could feel the glass vial in his breast pocket, like a medal chafing his chest. He shivered. *If they find the suicide capsule, I'm a big enough fish to torture. . . .* He reached into his pocket and let the matchbox roll off his fingertips into the slush.

He turned his mind to Ludmilla: Ludmilla was gone. As abruptly as she had come into his life, she had left it. For the first time in a lifetime of affairs and assignations, Chertkov realized he would never again know quite the same centrifugal force of romance; he was on the cusp of middle age, after all—and, even before the acquisitive Ludmilla, he had to admit, the girls no longer gave him a second glance. Perhaps she had never loved him after all, had mocked him while he slept, mimicked him to her roommates, laughed at his glasses and his fat. He was only as interesting as the latest magazine he finagled, an eager fool in a tailored uniform, a vacuum with roubles to spare.

There was no reason to stay: finally, there was nothing left to lose.

Chertkov had made his choice. He would run. Or die trying. He walked even faster.

# Chapter Seven

Prevadello kicked a crumpled beer can under a parked car, thinking, I've owned pairs of shoes that could walk this route by themselves, I've done this so many times. The mews was really a dogleg of an alleyway lined by the double-parked Saabs, Triumphs, and Volvos belonging to the professors and gallery curators and advertising types who slummed smugly in the Greenwich Village row houses above. Prevadello made his way past a vile-smelling garbage dumpster and found the padlock on the service door. The padlock gave a small shriek and a fine mist of rust fell on the back of Prevadello's hands. Inside, another door, unlocked, swung from rheumatic hinges as Prevadello gently pushed it open, into the dark. Only Kemper and he knew this back entrance, which Prevadello had found on a fire insurance map done of the Village building in 1937. Prevadello stepped in and shut the service door, hooking a tired latch to keep it closed. In the familiar blackness, he ran his hands along the wall, past the disconnected fuse panel, past what felt like an upright lamp, and opened the door handle.

The light burst in and a flurry of dust tumbled onto the gray concrete floor. A tang of fresh paint filled the safehouse's back stairwell. The basement door was directly opposite him; a fire hose lay coiled in the corner. Prevadello shut the mews door and shot the bolt.

He climbed the stairs to the third floor and opened the safe-room door. Kemper had already prepared his housekeeping cover for the meet: a disassembled Ampeg lay on the kitchen table, the tape recorder's innards in careful rows on clean newspaper. Prevadello noticed that someone had cut out the crossword for later and he remembered Kemper's fetish for word power.

Group must pay a service to keep the plants, Prevadello thought.

He eyed the fern frond at his elbow and slipped the safehouse key under the fern's earthenware pot on the mantelpiece. The rest of the Greenwich Village safehouse could have been anywhere—the upholstery was a psychologist's idea of cheerful and there were cellophane wrappers on the sideboard glasses and instant coffee, tea bags, cream and sugar on a New York skyline souvenir tray. Prevadello, who delighted in such details, noted the scotch on the sideboard was still Kemper's brand. Smiling, he took off his beret, lit a Camel, and tried to remember the last time he'd been here. Running the surveillance teams during a double game at the UN; that was it. Half a year's budget blown and nothing to show when the quarry went to the British instead. There must have been a girl, Prevadello reflected; there usually was. He settled his arms on the new windowsill; there had been renovations done recently—the carpenters' pencillings were just visible under the fresh paint.

The safehouse overlooked Washington Square, now bathed in the mid-morning sunlight. The square was alive again, as if the sudden sun had sprouted people from seed. One of them was Charlie Kemper, threading his way toward the Arch, past the pot sellers and the mock working-class NYU students and the sloe-eyed Puerto Rican girls, their placid kids aboard strollers. Prevadello watched Kemper cross the street and worked out where the watchers were. The watchers: how would Kemper run them? Probably a singleton trailing his cab and a trio rotating through the park—Prevadello thought the fellow with the *Wall Street Journal* was working the circumference of the fountain. Kemper always hand-picked his sidemen and they were the best: the fountain man casually moved to the right, stopping to decline an antiwar leaflet from a girl in her grandmother's shawl, her feet sandaled despite the cool. The watcher moved to a bench among the trees to the west, his shape now blurred by the sunlight falling in warm rectangles between the buildings and across the park. He's seeing Kemper to the door, Prevadello thought.

The scrape of the door came an instant later as Kemper moved inside. There was a pounding up the stairs and Prevadello remembered Rappaport's exercise fetish for his staff; there had actually been staircase races one year and Rappaport had shamed everyone by winning. The saferoom door sprang open and Charlie Kemper, a genuine smile wrapped around his angular face, made his entrance, everything moving at once from the nervous energy.

"You're here, partner," Kemper said, "good to see you again, it really is," offering his small hand while struggling to close the upstairs door. "Good. Have a seat. I'll join you in a moment. Coffee or . . . ?"

Prevadello shrugged no at the Nescafé and let Kemper fend for himself. "I brought you back the material you couriered me Monday—file's on the mantelpiece. Been busy?" Prevadello had settled himself on the couch; the new upholstery clung to his trouser legs.

"Very busy. Entirely different sort of pressure, this new job. Less waiting, more worrying, if you know what I mean. Quinn says hello, by the way. Wished to be remembered to you."

He's become an Easter egg of a man, Charlie has, Prevadello decided, all flash and shine, but centerless. "Still doing Group's books in blue pencil, is he?"

Kemper looked up from the kettle and pulled a face. "Oh God, no, we're on computer now."

*You certainly are,* Prevadello thought. "And Rappaport, how's he?"

Kemper took his time replying. "Growing like a weed, Group is, which means Rappaport's in his element, jawboning the NSC guys for budget dough until they're sick of the sight of him. He's *very* good at budget meetings." There was a pause. "Between you and me," Kemper said as he sat down in the rocking chair opposite Prevadello, "he's slipping otherwise. Getting sloppy."

"Sloppier, you mean."

Kemper ignored this and occupied himself with his attaché case. Prevadello never failed to marvel at Kemper's way with a stack of files—nothing was ever out of place. "You're looking well, Marty. Better than the last time we were here. That was the UN play, wasn't it? The fat Czech with the tan? Spring of '68?"

Prevadello decided to humor the small talk. "Yes. He ran to the limeys, I think. They must have had a better looking girl."

Waving his coffee cup, Kemper actually laughed. "A better looking boy. I didn't know myself until the briefing papers came through. He'll be happier with the broad-minded Brits than with us, I guess. Smoke if you want."

Prevadello said nothing and dug for his Camels and mouth-piece.

"I thought you quit, Marty."

"Tapering off. Only way to do it."

"Sorry to tempt you." Suddenly distant, Kemper might have been apologizing to someone in the next room for all the attention he paid Prevadello. It's his nerves, Prevadello noted. Maybe he's screwed up and somebody's kicking *his* pension around. "So if Rappaport's slipping," Prevadello said, "who's the new Messiah? Must be half a dozen spooks who'd kill for his job."

"Patience, partner, all in good time," Kemper said, taking a good bite of his Nescafé. "How's it feel to be back?"

"Pretty good. Not exactly voluntary, but it feels pretty good." Prevadello laughed softly and blew smoke. "Gets me out of the house." He waited. "Time to invoke the Old Partner's Act. I want some straight answers, Charlie."

Kemper examined him for a moment. "Old Partner's Act? Never give up, do you?"

"That's what you pay me for," Prevadello said evenly. "Or don't pay me for."

Kemper shrugged and said, "The pension was the only way I could think of. Sorry."

"Sorry—bullshit. How'd you fix my mail?"

"Takes a phone call these days."

Prevadello looked at him and then butted his cigarette. "Enough of the foreplay, Charlie. Who's going to save Group, win the war, get the girl?"

"You are, Marty."

"Oh, I see," Prevadello replied, stifling a sour laugh, "that's why you cut off my pension, to make a hero out of me? Come off it."

"I *thought* I was doing you a favor," Kemper said stubbornly, "giving you a chance to square things with Rappaport."

"You've changed, Charlie, you've gone carnivorous. You better make damn sure nobody eats you first."

"I've got it figured out," Kemper replied defensively. "I've done my homework."

"If I could live without taking your money, I'd do some homework, too: on your head, Charlie." Prevadello made a move to leave, shifted his shoulders, settled back. "You're going outside. Even if I'm an old hand, I'm outside. What's going on? Seen the light, have you? Want Rappaport's privates on a plate?"

Kemper put down his coffee cup. "It's an election year, Marty. Rappaport's about to screw up in a big way, even blow Group right out of the water. I've got an eye for the main chance, I grant you, but I want Group to survive. Which," Kemper concluded, "makes Rappaport expendable."

"Gone straight for the jugular, haven't you, Charlie? Big chance to take."

Kemper said nothing for a moment. "It's been a long haul for me," he said slowly, "a really long haul. I've paid my dues for Rappaport. In spades. So have you."

Prevadello rolled his beret into a sausage and tapped his thigh with it, thinking. "The new Messiah. Somehow I never saw you starting a new religion, Charlie." He reached for another Camel.

"Times change, partner." Kemper was opening folders now, mechanically slipping paper clips from one set of pages to another, his eyes on Prevadello. "You ready for my song and dance?"

"Whoa, slow down. I'm feeling coy. Start by telling me how badly Rappaport's screwed up."

Kemper stopped his fiddling with the manila folders. "Group has a Moscow contract I'll call TOPOL." Kemper spoke to his hands as he paraphrased the file, reading and weighing his words. "A traveling salesman, import-export, Greek. Sells gourmet food to the Party hard currency shops. Returned from Moscow Monday night. Tuesday morning, Group interrogation people in Athens kicked all the tires and gave him a clean bill of health," Kemper said.

He never took his coat off, Prevadello would recall afterwards. Perhaps Kemper's presence was extracurricular; it was certainly off the record, despite all the fan-dancing with the files. Kemper looked up. "Marty, Rappaport's running a real amateur show in Moscow. If TOPOL's right, the network handling CATALYST's been blown sky-high."

"That won't do détente much good, will it?"

"You're catching on, partner. O.K., here we go—it's Saturday, last Saturday night, downtown Moscow. TOPOL's having a drink in his favorite Armenian dive off the Arbatskaya with a source of his, an off-license taxi driver who diddles spare car parts on the Moscow black market. TOPOL's done a barter number with him once or twice."

"Or twenty times," Prevadello said.

"Or twenty times," Kemper agreed. "The cab driver's well into his second wind when he tells TOPOL late Saturday night the KGB goons commandeered his cab when their van blew a gasket. Evening rush hour, bars and restaurants hopping, cost him roubles, he's got a beef. KGB goons flag him down and throw this kid in the back, working him over the while, a real party. Kid's a mess and one of the more extroverted goons is shouting 'American spy,' 'CIA pig,' the usual stuff, all the way to the KGB suboffice at the Kurskii rail station, where they park the kid in the holding cell in the basement while the goons wait for the Dzerzhinskii Square boys to send another van. TOPOL buys his cabbie another round or three at the bar and gets the hell out of Moscow." Kemper looked up pointedly from his files. "We told TOPOL the boy in the cab was completely unemployable, not one of ours at all, paid his tab, and sent him on his way. Our people tell us the kid died in the cellars. We saw him meet a pair of dissidents we had our eyes on at the university. Right at the gates. As you said: very sloppy." Waving his hand at the cigarette smoke, Kemper frowned. "Rappaport's going to get his fingers burned, Marty. But good."

"What the hell's Rappaport thinking of?" Prevadello asked as he leaned forward, moving the ashtray from his knee to the coffee table. "And for God's sake, how much did the kid know?"

Kemper sipped his cold coffee, biding his time. "Your passionate heredity's getting the better of you." Kemper sucked a sugar cube while he continued. "The kid was a runner for a small network we cut the Vatican in on. Nice clean human rights stuff, Marty. NOAH's couriers—the kid ran verbals exclusively, never documents—the couriers clear the drops once a week, blind, and we get the material the same day. Rappaport figured it was nearly foolproof."

"I know all about foolproof, Charlie. Those NOAH people are going to die like flies." Prevadello laughed bitterly. "It's no go, Charlie. Every hood in Moscow's going to be on CATALYST's trail in the next twenty-four hours. Rappaport must be out of his small mind, servicing a mole in Moscow with choirboys and physics students."

"That's not your end of the deal, Marty. You're the mule: you bring us CATALYST, we'll do the rest."

"And then you bury Rappaport. The king's dead, long live the king."

"It's a milk run," they said, simultaneously, Prevadello burlesquing Kemper's voice. The two old partners considered one another, wordlessly.

Prevadello broke the silence. "Milk run, my ass, Charlie," he said calmly. "You tell me the last time Group went outside just to hold some Russian's hand at the border. Do you even know where this guy's supposed to appear?''

Kemper went very still. ''Vienna. We got word—''

Prevadello slapped the coffee table and Kemper flinched. ''Vienna! You were there, you watched the KGB grab Moravec back, right on the steps of the goddam theater. You're joking, tell me you're joking.''

''I'm not joking. We got word this morning.''

''I don't believe it. The Moravec grab puts me in the nuthouse and you want me to go back to Vienna. That's just great, Charlie. Next you'll be telling me you didn't know it was Vienna when you stopped my pension.''

''I didn't. If you'd let me finish—we didn't hear from NOAH until this morning. All the escape protocols were for Helsinki, Frankfurt, or Zurich. By air.'' Kemper lowered his voice placatingly. ''Honest. We heard this morning, by back-channel. I don't know how they did it, but NOAH got London Station word. It's Vienna. By train.''

''For God's sake, spare me your friend-of-the-common-man tone,'' Prevadello replied. ''Let me guess: you don't know when.''

Kemper donned his best winning smile. ''Well, it wouldn't be a milk run without a catch, would it?''

''You're something else, Charlie. You really are. How do I know it's him?''

''Rappaport's box of tricks.''

Prevadello gave a grim laugh. ''Not that old chestnut, Charlie.''

''Old habits're tough to break, you know that, Marty. Here, here's the key to the ring game.'' Kemper handed Prevadello a folder. ''Open it.''

The folder contained a schematic and a key to read the various configurations—five thumbtack heads in a row meant ''followed/abort,'' three heads in a triangle meant ''drop cleared'' . . . Rappaport's ring game. And under that, the cover to a paperback copy of Hoyle's rules for card games, the tear a ragged saw tooth.

''Rappaport and his bridge. He's really an egomaniac about it, isn't he?'' Prevadello observed. ''Still play with him, still in the first four?''

''Yes,'' Kemper said, very softly.

''I wonder how you sleep, partner.'' Prevadello dropped

Rappaport's kit into the folder. "What's the scoop on processing, then?"

"Papers to your old pal Cal Ruppert in Vienna, remember him?"

"Sure. I remember Cal. He freelance or what?"

"Part-time. Doing anti-terrorist chores for the Austrians. He'll have the emerg. passports, cash float, and the Stateside entry documents. And stay well clear of the embassy. Anything else, Marty?"

"Pack this." Prevadello handed Kemper his old gun.

Kemper hefted the pistol and then snapped one of the Colt's rubber bands. "You sure you really want this?"

"Just get it in the burn-bag, will you. I'm not flying with it. Where do you want our Russian friend for debriefing?"

"You find him first and we'll let you know."

Prevadello grunted, stood, put on his beret, and moved to the wall next to the window. The fountain man was still calmly reading the *Journal* and a pair of joggers was circling the park, their heads moving as they chatted, eyeing the window.

"Know what a miracle is, Charlie?"

Kemper was filling his case with his paperwork. "We haven't all had the benefit of a Jesuit education, Marty."

Prevadello watched the joggers veer back toward the fountain. "An effect which exceeds the available natural causes." Prevadello toyed with the fern fronds, recollecting the Moravec run going down in flames. ". . . but if this Russian makes it— I'll bet blood CATALYST won't—you've got one. The key's under the mantelpiece fern."

Crossing the saferoom to the top of the stairs, Prevadello heard the rustle of the curtains as Kemper alerted his watchers below. "One last thing," Prevadello said. "If I walk into another KGB sting in Vienna because Rappaport hasn't done his homework, forget about CATALYST, partner. I'll be looking for *you*."

And your silent friend, Morley Walsh.

# Chapter Eight

"Quit whining, you old bitch." The jackbooted guard tossed the sobbing woman into the street; she nearly fell at Chertkov's feet, but a Jew in the line wearing an astrakhan caught her just in time. "And tighten up the line! There's a citizen trying to use the sidewalk."

No one had dared reply—the line slowly closed in on itself, leaving the sprucely suited and intimidating Chertkov alone to march to the head of the docile queue. Until he had done his socialist duty in removing the woman, the militiaman in the hallway at the Ogaryova Street entrance had pointedly ignored the mid-morning line-up milling in front of him, chewing garlic and spitting. The militiaman made no attempt to mask the garlic stench when Chertkov presented his letter.

The upper corner of the document gave the guard pause, for the stationery Marta had stolen for Chertkov was calculated to impress: it bore the sword and shield KGB seal. "What brings you to OVIR, comrade?" the militiaman asked genially. He looked Chertkov in the eye and moved the garlic bud to his other cheek.

"The usual—a Jew's blotted his copybook," Chertkov replied. "Got a thing or two to track down."

"Never ends, does it, our job?" The guard winked and handed Chertkov his paper; the document Chertkov had forged was clearly out of the ordinary—Chertkov knew that from the sudden cunning respect on the guard's coarse face. Behind the guard, over his head, the portrait of Lenin needed dusting: a rime of talc fringed the cheap frame and the glass over the familiar face bore a gray velvet cast. The public portion of OVIR, the Jewish Passport Control office Lenin blindly surveyed, was a long room fronted by two ridiculous blue desks, each equipped with a taciturn OVIR officer. The hard seats on either side of the central aisle were filled with hushed supplicants, the elderly sniffling and bent, the middle-aged holding children quiet, the few young stone-faced, their whispered conversations hissing through the silence like rain. The place smelled of a papery must and the delicate scent of ink.

"Officer from State Security," the guard called to the uniformed woman behind the right-hand blue desk.

The woman did not look up from her paperwork but merely snapped her fingers once and turned a page in the dossier before her.

She loves the touch of paper, Chertkov thought. She has more feeling for the paper than the poor bastards she orders around like furniture. Chertkov placed his forged orders carefully on the blue desk—not so far as to be aggressive, but not so close to the edge of the desk as to be cowardly. The top of the OVIR woman's head was balding; she had the thinning, dyed hair of an old man.

The woman closed her dossier and looked past Chertkov to the guard at the door. "That Jew gives you any more trouble, have the greens pick her up. Or perhaps this fellow will take her off our hands, no? It's only a five-minute walk to the Lubyanka, eh?" She leered at Chertkov. The guard slammed the door behind Chertkov, who let a pale smile flicker across his face, in on the joke.

The forgery was in the woman's hands, her fingers grasping the slip as if it were a thousand rouble note.

"Don't see many of these, comrade . . . Uritsky, is it?"

"Yes, comrade-inspector."

The OVIR woman continued to stare at the KGB stationery. Then, her curiosity satisfied, she handed Chertkov his document, her face a blank. She stood and walked into the back office, motioning Chertkov to follow. *I'm sailing over all the fences, I'm flying,* he exulted.

The back office might have been anywhere in official Moscow—a desk, several mismatched chairs, the walls painted two shades of green, and a thin square of red carpet holding the floorboards down. A thick ledger lay open on the large oak desk. The OVIR woman motioned to the chair like a physician. "This is the register. Ever used it before?"

"One's the same as the next," Chertkov suggested.

This attempt at levity left the OVIR woman unimpressed. "Leave it open at the same page, comrade," she said sharply, passing her hand over the ledger. Then she was gone, back to her flimsies and rubber stamps.

Chertkov fought himself to a calm. Gently, Nikolai, gently. Eggshells, that's what you're dancing on, eggshells. He ran his finger down the list of Jews to whom the OVIR office had granted exit visas.

There were no departure dates given in the OVIR ledger. Only the names and OVIR file references appeared, numbered not by the person's internal passport number—for émigrés must renounce Soviet citizenship in order to apply for an exit visa—but by OVIR's own file system. Chertkov chose half a dozen male names at random, wrote the surnames and reference numbers down, and presented himself to the OVIR woman again in the front room.

She took his paper in her dry hand. "You are making progress with your investigation, then, comrade Uritsky?"

"I will need to draw these six files, comrade-inspector."

"Take a seat, Uritsky. Boldarev!" she bawled. "Boldarev!"

A slight, worried man with a limp appeared from a side door in rubber-soled shoes, a sorry specimen cursed with wide ears, his crumbling uniform collar powdered with distemper, a veteran's ribbon in his lapel.

"Yes, comrade-inspector."

"Boldarev, this is state security man Uritsky. Bring him those files." She fluttered Chertkov's list in poor Boldarev's face. "And bring us both some tea, Boldarev."

"Yes, comrade-inspector."

He says that in his sleep, Chertkov thought. Boldarev led Chertkov down a dark hallway, to a high-ceilinged room honeycombed with oaken file dockets, rank after rank of pigeonholes, thousands of them, a sepulcher of paper. Boldarev motioned Chertkov to a simple school desk and disappeared, as silently as he had come, into his hutch.

The silence of the place was overpowering; there was a fine winy smell of pre-Revolutionary dust tempered by the tang of ozone from the light bulbs high above, shrouded in their coolies' hats. Minutes passed. Five. Ten.

At a quarter to one, half an hour after taking his seat, Chertkov heard a door slam in the distance, loudly, and he had an uncanny sense of being entombed.

But it was the meek Boldarev, come with tea and an armload of exit files. "The others are out, under examination by the chief secretary of the Praesidium of the Academy of Sciences," Boldarev sighed. "The *Zhid* scientists," he added with infinite boredom, "are the most difficult." Then he slunk away in his silent shoes.

The exit files were each an inch thick, reams of personal and authenticating data. Chertkov, chastened, turned to the thinnest, but then had to discard Samonenko, R.N., immediately: the Siberian was too old. Next: Yakulev, S.L., aged fifty-three. Better. Yakulev's personal "testimonial" was first, countersigned by his "triangle," the head of his old fitter's department, the department Party secretary, and the fitter's trade-union organizer. Page after page of documents followed; questionnaires; countersigned copies of questionnaires; the transcript of two separate foreign-travel commission interviews, each stamped by the Perm regional committee; Yakulev's *objektiva*, summarizing his educational career and jobs held; a pair of medical certificates— Yakulev had had several operations since his first application in 1968; two sets of photographs, and more . . . page after page of carbons and colored duplicates. At the very bottom of the heap was the Central Committee foreign-travel commission sub-file, and, appended, a flimsy copy of S.L. Yakulev's exit visa.

Yakulev was a lucky bastard, Chertkov calculated; he had his visa in four years.

For the next two hours, Chertkov exercised every fiber of his limited patience, page after page, counseling thoroughness as he trudged through the exit files—a one-legged Muscovite, a run of Minsk Jews, a Leningrader married to an American from Boston. He summoned Boldarev twice for fresh fodder, coming close to finding a candidate once, until he discovered the fellow was scheduled to travel with a distant cousin.

By this time, Boldarev was growing familiar, showing signs of life, recounting his maladies with something like enthusiasm. "Doesn't bother me in the summer, you know, but the hip gives me the devil of a time come winter. Seizes up solid some mornings. Rheumatic, I think." He nodded, confirming his own diagnosis, before laying another four files on Chertkov's table and waiting for him to scrawl "Uritsky" in the OVIR logbook.

At five to two, while Boldarev dozed in one of the OVIR carrels, Chertkov found what he was looking for: a fifty-six-year-old bachelor, no immediate family in Moscow, a bookbinder once employed by the Moscow University Social Sciences book depository. Chertkov ran his finger across the file: RUBENSHTAIN, O.N.

The exit visa was issued for the Moscow-Kiev-Czechoslo-vakia Express.

The visa was valid for the week ending next Tuesday.

Chertkov left the sleeping Boldarev to the tender mercies of his superior, who continued her communion with the papers on her blue desk. At the OVIR door, Chertkov gave the guard a brisk nod and stepped through the lengthening queue. Once outside, he scanned Ogaryova Street; a street caricature painter was doing a good trade—two of the Jews were debating whether or not to sit for him.

A green Lada with KGB license plates stood parked not twenty feet away. Chertkov drew himself to his full height and, in what he hoped was the confident manner of an operative of the State Security organs, walked toward the car as the snow began.

It was nearly two-thirty as Chertkov drove southbound between the two great semicircular apartment blocks squatting like book ends on Gagarin Square, past the Leninskiy Prospekt Metro stop, but the street lamps were lit because of the growing storm and around their jaundiced haloes hung crystals of falling snow. Loaded down with the odd fruits of dozens of shopping expeditions, people edged down the snowy pavement like wary camels, their silhouettes bulging with booty. Rubenshtain's flat was the oldest building on the street, a side street that had broken itself against a huge pit, into which the city planners would someday pour an apartment block. A construction crane stood like a praying mantis on the lip of the pit, coils of cable too heavy to steal leaning against its single leg; a contemptuous solitary tree, its roots raw to the wind, endured at the pit edge. Chertkov drove carefully, circling the edge of the pit, and parked Marta's car at the back door of the apartment.

This address was a speck of prewar sandstone in the great gray sea of flats swelling from the southern boundary of Gorky Park to the Ring Road and to the hog's-back of the Lenin Hills beyond. The joke that season was that there were more Bibles than phone directories in Moscow. Chertkov believed it; after the two hours at OVIR, he would have given his right arm to be able to call the old boy's building before he knocked. But there was nothing for it now but to keep on.

Chertkov walked through the back door into the tiny lobby of the place and was greeted by a wave of ammonia. The floors had just been washed and Chertkov's boots left a track of footprints on the linoleum. Two old men were helping one another to the front door; one of them had his war medals on and was whispering encouragement to his companion, who carried the bottle. Chertkov nodded curtly and tapped on the concierge's window.

The concierge was a cheerful woman in her sixties; her obesity stretched the skin on her face taut as she smiled. She slid open her little window and Chertkov waved the KGB order in her face. The smile disappeared.

"State security to see the Jew Rubenshtain. Now. He in?"

"Yes, comrade-inspector. Apartment D. Up the stairs. Last door on your left. He's late up . . ." Her voice trailed off as she thought better of the conversation.

"He'll be awake soon enough, mother." Chertkov slid the window closed with his gloved forefinger. It's so easy, he thought, it's almost too easy.

There are never any light bulbs in Moscow stairwells, for the simple reason that light bulbs are a sometime thing, hoarded like gold. Chertkov felt his way along the banister, pausing at the landing to listen. There was silence behind the doors on the first floor and a quiet murmur of song from the second, a folk song from his youth. Chertkov thought of Sinatra as he rapped on the door with all his might. A line of light darted across Chertkov's boot tops from Rubenshtain's doorsill.

Chertkov growled, "State security. Open up, citizen."

The door snapped open, into Osip Naumovitch Rubenshtain's tiny room, no bigger than Chertkov's kitchen. Rubenshtain was dressed in his undershirt, pin-legged but with a barrel chest and a solid set of arms. The room, dark because Rubenshtain had covered the window frames with *Izvestia* to sleep, was stripped of everything portable and the walls were patched with yellowish squares where his few picture frames had hung. Rubenshtain's rumpled mattress lay on the floor and overhead swung a single sad bulb. There was nothing else in the room. Behind Rubenshtain the radiator lines beat a steady tattoo.

"Get dressed. And bring your papers—you're coming with me. The big boys want to see you, God knows why. And be quick about it," Chertkov said curtly. Rubenshtain's dark eyes flickered sleepily in disbelief for an instant but he wordlessly closed the door and bent over, reaching for his pillow.

"What about my crate?" Rubenshtain asked, gathering his papers. "It's already at the station. It could get stolen—it's all I have."

"Leave the flat open. You can meet the crate at the customs.

We won't be long; the general's place is on the way to Kiev Station."

At the mention of "station," Rubenshtain's face relaxed slightly. He pulled on a moth-eaten sweater with cloth patches at the elbows. Chertkov took in Rubenshtain's scarred sink and the melancholy plinking of the tap.

"Let's hop it, Rubenshtain. Not a good idea to keep the general waiting." Rubenshtain was fumbling with the stack of documents, trying to square the corners, some of them bent from the weight of his head on the pillow.

"I'll take those," Chertkov said officiously. "Can't be too careful, can we?"

And O.N. Rubenshtain handed Nikolai Chertkov his exit visa.

*One*, Chertkov said to himself, as he tucked the papers into his coat and then pointed to the door.

They walked downstairs without a word, Rubenshtain first. The stairs were barely visible in the murk—the concierge, her courage failing her, had shut up shop for the day. The lobby lights were out as well. "Back door," was all Chertkov said.

Marta's Lada already wore a second skin of melting snow over its KGB green. In the construction pit, a hockey game had begun, the pit bottom a small lake frozen and ringed with snow. Chertkov opened the Lada door and Rubenshtain waited submissively for him to unlock the passenger door, then dropped himself into an unhappy heap on the seat.

Chertkov reached across Rubenshtain and locked the door— only the driver's door had interior handles.

*Two*, Chertkov counted.

They said nothing for the next ten minutes as Chertkov drove through the slowly falling snow across the Andreyevski Bridge, over the river, and past the massive ashen bathtub of the Lenin Stadium fusing into the gray horizon to their left. Finally Rubenshtain could no longer restrain himself. "We are not going to miss the train?" It was more plea than question.

"I can't speak for the general."

"What's a general want with me?"

"That's for him to decide. I just drive."

Marta was right; the Lada's heater was a dead loss. Chertkov turned onto broad Pirogovskaya and decided to park on Abrik Street and walk the rest of the way: no point having the world see me driving a KGB car, he thought. As he turned left onto Abrik, Chertkov saw Rubenshtain was perspiring and his window was fogging over.

"I've . . . I've never been here before," Rubenshtain said. "I didn't know there was an office—"

Chertkov switched off the car and prodded Rubenshtain in the arm. "Shut up, will you? And lock the door."

Once across the big boulevard, Chertkov deliberately slowed his walk to a magisterial pace; it was all Rubenshtain could do not to break into a run. At the entrance, Chertkov opened one of the big twin doors and pulled sharply at Rubenshtain's sleeve to keep him on course.

The walk across the lobby's parquet floor had never taken so long; but Chertkov kept his tread even, Rubenshtain following—have to brazen it out. At her desk, Ekaterina was chatting with Madame Scriabinski about grandchildren and brandishing her knitting needles to make a point about discipline. The lobby, thankfully, was otherwise empty. Rubenshtain wandered momentarily toward the elevators, but Chertkov drew him away. "We take the stairs." Rubenshtain tried to look grateful for Chertkov's concern, but managed only a sickly grin.

*Three*, Chertkov counted, and we're almost there. I'll tie him with the laundry line—that'll keep him quiet until Olga gets back. Above them as they climbed, a floor polisher whined, obliterating the scrunch of their galoshes on the stair tiles. At the second floor, Chertkov nudged Rubenshtain into the hallway. Rubenshtain was sweating freely now, the whites of his eyes wide.

"Wait," Chertkov said, his hand planted on Rubenshtain's chest; he could feel Rubenshtain's heart beating double-time. "There's money in this for you, Rubenshtain. Play your cards right and you'll have a nice nest egg to spend in the West."

"What's the general want me to do?"

Chertkov slid the key into his own apartment door, opened it, and ushered Rubenshtain in, keeping himself at Rubenshtain's back. *Four.* "He wants you to help," Chertkov said in his smoothest voice as he locked the door, "that's all. Help."

"But how can I? I'm—"

In basic training, they had taught Chertkov that the blow was designed to stun instantly, but Rubenshtain must have been thick-skulled, because the blow Chertkov delivered behind Rubenshtain's ear simply drove him face-first into the wall, into the plate glass protecting Olga's favorite print.

The glass shattered and Rubenshtain groaned as the shards tore his forehead open. He stumbled and spun backwards, away from the wall, groping, his broken nose streaming, half-stunned, half-blinded by the bright blood pouring from the terrible cuts in his scalp. Rubenshtain wiped his eyes, but the blood flowed faster. Chertkov stepped backward, toward the door, his legs trapped against a footstool.

Rubenshtain steadied himself and found his balance, spreading his feet and raising his open hands. *He gets those hands on me and it's all over,* Chertkov thought. The sergeant who had taught Chertkov and forty-seven other conscripts hand-to-hand combat hadn't prepared the translator for one hundred and ninety pounds of enraged, bleeding human being attacking *him.* Chertkov kicked the footstool out of his way but the sound alerted Rubenshtain, who shook his head, the blood flicking off the ends of his sweaty hair and dotting the wall and the fragmented print's metal frame.

"Can't see," Rubenshtain said, taking a halting step toward Chertkov.

But that was only a feint, because Rubenshtain's next step was the first of four which carried him right at Chertkov, arms lashing for Chertkov's round face.

The first attempted blow missed but Rubenshtain's next, a roundhouse right, knocked Chertkov's glasses from his head and a reflex Chertkov never knew he had saved him from further damage.

Chertkov glanced about wildly, but Rubenshtain kept coming on, windmilling his fists, knowing Chertkov had only the advantage of sight; Rubenshtain was the bigger man, and thirty-five years of hand-stitching books gave him the strength of grip to crush the life out of his tormentor.

Chertkov pushed the footstool into Rubenshtain's path, but Rubenshtain heard the sound of its slide and sidestepped it, still frantically trying to clear his vision.

Circling was useless: that took Chertkov farther from the door and escape. *I must stand and fight.* Chertkov swung his hands back, searching for something, anything with which to slow the advancing Rubenshtain, to keep those big hands away.

Rubenshtain kept coming. Chertkov's left hand fell on the thick milk-glass lamp shade on the corner table. Grasping the blue china base of the lamp, Chertkov tipped it and nearly lost his only weapon, the light from the lamp dancing crazily on the ceiling.

"I can see you," Rubenshtain muttered savagely, sniffling back the blood from his skewed nose, his hands opening and closing; the movement of the light had given Chertkov away.

Then Chertkov clutched the lamp, swinging it back, all the way behind him, then forward, swinging hard from the hips.

The lamp caught Rubenshtain between the right ear and the eye, shade first, but he must have sensed the lamp at the last instant because he flung up his hand to fend off the blow.

The heavy milk-glass lamp shade flew off the light, cracked cleanly in two, spinning away over Rubenshtain's head. Chertkov swung again.

But couldn't.

Rubenshtain tried to hold the lamp away from his bleeding head with one hand, flailing at it with his other, knowing Chertkov must be at the other end.

Then it all went wrong.

The light bulb shattered in Rubenshtain's hands, and his head disappeared in a nimbus of blue-white sparks. There was no sound as Rubenshtain's body shook, the lamp suddenly an extension of his right arm, frozen there, as the current coursed through him. Chertkov watched, horrified, his mouth open, helpless.

Overhead, the three ceiling light bulbs dimmed and flickered.

Rubenshtain's knees collapsed, and, at long last, the lamp fell from his grip as his torso folded and his head lolled back like a broken doll's. Rubenshtain's death rattle echoed in the tiny room, going on forever.

Chertkov, his hands over his ears, ran to the kitchen and vomited into the sink.

It was a good five minutes before Chertkov summoned the courage to return to the living room, the half-empty pepper vodka bottle in his hand. In the middle of the room, not six feet from the door, Rubenshtain's upper body lay strangely akimbo, as if dropped on another man's legs; his head was slowly leaking blood into the carpet and one of his hands was blue-black where the electricity had done its work. Chertkov wanted to touch him, but couldn't, wanted to rearrange this . . . then he remembered the man in the monastery cell, all those years ago, the man whose package had made all this happen.

Made this necessary: Chertkov took a deep breath and then a deeper draft of the vodka.

*Don't stop to think about it.*

Very carefully, Chertkov unplugged the battered lamp and sat down. He spread the dead Jew's papers out on the table and made sure it was all there: birth certificate, his bookbinder's diploma, Rubenshtain's internal passport, a stack of clearance receipts for Rubenshtain's apartment and telephone, the receipts for the cost of his exit visa and of renouncing Soviet citizenship—and then the visa itself, a flimsy yellow slip of paper stamped at the Dutch consulate for entry into Israel. Rubenshtain's photo was stapled to the visa and, beneath the visa, Rubenshtain's train ticket to Vienna.

Chertkov spread the wings of the staple, slipped Rubenshtain's face off the staple and forced one of his own on. Rubenshtain's photo and the unused three of his own he tore to pieces. He pressed the staple closed and collected the papers. Signature; what of Rubenshtain's signature? Chertkov tried forging the bookbinder's hand but couldn't come close. Hadn't thought of that—with luck, I won't have to sign anything. With luck, Chertkov thought. With luck, Rubenshtain hasn't a friend in the world. With luck. Chertkov burned the torn photos and washed them down the kitchen drain.

Chertkov stopped to think for a moment, talking to himself. "An accident, Nikolai. You never meant to kill him . . ." *Keep moving*.

Now there was the matter Ludmilla had inspired.

Of all his possessions, Chertkov loved his records most. He had several dozen of them, and not the Soviet stuff either: Chertkov had bought and traded for one of Moscow's better collections of American jazz. But Chertkov's point of pride, his real treasure, was Frank Sinatra's *In the Wee Small Hours*. He took the album from its place in the rack.

Chertkov slid the album from its sleeve, admiring the rainbows of light on the grooved surface. "Can't leave this for those swine to play. Can't," he muttered. But the last act of the charade had to be played out. These records were the closest thing to a family he had. Chertkov took a deep breath.

First, his only Louis Armstrong record, sent from Berlin in '59. Chertkov pulled the disc from its sleeve and bent it over the edge of the table, slowly at first, then with a merciful twist that cracked the record in two.

"That's old Moldov's neck when they find I'm gone," he thought to himself as he let the pieces fall. Next came a pair of Dorsey albums, dedicated to Brezhnev's porcine neck, and then the Millers, dedicated to Gromyko's thin wattles, faster now, the middle twenty or so records going faster still, then Chertkov was into the heart of his collection, the Gershwin show tunes and Merman singing Cole Porter.

And, then, finally, the Sinatras. Chertkov sighed hard, for his work had winded him; his cheeks were flushed as with sexual success. "To hell with Moldov, to hell with Olga, to hell with

them all,'' he said slowly, stringing the words out, as the two
smashed Sinatra albums spun to the floor. Reaching over the
wreckage, Chertov shut his eyes and snapped the alloy tone arm
of his phonograph like a chicken bone. It sounded quite loud
against the silence.

He surveyed Rubenshtain's slumped body and then the rest
of the apartment. Then, methodically, thoughtfully, Chertkov
kicked carpets awry, tore books from the shelves, tipped over
the television, and threw open all drawers and closet doors. As
he carefully tucked his glasses inside the spectacle case Shykofsky had given him, Chertkov had a final inspiration.

He went to the bedroom. Feeling through Olga's lingerie, he
found her roll of American dollars, her hoard of hard currency
for emergencies—a new set of boots from West Germany, a
Swedish lamp . . . or a coat from Paris. Chertkov smiled grimly
and left the bedroom. In the living room, he dropped two fives
onto the heap of books and smashed records, then stirred the
heap with his boot, kicking some of the debris so that it lay at
Rubenshtain's feet.

*Welcome home, Olga.*

As he closed the door, Chertkov could smell something he
didn't at first recognize. Not until he reached the pavement outside did the smell strike a chord in his memory. In the tank . . .
outside Kursk, before his capture by the Germans . . . 1943: the
smell was the sweetish aroma of burning flesh—Rubenshtain,
I'm sorry, old man, but it was you or me.

Chertkov crossed Pirogovskaya Boulevard and turned down
Abrik Street, heading west, toward the river. The snow was
falling harder and a quartet of *babushki* were brushing the sidewalk clean. Halfway down the street, Chertkov saw someone
had already pinched the wiper blades from Marta's car; he had
forgotten to take them with him.

He drove north along the Savinskaya embankment, peering
out his side window and rubbing the condensation from the
windshield. To his left, the River Moscow had turned choppy as
the wind broadcast the snow in floury gusts. Near the Foreign
Ministry, he had to backtrack to find the overpass over the embankment to the Borodin Bridge. The bridge was already slick
with frozen snow and the traffic slowed to a crawl as a white-
out blossomed from nowhere.

The white-out passed as quickly as it came, and, directly
ahead, like a basket weave, lay the rail yards of Kievskii Station,
the electrified wires leading out of the yards like a cat's cradle

over the maze of track. It was eighteen minutes past three. The number 51 Czechoslovakia Express to Vienna left at five-forty. Chertkov left the car behind a broken-down bus parked off Kievskii Square and walked quietly down the side street, sliding in the fresh snow. With luck, Chertkov thought as he walked to the Station.

The customs shed stood next to Kiev Station, the shed no more than a cinder-block bunker with greasy wire-mesh windows. There was a tire retreading factory in the next street and the air above the rail station was thick with the smell of molten rubber. Chertkov, his glasses off to match the passport shot, stood in a crowd of some ninety Jews, their breath hovering over the yard. Behind the huddled émigrés, a van pulled up and another two families arrived; the train visible beyond the customs table was nine cars long—perhaps some three hundred passengers.

Chertkov felt for the spectacle case: it was still there. Someone, a woman, Chertkov thought, shouted from inside the shed and the crowd moved forward, hefting crude luggage and children toward the waiting customs men. Chertkov lifted the plastic shaving kit Olga had bought him for his birthday and clutched Rubenshtain's documents in his other hand.

"Next year in Jerusalem, eh?" said the man on Chertkov's right, under his breath. He gave Chertkov a wink. Chertkov was too stunned to do anything but wink back. Next year in Paris, more like it, Chertkov thought. The man's wife offered Chertkov a feeble smile; she was holding a young boy of four or five by the hand.

"D'you have a crate, friend?" They were some fifteen yards from the customs shed gate. Chertkov shook his head no, then remembered: "I sent it ahead; it's already at customs."

"You traveling light, then? No family?"

"I'm alone. Sold everything but the best. How about you?"

"Had a couple of crates built. You know women. Got their keepsakes. No knotholes, though."

"Why's that?"

The fellow laughed and his wife anxiously nudged him. "So's the KGB bastards don't *pish* in the holes, my friend." He winked again and Chertkov marked him a survivor. How long did this Jew and his frightened wife have to wait, Chertkov wondered, a guilty cramp probing his side; for a moment, he had allowed himself to reflect on Rubenshtain. Him or me—only way to look at . . . at what happened. I could be screaming my secret life

out in the cellars, on the wrong side of the electrodes while
Rubenshtain sat on his arse on a boat to Israel. Him or me: just
that simple. Who was going to miss the old boy anyway? If he'd
had any friends, he'd still be alive, right? That settled it—what's
done's done and to hell with worrying about the past: the now
is quite sufficiently dangerous. *Paris: my Jerusalem.* Then they
were at the gate and Chertkov knew he'd crossed the last line.

The customs officer at the gate wore an oversized peaked hat
tipped back on his head; he had to steady the hat while he gave
an abrupt wave and the émigrés moved through the sliding shed
door. Behind the door, a long table, its top scarred by decades
of luggage, fronted a half-dozen men, lounging and smoking,
hammers and crowbars in their hands, pointedly ignoring the
Jews.

Two young émigré boys lifted their family's crate onto the
table from its cart and the customs men unceremoniously tore
the top off. They methodically tossed the family's belongings
onto the table top, regardless of fragility. The customs man in
the peaked hat moved closer to the table, his notebook at the
ready, and opened a tissue-paper wrapped bundle with a stick
he had for the purpose: the bundle was a book.

The father of the family stepped forward; Chertkov saw the
tan edge of the ten-rouble note between his fingers as he lay his
hand on the table top.

"Any diamonds or gold, Jew?"

"No, sir. That is a mathematics text, sir," the father said
ingratiatingly. "I have approval for export. Here, I'll show you."
The father opened the text and deftly slipped the bill under the
book. The bill disappeared as the customs man flipped the pages.

"I see," he said. "Let's go, boys. Approved. Get the next
one up." He dropped the book into the crate and waved the next
crate onto the table. The father and his two sons hurriedly gathered their scattered belongings; the customs men were already
beginning to hammer the crate shut.

And so it went for the next hour. Some wheedled to no avail
and lost family heirlooms to the customs men; others struck
subtle bargains—a bottle of vodka for a candlestick, a samovar
for a doctoral thesis. Others failed in this grim commerce and
suffered the pain of smashed china and glassware, shirt collars
razored open, and "suspicious" keepsakes simply tossed aside,
as the customs men "searched for contraband." The sheer ran-
domness of the process made for a kind of sick improvisation,
as the bored customs men tried to entertain one another while

they pillaged. Clever packing schemes came to nothing as the customs men lifted, bounced, probed, flashlit, ripped and twisted; some crates magically passed through nearly untouched, but others were pulled literally to pieces. Chertkov watched impassively as one poor family was forced to run the inspection gauntlet twice, packing so hurriedly after the second going-over the husband tore a lace tablecloth nearly in two while his wife agonized.

Chertkov stood to one side, waiting. Two of the customs men had moved a pair of crates behind the table and sat on one, taking a break, smoking, their legs swinging, their boots banging against the crate-side above the carefully lettered name of Rubenshtain. Now or never, Chertkov thought, as he stepped up to the head customs man.

"I have a crate to declare, sir, that one there," Chertkov said, trying to point as casually as he could. The men on the crates continued their rhythmic kicking; one of them carefully butted his cigarette between the slats.

The customs man did not even look up from his notebook. "Wait your turn." A box of "Zionist contraband" lay at his feet; Chertkov could see a bolt of Chinese silk, nine or ten well-bound books, a beautiful gilt Tsarist centerpiece, several coats, one fur, all with the seams slit, and a bottle of French cognac—bribes or thefts, who could tell what entries the man made in his book? Chertkov moved quietly away.

Ten minutes later, without benefit of any signal Chertkov could understand, Rubenshtain's crate was shouldered to the table and two men attacked it with crowbars. He fared no worse and rather better than most that day: most of Rubenshtain's closely packed belongings eventually were returned to the crate. Anything with pockets was roughly sliced; discovery of hidden gold and jewels seemed to be the order of the day. Rubenshtain had apparently researched the customs process well, because, despite his trade, he packed none of the books that so troubled the inspectors, and no suit coats—and certainly nothing as adventurous as porcelain. His bookbinding tools and presses, all in handmade leather pouches, made it past the inspectors unscathed, but every single photograph Rubenshtain had packed was taken, for their frames, Chertkov thought.

Chertkov said nothing the entire time, his eyes meeting the head inspector's but once, over a set of tarnished dessert forks, which dropped soundlessly into the box at the inspector's feet, joining his other booty.

"Sign here for the confiscated silver," was all the inspector said, as the crate was pushed down the table to the carpenters. Chertkov hesitated for an instant then scrawled an illegible signature in the inspector's book, then followed the crate. At the end of the table, a customs man with a cart said, "Ten roubles to the luggage car," and spat.

Chertkov handed him the bank note and he and Rubenshtain's earthly belongings began the slow trek to the waiting train. It was a quarter past five, and the conductors were gathering; a stevedore in a dirty apron was pushing a water barrel up the stairs of a soft-class carriage. The luggage car was next. There the customs porter simply kicked the crate off and stuck his hand out for a further tip. Chertkov laughed at him, which was so unprecedented that the porter surrendered and walked back to the shed.

The crate stowed, Chertkov boarded the hard-class carriage Rubenshtain's cheap ticket entitled him to and found his seat. The carriage was a tyranny of parcels. Paper-wrapped cabbages fast by waxed cheeses, crushed string bags of baby clothes, and a catalog's-worth of bottle designs—thick milk bottles, long-necked five hundred gram vodka bottles, fat canisters filled with hoarded wine or *kvass*—lay tucked next to booted feet, away from light hands or mischance. Shouted Yiddish and cries mingled with relieved laughter; an ancient hatbox served as an ottoman; plastic bags pregnant with sweaters and books the KGB hadn't thieved propped heads against the windows. Wicker baskets grew butts of sausage and the occasional brace of chicken legs: the racks of the Czechoslovakia Express were loaded to breaking point, its floorboards leaked on by cracked herring and olive jars.

Chertkov took the window seat and tried to insulate himself from the chaos, his pathetic shaving kit his only luggage. He looked out the window and stared at the slow curve of the steel rails to the southwest and the Ukraine. At precisely five-forty Moscow time, the train shivered and began to move, gathering itself for the slow climb to the steppes.

Whatever lay ahead down the twin tracks to Kiev and the West, nothing would ever be the same.

Inside the green and yellow carriages of the Czechoslovakia Express, the chaos of leaving Kievskii Station had subsided: chatting children made tentative friends, eddying around oases of adult conversation, where the sole topic was what would happen once *there* was reached, the great Western cipher. Avoid this landlord above all costs; don't sell your champagne, save it for Rome, where prices are better; what *suveniry* did you bring to sell; all the news of the refugee pipeline—and the word would be passed from row to row. One of Radio Moscow's philosophers whispered in cracked tones from a speaker, his words heard only in the troughs of the noise: ". . . undeviatingly heading toward the Gosplan targets . . . territorial principle being worked out . . . new hydroelectric power stations on the Kama . . ." It was nearly seven and Wednesday's setting sun died spectacularly, melting into the trees to the west, casting the debris along the rail line in dull brass—piles of curling lumber, torn bags of concrete stacked like cordwood, and wild sculptures of rusting metal—sediment of the great river of Scientific Progress. Chertkov stole what sleep he could, waking for dislocated moments in the flickering carriage, lost, as the train carried his passive body deep into the underbelly of all the Russias.

Across the aisle from a quartet absorbed in a chess match played adagio, Chertkov watched out the dark window. Chekov's country rolled past, a region once composed of painterly wood-hutted enclaves now miniature Moscows with a few old buildings and *izbas*, the old gingerbreaded wooden cottages, war survivors ringed by the shadows of standard-issue flats and drowsy municipal offices. I fought near here once, Chertkov remembered, thinking of the muffled crash of cannon fire through the tank hull and the stink of cordite. He felt as sealed off from reality now as when they had played blindman's buff with the German anti-tank crews amid the trees and hills during the first counterattacks of the battle for Moscow.

He woke at one of the stops in the middle of the night. Outside, a single railwaywoman stood at attention at her station's platform, soberly watching the passing carriages, doing her duty in a cone of lamplight. Chertkov recognized her posture: the same military throw of the shoulders had tautened the Brusilov stationmaster's uniform on young Nikolai's dismal return from the Kiev conservatory as a child, before the war, before the GRU, before Ludmilla. Before this. At dawn, he reminded himself, I see Kiev. He tried to weigh the balance of good and evil in the omen, and tiredly decided it neutral.

Chertkov turned his cramped shoulder away from the gap between seat back and window glass, hearing Rubenshtain's last breaths dwindle to none in his memory. Chertkov shuddered, fighting on the frontier of sleep. On the opposite track, another in the endless litany of freight trains roared north to Moscow, a moving scar lapped by moonlight. For an instant, between the freight wagons, Chertkov saw a rank of storks, their pantograph legs bent, as the southbound birds rested amidst the stubble of the rail-side cornfields for the night. In the half-light of the train's incandescents, the nighthawks' round of chess began—one of the fanatics was playing against a book of chess puzzles.

And Chertkov dreamt, this time of hard prison light, the taste of sugarless tea, the drip of plumbing old in Dostoyevski's day, and of jackboot heels heard through the peephole, pacing. The pacing never stopped; the heel-clicks echoing off the cold stone were like small bones breaking. The real hell was the silence between the trapped sounds—no music, no voices, just the deep granite silence, the end of existence.

The Center interrogators began their work on "the conveyor" at four in the morning, when the will was soft—and then took their turns, around the clock, hard and easy, violent and comforting, sometimes for days, whatever it took to peel away the last defense. Chertkov dreamed of Butyrka prison, the red and white parquet of its entryway stinking of disinfectant, the green of its paint, the single glowing eye of the orange light above the guardroom, the heavy studded iron doors, and the sign over the entrance: *TO FREEDOM WITH A CLEAR CONSCIENCE*. He dreamt of the cells, the door with its thick hinged trap-tray for the bread and soup on the tin plate, and of the thoughtful half-moon depressions in the concrete walls on either side of the door which gave the eye at the peephole an uninterrupted view. And then the trial: standing in the dock, the fat microphone in one's stubbled face. A face? No, the imbecilic mask of the guilty, lost in the echo from the loudspeakers, the harsh glare from lighting banks, the prosecutor's narcotic harangues . . . then the midnight walk to the scarred firing wall at the foot of the Pugachev Tower, the smell of the serge hood, the unseen, unheard shots, and a gentle slide into—into what?

Heaven. Heaven was Paris. An open sports car in Paris, with the wind in one's hair and a girl at one's side. That would do for eternity, that and endless champagne. And he would have Paris, he, Nikolai Chertkov, son of a Brusilov welder, because he knew one dark secret facet of RAYMOND's life. As Chertkov pictured himself driving, no, flying through the fairyland of neon and shining shop glass on Rue de l'Opéra, the thrum of the Express a high-performance engine vibrating through his imagined bucket seat, Wednesday became Thursday.

# PART III

## THURSDAY–SATURDAY

"Exit, pursued by a bear."
*Shakespearean stage
direction*

# Chapter One

"Nothing yet, Cal? What about arrivals from the other bloc capitals? You sure?" Prevadello, speaking with Group's Vienna freelancer, Calvin Ruppert, Junior, looked past the Dorotheergasse sign, watching his dinner-jacketed waiter raise the café's awning with a long crank handle before the Thursday morning rain came to Vienna. The waiter waved, inviting Prevadello back to his snug corner table at the café; Prevadello waved back and pointed at the phone. He blinked, trying to concentrate; he had bet himself CATALYST would cross everyone up and take the air route.

"Not a breath of him on the Aeroflot red-eye. I've checked LOT as well, in case he tried Warsaw. And there's nothing on the manifests under old worknames, either." Cal Ruppert's quiet, professional voice had a smooth Oklahoma drawl, oddly American against the morning Viennese bustle outside the phone kiosk where Prevadello stood.

"O.K., fine. See you at the park." Prevadello bit off the start of a yawn and absently ran a finger over his unshaven cheek. His stomach was acid with jet lag, a pair of very strong *Moccas* at the café, and three straight days of worrying a crash defector run home.

He knew Vienna from the Moravec business. A Czech UN attaché the Group had nursed in New York for nearly a year was snatched by STB men off the steps of the Hotel Bristol, across the street from the Opera. Prevadello, Ruppert, and Kemper had the pleasure of watching the Czech intelligence men beat the daylights out of poor Moravec as the car pulled away. They must have known for days about the meet, and let him run West for the hell of it, Prevadello recollected; "the Bristol grab," as the incident was known in Group lore, was staged for spite.

Not much had changed since—the place still gave Prevadello the willies. Kemper had told him once that the Viennese were twice as likely to kill themselves as Londoners or Parisians—made you wonder about Freud. Here there were too many alleys, too many ways to get in and out. It was as if all of Manhattan were a rabbit warren like the blocks around Wall Street; too many ways for things to go wrong. But rabbit warrens cut both ways. Prevadello crossed the street and headed for a certain art supply shop, doubling back once to a druggist's to be sure, checking the windowpanes for telltale reflections and then stopping two corners east, eyeing the balconies. Nothing.

He browsed in the art shop for five minutes, finally buying a pocket sketch-pad and a pencil with the crisp schilling notes from the airport bourse. As well as its merchandise, the shop had another attraction for Prevadello: sidestepping a rank of easels, he left by the back door and found himself in a courtyard. Years ago, Kemper had grandly shown him the place, pointing out that Beethoven had lived over this very courtyard upstairs, but Prevadello ignored this memory, staying in the shadows of the gallery on the courtyard perimeter and walking another twenty paces to the cab rank. He didn't feel his back was clean until his cab crossed the throng of traffic on the Ring.

The cab left him at the entrance to the Stadt Park. Prevadello followed the paths to the pool near the Bruckner memorial. There a swarm of hungry pigeons cadged food from the Viennese on the benches and a trio of ducks pelted up and down the water, running on the foil-smooth surface, playing in the last warmth of the city before heading south through the Alpine passes. Their calls reminded Prevadello of the sea-rumble of Cape Cod and empty lifeguard chairs white in the morning sun.

Watching one of the ducks spin and dive, Prevadello knew Vienna would forever mean waiting to him. Not merely this disjunction of timetables, a half-baked defector run becalmed in the horse latitudes, but the waiting of a lifetime at the game. This one was the definitive wait, the one for the memoirs he wasn't about to write and which no security officer in his right mind would ever let see the light of day. The world could come to an end and still Prevadello would wait.

A strange voice said, "Fattening themselves for winter, I expect." It took a moment for Prevadello to realize the voice echoing from the trees was his; there was not another soul within earshot. The voice primed a *déjà vu*, a short-circuited memory of a hospital bench, too-even lawns, and white figures like ghosts drifting between the oaks. And Rappaport's single visit, meeting with him in a green office with shuttered windows and an apologetic psychiatrist, who told Prevadello all concerned felt he should "stay on," as if commitment were tour of duty. Prevadello blinked back the image, looking around his Stadtpark bench, lost, one of the quiet older persons, as his sentimental mother called them, the kind who need someone to talk to.

A scratching approached. It was an Arab, a park porter with gold teeth, making slow circuits of the paved park walk with his wide brush, murmuring to himself and nodding as he swept, sole proprietor of this corner of the park. Prevadello watched the Arab unfurl a small rug from his wheeled garbage can, remove his shoes, kneel, and unself-consciously begin to pray.

Feeling an intruder on this show of public faith, Prevadello strolled around the pool and found another empty bench. A wax paper sack containing a thimbleful of meal lay at the foot of the bench; he sowed a semicircle on the dying grass. The pigeons came, greedily, and Prevadello had a sensation of time not so much standing still as moving on without him. Perhaps this is the end of middle age, perhaps I've well and truly burned out.

He thought back to the last time he'd felt so diffuse. Drained by an exhausting homicide investigation—a real "heart-and-soul" the *Daily News* had called it, a double cop killing case in the middle of a tobacco store holdup that had taken the entire blistering summer of '61 to break—Prevadello had taken a week off in mid-September, staying alone in a small hotel outside Boston. He drove to the Cape, walking the dunes and filling his pockets with seashells, bits of worn glass, and pebbles sleek as silver. He walked all day, stopping only for coffee and a curling sandwich at one of the stands on the road behind the sand hills.

Near Marconi beach, a woman, perhaps twenty-five, walked a horse, following Prevadello, circling in and out of the waves, keeping her distance. Prevadello stopped, his shadow stretching out on the sand. She moved closer, her horse throwing its mane about as the sea spray splashed in perfect algebraic curves in the sunlight. They chatted for a while, walking together as far as Wellfleet. The woman was working her last weekend at the local vet's before returning to school. She wanted to find a farmer and marry him and care for his animals, she'd said. Prevadello seemed to remember her name was something with an A, he thought, disturbed by his fuzzing memory.

It was an image, he reminded himself now; I was in love with an image . . . perhaps I have a thing for girls with horses. A squawk rippled over the Arab's hissings. The ducks, tiring of their game, had left the pond and were preening themselves in the warm gravel at poolside. He remembered looking back across the Cape hills close-mown by the wind, wondering why he didn't have the courage to ask the girl to dinner; he knew well enough from her laugh she was intrigued, if nothing else. They could have spent a few hours over the fish and the wine . . . and dammit, it's all might-have-beens, he muttered. The Viennese pigeons scattered for a moment, then clotted together again, kicking and pecking at the meal.

Waiting . . .

A girl and boy on ancient bicycles, students in contrived frock coats on their way to school, rattled past the crouched Arab, their laughter echoing off the trees. The boy was weaving, mocking circus riders, oblivious of the ducks scampering back to the safety of the water, secure in his girl's attention. Then they were gone. Must be an occupational hazard, Prevadello decided, the loss of passion. He considered the proposition while the leaves collected at his feet, leaving a fine dust of mold on Prevadello's shine. Look at Kemper, Prevadello reassured himself; his one passion is survival.

Prevadello found himself turning the empty meal packet in his hand like an amulet. Some smoke, some fondle jewelry—Prevadello exorcised his demons by ritually murdering stray paper; he could feel the warmed wax coming off the paper as he recrossed his legs, shifting his weight. Someday the flight *will* be on time, with the right body on board, he thought wistfully: or the train or however it was the hunted human was making his run—and we'll all go home to a long bath and a decent meal. Boredom, Prevadello said to himself. That's my demon.

He dug in his coat for the pocket sketch-pad and began to draw Bruckner's statue to fill the time. Prevadello couldn't get the proportions right and put his pencil down distractedly. A contrail unwound overhead as a jet tracked westward. Prevadello watched for a moment and turned his mind to airlines and departure lounges and . . . timetables. Intrigued, Prevadello took up his pencil again and folded back a fresh page.

Whose timetable? he wrote. Kemper's? Prevadello stretched his legs and thought for a minute. Prevadello felt a bubble of acid burst in his belly. He delved for a stick of gum in his pocket, then chewed it placidly. Because, he resolved, thinking of the pension mess, because it's not a Group play. He stared into space, letting his mind drift.

"Nice day if it don't rain," said Cal Ruppert from his six-foot-five height, looking over Prevadello's shoulder. "Taken up the visual arts, have we?" Ruppert asked, offering a big hand and smiling down. Ruppert had a funny way of looking over the nose bent for him while parceling a consul through a Singapore riot. Those were Ruppert's wild days as an embassy Marine; now fortyish, Ruppert lived in Vienna with an English girl half his age who worked for Reuters—hiring on with Group when he felt like it, refining what must have been the most exotic stereo system in the city.

"You haven't changed—still the worst hair in the business," Prevadello said, tucking the sketch-pad away, and looking up at Ruppert's elongated frame topped with rough hair the texture of pencil leads.

"The girls like it, they like it fine," Ruppert replied equably. "You haven't changed either. Kemper changed?"

"Not a bit. Bought a boat, I hear."

"Then nobody's changed. Now we've settled that, mind if I sit down? All that standing at the airport's getting to me. Old age—happens to the best of us, huh?" The bench creaked as it took the weight of Ruppert's two hundred and twenty pounds; Prevadello had once seen him punt a football forty yards sitting down to win a bet.

"You'd like to know what this is all about."

"I guess," Ruppert said laconically. "Not every day I get to work with a living antique."

"Yeah, well, I thought I was safely out to pasture," Prevadello replied, shaking his head, "until Charlie got creative and stopped my pension."

Ruppert cracked a grin. "So that's what it was. I kind of figured they'd have to drag you back. How's it been for you?" Ruppert asked delicately.

"Since the breakdown? Pretty good. I cook a bit, read, garden. I like those little Japanese trees."

"Uh huh. Charlie said he did you a favor, that you were going stir crazy."

"He would say that." Prevadello paused and offered Ruppert a stick of gum. "I'm going stir crazy *here*, that's for damn sure. I was thinking about Moravec."

"Not exactly textbook, was it?"

"This one isn't either. Rappaport's got us a defector so hot we're not supposed to breathe the word embassy. Only problem is, nobody's figured out just when the guy's supposed to show."

"So Charlie said. Assuming this guy makes it out, maybe we should give him some running room?"

Prevadello unconsciously smoothed the wax paper bag on his thigh. "Been thinking about Moravec, too?"

"Learn from your mistakes, that's what my dad always said."

"Rappaport's, you mean."

Ruppert slowly shook his big head. "Shouldn't be so hard on the man. He's not as dumb as he looks. Old Charlie's got to take some blame too, screwing up that roadblock the way he did; we might've grabbed the poor guy back otherwise."

They sat in silence for a minute, the memory working on them. Ruppert spoke first, uncomfortably. "We go back a ways. Can I get a little personal?"

"Sure."

"You think too much, Marty, and it's contagious. You've got *me* thinking too much and we've only been on the job together two hours. Let's just do it: find the Russian and hand him over to the guys in the suits. Then we'll go to my place, get whipped, and I'll show you my new speakers. How's about that?"

Prevadello had to laugh. "Sounds good to me," he agreed.

"Glad we got that straight. Look," Ruppert continued, warming to his theme, "there's only the two of us and the KGB's bound to be pretty interested in getting this boy back. Once we find him, we give him some space. See what he does, let him come to us. You know, make sure we're not fishing the wrong pond."

"Be safer than a straight meet." Prevadello began folding his wax paper again.

"This place ain't exactly the wide open spaces."

"You got any ideas about the train station?"

"It's big enough for the Russians to stake out twenty guys in there. And that train's going to be chock-full of Russians, who'll be met by other Russians . . . jeez, it's needle in haystack time." Ruppert unwound himself from the bench. "You get some shut-eye. I'll see you at the Westbahnhof at noon. Take care."

"You too." Prevadello watched Ruppert lope away, the flats of his big hands swinging as he walked. The Arab was back at work, still murmuring to himself, none the quieter for his spiritual exertions. Prevadello gave Ruppert another five minutes to get clear, then eyed the morning clouds as he himself left the park; they were fissuring like cheddar as the cold front moved in. By then the morning rush hour had begun and there wasn't a free cab for miles. Prevadello walked the two miles back to his tiny room on the Schopenhauerstrasse along beautiful streets rich with broken light and the yeasty smells of wet tires and leaf rot, through a fine misty sun shower. Almost Irish, he thought, thinking of country pubs and firesides and books and fat beds; and then Geraghty. *Feed them what they eat,* the old boy had muttered into his whiskey; I hope to God I'm not the one on the menu. Prevadello checked his watch, calculating the sleep he could steal before his next vigil, his next port of call, the West-bahnhof rail station.

Waiting . . .

Waiting for a solo.

# Chapter Two

The flying dawn air smelt of burning coal and on the horizon Chertkov saw the domed glow of Kiev, with the smaller glows of the workers' townships flecked with the pinpoint fires of the blast furnaces. Just before this Thursday sunrise, a cat had woken him from a dream of a sun-bathed Parisian boulevard; a self-possessed girl no older than eight reached across Chertkov's chest to pry the frightened animal from the seat in front. "Here, Golda. Sorry, she's scared silly. Come here, Golda."

"That's an odd name for a cat," Chertkov said, stretching and moistening his lips and looking out. In the deep woods outside Kiev, a single headlight revealed a lorry bouncing toward the city along a dirt track. The girl plucked the cat free and stroked its back.

"Are you going to Israel, then?" the girl demanded, her voice hard with suspicion. Chertkov could only nod.

"Golda's not such an odd name there," the girl said quickly, holding the cat over her shoulder, and Chertkov realized who the pet's namesake was. Fortunately the surrounding seats held only sleepers—I will have to do better than that, Chertkov shivered, if I don't want a riot on my hands. He immediately left his seat for the next carriage, away from the girl and her political cat. He imagined the meows for a long time afterwards as the train slid south by southwest, toward the valley of the Dneiper.

There, Chertkov realized he had seen lights on the dawn horizon like this before, leaning on a dust-covered T-54 on a hot August night in 1968. All night the Mongolian infantry had marched past Chertkov's idled tank, its engine dead in a pool of frothy oil, their political officers shouting and swearing at them.

160

Poor bastards, Chertkov remembered thinking, walking all the way to Prague. One of their officers, a veteran, had told Chertkov there was better food across the frontier, but Chertkov didn't believe him. On the horizon, Chertkov could see the lights of the Czech villages; the first tractors would be moving about in the barnyards, now, the cows lowing, wanting to be milked.

This side of the frontier, better than a third of the tanks in Chertkov's tank regiment had broken down during the long drive south. The diesel fuel at the marshaling point was late, as were the maps, and rumor had it someone had been shot for losing the bloody code machines. So Chertkov, who did not speak Mongolian, had no translating to do, and with no coding machines to nurse, smoked and watched, wondering what the Americans would make of this mess. To Paris in forty-eight hours, that was the regimental battle cry: what a bloody joke.

And when the Red Army finally lumbered into Prague, no one was prepared for the vitriolic reception. Burning tires, braless girls throwing tomatoes, men screaming insults through the smoke—that was not what the political officers had told them to expect. Chertkov would never forget the solitary bicyclist, no more than a boy, weaving in and out of the tanks on Wenceslas Square, singing the Czech anthem. And no water, anywhere, not a drop: the Army had to truck fresh water in from Hungary.

And then even that changed, as the Czechs seemed to comprehend that the average Red Army soldier was as mystified by the reason for the invasion as the Czechs were outraged. The soldiers had never seen such a pretty place; and the store windows, with goods from Japan and America and England! His third day in Prague, GRU major Chertkov was pulled from translation duties and given a squad armed with machine pistols and wire cutters and assigned to find the clandestine TV transmitter the Czechs used to broadcast news and music. He never found it—the KGB finally found which part of the hydroelectric grid serviced the station and pulled the plug. Chertkov himself watched the last broadcast, a stark appeal for freedom that suddenly vanished. He went for a long walk around Wenceslas Square that morning, thinking over the first rumors of Red Army soldiers reaching the West . . . .

Chertkov sat up, his heart pounding.

The rail yards. Kiev. It was six in the morning and the snores began to diminish. The water had run out long since, except for tea; Chertkov's mouth had never tasted so foul.

He had imagined he was dreaming double, dreaming of Ludmilla dreaming of him. He shivered at the ingenuity of his subconscious, shivered at the recollection of her face, shiny with sun as they walked the circumference of the Alexander Park, the ship-lantern street lamps of the sunken park at their feet, and above, the floodlights of the Kremlin.

The train was idling; Chertkov could feel the diesels mumble in the glass pressed to his cheek. The KGB were not idling. Three of them were checking papers on the Kiev platform—they had a leglessly drunk young man in his twenties. He's skipped out on the draft, Chertkov thought. The fellow looked resigned more than anything; there was a bulge in his coat pocket that could only be a bottle and his eyes glistened like oil.

One of the KGB men looked directly at Chertkov for an instant. Chertkov blinked; then the KGB man was looking down the tracks, speaking out of the corner of his mouth to his assistants. Maybe it's the end of his shift or tea time—the bastard might have been thinking of boarding the train, Chertkov thought, to check papers.

*Safe.*

The KGB man waved to a conductress. She hoisted her yellow baton, holding it aloft as she jogged heavily to the train. The other two KGB men grabbed the young man by his upper arms and hustled him right off his feet, dragging him toward the station; his boots bounced like footballs on the platform.

Every rail station in the Soviet Union has a KGB prison cell.

The train began to move.

Vienna. Chertkov massaged the word.

"Pardon, but you are Klepikov? The lawyer? From Leningrad?" Chertkov swung his gaze from the midday clouds gathering and graying on the brim of the horizon to examine the face peering down at him, a deeply lined face, an oblong goatee astride full lips, and gentle, curious eyes: a civilized face.

"Me? No, you have the wrong man."

Then, almost too quickly for Chertkov to make out the consonants: "You must excuse me saying so, but you do look much like him. I thought—"

"Never been in a court in my life."

"Nor Leningrad? You do look familiar." The face was old-young, perhaps late forties, perhaps early sixties; the man's hair was swept straight back, as if the speed with which he spoke matched his pace through life.

"Leningrad? Yes, of course."

"Well, then, that will do for a start. If you are not Klepikov—
and you say you are not and I believe you—we will talk about
Leningrad. We have survived a night on this beast of a train;
care to celebrate with some lemon-grass vodka? On my honor,
I can vouch for its quality. I am Bronfeld, Adam Bronfeld. From
Leningrad."

*Rubenshtain, I am Rubenshtain.* "Of course, Rubenshtain.
That's me."

"May I?" Bronfeld dropped into the aisle seat, then unscrewed the vodka bottle in a single motion, then offered Chertkov the first drink.

"This *is* fine. Very fine." Chertkov let the alcohol glow in
his belly for a moment and then passed the bottle back.

"It is, my dear Rubenshtain, a terrible thing to lie about
vodka." Bronfeld took a deep swallow and settled the bottle on
his lap. "I am a cartographer, a mapmaker. I used to work for
the Navy in Leningrad, until they threw me out: refusenik. Access to state and military secrets. I waited twelve years. How
about you?"

Chertkov chose a number. "Four."

"Four, you must have connections."

Chertkov shrugged, needing the respite of a glance out the
window to reassure himself. There was snow ahead, a great wall
of white muscling over the sky.

"Connections are as good as the money that buys them,"
Chertkov said. "I had some money."

"Me, I had nothing but my pension and therefore a devil of
a time. I have relatives in San Francisco, state of California, on
my wife's side, God rest her. They wrote once, a year after she
died, six years ago—we had nearly all our papers in only five
years: I was almost home free. The letter comes and, *bang.* I
wait another six years. Did the KGB think I was going to America with state secrets, *me*? Life is a learning experience, eh?
Have a drink. You look pale."

"The train, I think."

"Drink up, drink up. Tell me about yourself, Rubenshtain."

"Thanks. Not much to tell—I was a bookman at the university textbook depot in Moscow. Sorting and shipping, that end
of the business."

"You are a reader, then?"

"No, we just shifted the stuff around. It was a job, slow
moving enough to give a man a chance to live a little in his
mind." Chertkov passed the bottle back, thinking, who would

have dreamed I would end up on the run with a philosopher-mapmaker, with a trainload of Jews for company?

"To you, Rubenshtain. Time, well, time comes and goes, but a man's memory of his country endures." Bronfeld wiped the neck of the bottle with the palm of his hand, then pointed it out the window. "For my part, I have drawn the coasts of this country more times than I care to think. Did you know that every map of the U.S.S.R. has a deliberate mistake somewhere?"

Chertkov shook his head. "Rubenshtain, such is our paranoid land. A state secret in every sandbar, under every harbor buoy. You know how much the coast changes in the course of a year, how many changes must be made to a chart while the wind and water eat the harbors and channels and spit them up somewhere else?"

"No idea, Bronfeld," said Chertkov, gently taking the now half-empty bottle from his drinking companion.

"Meters, sometimes tens of meters: enough to run a submarine aground or wash a mine ashore and blow some child to bits. Never-ending. Much like your books, I would think." Bronfeld pointed a finger at the carriage ceiling. "Not since Khrushchev was the kennel-master have I so much as touched a map, but I waited while the very coasts changed with the tides for my release. For a dozen years. For us, Russia changes her shape but never her color. Rubenshtain, I believe we Jews had it better under the Tsars, you know that?" Bronfeld's speech had begun to slow and he lowered his voice. "At least in those days you had somewhere to run when the Cossacks came. Now . . . the mystery of a new place, a new life, new persecutions, smaller ones—no doubt about that, but persecution nonetheless. Agreed?"

"A man can't hide his accent or the shape of his beard, can he?"

Bronfeld nodded and stroked his own goatee. "You are right." Bronfeld gave a shallow belch. "I can shave, but I will still be Bronfeld from Leningrad; you can grow a beard but you will still be Rubenshtain from Moscow, and that's that."

*I will never be Rubenshtain from Moscow, my friend:* Chertkov had another tipple and passed the bottle back. "Even in Tel Aviv, Bronfeld."

"Even in Tel Aviv," Bronfeld agreed sagely. "But I don't give a damn. I'm seventy, seventy years old, Rubenshtain, and I'm too old to give a damn any more. You know what they say, strike the nail and you only drive it deeper into the wood. That's me." Bronfeld sighed. "Here we are on a train with only one destination but we have lost our way nonetheless, Rubenshtain, lost our way . . ."

Chertkov said nothing and watched the snow clouds. He waited some minutes for Bronfeld to cease his silent brooding, but the Jew stared ahead, glassy-eyed and serene. Then his eyes fluttered and closed and Bronfeld's goatee rested on his chest.

"Do you want to talk about Leningrad now, Bronfeld?" Chertkov gently took the bottle from Bronfeld's open hand: Bronfeld was asleep. Chertkov finished the bottle and together, their heads jogging on one another's shoulders, the two of them slept as the train thundered on into the daylight.

Chertkov awoke. It was afternoon of the second day, twenty hours southwest of Moscow; Bronfeld still slept, his frame curled into his seat, burping occasionally as the train rose and fell. Vinnitsa. Zherinka. Ternopol: city-islands in the great sea of the Ukrainian steppe, imaginary places that appeared, grew, aged, and disappeared as the Express passed. Ten minutes of island here, eight minutes there, then onward, the train rolling and yawing like a galleon, creaking and groaning uphill, rushing down, sailing an ocean of snow crested by low, even hills, regular as tides. Chertkov grew used to the militia at the station stops, to the shouted abuse from those local passengers who knew the émigrés were aboard the train and where they dreamed of being; grew used to the shifts in personalities of the various conductors, some kind, some brutal, most uncaring; grew used to the endless horizontal blown snow that never seemed to fall but defied the earth and flew horizontally as fast as the train itself.

At dusk Thursday, the sun grew warmer and the snow-fields gave way to the infinitely variable browns and umbers of the treeless autumn steppe. Like a tempera painting, Chertkov had always thought, each twig and upright patch of wind-bristled scrub as clear in the fading light as if drawn. It was beautiful, all the more so because he would never see it again.

He dozed and was thrown abruptly awake: someone at the front of the carriage was having a coughing fit—the sound was identical to Rubenshtain's last breaths. Ashen, Chertkov stood and made his way to the couplings between the cars, needing fresh air. He hung to the entryway stanchion and found the rhythm of the train comforted him and dulled the memory of the dead man. What if someone on this train knows Rubenshtain: all Jews know one another . . . He stood there for nearly an hour, fighting his fears, before a gap-toothed conductor, one of the rough ones, chased him back to his seat.

The eyes that examined him on his return walk were curious: nothing more. I am going mad, Chertkov thought. In a moment, I shall scream, "I killed him! I did it!" But he did not. Bronfeld had taken up with a group of card-players in another carriage and Chertkov was alone with his fears, unable to sleep, his head aching from the map maker's vodka. His imagination ran to the faces of his long-dead parents and their apartment in Brusilov, their three high-ceilinged rooms and the communal kitchen, ripe with odors of six different meals cooking at once and the more subtle aroma of drying laundry.

Then he remembered the police coming at night, which gave him no rest at all; he chewed the inside of his lips till they bled and that calmed him. He watched a chess match, saying nothing, then walked the length of the train at sunset, watching the laddered shadows of the train, frames of a film on the hard soil and the splashes of half-frozen creek water under the bridges. Ahead lay the foothills of the Carpathians. As the hills swelled, Chertkov heard a child tell her mother the limbs of a solitary bare tree were shaped like the arms of a menorah.

Sundown, the second day: from L'vov in the southwest Ukraine to the Hungarian frontier takes the Czechoslovakia Express nearly five hours.

Chertkov had cadged some chicken and black bread at dusk from a couple from Petrozavodsk who had relations in Israel—he had not eaten since leaving his flat. Chertkov lied, he thought convincingly, to the couple about his dreams of working as a teacher on a kibbutz and left them to their illusions and their fears before the conversation turned to matters beyond his ken. What, for instance, was this Sukkoth they had celebrated a week ago? Mustn't press my actor's first-night luck, he warned himself.

In the twilight, he listened to the other voices, rising and falling in and out of sleep themselves. The coal-burning furnace in the entryway sizzled away; the conductors had had fish cakes for dinner and the whole car reeked of them. The cat Golda and her mistress were sleeping in an aisleway, propped atop a trunk, the only bodies in the car with any modicum of solitude. Bronfeld returned with another bottle won at cards and began a snoring marathon Chertkov resignedly managed to make a white noise. He had tried to dream himself to sleep, trying dreams of Ludmilla first, which made him despair. Then a dream, a childhood one, of a single small boat. Grandfather's he realized, slipping along the surface of the Don. But the dream faded. He woke, lost.

Outside, a firmament of lights: the collective farms of the southern Ukraine shone coldly through the gauzy fringes of a snow storm, like distant planets. In places snow had drifted across the line; there would be a sudden silence as the wheels sliced through the cushiony drifts. Chertkov wondered if the farmers knew where these night trains went, if they ever thought of . . . then he was asleep again.

At midnight Thursday, in the floodlit marshaling yards of Cop, a geographical afterthought tucked in the tri-corner where Russia meets Europe at the Polish and Hungarian frontiers, Chertkov woke when the couplings strained and banged as coveralled men changed the train's trucks to the European gauge. There is a time at night when dreams die, he thought, when one can no longer fend off the universals: how did I get here, he asked himself, surrounded by people I have all my life despised, but whose escape is my escape? He closed his eyes and imagined the beautiful streets of Paris and the reflections of the buildings on the surface of the Seine. City of light, city of lovers.

The image of Ludmilla's face percolated through Chertkov's mind all through the night, on this sealed train rolling through Hungary, rolling across the spine of the Matra mountains down the Danube plain: Vienna lay twelve hours away.

Ludmilla.

# Chapter Three

The two overnight train rides and the thirteen-hundred-kilometer round trip from Moscow to Leningrad and back, the line-ups—they had all been worth it. Her new lined coat belted tight around her broadening hips, Olga Kostova Chertkova straightened her back, drew herself to her full five feet, and deliberately kicked the loose linoleum tile; it chipped and broke, skittering across her apartment's lobby floor. Uncle Pavel will hear of this—the Housing Ministry ought to take care of loyal Party people—this floor was a disgrace. And now the elevator was out of service: another disgrace. Olga Chertkova hoisted her luggage and began to plod upstairs. Count your blessings, she thought. At least Nikolai will be at work and I can unpack my new treasures in peace.

It had been a pleasantly successful shopping trip to Leningrad for Olga Kostova Chertkova; she had had to buy this new piece of luggage to fit the four fine new dresses—handmade in Belgrade and second only to real foreign dresses, if you please—and the six black leather handbags from Poland she planned to trade for a fur winter hat. All in all, not bad. There was even something for the old man; she hoped Nikolai would like the battered little paperback life of Rodin she had queued for half an hour to buy. Some of the photographs had fallen out but Nikolai was mad for anything French and ten roubles seemed like a fair price for a temporary peace between them. There had been bad patches in their nineteen-year marriage before but lately Nikolai had been even more difficult than usual, even downright strange. Long, introverted silences, no sense of humor, and the peculiar way he had begun talking to himself . . . perhaps he

thought he was in love again, mooning over those witless girls
he chased. He thinks I don't know. My best friend Svetlana is
absolutely right: they *always* think we don't know. But we do.

Olga kept climbing. Why come home a day early, he'd bleat;
why not shop another day, you love shopping?

I missed you, Nikolai, truly, I'll say, just to confuse him.
Even though you're next to useless around the flat, at least, small
mercy, you don't drink like your wild friend Ferenko—who
should be ashamed of himself, carrying on the way he does
when the vodka hits him. Some son of an Academician *he* turned
out to be; his father must be spinning in his grave, may he rest
in peace. But the Army intelligence service is a good living,
much better than most, even if it isn't the Foreign Ministry, and
everything's found. And Nikolai's not a bad fellow, he's not
completely insensitive like most middle-aged Red Army men,
Olga decided for the thousandth time—he simply can't keep his
pants up.

Which was enough of a marital philosophy to see Olga Chertkova to her floor. She trundled her loot gamely to the flat's door
and felt her back pop into place as she gently deposited her
luggage. Heat's been off again, she noticed—I really *will* call
Uncle Pavel tomorrow. The door opened with its familiar click
and Olga, thinking better of straining her back again, nudged
her bags across the threshold.

And looked up.

Phlegmatic and practical, Olga was not by nature a screamer.
But she screamed now, her hands raking her cheeks, standing
stock-still in her smashed flat, because, more horrifying than
the crown of blackening blood around the poor man's torn head
or his fingers burned into claws, most horrifying of all was the
single staring eye, dull now, glazed with a final memory of life.

*He died with his eyes open:* Olga Chertkova would never,
ever forget that. She let silence return, afraid to move her hands
away. She was a brave woman, and after a decent pause and a
deep breath, she looked at the dead man again, willing herself
not to scream again.

She took a step closer and looked down carefully. Olga Chertkova did not dare actually *touch* the figure—there was so much
blood. Olga bent over, one hand on her pudgy knee, the other
pressed hard to her bosom, and waited for the thump in her
chest: was it him? She couldn't tell from the quarter of the face
free of blood: an uneven stubble and a lower cheek receding

into dark jowls. The jacket wasn't . . . no. And the hair, the shape of the head . . .

It's not Nikolai.

She began to breathe again. The shoulders were too big for Nikolai's slumped roundness and those awful shoes—Nikolai wouldn't be caught . . . Olga Chertkova gasped at the thought, she couldn't help it, that was the way the certainty formed in her mind.

No, not Nikolai—then who? Olga slowly, anxiously took in her violated living room. There had been a war here. The wall and carpets were speckled with dried blood and her favorite print, the expensively framed Serov, had been torn to shreds by the shattering of its own glass. The stereo and TV had been thrown over and fragmented records lay all over the floor.

Olga took several tentative steps down the hall.

The bedroom was the same—sheets tumbled into a heap, drawers flung from the bureau, closet doors wide open. Olga ran to the bureau and opened her jewel box. The brooch with the tiny emerald Nikolai had bought her for their tenth anniversary, her grandmother's bracelet with the platinum setting, the pearl earrings were all there. Some of her precious American money was gone, but, aside from the mess, nothing seemed missing. She sat on the bed and tried to slow her spinning thoughts. She looked at the bedside clock and with shaking fingers dialed the phone.

"You did the right thing, Madame Chertkova, calling me," Moldov said, thoughtfully wriggling his stockinged toes in a patched square of Nikolai Chertkov's soft red-wool Arab carpet. "The last thing we need is the KGB or the militia wandering in and out of here with their crystal balls. Can't have that, can we?" Olga said nothing. Moldov, his arm consolingly around his chief translator's wife, was watching the rubber-gloved GRU Security officer moving the limbs next to the body to make the corpse easier to move. "Never seen him before, madame, you're quite sure?"

Olga mutely nodded at Moldov. Her hands were still trembling and she wished they would stop. She was growing more afraid by the minute that Nikolai was mixed up in something terrible; she didn't like the very grave looks Colonel Moldov was giving her or the heavy way he tried to be nice, interrupting grandly when the pathologist asked her about the position of the body when she'd found it. Of course I haven't moved it, she'd said. Why would I move a dead stranger falling to pieces on my best carpet—to see if he was sprawled on my missing husband? She was shivering now and that was making her hands shake even worse.

"Do you have a friend you can call, madame?" Olga said she did and Moldov told her to spend the night at the friend's. Moldov released Olga Chertkova and gave her his overcoat to warm her, gesturing as he did so to Ferenko, who had occupied himself by nosing through the books on the floor. The two of them went to the kitchen while the Security officer had his assistants photograph the scene and ready the body to be taken downstairs to the gray van.

Ferenko bustled about with the tea preparations while Moldov drummed his fingers on the table top. "When do we tell the militia?" Ferenko asked, his hands on the kettle handle, waiting for the boil.

"We," Moldov said quietly, "don't do anything. Just you button up and make sure our tea's good and strong." Moldov was listening to Olga Chertkova's side of her phone conversation; she was talking about her jewels being there but Nikolai missing. Which was a bloody laugh, Nikolai Georgievitch Chertkov having had Moscow Center's crown jewels pass through his fingers every time the GRU's Washington *rezident* transmitted RAYMOND's encrypts. "Petrovski, a word with you," Moldov called, watching the melancholy procession as the Security officer's assistants moved the body out the door.

"Sir?" Lieutenant Lavrenti Petrovski was a resourceful GRU veteran handicapped with an embarrassingly high-pitched voice, which had cost him any hope of quick promotion, but this sort of dirty work would keep him occupied until he retired in two years' time. In the small world of the GRU's secret core, scandals were nonexistent; whether bloody domestic disputes, the occasional drunken rapes, the rare shootings—Petrovski cleaned up after them all, paying off, heading off, whatever needed to be done.

"How many murders have you seen in your day?"

"Forty-two since the war. Including this."

"Speculate, then: what do you make of this one?"

Petrovski peeled his rubber gloves from his fingers and assumed the circumspect air of the detective-inspector in the dock. "He died here, that's for sure. The blow to the head wasn't fatal. Neither was the loss of blood. He was electrocuted—the lamp fried him. I'd say within the last forty-eight hours."

"How can you tell that?"

"Blood pooling after death. He's pretty well unmarked aside from the head and hand. It must have been quick."

"Anything else?"

Ferenko poured two cups of tea and raised his eyebrows at Petrovski, who shook his head no. "My photographer's half-Yid," Petrovski said, "clever lad, likes playing the scientist. While he was taking his happy snaps, he says the fellow might be a Jew. So I checked."

"And?"

"Circumcised. There's one last thing. You'll want this." Petrovski handed Moldov an unopened air letter. "Jacket pocket. There were no other papers. Nothing. He's been picked clean."

"That'll be all, Petrovski. Good job, as usual. We'll have the militia to deal with this afternoon. Be in my office at two. General Savinski will be there, so spruce up that uniform, eh?"

"I'll do my best, sir." Petrovski saluted sardonically and left.

Moldov looked at the envelope, sipping his tea. "It's murder, and Chertkov did it," Ferenko said, fitting the tea cozy. "He's been diddling about in the black market and got in over his head. We'll probably find him at the bottom of the river."

"We'll find him all right, you can count on that. But the black market?" Moldov sighed and put the envelope down while eyeing his adjutant. "It must be remarkable," Moldov said, smiling thinly at Ferenko, "being as clear-thinking as you are. What makes you think his wife didn't do it? Have you seen her rail ticket, her receipts from the Leningrad shops?"

"No, sir," Ferenko said, blushing.

"But she didn't. She wouldn't harm a fly, would she, Ferenko?"

Ferenko stubbornly kept his silence for a long moment, then nodded.

"That's your flaw, my boy: I like my adjutants young and bland, like my veal; unopinionated. Don't muck up your fine young brain with opinions. That's the last thing Center needs." Moldov considered the envelope again, still listening to the phone conversation down the hall. "Listen. She's whispering. About you, I'd say. Chertkov's wife doesn't like you, Ferenko. Don't compound it by nosing about in her flat. Leave the books and the blood to the militia. That's no concern of ours; we have enough on our plate staying a step ahead of the KGB. Now," Moldov continued, "what do we make of a missing translator, a dead Jew, and an envelope?"

"I don't see, sir."

"There you're wrong. I'm the one with the bad eye. You *do* see," Moldov replied patiently, handing Ferenko the envelope. "Have a good look: tell me what you see."

"An envelope, an air-mail envelope. Soviet made. Addressed to Israel. No stamp."

Moldov swirled his tea in his glass. "Israel's not an unusual place for a Jew to mail a letter."

"But sir, look at this." Ferenko held the envelope's reverse for Moldov to examine.

In that moment, Moldov realized what the return address meant, what the cold body in the back of Petrovski's gray van meant, even as Ferenko said, "It's not Moscow: it's Vienna, in care of the Jewish Resettlement Commission. Maybe that's why there's no stamp, comrade-colonel, because he was going to mail it in . . ."

"Bloody hell!" Moldov exclaimed, nearly spilling his tea as he stood. "Bloody hell, Ferenko, I'm getting slow in my old age! Madame Chertkova," Moldov called, shoving the kitchen table away, "I need your telephone."

# Chapter Four

"Baggage handling fee. Dollars or koruny, Jew, come on, we haven't all day."

Friday morning.

Bratislava: on the east bank of the Danube, the Czechoslovakia Espress's last stop in the East.

Bronfeld, sitting next to Chertkov, looked at the leering Czech porter with distaste and reached into the mildewed depths of his ancient coat. A green glass bottle appeared in the old man's hand and he tossed it lazily to the Czech. The porter was already drunk and nearly dropped the bottle.

"Good thing I caught it, Jew," the Czech roared in guttural Russian. "Or you'd have paid through your Yid nose." The porter tapped his own nose with the vodka bottle's cork, lowered the neck, and pulled the cork out with a cracked tooth. He took a deep draft and moved on to the next victim, forgetting Chertkov in the window seat.

Throughout the train, the scene was being repeated—and woe to those who had not budgeted for this last corrupt toll. The blackmail was simple and effective: hard currency or vodka for "baggage handling" or the porters threatened to throw the émigrés off the train before the Austrian frontier. As he huddled closer to the window, Chertkov's belt felt loose against his belly: I've lost five kilos since this nightmare began. And I am going to be sick if this car gets one degree warmer. Trickles of condensation ran down the window next to Chertkov's face.

The shouting porters left the car, arguing over a bottle of Georgian brandy. Someone at the back announced in a querulous voice that the border was fifteen minutes away.

No one clapped.

Chertkov looked at the old man next to him. Oblivious to the stench of fear and fatigue in the carriage, the old man had shown his deep concern for the dangers facing them all before the last hurdle: he was fast asleep again.

Chertkov's heart felt as though it would burst. Fifteen minutes.

At eight in the morning, the train-children should have been playing in the aisles and the older folk brewing tea and comparing how badly one another had slept, but on the train, no one spoke; even Golda the cat recognized this stop was different from all the others. The silence of the place, a spit of concrete set in a clearing, was the silence of the guard hut, of paper and dust, of no man's land, the artificial silence of an artificial border. Outside, on the platform beside the halted train, the Czech border police were chatting with the conductor and fingering the carbon flimsies on his clipboard. At the far end of the clearing, at the peak of the bridge across the Danube, the Austrian flag slowly untwisted from its pole; the shadow of the flag crept down the tracks, then disappeared as the wind died.

Chertkov leaned against the windowpane of the motionless carriage, peering through the drabbled glass. Past the end of the platform, a gravel strip some twenty yards wide drained away into the trees like sand on the shore; half-hidden in the fringes of the fir-limbs Chertkov could see a Czech guard smoking and staring, his jackboots settled into the thin new snow, his rifle nestled papooselike against his back. Couldn't you use a night in the fleshpots of Paris, Chertkov mentally whispered to the silent guard, instead of standing up to your ankles in snow, watching me watching you? After a last economical drag, the Czech irritably threw his cigarette onto the gravel and, shifting his rifle to his other shoulder, spat eloquently at the train.

Directly below Chertkov's window, another Czech soldier, a short, splayfooted corporal in rimless glasses, whistled as he played a convex mirror on a pole beneath the carriage, examining its suspension and the rat's-nest of hydraulic lines for any countrymen misguided enough to try to escape on his shift. The Czech was quite cheerful, as if this task were the last of his duties for the day—or perhaps he had taken his comrade, the sullen sentry in the trees, at cards: yes, Chertkov thought with sudden inspiration, as the small guard played his mirror like a dentist, the short one won the pot last night. The Czech moved on to the next car, still whistling.

Their backs to the wind, the border police and the conductor shared cigarettes, the conductor making a point of using his sophisticated lighter; he showed it to one of the security men, who, having checked the papers on the clipboard, weighed the lighter respectfully in his gloved palm and made a joke before handing it back. Come on, boys, Chertkov urged, let's get it over with; his mouth tasted suddenly metallic and Chertkov realized he had unconsciously chafed the inside of his cheek raw—he swallowed and tasted blood as he watched the conductor eye his stopwatch. With an oriental slowness, the clipboard made the rounds one final time as the conductor's manifests were signed and stamped and signed again.

Chertkov watched a man at the front of the carriage stand and theatrically make for the washroom in the next carriage. Bronfeld pinched Chertkov's arm as he said something in Yiddish, but, out of the corner of his eye, Chertkov had seen one of the Czech security men begin to jog, the skirt of his greatcoat bouncing off his knees as he ran: it was the small one, the corporal with the rimless glasses. In the entryway to the guard hut, a soldier held a phone, his mouth wide.

Why are they shouting, a voice cried from the rear of the car.

Like spectators at a tennis match, every passenger on the platform side of the carriage had turned their heads simultaneously, fearfully watching the charade between the small Czech corporal and his colleague with the phone.

*No.*

This is a nightmare, a girl said matter-of-factly, before her father clapped his hand over her mouth. What is happening? another anguished voice cried, the first of a chaotic wash of advice, shouted prayers, and wailed curses filling the carriage's stale air.

Chertkov knew: KGB. *I am dead meat.* Let them shoot me, he thought; I've come too far to be dragged out of my seat. *Move:* Chertkov stood and stepped over the startled Bronfeld into the aisle, making for the platform between the carriages. In the distance, the guard in the woods unslung his rifle and trotted out from the trees, leaving a trail of bootprints in the morning snow.

Chertkov hesitated. Head count, they'll do a head count—then it will come down to papers . . . and what if they have a name, else why would they have stopped the train?

A siren began to sound, rising in pitch, wailing.

But inside the Express, it was absolutely quiet, save the low voices halfway down the carriage, the staccato conversation of the STB man and a Russian in an overcoat ordering the seated men to stand, working quickly, a glance, a line through a name, then on to the next bench seat.

The aisle seemed endless, a blurred catacomb of heads and seat backs. The STB man cleared two men and ordered them to sit down; Chertkov could sense their relief, their abrupt disappearance into the inspector's wake.

A scrape of jackboots. "Where the hell do you think you're going? Papers." Russian: I've drawn the KGB man. Chertkov said nothing and handed the visa to the white shape in his face; a cap behind—the Czech waited.

*Mother:* if you're listening: save me.

"Rubenshtain, O.N. Born 12 July 1916. Poltava." The voice was sharp, a showman's voice, that of a man who likes his power. The Czech's hat had tipped down.

The list.

"Take the bloody thing, Rubenshtain." Chertkov reached randomly into space and felt the visa press into his shaking hand.

"Right. Got him, lieutenant. Next, you there, stand in the lieutenant's presence. Come *on*, Rubenshtain, get your Jew-carcass out of the way. Think you're part of the furniture?"

Chertkov stepped around the two inspectors and felt for the support of a seat back as he moved. Which way now? I am walking forward. To Austria.

As soon as he reached the haven of the partition at the end of the passageway, Chertkov slipped his spectacles on and peered out the window. The train was ringed by green-uniformed guards, perhaps thirty of them, their rifles unslung. Two of them were talking, one jerking his thumb at a gleaming green Volga parked on the platform.

Chertkov pocketed his spectacles and heard a door slam.

The KGB man and his STB assistant had left the car.

A baby began to cry and a swell of whispers swept down the carriage. Chertkov looked out the window again. A half dozen guards crowded around an officer, who pointed sharply at his men, gesturing them to the train—to the carriage behind Chertkov's.

To the carriage behind.

"They've got someone, the bastards," said a man with his

head pressed to the glass. Chertkov couldn't see anything for a moment, then a many-legged shape detached itself from the train, dragging something. A woman . . . and behind her, in a soldier's arms, a child sprawled, crying. The Volga moved, all was movement, the car moving toward the struggling huddle of soldiers and their burden, the KGB man striding behind, a terrifying dumb show . . .

"What are they doing to the lady, mummy? What's she done?" Chertkov knew the voice: it was the girl with the political cat.

The siren stopped, its dying moan fading into the trees. The Volga's door swung open and the huddle pressed itself to the car, delivered itself of its victims, and then the KGB man waved, an arrogant flinging of glove against the sky.

Suddenly, it was over. The Czechs stepped back and made their way to the tiny sheet-metal office at the end of the platform: one of them gave the engineer a wave. A bell clanged far ahead, followed by a great sigh as the train gathered itself. There was a shout and the blast of a steam whistle and, gently, infinitely slowly, the train began to move. The train pulsed as the couplings took the weight and Chertkov's carriage, rocking gently like a ship at its moorings, edged past the end of the platform at a walk, slowly moving toward the bridge across the Danube and Austria.

No one said a word. Each passenger willed the tons of metal across the frontier, meter by slow meter. Chertkov thrust his trembling hands into his pockets. *The sun shines and I can walk on water:* the first iron plates of the bridge appeared, the low buttresses, the first railing, the water of the Danube below, slow, plastic, malt-brown beneath the overcast sky.

He opened the door and stepped across the platform between the carriages, walking to the rear now, back to his seat next to Bronfeld, his pace identical to the train's, so that the landscape seemed to stand still as he worked his way down the aisle.

Bronfeld had taken his old seat and was staring down at the river; Chertkov placed a warning hand on Bronfeld's shoulder before he could speak.

"They got someone," Chertkov said as he sat down.

Bronfeld looked up and nodded. "I was worried about you."

The carriage was halfway across the bridge now, the wheels squealing. Barbed wire spiraled around the bridgework and a chain of rafts swung on the Danube's current, buoying nets that fished for men on the run; on the last raft, a pair of guards sat watching the train pass above, a machine gun mounted between them, pointing west.

"We're almost there, Rubenshtain."

"Yes. We're almost there."

Someone began to sing uncertainly in Yiddish, another voice caught him and then the carriage was alive with the song; Bronfeld began to sing, a gloriously tuneless voice, slapping Chertkov on the shoulder.

"Sing! Sing, Rubenshtain! *Mazel!* We are free!"

Ignoring his companion's cheer, Chertkov reached for his single piece of luggage, standing over the startled Bronfeld to pull the case off the rack.

"What's wrong, Rubenshtain?"

Chertkov sat down and sprung the luggage open, searching. From his valise, he pulled the spectacle case Shykofsky had given him at the laundry. The singing uproar continued; Chertkov had to shout to make himself heard. "Adam. Watch this for me. I'll be back in a minute. Don't worry, we'll have our vodka in Vienna together." He placed a finger over his lips and stepped into the aisle.

"Adam. Don't worry." Chertkov gave Bronfeld what he hoped was a reassuring tug on the arm and walked to the carriage door. He turned and Bronfeld gave him a confused thumbs-up. Chertkov opened the door.

On the platform, he looked out to the west, between the carriages down the track. A contingent of Austrian soldiers was drawn up on the Austrian side, a rank of men in parachutists' smocks and jump boots.

Chertkov was trying to puzzle this out when he felt a hand on his shoulder. Chertkov reached for his spectacles and fitted them.

"Someone always comes out on the bridge," the large, sour-faced conductor who had boarded at Kiev said. "Against the rules." The conductor, one of two men of his profession among the twenty women working the last quarter of the route, had his cap tilted back on his head as he packed his pipe. His bulk was inflated with the pockets of his uniform, which overflowed with paper, ticket stubs, and timetables; he wore a tea strainer and a ticket punch hanging from a chain at his generous waist.

He shouted over the whine of the wind, "You a Yid, then?" The conductor thrust a big thumb deep into his pipe and screwed the tobacco flakes into the bowl.

Chertkov nodded, and the conductor shrugged in response, a masterpiece of concision spanning three centuries of hate. "Think it's any better there?"

Chertkov said he didn't know. Behind the conductor, over his shoulder, two KGB men on the Bratislava platform were waving frantically as the train crawled across the bridge. Chertkov glanced down; the soldiers on the raft were suddenly alive, one of them swinging the gun upwards.

Over Chertkov's head, a sign read "Republik Oesterreich."

They were in. As the train clanked farther across the bridge, the green uniforms on the Bratislava side slowly turned and walked disconsolately back to the guard hut as an officer ran at them from the station itself. Then he, too, slowed to a walk and watched the train pull away.

"Well, I see it once a week and it does damn all for me, I can tell you. Vienna, that is. The chocolates are good, that's about it. Nice to take some home, but give me Moscow any day. Least a man knows where his next meal's coming from at home." He put his pipe between his steel teeth and lit it; the smoke disappeared in the slip-stream of the train. "What's the matter with you? Don't value your own opinion enough to speak?"

Chertkov said nothing, thinking of Bronfeld and his twelve-year wait. "Tell you what: we won't miss your kind, not a bit. Like flushing the john, this run is." The conductor raised his cap and set it at a less provocative angle on his big pale head. He pulled an imaginary chain and winked at Chertkov, then laughed, moving his eyes about like a circus clown, pleased at his wit. The conductor threw his match over the side of the bridge and winked again. "Mind the step, eh?" The conductor wrapped his hand around the door handle.

"Wait," Chertkov said. "What are the soldiers for?"

"Arabs. Austrians're scared the Palestinians are going to blow your lot to kingdom come." He laughed again and pulled the door closed, winking as he went, his face saying, What else can you expect?

Chertkov remained between the carriages, watching. The train crawled along, rocking the last few meters of the bridge before the line spread into the maze of siding off the main line.

*I cannot believe this:* the whole mad scheme is going to work, he exulted. I must keep my face grave, Chertkov thought, but the corners of his mouth would not remain set. As the train pulled even with the troops on the siding, Chertkov began to

beam, his smile the delirious grin of a man beating all the odds.
I have survived, said a voice in his head—and you have killed,
whispered its reply.

Sobered by that thought, Chertkov worked out the odds. The
KGB Vienna *rezidentura* numbered over twenty men—and if
they missed me at the border, he knew, they will surely try again
in Vienna.

The train stopped and the Austrian troops boarded, boys on
national service, most of them, Chertkov calculated, big-
shouldered farm lads with slow, gentle voices. The troops passed
out chewing gum and made a special effort with the children,
showing them their canteens and the insides of their ammunition
pouches. Behind them, the customs men checked and ticked
and stamped, their Old World politeness a shock after the Czech
border police—the customs men spent all of half a minute with
Chertkov, casually inspecting his few belongings and then nodding him on his way back to his lookout between the carriages.
The Soviet Jews warily watched the soldiers, these young, heavily armed Aryans, chatting easily in German; the faces of the
older passengers alternated between relief and skepticism—had
these very tracks groaned under commandeered cattle cars
headed for obscure Polish towns, guarded perhaps by the fathers
and uncles of these cheerful boys?

The customs men retreated, their mysterious marks left on
passports for the émigrés to compare. The train started again,
and two Austrian soldiers moved past Chertkov with curt nods,
holding their machine pistols close to their chests and scanning
the trees lining the track. There was a muffled bang behind, but
it was only a sweets vendor, his cart loaded with foil-wrapped
chocolates and blocks of nut brittle. Chertkov propped open the
door for the epicene-faced vendor, who gave him a gushy *"danke
schön"* as he rolled his cart past.

Chertkov had no time to mull over this Western decadence;
he rested his hands on the window ledge and tried to see down
the track, but the curve of the rail line meant all he saw was the
long string of carriages ahead. Following the chicane curve, the
engine swung gracefully back and disappeared into the deep
forest.

In that instant, Chertkov realized that as it rounded the apex
of the S-curve, as the cars arced wide, *no one could see his
carriage door*.

Chertkov removed his glasses, put them in their case, and
held the case close to his side. He hauled his round shape over

the side of the locked half-door, his feet seeking the step below.
*There*. The carriage suspension whined and rolled and Chertkov
was flung flat against its side; then his feet swung free as the
carriage banked the other way, into the S-curve.

*Now*.

He pushed hard, too hard, as the centrifugal force alone took
him well over the rough aggregate of the ballast bed and sent a
badly frightened lump of translator sprawling into the evergreen
scrub at the edge of the forest.

The noise seemed inconceivably loud to Chertkov, his feet
over his head, his back spiked in a dozen places by broken
boughs and fir needles. He kicked himself out of the bush that
held him and tumbled backwards into the shadows of the trees.

The last carriage of the train trundled past, the two guards on
its rear deck swaying like sailors as they studied the trees over
Chertkov's head, and, incredibly, paid no attention to the di-
sheveled Russian putting his spectacles on, waist-deep in the
undergrowth not twenty feet below their post.

The train shrank down the track and arced into the forest
beyond the next curve, the two soldiers diminishing into min-
iatures, then two white dots against the green of the carriage.
And then the train was gone.

Chertkov looked for the sun and took his bearings: west, west
to Vienna. For some minutes, he fought his way through the
bush, sometimes backing into the denser scrub between the great
trees, until he found a path along a small brook. This he followed until the path petered out in a glade.

Voices.

Men: he could hear, quite clearly, two or three voices, German ones, shouting numbers. Chertkov pressed himself against
a tree and searched the surrounding woods. He found them.
Four men in uniform jackets with shiny red plastic vests, standing around a tripod. One of the men left the others and dotted
a tree with blue paint.

A theodolite—they were surveyors. And, in the shadows beyond the edge of the glade, stood a truck, "Schmidt und Ehr-
lich" painted on the doors, with that most magical of words
below: *WIEN*.

Chertkov felt for the roll of American dollars in the seam of
his woolen shirt and began to walk toward the surveyors.

# Chapter Five

Ruppert and Prevadello, surrounded by a crowd of some hundred Russians waiting for the Czechoslovakia Express, stood posed like mannequins on platform five of Westbahnhof rail station.

"This is just like yesterday. We could film a remake of *War and Peace* right here, right now," Ruppert was saying, indicating the crowd with his new red mittens. "There's enough extras for the whole battle of Borodino."

"Think of it as a welcoming party, Cal," Prevadello said, showing his teeth. It's a burial party, he corrected himself. The wind, bravely attempting to gather itself again, sent stray leaves scuttling like crabs across the platform. There could be a platoon of KGB hoods here and I'd never know. Prevadello stamped his feet; it was a cold like Korea's, rat-faced and eager to set its teeth into his bones. Prevadello's insides lurched and his eyes still smarted from jet lag, but he nonetheless gazed doggedly down the rail line to the east. Throw a stone far enough down this track, he mused, and it'll come back part of a five-year plan. He turned his back to the wind. It's twenty years on and I'm still commuting, Prevadello thought, and the trains are still late.

The night before, after a bachelor meal at Ruppert's as his girlfriend worked late at Reuters, they had gone to a dismal nightclub enlivened by a riotously funny bartender, an acquaintance of Ruppert's who told sly Viennese jokes and specialized in impersonations. Neither drank much, and Prevadello fell asleep in the cab and Ruppert had to wake him to get him up the stairs of his hotel. He woke at seven, still jet-lagged, bathed, and took a stroll around the Ring, content to drift the sidewalks.

"In Vienna, things are slow," the bartender had said, "slow like double-cream." And Prevadello remembered then that was how Moravec had taken his coffee the times they had met at Lehmann's on the Graben before the Czechs grabbed the slender diplomat back.

The trains from Bratislava in western Czechoslovakia terminate here, mein Herr, the elderly woman in the *Bundesbahnen* uniform had told Prevadello. *Ja, ja,* the Moscow train too. Be sure to see Stephankirche as well, mein Herr, the woman suggested as she handed Prevadello a timetable. And *wilkommen* to Vienna. The cathedral—or anywhere warm, Prevadello decided ruefully.

Ruppert wore a ski hat, which only made him taller, and a thick woolen scarf, his cheeks ruddied by the crosswind. He touched Prevadello's arm. "You can wait in the car, you know. It's warmer there. This train's sometimes hours late. Depends on the bastards at Soviet customs." Prevadello declined politely, his trousers flapping occasionally as the wind picked up. Ruppert, who was used to the cold, shrugged beneath his coat. A slick black valise stood at his feet like a freshly washed terrier. In it were the alien clearances, the passport, all the papers the diplomatic pouch carried this morning for the new arrival.

If he comes, Ruppert thought; he had seen his share of these schemes go down the tubes at the last minute. His nose began to run. He wiped it and looked at the thin coat the chunky Italian case officer from Washington was wearing. Ruppert sniffed as a thread wafting from Prevadello's coat caught his eye. Good reason to be on contract overseas, Ruppert decided. God knows Marty's cheap but the guy ought to buy a decent coat. He sniffed again.

"How late are they now?" Prevadello had turned, the wind blowing his hair forward over his ears.

"Twenty minutes. It all depends on the Russian customs, you see, Marty. They can do whatever they like."

"So you said. Could you please bring us some coffee from the car?" Prevadello drew his gloves tighter, feeling the cold leak past the seams between his fingers. He moved to the end of the platform and stood alone. His inability to speak German bothered him, should something go wrong. It's been nearly half an hour. If he's gone, he's gone. That's all there is to it. And if he's gone, he's in far hotter water than I'll ever be, Prevadello estimated. The minutes passed, growing to five and then ten.

Prevadello shifted his weight and felt something brush his

cheek. He plucked in the air for a moment and a long thread came away from his shoulder seam. Feel the cold more when you're older, Prevadello thought ruefully; old men wear long johns and I've forgotten mine. Korea: he remembered the GI long johns, the snow drifting like a smoke screen across the tops of the bare hillocks, the groan of cold engines, and the heatless northern sun, cool as ceramic behind the skidding clouds. Prevadello tugged the thread and snapped it free just as Ruppert returned with the coffee.

"Coffee. Phone call just came through at the stationmaster's. Train's over the Austrian frontier. Put anything in it for you, Marty? I've brought schnapps. . . ."

Prevadello took the styrofoam cup and smiled. "No, thanks, Cal. Thanks for the news. Good coffee."

They killed a few more minutes debating the World Series, but the tension soon wore on them both, and they lapsed into silence, listening to the musical Russian babble of the relatives around them. Ruppert walked the platform in straight lines, patroling, scanning the crowd, while Prevadello, a fixture next to an advertisement for Rothman's, stared off into space, much occupied with the same two-headed problem he had faced yesterday and might face tomorrow, if this weren't the train: when and where? He and Kemper had once waited a week in Boston for a Hungarian steamfitter to work himself clear of the hoods on his freighter. *That* had been a wait, but the operation had worked . . . who knew about this one? And there had been a dozen men on that case. Here there was just Ruppert, Ruppert and me.

"There it is, that light there!" called Ruppert.

They all stood and watched the train grow from a pinprick of headlight to a great slow thing, throbbing to a stop at their feet. "There's nine cars on the train," a bright voice said in perfect French over the noise of the idling engines and the singing compressed air, but Prevadello was too busy to mark the speaker. "Cal, watch the gate, please, I'll stick near the first carriage," Prevadello said.

The train stopped and suddenly all along the platform a wild dance whirled; baskets and luggage were levered out of the windows, curious children eyed the Roman letters on advertising hoardings for Agfafilm and the Staatsoper, exasperated husbands and wives ordered and countermanded orders in a half dozen dialects as plump Austrian conductors slipped nimbly through the throng like halfbacks, leading with their briefcases.

Crying relatives embraced as mystified children watched, and the porters were having a field day with the émigrés' crates. Prevadello found a foothold on a lamp stanchion and climbed precariously, a file photo of CATALYST in his hand. By now there was a first-class bottleneck beyond the platform entrance; behind the entrance stood a trio of Viennese police, huddled jealously around their walkie-talkie. At the back of the crowd, the Austrian soldiers who had boarded the train at the frontier were sticking together at the rear of the crowd, their automatic rifles slung over their arms, anticipating their lunch beer.

Prevadello saw him first, wedged between the soldiers and a family of five, a pale round fellow in a cloth cap, fumbling with something in his jacket. A pair of spectacles with thick black frames emerged and were fitted to a face even fatter than the one in the photo Prevadello held in his hand. "Got him," Prevadello called to Ruppert in midair, as he jumped from the lamppost. Ruppert, already towering over the throng, had himself climbed an iron fence railing to see.

This is the train, I can feel it in my bones.

"The envelope, where's Rappaport's envelope?" Prevadello muttered as he trotted along the platform edge. Cops and robbers: he found the envelope and tore it open. Prevadello stopped, scanning the platform to make sure CATALYST was still in view. He shook the envelope's contents into his hand.

"What'll he think of next?" Prevadello wondered, moving toward the crowd of soldiers, the torn paperback cover in his hand. The Russian was shuffling slowly behind the soldiers, his head swiveling nervously, wondering. Prevadello turned and indicated to Ruppert to circle and cover the open end of the platform.

Prevadello waited for the Austrian soldiers to pass and cut behind the Russian, calculating there were ten paces to go between himself and the pillar with the no-smoking symbol. Slipstreaming the Russian, Prevadello held the cover in his fingers, bracing his shoulder. Five four three two *one*: Prevadello hooked one hand around the pillar and lowered his shoulder, neatly pinning the Russian to the pillar and shoving the cover in his face.

"What the hell do you think you're doing?" the levitated man yelled into Prevadello's startled face. "I'm a British citizen! Who in blazes are you?" Prevadello let go of the man's lapels, his mind racing. He did his best Italian apology, pointing weightily at the train. Drained of his ire, the British tourist stood rolling his eyes at the beatifically smiling ex-detective as if he were extraterrestrial.

"Bloody Eyeties," huffed the British tourist as he squeezed into the crowd and just then Prevadello remembered their man had God knows how many languages to his credit. Prevadello cut behind an elderly woman bearing a handmade sign reading "Ostrovski," following the cloth cap into the throng, to be sure.

But not ten steps into Prevadello's pursuit of him, a plump woman in hiking boots and a tartan skirt hailed the cloth-capped man in a broad Lancashire accent; their subsequent greeting suffered from Prevadello's handiwork at the pillar—the British tourist kept an angry eye peeled for his first welcomer despite the embrace. "We got zip, again, Marty," Ruppert was calling. Prevadello waved the British tourist through and made a slicing movement across his throat in case Ruppert got ideas. Behind Ruppert, Prevadello could see the platform was clear again. "Keep an eye on the Austrian cops if they check the train, Cal, O.K.? And see if you can't round up a copy of the passenger manifest."

Ruppert lowered the antenna on his walkie-talkie with a slap of the hand. "Same drill as yesterday, Marty?" Then Ruppert was huddled close to the radio again. "I just caught the embassy transport mobile line on this—" Ruppert shook the radio "—and Farmer, the dispatcher, says Soviet radio traffic out of Bratislava's right off the graph. They're going nuts over there about something, that's for sure." ·

"What about the hoods at the Vienna embassy?"

Ruppert beamed. "A cast of thousands, apparently, like pay-day. You'd think they just got a fresh shipment of tape decks at the PX."

"Well, that's a plus. At least they've got their hands full, too. You make anybody?"

"Two: knew 'em from the mug shots of Soviet embassy staff."

Ruppert's walkie-talkie bawled and he held it to his head. "Sorry. Nobody on the train. My friend the stationmaster must have taken a shine to us yesterday—he's already got the trainman for you to chat with."

"It's a tourist town," Prevadello said, "they're just keeping the customer satisfied." He butted a cold Camel on the platform. "Let's do this indoors. I'm freezing." Charlie Kemper, he thought as Ruppert gathered his men and led the way, thanks for the milk run.

* * *

Ruppert found them an office smelling of wet boots and old cigarettes in the station basement, an office barely bigger than a broom closet, but blessed with an enormous Victorian radiator that tinked and thumped with steam. Prevadello drew the green blind on the door and swung forward in his chair and considered the papers on the desk, a hulk worn dull by years of coffee spoons, the bare wood tinted brown-black with the ink of thousands of newspapers. The trainman was an Austrian, slow-moving and sadly formal, and he leant over his papers on the desk like a Dickensian solicitor, folding the sheets back and forth as he worked his memory.

At last the trainman looked up, his small eyes confused. "Herr Inspektor, there is an irregularity here." His English accent was comic-opera German, with rolled r's and clipped consonants.

"What kind?"

"The Soviets took a woman and her child off on their side, at Bratislava, that we know, Herr Inspektor. But it appears that the count we did on our side of the border was short three, not two."

"What was the name of that additional person?"

The trainman repeated his slow, dignified search through the manifests.

"Rubenshtain. A Soviet Jew. I would say he left the train on the frontier. I cannot understand how this happened, but unfortunately it is true." He formed his features into a mask of painful regret: I shall still be filling in forms about this long after you've gone, his eyes said.

Prevadello waited for a moment, then asked, "This ever happen before?"

"Not ever. No."

Prevadello thanked the melancholy trainman and Ruppert ushered him out, then closed the door. They were alone.

"Figure they've grabbed him?" Ruppert had lowered himself into a folding chair against the wall. He watched Prevadello take off his beret and set it down on the worn desk.

"They grabbed *somebody*." Prevadello sat silent, then ran his fingers through his hair. "Behind the Curtain, O.K. You know he's not going to trust anybody if things go wrong. I'd duck out too if the KGB was having coffee and doughnuts at the border waiting for my train. But," Prevadello said, bemusedly spinning his beret, "he doesn't trust *us*. Unless he's run to somebody else's loving arms, not making this meet, this way, means the game's on his terms." Prevadello kept spinning the

beret, then looked up at Ruppert. "So we do the circuit again."
Prevadello swayed slowly in his chair, mumbling Italian curses.

"I love it when you talk dirty to me." Ruppert said, winking.
He'd heard them all before. "Come on. We'll get him. Besides,
if he doesn't turn up today, I know a Hungarian place on the
Maysedergasse, they do a great goulash. And the desserts . . ."
Ruppert, kissing his fingers, opened the old office door. "If
you're a good boy, we can listen to my stereo afterwards."

"Cal, you missed a fine career in hospitality. Just take me
somewhere where you don't get KGB with your brandy."

"Loosen up. You too can learn to love overseas pay."


The Studentenheim Rudolfinum at Mayerhofgasse 3 was nearly
empty; the place was a jumble of barren hostel rooms, impec-
cably clean, but vacant except for Chertkov and three heavyset
American girls with orange knapsacks who stayed well away
from him when their paths crossed in the echoing stone hall.
The surveyors had dropped him off at three that afternoon, and
Chertkov had slept until five. Over his bunk bed was a small
multilingual sign reading UNLIMITED SHOWERS, and, more irritably, CURFEW 22.00 HR. Below the sign hung a lamp made
of pink plastic that seemed ready to melt as he read his map by
its faint light.

The man at the desk hadn't even asked for his passport: this
was October, the student tourists were long gone, and Chertkov
had American dollars—the man had even told him what a good
rate of exchange he was getting. Chertkov spread his new Falk
map of Vienna out on the rough coverlet. He had bought the
map at the tourist kiosk after the surveyors had left him there; it
took him a few minutes to sort out the map's pleats. Then he
drew the spectacle case Shykofsky had given him from his
pocket.

He opened the case. Slowly, and with great care, he peeled
back the cloth lining of the case and drew out the rice-paper
address list and the torn paperback cover. Chertkov tore the last
of the lining off, and there, pressed into the case's thick card-
board, were three bright yellow thumbtacks.

*Next year in Paris.*
Or tomorrow.

# Chapter Six

"I'm betting on the goulash tonight. I'm betting he's on the train tomorrow," Ruppert said as he slowed the BMW, his big hands holding the map on his lap. It was just past seven and Vienna was unlocking itself for the evening, all the baroque stone surfaces alchemically changing to soft light. "Right on schedule. Not bad for driving on a Friday night, huh?"

"A. J. Foyt, look out." Prevadello opened the BMW's door and walked down the alley. He played his flashlight ahead of him. This dead-drop, the fourth of Rappaport's fall-backs they had checked since two that afternoon, was a lamppost in an alley behind the Raimund Theatre, in the Sixth District, not far from the Westbahnhof. They had worked in concentric circles, moving in from the outskirts of the city as they searched. Prevadello's footfalls chased a small dog from the shadow of the lamppost, a mast shoved into a fragmenting deck of flagstones. He played the beam over the creosoted wood.

Nothing.

He walked back to the car and tapped on the window. Ruppert opened the door and raised his eyebrows. "We keep going," Prevadello said, "we get the whole nickel tour." Ruppert drove fast, heading northeast now, alarmingly fast, passing trucks on the right and committing all manner of offenses. "Love the car, tune it myself, you know. Brake jobs, lube, everything. Want it done right, gotta do it yourself," he said as they sped down the Mariahilferstrasse.

"What's next?" Prevadello asked, involuntarily bracing himself with his feet.

"That tram-stop shelter just this side of the Ring, for the

forty-eight-A car. I got out of the shower this morning, thinking about it: notice a pattern forming?''

Prevadello didn't dare take his eyes off a tram car Ruppert came perilously close to sideswiping. "No. Enlighten me.''

"All the dead-drops are near theaters. Funny, huh? This next one's near the Volkstheatre. Figure it's deliberate?''

Prevadello said he didn't know and then asked Ruppert if he'd ever had an accident.

"Rolled an Alfa once," he said matter-of-factly as he slowed. "There. That's the one." The BMW's hood bobbed and trembled for a moment after the car stopped, but Ruppert paid no attention to the results of his breathtaking stop. "Should be at the far end of the bench, remember?'' He was studying Kemper's copy of the ring game.

"Should be," Prevadello said and stepped onto the sidewalk. This quarter was dominated by the backsides of the Hapsburg buildings sitting monumentally astride the Ring. Ruppert was right—Prevadello could see the Volkstheatre to his right, diagonally across the Museumstrasse. Rappaport must know every inch of this patch, Prevadello thought, it's all real estate, as he stepped inside the shelter.

The bench in the tram-stop shelter was crowded with couples and kids in nervous, chatty groups and the quiet clusters of little old women who seemed to populate most of the city. Prevadello moved through the crush to the far end of the hoarding, a handful of change in his hand. He turned to face the wall and dropped five or six coins at his feet.

One or two people called out and pointed out the path of the rolling change; one elderly gentleman wearing a Tyrolean hat even stood up from the bench to help. And next to the gentleman's newspaper, shining bright as the day they were made, was a neat line of yellow thumbtacks.

*Hark the herald angels sing . . .*

Prevadello straightened and followed the old gentleman's cane to the schilling next to the arty-looking girl with the Künstlerhaus shopping bag. Within minutes, after much shuffling and bowing, Prevadello actually got all his coins back, thanked everyone profusely in pidgin German, and was rewarded with a tram sheltersful of restrained non-response, the Viennese reflex with the foreign. The tram came, and Prevadello made a show of examining the route map while his guardians boarded, their ways home brightened by the silly *Auslander* who could not hang on to his money.

Prevadello walked back to the car on air: the goddam thing was going to work, the Russian *had* made it out. Thank God, thank Calvin, Jr., thank Geraghty's mad Irish luck, thank *me*. Ruppert flung the door open and blew him a mocking kiss. "You look fat. Guess we got word, huh?"

"Touchdown," yelled Prevadello, pounding Ruppert's arm.

"Teach you to have a little faith in your fellow man," Ruppert whooped as he turned the key. "What were they?"

"What were what?"

"The tacks, genius, the tacks, how were they set?"

"In a line. Three in a row."

Ruppert was heading north now, to the embassy, the BMW's gearbox threshing away as he downshifted. "Unless my memory fails me, you've got a meet on the Graben," he said, passing Prevadello the ring-game key.

Prevadello nodded, thinking; the Graben was the central pedestrian mall. He was already working out the problems. "Going to take in some shopping while you're at it, huh?" Ruppert offered. "One of the embassy guys got this leather coat at this shop on the Graben, knock your eyes out. Two hundred U.S. Damn cheap, considering the exchange," he added encouragingly.

"No, thank you," Prevadello said, rereading the key. "Have to consider my pension. Let's have that dinner. My treat."

Ruppert began to laugh, then stopped and looked over at the unlaughing Prevadello; he drove the rest of the way to the Hungarian restaurant wondering about the strange turns of Marty Prevadello's mind.

Prevadello peered at the luminous face of his watch: five minutes past ten. He sat in an aisle seat, an *International Herald Tribune* folded in a triangle on his lap in the back row of a tiny cinema two flights up from a garishly lit marquee. Perhaps forty paying customers, most of them kids, were watching a badly dubbed version of *The Lavender Hill Mob*, giggling at the quixotic thieves. Ruppert had left his seat twenty minutes ago to engineer the meet, holstered and hatted, the tools of his trade stored, improbably, in a battered old leather book bag, the kind with the leather flap and three slots for the metal hasp; Ruppert's bore his initials.

There was a car chase on the screen and the kids were shrieking when Prevadello left. At the top of the creaking stairs, the sullen usher hadn't moved since taking their tickets, except now a girl had joined him, a pallid creature with dyed hair sitting athwart his legs; she stuck out her tongue at Prevadello as he passed.

In the plaza across from the cinema, Prevadello walked behind a kiosk plastered with handbills and theater posters, the newspaper beneath his left arm, counting down the remaining minutes, blindly looking at the menu in the restaurant window above which hung the buzzing neon EUROPA-GRILL. Inside, the waiters were at the bar, gossiping and comparing tips, while their tables stood half-empty.

The clock over the grill's bar said ten-eleven.

Just like him to read a menu at a time like this—he's cool, I'll give him that, Ruppert thought, watching Prevadello from his café table, drinking his second coffee. Ruppert had been surprised to see the change in Prevadello, the long silences where once he had wisecracked, the new ways he fidgeted with that beret of his all the time. He'd cut back on the smoking, that was a good thing, but he looked like he needed a long spell in the sun someplace. Or a woman: God knows, he could have had his pick ten years ago. Maybe it's his clothes . . . for a detective, a well-dressed breed, Prevadello dressed like the kind of office drone you find in the back of a skin magazine shop. Talk about square; but you couldn't blame the clothes if the guy inside just wasn't interested. I know I'd go crazy without Carol, but to each his own, I guess.

Ruppert looked through the café window down the Graben, wondering why there were so many philatelist's shops in Vienna but you couldn't even buy a Mars bar after dark in this capital of chocolate. I'm not complaining, he noted to himself, for me, it's a fit, Vienna, what with Carol, the flat, my stereo. Prevadello hates the place, you could see it in the way he's always on edge, but that's because of Moravec. That's his problem, Ruppert decided, Marty's a perfectionist, that's why the women steer clear; he won't forgive himself his own mistakes. What might have been an attractive intensity when Prevadello was younger was becoming . . . what? Becoming small, Ruppert concluded, and small wasn't a word he'd ever have used in the same sentence as Marty Prevadello. The guy needs a change.

Ruppert dropped a tip under his coffee saucer and picked up his old book bag; he could feel his radio slide about among his odds and ends of homemade wiretapping gear, his favorite Rolleiflex camera, first-aid kit, and that book on clouds Carol had bought him. He had stared at the sky long enough in a career spent waiting—might as well learn something. Besides, Ruppert was a practical man, and weather in his world was something one anticipated. That was the answer to staying sane in this business, he concluded, anticipating. He moved into his position, the tree next to the cab rank, thirty feet from the meet; they knew there was a second entrance from their trek here after dinner, which was bad news if the KGB felt like dropping in but there was nothing to be done—you just had to figure the Russian knew what he was doing. Here we go, he thought, as Prevadello, still checking the shop windows, paused before closing in. Ruppert did a slow circle around the tree, calculating: a couple in a Volkswagen, arguing; four kids, doing nothing in particular; and two old men, deep in conversation, and Ruppert caught the word Goethe. He completed his circuit and saw Prevadello idly doing the same drill. Say what you like, Ruppert thought, he's got the goods, that one. Prevadello moved into the reach of the street light at the head of the stairs and turned his newspaper over. *Going downstairs.* Ruppert, his earphone jacked into the radio in the book bag, put his bag down and settled in to wait, his Rollei, primed and loaded, on its strap beneath his coat.

Prevadello moved several steps along the sidewalk, stepping over a line of chain demarking the sidewalk from the stairs, then into the harsh light of the stairwell and squinted to check his back.

Clean.

He went down the stone stairs, his eyes still slightly dazzled by the overhead light. A bus went by, very close, and Prevadello shut his eyes for a moment and then he could see again. He stood in the eerily beautiful stairwell of the underground public lavatory.

And to his right, half-hidden behind a heavily shuttered iron-grille service door, the round fellow with the heavy spectacles was turning a copy of *Paris-Match* over and over in his hands. Above them, the entrance-chain swung between two ornate pillars, its links still rattling from the brush with Prevadello's coat.

Stepping down the last stair, the bespectacled man pressed the magazine between the buttons of Prevadello's coat, and then, with a snap of his hand, indicated the door at the bottom of the stairs. Prevadello backed down the two stairs; it wasn't much of a precaution if somebody really wanted to jump him, but at least he was going to see it coming.

"We were expecting you at Frankfurt," Prevadello said,

keeping his back to the wall. "It's good to see you here, Nikolai."

Chertkov said nothing for a moment, then inclined his head
to the door. "Frankfurt," he said in a well-modulated voice, an
actor's voice, professionally calm. "Maybe KGB expects me
there, too?"

Prevadello stopped. "Nikolai, we haven't much time. If I
have to move you, I want to know enough to protect myself,
understand?"

Chertkov was chewing on the backs on his knuckles on his
free hand, keeping the magazine between Prevadello's coat buttons. "Move? We will move inside, please. I wish to wash. We
will talk there." He opened the door and gestured Prevadello
inside.

The public lavatory looked recently restored and was surprisingly elegant, with marble sink tops, burnished wood doors,
and copper fittings. An elderly night attendant sat like a gnome
on a toadstool, reading a tout-sheet. In the corner, two boys
were pulling records in and out of shopping bags and arguing
about jazz, their German studded with " 'Giant Steps' " . . .
" 'Giant Steps.' "

Chertkov walked over to the sink and lay his half of the Hoyle
paperback cover on the counter and turned the torn edge toward
Prevadello, who dovetailed his to the zigzag tear.

"Good," Chertkov said. "Professional." He rolled up his
sleeves and opened the art deco taps. "Pay the man, please. It's
twenty schillings."

If only you knew, Prevadello thought. He crossed the floor
and dropped a hundred-schilling note in the tray and asked the
attendant, "Speak English?"

The old man looked at the bank note and tapped his ear; his
hearing aid fell into his palm and he philosophically pocketed
it. Prevadello took a pair of towels and declined the change.
Before he spoke again, he waited for the two boys to leave,
continuing their argument about John Coltrane as they pounded
upstairs into the night.

Tossing the towels onto the counter, Prevadello sat on the
sink edge and lit a Camel, then the separate parts of the paperback cover, making sure they were consumed. Prevadello
opened the taps and rinsed the sink.

Chertkov moved his back against the sink, resting there. Prevadello did not move. Chertkov plucked at his hair, running his

tongue around his lips like a cat, frowning as he worked out the vocabulary.

"What is your name, please?"

"Silvestri." Prevadello did not offer his hand, for Chertkov had the knife within reach. "You are Nikolai Chertkov."

"I am. You are from Paris." He didn't pronounce the "s," and the Russian had phrased the sentence as more of a statement than a question.

That crazy electric feeling bumped up Prevadello's spine. He hesitated. "No. I am from New York."

"I was expecting someone from Paris."

"Why?"

"Take me to the French Alps and I'll show you." Chertkov continued washing.

"Why? What's there?"

Chertkov stopped and looked at Prevadello's reflection in the mirror. "Can you arrange this? Have you the authority?"

Prevadello said he did.

"Then I tell you what you need to know. If not, I am a dead man, understand?"

Prevadello nodded and waited.

Chertkov was washing his underarms and back now, slowly and thoroughly, as he spoke. "I have insurance." He turned his trouser pocket inside out and produced a torn square of map, the place names in Cyrillic. "Southeast France, near the border of Switzerland. Get me there and you will have answers. Interesting answers. That's all. You know and I know I am no good to you dead. Things have happened in Vienna before. KGB has very long arms. That is our agreement, you see. First I get my insurance. And then you will have a live Chertkov." Chertkov returned to his ablutions.

In the mirror Prevadello watched the soapy water run down Chertkov's hard Buddha's belly; tufts of hair sat on Chertkov's shoulder blades like abrasive pads. "What's the insurance?"

There was no answer while Chertkov patiently dried himself, using both towels. He tucked a chubby hand into his pants pocket, toying with a cache of coins. "I have used my brain, I have thought things out . . . I know what I will find saves me. Believe me, I know this."

Prevadello let the words hang, his gaze never leaving Chertkov's face. "Why trust me to take you there?"

"It's not a matter of trust, Mister Silvestri. You have no choice." Chertkov gave a magnificent shrug. He stood away from the sink, stroking his belly unself-consciously. "Silvestri, you are a professional. Improvise."

Prevadello, watching the elderly attendant mark off his bets on the tout-sheet, worked out his own stakes. Chertkov had not only sprung the case wide open, but had rewritten the rules. The bet's simple enough, Prevadello thought: trust my guys and I can't trust the Russian. Trust Rappaport and Charlie Kemper? Interesting notion. What got me here? A milk run that was never a milk run: so we go solo. Together, me and Ivan here.

The very flavor of the paradox attracted Prevadello's anarchic streak. For once to be the pursued rather than pursuer, to turn his tepid world—and Kemper's and, most blessedly, Rappaport's too—quite perversely on its head: it was irresistible.

Prevadello reached for the radio inside his coat. "Ruppert," he said.

"Yessir."

"Stand down. It's over."

"Good to hear it. Everything O.K.?"

"Yes, but we stay outside, O.K.?"

"How's the parcel?"

"Our friend is alive and kicking and very, very clean." Prevadello gave Chertkov what he hoped was a winning smile. "Let's call it a night. I'll need a clean flight to Geneva tomorrow. I'm going to France for a day or two," Prevadello said. "Trust me. Marty's caught a live one."

"Got just the place for a good night's sleep." Ten minutes later, in Ruppert's BMW, Prevadello saw the snow start again, the clouds of flakes billowing like midsummer laundry. They were on the autobahn now, driving flat out, out of downtown Vienna, past the gray geometric housing districts of the Gürtel, the car thrumming over the glazed concrete toward Ruppert's favorite safe hotel. Chertkov was already asleep. Why not? Prevadello dropped his chin to his chest and began to nap, the amber highway lights growing and receding like uncertain sunrises through his closed eyelids.

The hotel was nondescript, an anonymous brick three-story where nothing matched, its walls and winding corridors seemingly papered from a sample book, the rooms furnished with cast-offs Prevadello remembered from the downtown YMCA in Queens: rachitic beds bowed like hammocks, big chunky chairs with slabs of sour foam for cushions. You couldn't even call it a seasonal place—spring, summer, winter, or fall, the grandly named Hotel Franz-Josef was as changeless as its curt proprietress, Fraulein Menzel, a bony spinster Prevadello imagined had been born there, spurned her only suitor there, and would die there. But Ruppert knew both the hotel, its approaches, and its phone lines inside out and the only other clients were a quintet of German pensioners who bickered as they watched a minuscule television, drinking peppermint schnapps.

Ruppert babysat Chertkov in Prevadello's room, dinner being a bottle of vodka, black bread, and a tray of cold meats he had bought at a delicatessen; Prevadello used the telephone in Ruppert's room—Ruppert, having performed his mysterious craft, pronounced the line clean—and returned to a vain conversation with Chertkov. Prevadello cradled the receiver against his shoulder and read the business card: "IMPACT COMMUNICATIONS Overseas Telecommunications For the Professional Traveller"; Prevadello flexed the card while he waited, absently testing the paper stock. He counted the rings and on the seventh pressed the disconnect arm, released it sharply, and began to dial the WAVE exchange with the line still open. The wrong number tape came and went and then the WAVE operator answered, her voice calm as codeine. "Good evening. Your client number, please."

Prevadello gave the number belonging to his old workname and waited. In the background a speaking clock said something in German in its synthetic voice. "Number, please."

"What's the local time in Washington, D.C.?"

A second to look up at the bank of wall clocks—Prevadello had visited the Bonn WAVE exchange once with Kemper on a walking tour—and then the operator replied, "Seventeen thirty-six Eastern Standard, sir." Prevadello tipped the card toward the bedside lamp and read the number slowly. Prevadello nearly said something else to be kind, but the electronic breeze rose to a gale in his ear and then the line was open and ringing. The operator at the other end must have cut in too early, because suddenly Kemper himself was there ". . . to the south. Hold, will you, Ed, I've got somebody on the overseas line. Hello?"

"Lou Silvestri, Columbia Importing here," Prevadello said. "We finally have some news on that part you wanted, for the European project."

"Hang on, this pen's died." In the background Prevadello could hear a girl saying, "A slightly darker blue" and imagined Kemper was having his carpets re-done and then a chattering telex drowned her out.

"Sorry about the delay, sir," Prevadello added. "You know what these shippers are like if the forms aren't filled out right."

"Understand. O.K., shoot."

"We've traced the part in Vienna just fine, sir, the one you were looking for. Got it right here in the office, safe and sound." Prevadello waited: *say the word, take him off my hands, bring us in.*

"You have the part," Kemper said. "Part confirmed. What are your plans?"

"Correct, sir, we have the part." What are *my* plans? Prevadello hesitated, switching the phone from one hand to another. "What we're thinking of, sir, requires we transship the part via Geneva, with a layover in France for a day or two. That a problem for you?"

"Hold, please, I have three lines going." There was a crackly silence for fifteen seconds, then Kemper said, "Do what you have to do. You know your business. Anything else?"

*He wants us to run.* "I didn't catch that, sir," Prevadello began again, "would you repeat?"

"Transshipment via Geneva and France is approved," Kemper said flatly, "repeat, approved."

"Vienna-Geneva-France approved," Prevadello said slowly. "I'll call to confirm transshipment."

And then the WAVE exchange blipped once and receded into a dial tone.

"A milk run. *Bastardo.*" Prevadello flung the phone down and rapped on the thin lath-and-plaster wall between the two rooms. Next door a bed squeaked and Prevadello heard Ruppert trying out his novice Russian as he reassured Chertkov, and then a rude silence.

There was a knock at Prevadello's door. Ruppert had his holster on, its flap open. "What'd Kemper say?"

"He didn't ask one damn question." Prevadello ran his fingers irritably through his hair. "Not one. What the hell's Charlie running, a charter service? I'm ready to strangle him. He's okayed France."

"Down, boy, easy—it's no big deal. We take Nikolai for a little sightseeing, he does his thing under our watchful eye, then we pack him off. Piece of cake. I take it you don't feel so great about it?"

"What's done's done. I'll do my bitching stateside." Prevadello began to take his thick shoes off. "How's he doing?" Prevadello asked quietly; Ruppert had left the door ajar.

"Nothing wrong with his appetite, that's for damn sure. He's whistled through all the cold cuts and most of the bread. And pretty damn calm."

"Drinking much?"

"Five or six shots. Hasn't exactly freed his tongue. I did my best 'how to win friends and influence people' number and didn't get a peep out of him. And watch your smokes. He's already finished the pack I bought after dinner. What's the plan for tonight?"

"All three of us in the big room. You mind the floor, Cal? I'd like you on watch there."

"Best doorstop you ever had," Ruppert replied cheerfully. Then, after a beat, "What's up come morning?"

"Tomorrow we split up. I want you here, doing your man-about-town number, decoying for me. I'll take Nikolai alone. We still clean?"

"I'm going to take a stroll around the block. You try your luck with Nilokai, see if you can open him up." Ruppert handed Prevadello his 9 mm Luger from his shoulder holster. "Back in fifteen."

Prevadello nodded and went to the door of his room. The Russian had his feet on the coffee table, the vodka bottle close by in an ice bucket. The light from the television tinted Chertkov and the crazy-quilt walls an acetylene blue; he was watching a soccer match and someone had just scored. Chertkov looked at Prevadello briefly, then returned to the goal celebrations. "In the West, do they always kiss after goals?" he asked incredulously.

"We're going to France tomorrow."

Chertkov turned from the television, then hoisted his vodka bottle. "Now you're talking," he said in word-perfect fifties American. "Vodka? In my experience, vodka settles a traveler's stomach. Have you a cigarette?"

"I'll have a shot." Prevadello made the mistake of offering his Camels and Chertkov took the whole pack, lighting up immediately. "These are very good. Are we flying to France?" he asked as he poured.

"Yes. I've arranged a private plane. We're not going near the big airlines."

Chertkov, impressed, slid the glass of vodka toward Prevadello. He inhales like a jet engine, Prevadello thought—he's a mess of nerves inside, despite his exterior. "A private plane, that is very wise of you," Chertkov said. "You know, you expected me in Frankfurt. I expected you to be French."

"And I expected you to talk."

"Precisely." The Russian's eyes were fixed on the television. For several long minutes he said nothing. Then, chain-lighting his second Camel, he looked directly at Prevadello. "I have been very, very lucky so far. I will not test my luck by talking to anyone before I get my insurance. Tomorrow we will see."

An hour later, as Chertkov snored and Ruppert's long, restless legs thumped against the door panel, Prevadello lay awake, listening to the traffic in the distance. Tomorrow, he thought as he stared at the plaster ceiling medallion, tomorrow will decide who we are, each of us, down to the bone.

# Chapter Seven

Ruppert had seen them off, safe and warm in the confines of a hangar at Schwechat airport secluded behind a row of NATO fighters. The hangar, crowded with a grab-bag of aircraft in various stages of demolition, was typically Ruppertian: tools all over the place, seemingly no one knew exactly what was going on, four or five different languages might get one what one wanted—or might not, but after a half-hour's delay, it all worked beautifully. Ruppert himself sealed the four-seater Beechcraft's doors and crossed his fingers as the aircraft taxied away. That had been three that afternoon. Since then, the flight from Vienna to Geneva had been notable, from Prevadello's point of view, for the grave silence of both Chertkov and the dour pilot, and the Saturday evening sun splintering on the ice fields crowning the wedding-cake mountains.

Hannibal had told his troops these mountains do not touch the sky. Prevadello didn't much care precisely how high the massive peaks were; the measurement that turned his stomach was the stone's-throw between the chartered Beechcraft's belly and the grasping trees and rock outcrops below. So this is where I cash my check, he thought, in one of these mist-filled valleys so rugged the Swiss Army absolves the region from its annual maneuvers: no enemy had contested this terrain since the Carthaginians. The little aircraft was doglegging up the alpine passes on the Swiss-French frontier, its shadows blending with the Saturday dusk on the granite mountainsides, its prop wash beating down the tops of the trees in its path: they had filed no flight plan at Geneva airport and the pilot, a close-mouthed New Hampshireman named Albee who had flown in the Berlin Airlift, appeared to have a pathological hatred of radar. Prevadello found the apparent speed hair-raising; he couldn't see individual trees in the twilight, just a phosphorescent blur too fast to focus on. He eyed the navigation lights on the wing-tips—they seemed to be *below* some of the tree tops. Prevadello made himself concentrate elsewhere.

Albee had spoken once, while the Beechcraft dipped and bounced in the eye of a small but fierce snowstorm not ten minutes after takeoff. "Hell of a party you got here." There was no "sir"; Prevadello pegged Albee as the kind of man who did things by the book and chauffeuring a spook and a runaway Russian was not his idea of by the book.

"Keeps life interesting," Prevadello had replied, gripping his armrest. Those ten words had been the extent of the conversation since boarding the Beechcraft. Chertkov had slept peacefully since the Geneva flare path disappeared beneath the wing-tip at six that evening, his head nestled in a blanket against the Plexiglas window panel; Prevadello marked him up a notch in his estimation. As they flew over the River Rhone, Prevadello, starved for conversation, had tried to engage Albee by pointing at the gleaming water, but Albee eloquently flipped his silent headphones over his ears.

That was twenty minutes ago. Albee swung the flex of his map light out of his way and headed the nose of the aircraft to the southwest for his run-up. The Beechcraft began to climb to a less disturbing altitude. "Where are we landing?" Prevadello asked.

"Wouldn't call her a landing. Ain't even going to get the tires warm. I'm outta there." Albee tapped his pipe into the ashtray. "There's a civilian airport at Aix-les-Bains, the place with the mineral baths on Lac du Bourget. Ruppert's arranged for the car at the field and finessed customs for you." Albee's tone said, "And the best of luck." Below, the lights of the lake-side town glimmered through thin silky clouds.

Chertkov shuffled his shoulders deeper into the cheerless little Renault, the only car the Aix rental office had left after hours. A bored mechanic had filled in the forms and fitted a set of snow chains to the rear tires—there was a blizzard in the offing, the forecasts said. Then he handed Prevadello the keys and slipped gratefully back to doze at his desk.

As Prevadello, his car seat rocking on loose mounts, drove the first few kilometers from the airport, Chertkov was preparing a preamble, a statement of belief, a moral timber to prop

the shaky house of second thoughts he had lived in daily . . .
for how long? A broken sentence rose in blebs on his cheeks
and then faded. Truth, Prevadello urged silently, give me the
truth. He offered Chertkov another chance at the vodka but was
rebuffed with a grunt. But then, abruptly, Chertkov was off and
running, talking to his reflection in the window glass, searching
the Alps, to break the claustrophobia of the whinging little car.

"We are all double agents in Soviet Union, just to survive."
Chertkov shot a spark of tobacco out the window and looked
back in the wing mirror at the tumbling ashes; he's a child, a
peasant child, Prevadello judged. Chertkov continued, "You
don't believe me. I tell you: my family's apartment in Brusilov
was a good place. When I was seventeen, Stalin purged the Red
Army. The streets at night were alive with the NKVD trucks,
State Security men coming and going. In our building, there
were many Red Army officers and their families. Things got so
bad the Red Army men asked the building committee to close
the stairs between midnight and six. The officers couldn't sleep,
thinking the boots were coming for them, waiting for the noise
to stop at their floor." Chertkov blinked at the memory. "They
shot a friend of my father's."

Chertkov's earlier coolness had vanished. You could break so
easily, Prevadello thought; you could shatter. Decompression,
the psychologists used to call it at the Police Academy lectures,
a fancy name for shock, and Chertkov had the symptoms: seepy
eyes, compulsive smoking, the grasshopper leaps of logic. The
Russian blew smoke out the vent window as they passed a single
truck struggling up the slow lane, groaning against the pitch of
the incline. Prevadello let him chatter on. At this point, any
voice but his own was a small relief.

"I like Sinatra," Chertkov said feelingly. "I think often of
what he stands for, his philosophy. He is a master of melancholy,
like Cyrano, you know? I've always made a mess of love. I
should have been born French. Russian women do not appreciate me, they think I'm a philistine from Kiev. I'm really very
cultivated. And very melancholy, because of my romanticism.
Distant. So I love, which lifts one for a while. Then I lose.
'Guess I'll Hang My Tears Out to Dry,' do you know that one?
It's all there.

"Romantic, maybe more romantic than a woman, spying is.
On the edge, do you see? Like falling in love all the time. The
trust, the betrayal. The danger. All the great spies are more
addicted to that than to ideology. Being a double agent is like

being in love with yourself twice, do you see? You love your real self and your secret self. Twice.''

Chertkov wrapped the blanket around his shins; the little car was drafty and they were still climbing. "My wife was not getting any younger. No children. She began to bore me, but her family has the connections, the apartment, the clothes. So I did not dare divorce her. I had an affair with a girl from Georgia, very lithe, a gymnastics student at the university, but she went back to Tblisi when spring came. I could never visit her, and she could never visit me. I was very unhappy.''

Prevadello said he was sure he was. Chertkov sighed and continued. "I was very unhappy." There followed a long silence. Chertkov drank for a minute and stared outside at the dark trees, their tops burnished with the feeble moonlight. Prevadello knew silence's multiplying effect on some subjects—the longer the interrogator waits, the greater the urge to fill the silence. The notion that time can be conquered by stuffing space is an almost irresistible temptation once a certain point is reached; the dam breaches as a matter of course. Conscious of having baited Chertkov's talkativeness with a measure of peace, Prevadello waited.

Chertkov motioned for the vodka. Steadying the wheel, Prevadello reached under his seat and handed Chertkov the bottle. They were climbing almost continually now, the lights of the oncoming traffic growing and exploding like photo-flashes as the cars rocketed downhill. Prevadello had the wipers going, flicking away at the flakes like spider legs.

Chertkov took a swig, saying, "Here's to our voyage of discovery." Chertkov began again, the bottle in his lap like a stray cat, jumping his hands about in short, forceful gestures, like a chef disjointing meat. "The Russians talk and drink to do nothing," he said randomly. "We Russians must learn to be like the Americans, and learn to listen as we run, or we will never amount to anything. Silvestri," he said thoughtfully, "I will tell you a story, a short one. New Year's, 1970. I was at a party with my old friend Domichev, drinking a bottle of vodka just like this one—we went through GRU school at the Center together, we're good friends. Domichev is even drunker than me, and a bragging man. He's a mathematical type, he's just been transferred to ciphers and codes at Moscow Center, where he's seen some fabulous material from the West. I flattered him, I wanted to hear more. 'Ah, Peter Vladimirovitch, you are a great cipher officer,' I said, 'have some more of our vodka with me! Go on, tell me about this miraculous source of yours!' And he does. But he had not heard much, only two things: once in a while, this source needs cash—and Center does not even blink. Off it goes. And there is one other thing Domichev says: there is something French in his background, something happened to him in France. In France . . .'' Chertkov's voice faded, then drawled into nothing.

"What about France?"

"Later. Not now. Now I need some sleep." Prevadello might have been in Manhattan for all it mattered to Chertkov; the Russian did not budge. Still resolutely in control, his eyes had fallen shut behind his spectacles, the burned-out Camel in his cupped palm, like incense. And so they drove for the next hundred kilometers, the only sound the beat of the tires on the autoroute.

And when Chertkov's handed over to the head office boys, Prevadello bet himself as he drove, it's a family reunion; they'll all be lining up for the photo, hugs and kisses, Prevadello thought wryly—drinks with Rappaport and backscratches all round. He thought of Kemper, too, and imagined his old partner secretly standing on tiptoe when the flash bulb went off.

They had stopped on a bridge; below them, a mountain creek ran blindly in the dark. Chertkov had spread Ruppert's map on the seat and was pointing to a small cross two kilometers down the road. "Abbey," Chertkov said, digging his fingernail into the cross. "That is the place." He waved south and Prevadello slipped the Renault into gear. The headlights picked out individual trees, but behind the front rank of spruce, the forest ran unbroken to the western skyline. Below them, to the east, its surface a pale photocopy of the surrounding hills, lay the shining lake.

"Yes, yes, I remember this now," Chertkov said fervently. "Here. Stop here." As the Renault bumped to a halt, Chertkov swung his door open and stood on the door jamb, staring up the mountain road into the trees. Then he strode off into the snow a few paces, his hands on his hips, Ruppert's borrowed coat hanging off him like a tarpaulin. He was talking to himself in Russian, pointing and miming uphill and down as he muttered.

Chertkov came back to the car, his face pursed around an unhappy mouth. "A few more minutes, please. It was summer the last time, and the snow changes things. A few minutes," he repeated, scanning the horizon. "I haven't seen it yet."

"Seen what?"

"It is in my memory," Chertkov said calmly. "We are very close." The Russian walked to the front fender of the car; ahead, the monastery looked down on them, its shadowed façade pocked with soft yellow niches of light the color of the slim moon above.

"I remember now," Chertkov shouted. "We are absolutely right! Drive," he ordered, dropping into his seat. "Slowly, please. I must think." Prevadello had the Renault in second gear for traction and for a moment he thought he had stalled the feeble engine. But the car sprang forward as Chertkov called out, "Left" urgently and then they were climbing a paved path no wider than a cart-track. Along the beams, Prevadello could see dark wooden grottoes among the trees: the Stations of the Cross, he calculated—we're on the grounds.

"There!" Chertkov had lowered his window and was pointing to the brush. "Stop! Stop now!" Prevadello reached across and held Chertkov's bicep or he might have leapt bodily through the window. "Nikolai, wait for me." It was bitingly cold for October, an Alpine cold that mentholated the lungs. Prevadello switched on his government-issue torch. A depression in the carpet of snow to their right twisted behind a stand of firs, disappearing into the headwall of a ravine.

"There!" Chertkov led the way at a half-run along the path, with Prevadello bringing up the rear, his torch casting enormous shadows against the snow. There was no slowing Chertkov. Prevadello followed, the oversize coat Ruppert had lent him rustling like bat's wings, playing his flashlight on Chertkov's leaping back. They were circling the ravine, sliding down the path like skiers where the ground pitched down, their arms flung out like scarecrows'. Whooping in Russian, Chertkov ran around a haystack of drifted snow and Prevadello nearly fell over the rim of the ravine as he skipped over a small culvert to keep up. The haystack was a grotto sheltering a statue of the Virgin, snow-shawled with a lace of flakes and glowing whitely in the reflected torchlight, guarding the cemetery gate.

Then they began to climb.

They climbed past the gate and up the cemetery path, past snow-crowned graves like the keels of upturned boats, sometimes knee-deep in snow, halting a few short feet from the abbey walls. Prevadello saw Chertkov drop to his knees and for a paralyzing moment thought he had a madman on his hands, but Chertkov was clawing at a door latch, his breath whistling in clouds of condensation caught by Prevadello's flashlight before they dissolved. There was a rattle of iron and the gasp of rotting wood giving way and then the door sagged into the snow.

"Hell, you didn't have to tear it off the hinges," Prevadello whispered.

Chertkov's voice was sharp with excitement. "Now. Bring the light."

Inside the shed, Chertkov jumped atop a workbench and gestured impatiently for the flashlight. Prevadello handed it to him, willing his ears to hear the first sound of the monks coming to investigate. But there was nothing.

Chertkov played the light and tested the soft wood with a trowel, muttering in Russian. With an exultant shriek, he pulled a round shape from the crumbling wood in the elbow of a pair of beams deep in the eaves and clutched it to his chest. Chertkov's eyes shone as he motioned for Prevadello to step closer with the torch. In one hand Chertkov held a milled metal canister, pewtery in the light of the torch. He began to unscrew the canister.

Prevadello heard the slam of a car door.

Below. At the intersection.

Looking out the shed's side window, Prevadello put Ruppert's binoculars to his eyes, kicking himself for not demanding infrared night glasses.

French police? The KGB? Or even Rappaport's hoods, hunting renegades? They were professionals: two men, maybe a third, arrayed themselves against the rim of the snowbank. One of them had a telescopic sight. His mind capsized: there's but one way out and they're sitting on it.

Why haven't they shot yet? "They'll only shoot to kill," Prevadello muttered, answering himself. "Give me that canister, Nikolai, we've got company."

"KGB?" Chertkov was screwing the canister lid back into place, his face drawn open in panic.

"How the hell should I know?" Prevadello wedged the flashlight in the fork in a tree and aimed the beam downhill. "Come on, hand it over."

"No! This is my insurance, my . . ."

Prevadello pushed Chertkov backward into the snow and put a boot on his chest, his old rubber-band-wrapped .32 Colt in his hand as he spoke. "I'm not kidding around, Nikolai. Let's go."

Chertkov gave him the container.

"I don't know how this worked, Nikolai. If you set me up

for a burn, I'll scramble your eggs for you. Now, move. We circle uphill.''

Below them, a pair of headlights came to life and panned across the trees, bobbing like Japanese lanterns. *Oh my God,* Prevadello thought as he flailed through the scrub along the ravine's lip, waiting for the first buzz of the silenced bullet, *I've hit the jackpot.* The light went out. O.K., so they've figured out the flashlight gambit, genius, now what? Prevadello asked himself.

Then he and Chertkov were at the roadside, throwing open the Renault's doors, Prevadello at the driver's door, listening.

Nothing yet: they'll be screwing on the silencers and taking off the safeties. Prevadello forced himself to think: advantages first. One: we've got altitude. Two: we've seen them—they haven't seen us, or they'd have shot by now. Three: the trees'll give us some cover. Disadvantages . . . he opened the Renault's door. He'd weigh those afterwards. If there was an afterwards.

Thank God and all his angels: the Renault turned over instantly and he had the car in gear and climbing. In the rearview mirror, Prevadello, driving in the dark, imagined he saw a shape settling into the snow at the square in the center of the intersection, a trapezoid of black amid the gray-white. Marksman or monk, whatever it was, the shape seemed a long way off and then was gone as the car reached the crest of the mountain, squarely facing the side of the chapter house.

A line of chimney pots atop the monastery appeared to spring like a conjurer's trick from the profile of a single stack, as if someone had pulled a row of children's cutouts along the roof top; Prevadello was getting a lesson in baroque perspective as he swung the protesting Renault around the circular drive. There was a carriage house to the left and several heads appeared in its ornate window frames. Prevadello saw the gate at the far end of the drive, its wrought-iron work filigreed with snow, a single gas-lamp burning overhead. The monastery was the only light for miles—Prevadello could see the lights of Chatillon winking across the lake through the thermals to the north. He downshifted as the drive split around an island of naked birch, sending gravel raining. Prevadello would worry about maps later; he fixed the lake, knowing that way lay east.

Charlie Kemper, you sold me a milk run, you bastard, and set Moscow Center on my backside instead, Prevadello muttered to himself. In the passenger seat, Chertkov was shivering, open-mouthed, his hands braced against the dashboard. Prevadello pushed the accelerator to the floor, relying on his memory and the thin rind of moonlight to guide the little car downhill.

Down, down they went, straight for the Peugeot, the Renault's rear end drifting free for a mad moment when Prevadello overbraked badly. He dropped the unhappy gearbox into neutral and let the car head straight down the tracks he'd cut on the way up. Six feet of clearance, Lord, he said to himself, that's all I need. That and a . . .

One more rise.

Over the top . . . as Prevadello let the clutch in, just enough gas . . . the men outlined in the moonlight below seemed to hesitate for a second and then dropped to the snow. There must have been someone in the Peugeot, because its lights came on and the Renault was caught full in beams.

Prevadello was dazzled but at the very edge of his peripheral vision he saw the dark track of trampled snow. He spun the steering wheel, hard, and then the Renault was axle-deep in the snow of the footpath between the Stations' wooden grottoes, veering away from the pavement, slamming its shocks to full compression and swimming for an instant, tipping, swinging drunkenly off the road, caught by a drift of untracked snow, tilting, then the chains caught and the engine screamed in low gear: we hit a boulder, all the oil in the sump'll be gone in an instant . . .

*In another moment I'll be dead.*

Prevadello punched the headlight switch and saw the tree branch at the last horrifying instant, a limb thick as a horse's neck coming at him eye-high—

"Down!" a voice shrieked and it was his own.

Prevadello shrank himself into his seat and felt the roof buckle and then, in the last possible slice of time, the Renault's nose dropped and the little car flew down the snowbank and bounced crazily onto a single tire, the driver's-side fender catching the Peugeot square-on and sending the other car slewing into the ditch.

His ears ringing with the shriek of sheet metal, Prevadello felt the Renault on the verge of a spin, but the chains held and they were away, doing forty-five plus on the northbound arm of the crossroads, the overstressed suspension squashing along— but they were away.

"Bonus points for that," Prevadello said fervently, watching the Peugeot wobble and tip nose first into the ditch. In the mirror, he could see Chertkov's head in silhouette, staring backward down the road; fear and a supple back had helped the Russian somehow wedge himself in the back seat. As the Renault slid down the last incline, Prevadello slapped his hands furiously on the steering wheel and yelled, "Hope to hell you're worth it, pal."

Prevadello turned on the high beams. One came on—the collision with the Peugeot had finished the other and the world was white against the night. "How . . . how did they know we were here?" he gasped. Prevadello felt along the dashboard: amazingly, the windshield glass was still in one piece but there was a gale blowing around his legs and head regardless. "You all right?" he shouted to Chertkov over the rush of frigid air.

"All right. We have been shot, no?"

"Nothing vital." Prevadello felt himself shaking; a bullet had clipped Ruppert's best coat and an elliptical gash lay open to the night wind. The instrument gauges still worked—there was still plenty of fuel—and Prevadello realized he was doing nearly sixty on the downhill straightaway. He slowed, which, he thought sardonically, meant the brakes worked too. "Somebody's damn mad at us, Nikolai, I want some running room. Find the map in the guidebook. We're heading north on the D914. Next to the lake, O.K.?" The ceiling light worked; Chertkov's face was at Prevadello's elbow, bent over the map.

"I think we are ten kilometers south of the village of Conjux. Stay on this road."

Prevadello tried to think. That was incredibly fast footwork. Or was this a border incident before the main event? I wish I had *me* working for me, Prevadello decided as he slowed the Renault to make a fallaway curve. He downshifted and let the chains flail the snow as the car switchbacked the stairstep hairpins of the mountain road. The Renault stank of vodka; the bottle had smashed in the mad descent down the monastery path.

Funny thing was, Prevadello had no more pity for himself than those he himself had tracked; his own pitilessness brought him a measure of calm and in that respite Marty Prevadello began to stitch together a life line.

# Chapter Eight

Prevadello tapped the brakes carefully. A veil of snow was falling, washing through the headlights. In the hairpin curve below nestled a solitary building, a climber's hotel, barely more than a farmhouse set into the hillside; downhill, the parking lot lay beside a stand of firs, their limbs bowed with new snow. A floodlight jaundiced the snow the plows had pushed halfway up the pole which held the lolling sign: AU PETIT HÔTEL. The hotel's front bow window was dark but a small glow leaked beneath the curtain in the red front door. The snow burned sky-blue in his headlights for a moment before Prevadello extinguished them, switched off the ignition, and allowed the Renault to free-wheel into the lot: it was just past nine.

"Let's have a look at the canister, Nikolai, see if it's all it's cracked up to be."

"Yes," Chertkov said, his voice small, for he sat well back on the seat, his broad head in outline against the snowy backdrop. Prevadello tapped the brakes once more and the tires were silent.

The light from the hotel sign was enough.

Prevadello retrieved the canister from his pocket and forced its lid. An evil-smelling red flour powdered his hands; the rubber seal had rotted away. He brushed off his lap and lay the canister lid to one side; Prevadello could feel Chertkov's breath on his cheek as the Russian leaned forward between the seats.

"Dessicant's gone."

"Dess . . . ?"

"Keeps it dry. This stuff's slowly rotting."

A fragile roll of documents, brindled with fungus—that was all.

"This it, this what you wanted, Nikolai?"

Chertkov, his head wedged between the seat backs, said excitedly, "Yes, look, there they are!" He ran his fingers over the tight roll of documents and then clapped his hands. "Beautiful, aren't they, beautiful."

"Calm down." Prevadello gently smoothed out one of the documents on his lap, with its yellow shell and the French legalese, burrowing through his high-school French—then it dawned on him what they were.

They were bonds, Royal Dutch Shell bearer bonds, each worth ten thousand pounds sterling, and there were over two dozen of them, curling and crumbling in the aluminum canister. Prevadello did a rough reckoning: a quarter-million pounds sterling compounding nearly thirty years . . .

*Madonn'*: a million pounds.

"How'd you know this stuff was here? This a Center dead-drop?" Prevadello was still looking down at the bonds. "Are you robbing the Center?"

Chertkov looked horrified. "No, no. I put the canister there."

"*You* hid it?"

"Yes. During the war. I didn't know what the papers were then."

"You're an expensive item, now, Nikolai. Let's see about getting you home in one piece."

Prevadello scanned the parking lot—a Peugeot and a Simca, both old, a Volvo under a meringue of snow, a fat Citroen too close to the door. All French plates. On the right, a pair of BMWs, one rather the worse for wear. He made his decision; go with the newer one and hope, despite the German plates.

"I'm going to leave the car for a moment." There was no reply. Prevadello looked over his shoulder and their eyes met, Chertkov's wide again. Prevadello turned and pointed over the top of the steering wheel.

"See that car? The beige one?"

"With the ski rack?"

That gave Prevadello another idea. "Yes. I'm going to run an errand. Here's my gun."

There was a sharp intake of breath at his ear.

"It's a baby Colt, a .32. It won't do much damage unless you aim for the gut. I won't be long. Don't," Prevadello said, "shoot me."

"No, KGB only," Chertkov replied, and grinned.

*And we're in love again:* Prevadello opened the door and felt the wind-honed November cold. He opened the trunk and retrieved his getaway kit, the coffee thermos, and Ruppert's corned beef sandwiches, then gently lowered the trunk lid. Prevadello tapped on the window and Chertkov fumbled with the latch before the window wound down.

"Coffee and sandwiches. No more vodka, I'm afraid." He nodded at Chertkov. "Behave yourself, Nikolai. We can't afford any more screw-ups."

Chertkov blinked but the gun had reassured him; he was ready for the wait, the black nose of the gun steady. Prevadello turned and walked quickly to the BMW 2002 with the ski rack. Working fast, he took the rack off first, tucking it under the back wheels. The car was new, the plates freshly mounted, thank God. M/RW 1567: not bad, he thought. No double digits to stir the memory. Prevadello walked around the car and wedged himself between the front fender and the snowbank. He unrolled his leather tool kit on the BMW's hood and knelt; the front plate came away with two twists of his screwdriver. The snow was falling harder now, but he took no chances, twisting off a fir branch and brushing away his footprints. He left the BMW's rear plate untouched. They won't notice until they get home, he thought, God willing and the dam don't break. Prevadello threw the ski rack over his shoulder and jogged quietly back to the Renault, praying there would be no traffic. Or snowplows, he thought sourly, to wake the night clerk; just my luck if I have to dig the car out as well.

Pulling the Renault's plates from their clips, he slid the single German plate in. After a tussle with the adjustable grips, the ski rack fit on the roof; half its paint had been peeled away by the tree limb. He walked downhill in the dark, to where the hairpin fell away, following the gutter. He dropped the French plates between the bars of a storm sewer and heard a clatter against the stones below. A minute later they were off, Prevadello with the weight of the Colt once again against his ribs. Changing the silhouette, he'd called that once. In the classroom. In a different age.

"What are you looking for?" Chertkov's shoulders were against the window, his hair scratching a circle in the condensation. Chertkov had his hands crossed over his chest, looking dead ahead.

"A gas station." They had seen no one as they reconnoitered

the town, but now a crowd of men and boys, Saturday night hearties, crossed the street in front of the little car; Prevadello kept the Renault moving, ignoring them.

"They will all be closed."

He turned his head sharply. "Oh, for Christ's sake, *think*. We need an hour's peace. Use the guidebook. Find me one off the beaten track."

Prevadello's anger left no mark. "Follow this street around the square," Chertkov said flatly. "I am trying to see the map. There is a station ahead. Next left, past the square."

For a moment, Prevadello actually debated whether or not to apologize: leave it, give Chertkov something to think about, he thought, peering over the steering wheel once more, forcing himself to watch the street corners for signs of trouble. Any other time he would have found the village attractive, with its old brick and chimneys breathing smoke. But the shadows unnerved him as much as Chertkov did: the Russian was very hot property—and the reach of the Center's claws had already fallen short once, which spelled sheer luck in Prevadello's books. The shadows weren't alone in worrying him: so did the two boys on the corner and the lights in the windows and the curtains with the small town behind them. The very ordinariness of the place alarmed him. He turned the car down a side street, then followed the perimeter of the square; a couple embraced near the statue in the square's center, their breaths mingling.

"Look for Rue St-Sulpice." Chertkov was holding the *Michelin Guide* high, to catch the street lights. "On the left again, I think."

"Good. I see it. Great." Prevadello flexed his hands, fighting cramp. There was a big folding door at the service bay entrance. On either side, a bakery, dark, and a camera shop, shutters drawn. He drew the Renault up as close to the door as he dared. Taking the Colt in his right hand, Prevadello felt in his pocket with his left. He turned and eyed Chertkov.

"We are going for a walk, no?" A broken smile. Chertkov was nervy; his voice had lost its professional, lubricated quality. He stank; the thought of having to use the gun at the hotel had sweated him.

"No. Keep your head down, it's Saturday night, there'll be passersby. Back in a minute."

At the garage door, Prevadello reached in his breast pocket for the tool kit. The lock didn't need picking; two shots with his steel hammer and the body of the lock fell out of its collar onto the floor inside. Prevadello considered an alarm system and then dismissed the idea. This is a small town in the French Alps, not West 75th, he thought, rolling the garage door up as quietly as he could. The warm reek of burned oil and then the sweetish odor of axle grease rose to his face. Somewhere a tap dripped. Prevadello checked the entryway and moved an empty jerrycan into a corner, listening. There wasn't a sound for miles. He kicked the failed lock under the back workbench.

"We've got a home for the night, my friend," Prevadello said, getting into the Renault. The little car fit easily into the bay. "I'll be fifteen, Nikolai. Try to get some shut-eye." He got out and listened to the street. Nothing. Move it, Marty, he said to himself. All you need is a *gendarme* on his way back from the tavern and you're sunk, pal. He pulled the door down, lowering it the last six inches as slowly as its weight would allow. Through the doorway off the work area, he could see a phone hanging next to a Pirelli calendar. "You better be manning the phones, Charlie," Prevadello muttered. He felt for alarm wires along the door frame—there were none—and then crossed to the service counter.

The phone worked.

A kerosene heater stood cold in one corner of the office; without the heat, the service station windows were beginning to mist from his breath and Prevadello knew that would set a sharp-eyed cop on edge. He turned from the glass. He dialed the WAVE exchange, knowing he had only one shot at this phone: two tries and the Bonn tracers would have him. "Operator, I need D.C. Station for Kemper. K-E-M-P-E-R. Kemper's on the Group executive list." He hung up and pulled a Camel from his coat, muffling the flash of the Zippo with his gloves. Charlie baby, he thought, you better have the goods this time, or your half-baked operation's going to blow up in your face. Checking his watch, Prevadello switched hands and began to doodle a big question mark on the back of a *MotorSport*.

"Kemper."

"Hello, Charlie, Tom Wade here. Had a time getting you."

"Tom? Oh, *Tom*. Where are you?"

"Oh, I'm around."

Another pause. "Have you got the package?"

"In the pocket, partner. CATALYST's got news." He waited. There was a silence. He's lost already, Prevadello thought, he's got steam coming out his ears, he's thinking so fast.

"What do you mean, news?"

"You hear more when I'm good and ready. And I'm not ready."

"Where are you?"

Prevadello wrote CATALYST in big block capitals then carefully crosshatched it into oblivion. "You must be joking." A truck stopped and parked in the square and the hiss of its brakes set Prevadello's teeth on edge; every street noise seemed huge.

"I . . . I don't understand."

"Well, you sure as hell will. Turns out our friend CATALYST is a GRU translator with access to the family jewels—some minor defector, some milk run." Prevadello linked a series of dots and made a star. "You have any Group teams out here already?"

"No, Tom. Only Geneva station and Vienna, you know that."

"Wish I could believe you, Charlie: you still listening?"

Kemper was licking his lips; there was a dry snick before he replied. "Yes. I'm trying to follow."

Prevadello drew a hard slash across the magazine cover. "Try a whole lot harder, Charlie, 'cause it's me and a Russian tangoing around out here, and I'd really like to off-load this particular milk run. Before I get shot at." Faster, he warned himself; they'll have the tracing computers cranked up in Bonn. "Again."

"Shot at?"

"Shot at. Any news about that?"

"No, Tom. Hang on." He's writing, Prevadello guessed. Or somebody's writing for him.

"I don't have time to hang on. Tell me how I dump this Russian. He's too damn hot for my taste. And step on it, I know about those tracing relays in Bonn."

"Uh, my understanding is that Walsh is already in Vienna, or damn near."

"Walsh? And who the hell is Walsh?" And now it's old home week, Prevadello thought. "You dragged me from a comfortable chair and a warm place by the fire for this one, Charlie. Who the hell's Walsh?"

"Walsh is Group's legal counsel."

Prevadello felt his gorge rise. "Was that the plan?"

"What plan?"

"Was Walsh cut in on this? Was that the plan, to do Walsh's dirty work?"

Silence.

"You tell Walsh to shove his plan," Prevadello said furiously.

"I've run with this thing too far, understand? CATALYST's going nowhere unless I control the handover. Tell Walsh to get on the next flight to Geneva and to hope and pray there's a message for him at the Swissair desk at Cointrin. We're going to take this one step at a time. See you."

"Take care, partner—"

"Tell me about it." Prevadello let the phone drop into its cradle and checked his watch again. The Bonn tracing gear couldn't get much closer than Grenoble in time, if Prevadello remembered the WAVE protocols. He thought for a moment, picked up the phone again, and dialed Geneva long distance directory assistance. There was an oversize wall map of Europe behind the cash register; Prevadello ran his finger across the pork-chop shape of Austria, calculating. Vienna-Geneva by Air Force jet . . . ninety minutes tops. "Swissair, Cointrin Airport, Geneva, please." And, at the apex of Lac du Bourget, Prevadello found a landmark at once isolated and close, a canal called Savières that ran from the lake to the River Rhône.

A harried girl came on the line and Prevadello left a simple message for Walsh, repeating it three times to be sure, then rang off. He stubbed out his Camel into a smear of damp paper. A set of headlights climbed the walls of the buildings opposite, setting the Fina station's dirty plate glass on fire. The car passed, a Fiat 124 roaring in too low a gear, its taillights washing the pavement with twin red streaks. By the time the Fiat's exhaust died away, Prevadello was at the Renault's passenger door.

"Time for a chat, Nikolai." Chertkov was shocky and pale and Prevadello shook the Russian to his feet. "Let's start with your papers." Chertkov rummaged through his coat and produced a bent sheaf of documents.

Prevadello moved into a slat of blue-white street light in the middle of the garage floor, turning the pages. Prevadello waved the packet of Soviet travel papers. "Did NOAH do these for you?"

"Yes." But Chertkov lied badly under pressure, hopelessly, without conviction. The missed hit at the monastery had robbed him of his earlier bravado. He slumped further in the Renault's seat, his elbows on his knees, his hands propping his round chin.

"But NOAH was finished. That's why you ran. Why use their papers?"

Chertkov, who hadn't answered, let his hand flop dejectedly from his face, his hair standing from his head like shorted wires.

" 'Ruben—shtain, O-Osip,' I think it says, Nikolai. Why?"

*My God:* suddenly seeing the whole cynical scheme, Prevadello faced Chertkov. "Because Jews're the only ones who're issued exit papers . . ."

Prevadello stepped out of the light and looked at Chertkov. Utter misery played across Chertkov's face and Prevadello could make out a track of tears on his cheek, dribbling from the misty, blank eyes.

"You didn't kill him, did you?"

Chertkov's tears were too much for his fingers to contain. He nodded once.

"Why couldn't you have taken down a KGB man, for God's sake? You better hope the Israelis never hear about this."

Chertkov blinked and looked at Prevadello, morosely rubbing his jaw. "It was an accident . . . you won't tell them, will you?"

"I've got enough to worry about without Mossad, I can tell you." Prevadello put his arm around Chertkov. "Look, you can't hate yourself for something like that," Prevadello said, hating himself for cheerleading, and even more for saying: "It was operational. It happens." *Don't crack now, Nikolai.* "O.K.?"

"O.K."

"All right, Nikolai, that's better. Facts time: we're alone out here. We've run out of running room and friends as well. Moscow Center wants your hide, we're in France illegally, and Washington doesn't much care one way or the other, as long as we take the heat. So it's unanimous. Which means we had better put our heads together or you're going to end up dead and I won't be far behind. You follow me?"

"I understand."

"We're outside now. I can't keep running with you forever; sooner or later, you have to go inside, understand? I'll have to hand you over. And I have one chance, you have one chance, to get the handover right. That could have been my people back there, you know. Things could be that dangerous."

"It is possible. Can I have a cigarette please?"

"Make it last; I've only five left. If the monastery team were Americans . . . we've got problems. But we can still try to control the handover. We've got the advantage until we go back inside."

Prevadello lit him a Camel and passed it over; Chertkov held the cigarette to his lips carefully but the burning ash still quivered. "Thank you. As you say, we cannot keep running. Where are we going next?"

"Let's talk in the car. We'll take it from the top."

At ten, they left the village the way they found it, the snow falling and rowdy mountain boys shouting and roughhousing in the drifts. Prevadello drove slowly, circling down side roads, doubling back, navigating due north by dead reckoning, avoiding the main road. Chertkov had wrapped himself in Ruppert's favorite beach blanket; he had "Monaco Grand Prix" upside down across his chest. "I will begin now," he said, after his third wordless Camel. "During the war. . . ." Chertkov stopped, his voice collapsing into a sigh.

"Nikolai, we haven't time. Talk. Any way it comes out. Just talk."

Chertkov took another deep breath. "I was a prisoner of war in '44. I was taken from the prison camp, to Lyon, to work in a factory. There I met a Communist named Jacques, from Marseille. He died." Chertkov had stopped again, peering into the night. "His Communist resistance group smuggled me out of the factory. Jacques said the Resistance needed me, they had many foreigners in their ranks they could not trust because they could not question them. I left the factory in a truck, but we crashed in the mountains, near the monastery. The Communist escape chain to Switzerland used the monastery where I hid the canister—I was taken there after the crash. I found the driver in the monastery sick room, very badly hurt. He gave me the bonds, to hide them; there was someone in his group he did not trust. I hid them for him, but when I came back to the sick room, he was dying. He had told me there was one man I could trust in his Communist cell, a Russian." Chertkov snuffed his half-smoked cigarette with his finger, saving it. "His name was Igor. After their colleague died, I was taken to the next stop in the escape chain, a village near the Swiss frontier, Petit-Egremont. Igor questioned me in Petit-Egremont all that day, asking me everything, Stalin this, Molotov that, what did I think of the West, did I believe Roosevelt, turning my head inside out. The next morning he said, 'I can help you' and that night they smuggled me from Petit-Egremont across the frontier. A week later I was in Moscow, via the Soviet embassy in Berne. I was very lucky. Stalin liquidated thousands of Russian prisoners of war who had seen the West. In 1953, after Stalin died, I met Igor on the street in Moscow. I had a bad job translating in a publishing house, very sensitive because of the censors. He told me he would help me enter the Military Institute of Foreign Languages. That was how I became a GRU officer. Igor is dead now, too. His heart, I think, in '64. I went to the funeral."

Prevadello had parked for a time, the Renault idling in a trucker's rest area, well away from the highway lights. "I tried once, in Prague, in 1968, to defect. I was part of the invasion, very confused by what I saw. We had been lied to so badly. I went to the French embassy there, but the man at the door was too frightened to let me in. So I went away.

"Life was very boring after that. Then one day, January 1970, I was swimming in one of the pools near the Kremlin. A man asked me in French if I would have a coffee with him. We went to a coffee house near the Botanical Gardens. He made me a proposition, saying his people have been looking for me for two years. You came to us in Prague, yes? he says.

"I said, what the hell are you talking about, and got up to leave."

"Very sensible of you, Nikolai," Prevadello said.

"He says, no, I have a plan: listen. All right, I said, we'll do a deal: get me a way out of the USSR and I will work for you. This can be arranged, he said. Not so fast, I said, because I wanted papers ready, good ones: this was a very serious business. It took the Frenchman two months to put everything together. Then we begin. I sold only first-class material. Bloc security conferences, Central committee memoranda, briefings for bloc military maneuvers, economic summaries. Hungarians, Poles, Czechs, I spit on them all. Do you understand?" The question was purely rhetorical, for Chertkov stopped only long enough to draw breath. A wash of headlight scythed black crevices and pits on his round face, marking his features with Caligarian shadows. Looking at him, Prevadello remembered that Rappaport spoke French. And had used kids as part of his operational handwriting. And had been Moscow acting head of station in the fifties.

"They loved me. Life was wonderful." Chertkov gave an odd giggle, like a schoolgirl's, glancing to see if Prevadello appreciated the great affection the Frenchman had for his prize. Prevadello nodded, careful not to break Chertkov's rhythm, feeling the momentum of his story carry Chertkov into the world he had invented for himself.

"The Frenchman was very, very clever. At first we used children's sailboats, the kind you push with a stick. My contact brought a boy to the concrete pond. The film's in the hull of one boat. We switch boats and go our own way. In my boat, I get a photo of Swiss account passbook, see the money. The scheme worked all through for the summer of '70, great. That winter, we used dead-drop lockers at a gymnasium. Then the Frenchman's kid tired of boating, so we used a baby carriage, met in parks, fed a baby the film. Great. Then, the laundry. Brilliant.''

"The laundry?" Prevadello interjected.

"Yes. The embassy laundry—napkins, tablecloths. NOAH picked up the product at the pool and folded the film cassettes into the embassy linen. Simple. Clean.''

"Clean," Prevadello agreed, suddenly realizing what Rappaport had accomplished.

"Then at Moscow Center," Chertkov said, pitching his voice lower, "I hear rumors of 'our star American agent' or 'the man over the water.' Just whispers. Scraps. Thin soup, I call it, but hot enough to boil me alive. NATO is a sieve. If the French know, the Americans know.''

"When did you first hear about a mole?"

Chertkov lowered his eyes and probed his ear. "I don't know. Maybe two years. Maybe more. I don't know.''

"What did Center call the mole?"

"RAYMOND.''

"Where does RAYMOND work? Have you ever seen a photograph of him?"

Leaning back against the seat, Chertkov made a show of chewing his thumbnail. He cocked a spume of eyebrow as if to say *ask him*. "I don't know. I don't have everything yet. It will take time.''

"Is RAYMOND a Communist?"

Chertkov canted his head in puzzlement, then grinned, badly, tilting his head, trying to include Prevadello in the joke.

Prevadello didn't laugh. "Love or money?"

Chertkov rubbed his fingers together, like an Arab trader. "He is very bourgeois, RAYMOND. Money, that is the crack in his head.''

And not in yours. Prevadello set the Renault in gear; the highway was deserted again. "Why the French? Why them?"

"The British are blown. The West Germans the same. France had DeGaulle, a very great man. The Russian people need a DeGaulle, a leader of vision, a nationalist. Our nation is disappearing . . ." Chertkov sighed. "The French are a civilized

people, lovers of art and music and women—'' he traced a silhouette in the air, grinning ''—it was a civilized choice.''

''I seem to remember a Reign of Terror in there somewhere,''
Prevadello observed drily. He let the Renault roll down the truck-
stop entrance and set off north again. The snow was falling
patchily now, as they left the mountains for the lake valley.
''And the French,'' Prevadello continued, ''are as porous as the
rest.'' Rappaport, Prevadello calculated, should have a real future at the French National Tourist Board. Prevadello's other
half, the interrogator, had breached the membrane; he was re-
born, operating in tandem again, effortlessly after the time away.
And the ease of shifting back alarmed him. But he watched
Chertkov dispassionately nonetheless.

''The bloc security services had a conference in November,
two years ago. I was translating. GRU has a pool of interpre-
ters—I was best qualified to speak the Balkan languages,'' he
said. ''The Directorate chiefs were gloating about a source called
RAYMOND; they said they had memos of the American's ABM
discussions at the White House. They knew the index references—they could compare RAYMOND's films with the index
numbers to request what they were missing. They even knew
which branch of government used which binder. State Department was one kind, CIA another. It goes that far, you understand? Moscow Center had seven GRU officers processing
RAYMOND's take every weekend for the Monday Politburo
meetings. It goes straight to the Central Committee. They call
RAYMOND Father Frost; every Monday is—the holiday, the
name?''

''Christmas.''

''Christmas, yes.'' Chertkov nodded, waiting, the muscles
in his cheeks working.

Prevadello sat silent for a long minute. They were still on the
highway, the tires leaving twin sutures in the snow. ''Who's
running RAYMOND?''

''Moldov,'' he said simply. ''Moldov's been running him for
years.'' Chertkov was remarkably calm again.

''American Directorate, GRU?'' Prevadello, his voice flat,
might have been asking after an unpopular relative. His eyes
were fixed on the road ahead, seeking space.

''Yes. We . . . *they* recruited him.''

''Why isn't the KGB running RAYMOND? They'd love an
edge like that over the Army.''

Prevadello's eyes came back to Chertkov's with a suddenness

that stayed the Russian's tongue for a moment. "Missiles are military; Central Committee argued but the Army won." There was a pause which Prevadello made no move to fill.

Chertkov did. "KGB grows too strong—the Party had the balancing act going. They had to give the Army a crumb."

"A hell of a crumb—RAYMOND's the whole loaf."

Chertkov said nothing, chewing his knuckles, his eyes fixed on Prevadello. The enigmatic smile again: Chertkov shook his head slowly. He lowered his head and scraped at his scalp, muttering. Then he spoke up. "That is of no consequence now. I want to stay alive." Chertkov extended a wet thumb at Prevadello. "And you want RAYMOND."

And RAYMOND, Prevadello thought, changes everything.

# PART IV

## SATURDAY / SUNDAY—MONDAY

"La trahison, c'est une question de temps."
*Talleyrand*

# Chapter One

Still no word.

Pulling his braided uniform sleeve over the watch given him by his mentor, the elderly, mustachioed general who had worked with Dzerzhinsky himself, Moldov rubbed his good eye; the new salve wasn't working. The pain was so bad Moldov had shut off the overhead light and sent Korilov to the Moscow Center dispensary for painkillers. He sneezed again, wiping his nose on a matted old handkerchief. A phone rang down the hall, endlessly. There was no one else in this wing of Moscow Center this hour on a Sunday night; in the cluster of offices flanking Moldov's directorate office, his coveted red light glowing and forbidding all entry, only the code boys kept watch with him, their station electronically sealed from the rest of the wing; transcribing the Ottawa embassy signals. The phone still rang. Curious. Maybe they're testing the phone lines again. The Kremlin wanted to know everything immediately. Immediately? Good news or bad? What is the use of that, Moldov asked himself; bad news should be savored, he thought. We forget that these days. Savor the bad news—it lends perspective to the good.

So. We wait.

The small clock on his desk made the only sound, its tickings like ice cracking; the hands had nearly reached midnight. Moldov had known real loneliness before, sitting in this chair in this spartan office with its special green desk lamp and his *vertushka*, his high-security line to the Kremlin, now hard-wired to the microwave link in the codes room. Over the last hour, Moldov had broken away from his desk now and then, to ease the stress; he had gone to stare fixedly at the big French

1:50,0000 scale National Survey map of the Haute-Savoie on the end wall. As the news came through, Moldov had penciled in the hit team's track lines on the map himself, marking off the times as the team's Morse transmissions, recast in digital bursts of noise, were read off the link, decoded, and relayed to him on the *vertushka*.

They must be bloody close: the GRU *rezident* had RAYMOND's message and his orders to release the team within minutes of its reception at Moscow Center at two o'clock this morning. The operation had been in place within an hour thereafter, and the hit team had picked up the trail at the airport at Aix-les-Bains. Everything depended on speed now. But even then, the team was working in the dark, and if they lost the trail . . .

I must keep busy. Moldov re-scanned the interrogating officer's Leon case report ''. . . highly motivated by religion . . . contradictory language, possibly a code . . .'': tell me something I don't already know, Moldov muttered acidly. I'm slipping, Moldov thought; when I was young and hungry, I would have been behind the desk against the cellar wall in the half-light, watching Leon's interrogation, making certain the right questions were asked. Or, sometimes, in the more difficult cases, making certain the right answers were ''engineered'' before things came to their natural conclusion.

Moldov looked at his jotted notes and tried to glean from the arrows, questions marks, and multiply-underlined phrases what the devil the young bastard had been talking about. Or not talking about. The attached medical officer's report recorded the drugs administered to keep the subject conscious, including a final jolting stimulant to get him down the homestretch; then the time of decease and the carbon copy of the death certificate for the Center archives.

What a botch. And now it might be too bloody late. Moldov's eye ached. A pulse of pain bounced from his temple to the socket of the good eye and back again. This Leon boy was a fool; Moldov disliked nothing more than fools. Leon's interrogation at the Lubyanka had nearly surpassed the record set last year by the Estonian diamond smuggler, but that one unfortunately died before finishing his ''processing.'' This Leon had died too, but he had yielded more, page after page of material, a strange, garbled tale.

What's all this trash about arks and animals speaking in tongues, Moldov wondered. Pity there isn't a war on: a stint at the front would have done you the world of good, my young friend Leon, Moldov advised, and driven your fanatic notions from your head to boot. Fanatic was right; the boy had withstood the water baths, the electric prods, and pincers for well into the tenth hour before beginning to crack, his replies couched in strange turns of phrase. Speak Russian, why don't you, it would have gone easier for you. But no, Moldov thought, the fanatic has to play out his martyrdom.

Perhaps, just perhaps, I should have talked to this boy Leon myself, without all the processing equipment, led him by the arm from his cell, taken him for a walk around the exercise yard, offered him a smoke. I have a way with the younger ones—a joke here, a knowing laugh there, the jolly uncle. Maybe that's what I should have done. Might have done better. Really, how crude this is. And look at this transcript: all those bloody animals . . . how frustrating it had been. Moldov had even consulted a Bible, requisitioned specially from the Center archive, to try to fathom their meaning. Moldov's headache had grown and a crescent of tears welled in his eye. Moldov grew drowsy and a childhood picture book of the ark and its paired cargo swam in his mind.

Then a phone rang again and this time Moldov realized it was his, the warning light on the *vertushka* winking as it pealed. The voice on the line leaped at him, a weak voice grown tense and fast. "Sergeant Tizkhov here. Codes."

"Report, then." Moldov scrawled a rough circle on his notepad while he waited.

"Geneva's just radioed. The team's missed their last transmission deadline, sir," Tizkhov said, sounding worried. "Should I try to raise them direct?"

Moldov stopped his circling and shook his pen. "No. We maintain radio silence. What the hell do you think the Americans have all those listening satellites for?" He shook the pen again: it *had* run out of ink. "It'll be all right, Tizkhov. Patience." Moldov put the *vertushka* back in its cradle.

Moldov examined the steadiness of his fingers. My old woman's right. The nerve is going. But there is yet a way out. Ten years ago I'd have had the bastard dead and buried by now. The quote from the New Testament he'd been reading before dribbled into his mind: "The tongue is the whole wicked world; it infects the whole body." Suddenly, it might all slip away, the car, the big office with its three phones, the *dacha*, the doctor's solicitous monthly visit. All gone. Attack: I must attack. He absently looked at his watch. *Concentrate.*

The buzzer on his desk sounded and Moldov pressed the button opening his door. A GRU courier officer entered, his face damp with melted snow and his motorcycle boots raising soprano squeaks on the linoleum. Moldov looked at him expectantly, but the courier merely dropped a file on the desk and saluted.

"Where's this from, then?" Moldov asked. There were two big patches of white flesh around the courier's eyes where the goggles broke the wind. He looks like a carp, Moldov reflected.

"Comrade-colonel Chuikov, sir. Sent it over on the double, sir—I nearly spilled my motorbike twice. They signed for it downstairs."

"Get out, I'm busy."

The courier blinked once and left, easing the door shut. The file was sealed with wax and Moldov was calculating the best way to open the file with his bare hands when the phone bell came to life. "Moldov."

The voice at the other end was abraded by the lines.

"Speak up, I can't make you out." The voice became a steady hiss, like the sea. If Security's going to test the lines, they ought to damn well tell me beforehand; Moldov hung up. The medallion of wax cracked and Moldov absent-mindedly tipped the lamp to see better. The file contained a single sheet. As he read, Moldov began to laugh. Is this what I have come to after all these years?

The single page formally requested permission from Moldov as Directorate head to forward the name of Major P.V. Shkarenski to the State Security organs for "further inquiries," it said; Colonel Chuikov had reason to believe Shkarenski was guilty of "moral turpitude and conduct unbefitting a Red Army officer."

He's screwing your wife, Chuikov, and you want me to turn him over to the greens; there's a pig in my office and you're sweating because your wife can't keep her knickers on. Moldov spun the paper to one side and rubbed his temple. Korilov was taking his sweet time. Moldov looked at the big French map again. The team must be damn near on top of them by now.

In the anteroom, Korilov was fussing again. Moldov sneezed, which only worsened his aching eye. "Korilov! Hurry, will you? This pain's bloody awful."

A figure bearing painkillers and a miniature samovar on his

tea tray stepped into the door frame. Great bellowing barks met him—Moldov had another of his sneezing fits, bracing himself with one hand on his desk, the other covering his bad eye; papers spun like maple keys to the floor. "And get me RAYMOND's file too," he muttered between explosions. "Once we finish Chertkov, RAYMOND's going to earn his keep." He sneezed again. "Just like the rest of us." Moldov reached for his *vertushka*.

There was no signal on the line.

Moldov looked up and said sharply, "Korilov! What the hell's happened to the phone?" But the body backing through the door belonged not to Korilov but colonel-general Savinski, the Chief of Internal Security. And, dear God, behind him, in the civilian suits . . .

The grim-faced Savinski spoke first, waiting a moment for one of the suited men to shut the door. "This is—"

"State Security. Do hang up, will you, please? The telephone is quite useless, I can assure you. And have your tea," the dark fellow in the suit interrupted genially. "We can wait." He smiled thinly at Moldov first, then Savinski, like a reluctant undertaker. His companion was tapping the leather between the fingers of his imported gloves with his other thumb, his eyes never leaving Moldov.

"I believe," Savinski began again, "you have a certain Chertkov attached to your office?" The "comrade-colonel" was noticeably missing. Savinski was clearly embarrassed; he opened his mouth to continue, only to have the dark KGB man interrupt again.

"He is a translator," the KGB man said easily, still smiling his horrible smile. "Go on, do have some tea. And take your medicine."

Moldov blinked, hard. It couldn't be. . . . Fighting his nerves, Moldov poured the tea, the jet of liquid trembling as it arced into his cup. Moldov lifted the capsule to his lips and hesitated, risking a glance at Savinski, who looked like death. Where was Korilov?

"Yes, Chertkov worked here."

"And this Chertkov has translated at your side at interservice conferences with our Pact allies? At Warsaw, Prague, and at Bucharest?"

Moldov nodded; he didn't want any tea.

"You requested him personally?"

Moldov nodded again and put the capsule down.

The KGB man lost his smile. He looked at his colleague and shook his head. "Have we a record of these arrangements?" he asked. His colleague, still tapping his gloves, nodded slightly. "They were forwarded to us."

*Forwarded?* From my office? Moldov wanted to shout, but held his tongue. It's awfully hot in here, he thought; I'm having trouble breathing.

Sighing hard, Savinski stepped back from Moldov's desk, narrowly parting the blinds, standing motionless, staring at the night lights of Moscow. Moldov felt sick: *Savinski's going to let me hang.*

The first KGB officer drew Korilov's chair into the light and sat down. He smiled. "Finish your tea, citizen. Then you can tell us all about the translator Chertkov and this NOAH business . . ." He looked meaningly at Savinski's back before continuing, ". . . over a cup of *our* tea."

"But we have tracked Chertkov down. He will be dead in a matter of minutes!"

"Calm yourself, Moldov, please. This is a small room; no need to shout. Did it not surprise you that your subordinate, an officer with access to very sensitive state material, did not report for duty for forty-eight hours? That he killed the Jew Rubenshtain? That he has been successful in reaching the West?" The KGB officer tapped a finger on Moldov's desk. "We have just learned the operation to liquidate Chertkov and his American escort has failed, which surprises me. Does that surprise you, Moldov?"

"Yes. Yes, of course it does," Moldov said, his eye hurting more than he had ever thought possible. The internal, it started with the internal—*and now the greens are inside.*

"Well, it surprises me too. In fact," the KGB man continued "there have been far too many surprises in this affair. There will be no more surprises, Moldov, that I can assure you. We will be making all future arrangements." The KGB officer dispensed with the conversational tone and shouted out the doorway, "Get his coat!" and Moldov saw Savinski, still unable to bear looking at him, flinch.

The two KGB men took Moldov away, using the back stairs and the freight corridor, finally leaving through one of the underground garages. The moment before the *voronok* pulled up in the laneway between his office wing and the Center's outside wall, Moldov looked back at the light in his office. A uniformed figure stood in his old window, looking down steadily, as if he wanted to be seen; too thin for Korilov, too tall for Savinski, watching, immobile. Moldov strained his good eye at the officer, not recognizing him until the moment the van doors slammed shut: it was Ferenko.

# Chapter Two

It was time.

Prevadello pulled his overcoat cuff over his watch and wiped the Renault's front window with the fabric, moving the Colt along the dashboard as he rubbed. There was no sign yet, just the trickle of snow through his view of the short causeway across the canal.

"Perhaps they will not come?" Chertkov smoked the last of Prevadello's Camels, a fingernail between his teeth as he too stared at the empty night.

"Don't make me laugh." Prevadello started the car and let the heater run for a minute. "They'll come, Nikolai. My guys don't want Prevadello the genius on the loose with their prize defector. They'll be here all right. For years, until you came along, Moscow Center's been airtight." Prevadello checked his watch again. "You don't think they'll turn up? Count on it, because you've got the keys to Disneyland. If there's one hand-over they want," Prevadello said, "baby, it's you."

Waiting: he tried to shut his eyes but couldn't coax the sleep into his head. He needed to be physically rid of Chertkov; Prevadello had had his share of bad days in his squad car, but this combination of the compulsive running and the cramped car was unnerving him. *Finish it.*

A set of headlights splashed blue-white on the shadows of the hill behind them and then stopped. "Get down, Nikolai. Come on; take the gun. Don't move. They mustn't know you're here."

Thirty feet of concrete causeway spanned the lift-way of a canal; below, the waters of the Rhône stood black and cold between two great stone walls, backlit by the glare of a solitary mercury light. The canal's mortar beads were rimed with ropes of snow, like chenille on rough cloth. A single railing and half-filled footprints marked the pathway across. The walkway's yard-wide concrete pads lay in the shadow of the great shapes housing the lift mechanism, steel boxes the size of freezer chests, freck-led with key locks and ports for the lock-master's tools. Below, the spillway water lapped unseen, fringed with fine new ice.

The idling Audi gleamed in the Renault's lights on the far side of the bridge—Chertkov thought he could make out the glow of a cigarette or a pipe for a moment, but the pinprick of light disappeared as the car door opened. There was not a sound but the canal water's lisp. The car's driver was a large man, who pressed loose strands of hair to his scalp as he walked. His hands were turned out, his elbows splayed wide of his body by the girth of his arms. He stopped and waved, his features cut like scars by the street light overhead.

"I understand," Chertkov said, shuffling his feet on the car mat. "Keep quiet," Prevadello replied under his breath. "And don't dare leave the car. You're not here, understand. I'm going to try to buy us some time." Chertkov heard his friend Silvestri say something else but missed the flow of the words. Now the heater was off, his glasses were fogging over; he daren't clean them for fear of the man across the bridge—he may think I have a gun, Chertkov thought. Silvestri touched his arm, half in warn-ing, half in good-by, slammed the Renault's door, and began to walk across the bridge, smoothing his beret as he walked, a short fellow with pigeon toes. His shoes squeaked in the snow.

My feet are cold: Chertkov rolled his boots back and forth in the car matting, trying to infuse some warmth. I am going to stop running, he thought; it all comes down to this.

Silvestri was across the bridge now, within ten yards of his contact, moving closer, five yards, two yards, then stopping. He wants to see into the man's eyes, Chertkov said to himself. He wants to see the whites; I wish I could see too. Then they were speaking, in English, slowly, carefully, choosing their words, their voices barely audible through the car window, Silvestri's soft accents giving way to the deeper, harder voice of his con-tact, like cello and bass.

Silvestri shrugged, his arm swinging free, pointing north, to Geneva. His contact looked over Silvestri's shoulder and nod-ded. The two voices stopped for a long moment and then Sil-vestri spoke, lifting his hand to his side noncommittally, as if indicating the fine points of the canal. He spoke at length, his contact watching him, nodding. Silence: the contact shook his head.

Yes or no? Bastard, Chertkov thought. He's lied; the deal's off. Chertkov bit his lip, nearly shouting a Russian obscenity. Silvestri half-turned, jerking his thumb over his shoulder. The contact turned away completely and Chertkov heard a train whistle in the distance. Silvestri turned and began to walk back.

Chertkov shifted his gaze to the other man. Was something wrong? The big contact man was bent over, searching his coat, checking papers; it was typical. Chertkov, relieved, reached behind his ears to take off his glasses, to clean them. Silvestri kept walking, very slowly. Chertkov groped in his pocket for a scrap of tissue and in that moment he sensed the man across the bridge wasn't writing any more. Ten meters beyond Silvestri, standing very straight, his elbows akimbo, holding something.

*No.*

Clasping the gun, Chertkov reared up in the small seat and switched the Renault's headlights on. Below him, on the causeway, the contact froze, his upturned face full in the beams, and Silvestri, swinging his head to the Renault, was shouting something. Chertkov flung the car door open, the gun in his hand, hearing Silvestri shouting, "Get down, damn it!"

Then Chertkov was falling, spun sideways and driven to his knees by a paralyzing spasm of pain, his spectacles catching the light from the mercury lamp for a midair instant before they cartwheeled away, the unfired Colt tumbling away too, landing soundlessly in the rutted snow. Chertkov's brain registered the fall: *Can't breathe.* Silvestri was running, shouting, and the street light seemed to bob and spin.

*Mouth tastes of blood*—Chertkov tried to lick his lips.

The fire in Chertkov's chest was unbearable. His eyes were still open but the light was skidding into a blackness, pooling and spreading like oil on water . . . *I would like to go to sleep* . . .

For a final instant, Chertkov's optics revived and he saw the lilies, bobbing and spinning on the light. Then a darkness far stronger than the first, tinged by a sweet wave of water lily, claimed him and swept him down.

*Merciful Christ:* Prevadello ran, slipping once, balancing and propelling himself from steel box to steel box with the flat of his hand, like a slapstick drunk. There was no cover. *Twenty years at it and I'm under fire, unarmed, and in the open.* He dodged, his body seeking cover in the folds of his madly flapping jacket as he tried to see uphill past the dazzle of the Renault's beams. The car door was open. Chertkov was down . . . *Madonn'* . . . Prevadello held a length of tubing and swung himself behind the bulk of the lock mechanism. He could hear his breath, whistling gasps of mist. He had lost a shoe; he could feel the snow melting through the sole of his sock.

*He thinks I'm armed: he's waiting.*

Prevadello pressed himself flat, then peered carefully down the causeway from the shelter of the steel lock housing. Walsh was moving, not toward the trapped Prevadello, but away, his shape lumbering through the headlight beams, swirling the snow around his legs like stage-smoke, his trousers painted for an instant in white latex. Prevadello stood, rigid, his breath choked off, the echo of the single shot echoing around his head. A high mechanical whine—the engine asthmatically struggled to turn over—"he's flooding it," thought Prevadello.

An oath carried over a new noise: the singing hum of a failed ignition. Behind his car, scrambling up the far rise, Morley Walsh swam from tree to tree in the sea of snow, a smear of black melting into gray, disappearing into the harbor of the firs, into the forest.

*Walsh was theirs.* Prevadello sagged, letting his softening belly collapse onto his knees. Panting, he propped himself up with an open palm, wrist-deep in the snowbank; the fresh flakes dribbled down his glove cuff. "So long pension," Prevadello said to himself, bending to loosen his lost shoe from the drain grille set in the causeway. The distant thrashing in the woods faded into the water-sounds of the spillway below. His beret too had fallen into the snow; Prevadello retrieved it, spun it on his forefinger, and pulled it onto his head. You, Marty Prevadello, have been set up with a capital S: God, how could I have fallen for something so crude? Could I? You bet. Absolutely. Ten-four. He had a sudden chill and tightened his collar. "Morning, Charlie," Prevadello muttered, "and how's the new boat?"

Nikolai.

At the far end of the bridge, next to the little car, its lights still burning full-on, a broken bundle lay in the snow. There was a wisp of condensation, a small one . . . Prevadello began to run.

Beneath the open door, its glass punched opaque by the shot, Chertkov lay twisted, his round face in profile, and half-buried in the snow. Prevadello knelt and edged the Russian over onto his back. He saw the great hole in the front of Chertkov's borrowed coat and felt the stickiness at the same moment. "Mother of God." He lifted his fingers off Chertkov's chest and the blood covered his hand like wax; the steam Prevadello had seen was blood cooling.

He wiped his hand in the snow. No matter how many times you saw a dead human being, Prevadello thought, each was different—you could never be prepared for the absolute singular loneliness of their end. He crossed Chertkov's arms and gently straightened his legs. "Good-by, Nikolai: you deserved better, much better, from me." Prevadello stood there for a moment and then crossed the bridge to Walsh's car, determined to finish what Charlie Kemper had started.

There was nothing in the glove compartment but an Avis rental agreement in the name of Perry. Under the passenger seat a briefcase lay in a pool of half-frozen snow. Prevadello moved the briefcase to the Audi's hood. He slit the spine of the briefcase open with the Renault key, then tore the plastic side off, letting the briefcase empty itself in the center of the still-warm hood; the night smelled of radiator and raw gasoline. There was little for him to examine. A checkbook, personal—name of Arthur J. Perry, no stubs, drawn on an account with a Geneva bank, Banque Carrière et LeComte; Prevadello tore off a blank and pocketed it. There were half a dozen credit card carbons, American Express, also in the name of Perry; a bottle of duty-free cologne; and a day-old *Wall Street Journal*. Nothing, in short, to indicate Walsh had come to kill Nikolai Chertkov but the box of 9mm copper-jacketed Browning ammunition and the spare six-round clip for Walsh's FN handgun Marty Prevadello held in his hand. And why not one for me, he thought.

*Because those weren't Moscow Center's orders:* Chertkov was the prize—I'm just another passenger. He walked back across the causeway to Chertkov's curled body. The snow had begun again and now the flakes weren't melting as fast on the Russian's face. A terrific rushing sound surrounded Prevadello and filled his mind for a mad moment with helicopters, the cavalry come to the rescue, to resurrect Nikolai, to ferry them home to Geneva.

But the noise was only the canal overspill: the automatic sluice-gate was ratcheting open, its gear meshing hollowly, like clogs on cobbles as Prevadello stood over his dead friend. Prevadello knelt next to him, to lift him into the Renault.

Then, kneeling there, the old instincts took over and Prevadello began to search Nikolai's pockets. His Soviet exit papers were there, several schilling notes and one American twenty-dollar bill in his trouser pocket; his Russian overcoat outer pockets held nothing—Prevadello turned the coat's rough fabric back, separating the blood-soaked coat and shirt from one another, and felt along the overcoat lining.

In the bottom of the lining pocket, six inches below the bullet hole, Prevadello found a stiff rectangle of paper. He carefully palmed the paper out of the pocket, protecting it from the dank cloth.

He held his find over Chertkov's body, turning it into the pale light from the mercury lamp.

There in his hand was a photograph, an old one, its treated surface veined with age and wear, of four men standing before a fireplace, raising their wine glasses to the camera. The wine bottles on the table were French; Prevadello could make out the name Médoc on the one nearest the lens, and a packet of Gauloise had been tossed carelessly between the bottles. Something spoke of the war to Prevadello and then he realized a Sten gun hung from the back of one of the chairs.

The Resistance, Prevadello decided, as he scanned the faces. Three of them meant nothing to him, one tall and dark, and rather fine-boned; a short, blunt blond; and an older man, graying, a priest—they were the sturdy weather-worn faces of men temporarily escaping the stress of secret lives, hard, determined men, anonymous in their mountaineer clothing. But the fourth . . . Prevadello had to look twice to be sure, but as he focused on him the second time, there was no doubt about the identity of the young man standing second from right, next to the priest wearing the leather bandolier.

His hair was thicker, and cropped; that much about him was different, but the face was that of the man who had just shot Nikolai: Morley Walsh. Prevadello looked back across the causeway and then down at Chertkov's body.

This killed Nikolai, Prevadello thought, as the certainty held him, this photograph. Walsh shot him, but the photograph killed him. Chertkov's gamble had brought him here, inescapably; what he had trusted as his insurance—trusted more than me, Prevadello emphasized to himself—was his death warrant. "My sweet Lord, comrade," Prevadello whispered as he gazed at the dark comma in the new snow where Chertkov had fallen, "you came a long way to die."

Somewhere in the forest behind the Renault came a clicking

of iced tree-branches, counterpointed by a walkie-talkie's rasp, and from the dark bristling firs one shape detached itself, then another. Prevadello put the photograph in his pocket and stood, medallions of broken safety glass clinging to the knees of his corduroys. Then there were four or five of them, one of them playing a torch on the sides of the trees and the tumbled snow, as they moved slowly down the hillside, easily, like hunters.

# Chapter Three

Beyond exhaustion, Prevadello had first slept badly, then worse, not falling off until dawn in the small Old City *pension* behind the cathedral. The eternally wakeful Ruppert, conspicuous by his absence at the canal-kill, reappearing in the shadows of Place Bourg du Four had handed Prevadello the keys to the best safe-house the Group had in Geneva; an anxious Swiss matron in curlers had greeted Prevadello at the door with a cup of cocoa and seen him to his room.

Prevadello chose not to remember much of the drive from the canal to Geneva. Not that he would have remembered much anyway, after the sedative Charlie Kemper had urged on him as Kemper's watchers packed Chertkov in a body-bag. Un-history, the scavengers, Group's clean-up technicians, called their task. Prevadello watched the scavengers carefully brush over the traces of the two cars and the footprints on the causeway, and, finally, the blooded crescent where the Russian had fallen. A tow truck had come for the Renault, and Prevadello remembered watching the winch hoist the little car and take it away to God only knew where.

Then, in a *pension* bed smelling of bleach came sleep, fitful and shallow. At daylight, the jangling telephone, painfully close to his ear, registered first as the round bell to an imaginary fight; the clang mixed with the aroma of sweat ("get the hands up, *up!*") and the crowd's roar . . . at that moment, the old image dissolved; Prevadello realized the sound was the phone. Switzerland: the rhythm of the bells was all wrong for Manhattan and the rococo plaster over his head certainly was not his own ceiling. Yes, Geneva. He had coughed, spraying cigarette ash from his night-table ashtray onto the carpet. Kemper's harsh voice roused him from the dream and rang around Prevadello's head as the cab deposited him down the street from the Geneva Station. Coffee for breakfast, he thought, as he found his bearings and began to walk, half an hour late for his debriefing with Kemper.

A limousine cruised past him as he crossed the street, its windows smoked opaque, its body work polished as only tax money can make it. Prevadello remembered the arms talks began tomorrow not half a mile away; even now the pencils were sharp and the scratch pads laid out in neat geometrical patterns on the boardroom table tops. He pulled his beret lower, to contain his wild morning hair, unwashed without his trusted shampoo, and pressed open the shiny brass door.

Group wits called the place Lubyanka. The ugly three-story heap was formerly a British insurance company's Swiss headquarters, but as Empire faded, head office sold the place to the American government, at a premium, despite the sacred special relationship. Group had the entire building; in the sixties, a Justice Department branch specializing in laundered money had the first floor but the lawyers were driven out as Group expanded.

Insurance company to spookhouse: Lubyanka, Prevadello reminded himself.

Geneva Station was unearthly quiet, even for a Sunday. At the double doors, a thin fellow with a blond brush cut, pinkish eyes, and a name plate that read "May" greeted him effusively, like a lost cousin; May had been the fur-wrapped novice in the trees with Kemper last night. Ignoring Prevadello's rumpled clothes, May fawned over him and made him sign three separate books. At the far end of the corridor, a small man genuflected before a disembowelled photocopier, probing its entrails. That was it. There was not another soul in the lobby, no extra talent pressed into service at the telexes, no cars coming and going, no ringing phones, *niente*. May flourished a laminated necklace pass, complete with Prevadello's old NYPD ID photo and a plastic thong that caught in his hair. May then summoned the elevator like a floorwalker and grandly pressed the buttons, which only added to Prevadello's growing irritation. The elevator was brass and no bigger than a time capsule, though somehow room had been found for a cuspidor, a relic from the days when Bud Dineen, Group's first Adviser and Rappaport's predecessor, a Texan with a penchant for a chew of Red Man, had run the ranch. Prevadello shook his head; Dineen had retired in 1965.

The second floor was equally dead. Not until Kemper strode from a doorway was Prevadello certain he had it right. Kemper looked surprisingly spruce as he bounced Prevadello's hand in his own.''

"Partner. Superb, as always. The best, really. Come on in, Marty, Catering's done us up a breakfast spread."

"Sorry I'm late. Still feeling a bit fragile."

"Not to worry, coffee's on."

Before Prevadello had a chance to contradict Kemper's sense of the superb, the door swung open and the long lithe shape of Theodore Bradford Rappaport, Intelligence Security Adviser to the NSC, unwound from the biggest rosewood desk in the trade like a jack-in-the-box with a newscaster's face.

*Shiiiiit*, Prevadello registered, *it's the head creep himself.*

"Well, well, back from the wars, and looking hungry. Sorry to cut your dreams short, Martin, but today's shaping up as a busy one."

The understatement of the decade, Prevadello thought, sticking out his hand by reflex, once the White House hears about Walsh's disappearance. Chatting nonsense, Rappaport shook his hand and wrapped a long arm around Prevadello's squat shoulders. The comradely arm was unprecedented; Prevadello had never seen Rappaport look so sleek. Prevadello was mystified: there's been a feeding, he's fat, that's for sure; a full seven courses' worth. Rappaport guided Prevadello to the outsize desk's matching rosewood credenza, where the caterer's boxes had been opened, the coffee cart come and gone—he must have expected the Secretary of State, Prevadello thought. There's enough here for the Secretary's fabled appetite, as well as his underlings, he added sourly.

Nothing had changed about Rappaport. The same relentless ease, the same unnerving ability to shut himself up like a fan, the same classless clues to his life of privilege, the accent, the very texture of his hair. But surprisingly from Prevadello's experience with Rappaport, the telephone was silent. Or telephones: there were two of them, a pair of upright phones the Hapsburgs might have used, a property-mistress's dream, trimmed in gold-leaf, one raven black and the other a dull red, still as sentries to Rappaport's left. Strange; Rappaport was usually tethered to a telephone most of his waking hours. Rappaport had another bite of the *apfelstrudel* and a cascade of flaky crust fell to the desk top; his sweet tooth was legendary. Kemper had commandeered Geneva station's best silver coffee service for the occasion; he gamely poured Rappaport another cup.

"This *is* good, isn't it?" Rappaport commented. "Charlie, cut Martin a piece, will you?"

"No, thanks. Somebody mind telling me why I'm getting the Mr. Wonderful treatment when the operation's all over the floor?"

"All in due time," Rappaport replied calmly. "Don't mind us for a few minutes. Take it easy," he added dismissively.

Prevadello, still stiff with sleep, stood next to the roaring fireplace, sipping a cup of black coffee, while the other two fussed over a dossier like boys with contraband, trading acronyms like Green Stamps—something called the "NIE SLBM estimate" was the hot topic. What the hell's up, Prevadello asked himself. By rights, Rappaport's masterstroke was a fiasco: he'd lost both Walsh and Chertkov . . . plus Lord knows what else in the binders. *I must concentrate.* Closing his eyes, Prevadello tried to think, but nothing came through the warm haze of fatigue. He forced his eyes open.

Listening to Rappaport and Kemper talk missiles, Prevadello hoped to hell the electronics people had sanitized the board room, then discovered he really didn't much care: Moscow Center had had their ear to the wall long since. He sipped at the coffee, looking out the casement windows on the far side of the room. The game's over: it's time for us all to decide just who the hell we are, bones and all. He sipped his coffee again.

Closing his dossier, Rappaport condescended to address Prevadello. "Done, Martin. Coffee all right? Need a refill?"

Prevadello said nothing and shook his head no, moving back to the fireside.

"You mustn't be as down as you look, Martin. You've done damn well. Stop thinking so much. It's over," Rappaport continued, while locking the dossier away in the office safe. "You're exhausted. I promise I won't keep you long." He pocketed the key and recorded the deposit in his daybook, writing in block capitals with a gold-filled pen.

There was a burning knot at the edge of the fire and Prevadello flicked the coal back into the flames with the tip of his shoe. "I'm used to waiting," he said quietly, listening to the starlings' patter outside on the stonework above the windows. For a moment Prevadello thought of spring and spring in a new place; he had a sudden and uncharacteristic urge for the sun, for summer heat and the rescue of shade. The knotwood broke, collapsing in a confetti of sparks.

"There. What's lockable's locked. Let's keep things informal," Rappaport said, leaning forward and making a tent of his fingers. "I'll pursue loose ends—you just talk. Excuse me." Rappaport gave an adenoidal sigh and then blew his nose. "This dry electric heating always knocks my sinuses for a loop." He produced a spray bottle from his jacket and inhaled. "Shall we begin?"

Prevadello looked at Kemper. "This off the record? No tapes, no notes?"

Kemper hesitated, then shook his head. "There won't be a report, if that's what you mean."

"That's what I mean and good luck," Prevadello said. "From your chat, sounds to me like Walsh has been peddling CIA draft copies of missile estimates in the middle of an arms summit, not to mention what he's flogged since Center got their hooks in. Doesn't take New Math to figure CIA's going to want a security inquiry."

"Oh, Martin, you *have* been away too long," Rappaport said, shaking his head. "That stuff's cooked up, it's chicken feed: you know me better than that. You think CIA *knows* they have a leak? Even if they did, I doubt they're going to admit it's their copies gracing Moscow Center's top table by coming after *us*." Rappaport was massaging his temples, smiling a small smile. "Makes for very bad CIA image at the NSC meetings, having your organization leak all the way to Moscow."

Rappaport gave a cynical click of the tongue and looked deprecatingly at Kemper. "Besides, CIA doesn't have too many friends just now." He pursed his lips into a droll grin and tapped the desk top with his forefinger. "And one doesn't intend adding to their admirers at one's own expense while doing a deal like this. Taxpayers' expense, maybe, but not mine. Didn't say that, Charlie, did I?"

Kemper smiled right back. "No, sir. Accountability's the word, sir."

That's what you would call it, wouldn't you, Prevadello thought, a deal: espionage as real estate.

"I know that look, Martin," Rappaport said, his voice deliberately even. "But one might as well diddle the Russians' SALT calculations while one's at it. Point?"

Prevadello said nothing.

"Nice to have my opinion seconded," Rappaport said dryly, and blew his nose. "Ready?"

This doesn't call for preamble, Prevadello decided. "Seems Walsh was a compulsive gambler," Prevadello began, ignoring Rappaport's invitation. "Mainly commodities. Lost a pile playing copper futures. The ponies were too blue-collar for him, I'd guess."

"How do you figure that?" Rappaport, making notes in his minuscule handwriting, might have been talking about the weather instead of his hand-picked subordinate's secret weakness.

"I ran a check on Group phone records—Charlie's, some of yours, Walsh's."

"Charlie, let's have the computer security people in for a chat when I get back. First thing," Rappaport ordered, looking not the least unnerved. "Very enterprising of you, Martin."

"Very informative, too. Walsh called his stockbroker hourly some days. By late '69, about the time you hired him, Walsh was into copper futures in a big way. He did well for a while, I'd guess with the help of somebody's Chile desk. Then something went wrong; he had a margin call for twenty-five big ones in early 1970. We're puritans, we don't encourage our officers to come clean about a gambling habit. So Walsh went hat in hand with his free samples and made his sales pitch to the Russians. I'm surprised it doesn't happen more often." Prevadello looked into the fire, watching the dance of the flames; he could feel Rappaport's stare on the back of his neck.

"Center must have drooled," Prevadello continued. "They knew what Walsh's material could mean to their arms talks strategy. Even so, he had all the makings of a first-class headache, because when Center took him on, they paid his debts—which must have played hell with Center's sense of frugality. Walsh's brokerage records suggest he played for the big one until the very end. Maybe he thought he could gamble his way off the hook before things got too hot." Prevadello sipped his coffee and then rested his cup on the mantelpiece.

"But then NOAH began to crack. Walsh must have guessed Chertkov could finger him. If Chertkov defected, it was game over for Walsh. So you let him betray NOAH, knowing Chertkov would run."

Rappaport blew his nose again. "NOAH was there long before Walsh," Rappaport said equably. "We didn't have to engineer that end of the plumbing; it was already there." Prevadello felt

Rappaport looking at him over the top of his coffee cup. *That* was too smooth, Prevadello registered—there's more, much more. "Why the hell did you never let the security people take a run at Walsh? He was Moscow's man for two years!"

"There is nothing to discuss. Morley Walsh's self-indulgence led him to do business with Moscow Center. Everything else is none of your concern. Clear?"

"No."

"Have it your way," Rappaport said mildly. "I personally have other things on my plate. Just what did Chertkov—I can call CATALYST that now, I suppose?—what did Chertkov want at that monastery?"

"Never told me. He kept calling it his insurance—whatever it was, he thought he had something on Walsh." The lie left Prevadello unmarked and unmoved; the untruth was no more than a bit of lint slipped from the pockets of his memory. Rappaport lowered his cup and carefully nestled it into the saucer. "Speculation," he said briefly. "Your theory, Charlie?"

The tambourine sound of the sugar mill stopped. Kemper put the mill down and chewed a mouthful of pastry, nodding. "A Center document cache might fit," Kemper said slowly. "If Chertkov intended to double back, he'd need to get himself across the Curtain if he ever had to run. Center would have records of passport dead-drops—Chertkov could have found out. It's possible." Q.E.D., Prevadello thought; except this cache was forty years old. And the best of luck to you, plausible Charlie Kemper.

There was a phone ringing unanswered in the office across the hall; a clip of heels responded, then headed toward the elevator. The codes room was upstairs, Prevadello remembered.

"Any unusual air traffic?" Prevadello was walking and talking, moving across the room, drawn to the window again. Below, a rank of cars was being tended by the Group jockeys; an overweight Swiss cop strolled by, ignored by the American drivers.

Rappaport woke from his silence. "Why d'you ask?"

"The hit team had to get out fast, I would think. The French are pretty quick on the draw, aren't they?" Prevadello wondered, one cop to another, what the gendarme below would make of Rappaport: rich American, someone to defer to—no parking ticket.

Kemper cleared his throat, looking at Rappaport, who was occupied with the state of the plaster moldings on the ceiling.

"Yes, well, there *was* an unscheduled Aeroflot freighter flight to Sofia last night, three passengers, all with Bulgarian passports, one in wheelchair, in addition to the crew. No waybills, no known freight."

Rappaport looked at Prevadello with renewed interest. "That pacify you, Martin?" Rappaport tilted his chair back and tucked his hands behind his neck, his flexed elbows looking like enormous antennae on either side of his Borzoi's head. Rappaport's skin was the color of fresh brown eggs; there was a tan line at his throat and Prevadello pictured him, goggled, under the sun lamps.

Prevadello nearly said, "It'll all be in the report," but merely shrugged. "Any action at the Soviet embassy? Radio traffic going through the roof?"

"All that and then some," Rappaport said. "They're transmitting to beat the band." Rappaport let his chair return to the horizontal, bobbing for a moment like a tin duck at a shooting gallery. "Figure they'll want Chertkov's body?"

"Would you claim Walsh's?" Prevadello sensed Rappaport's back stiffen. Come on, Prevadello thought, let's see some fireworks. Rappaport hesitated, a shade too long, Prevadello thought, and then composed his face into his talk-show grin.

"No," he said shortly. "I suppose I wouldn't at that." He rubbed his eyelids. "Must be getting old. These contact lenses are driving me crazy."

One of the ornate desk phones rang and Rappaport waved at Kemper to answer it. So close, Charlie, Prevadello thought, so close—you can smell the waxed paneling and the freshly washed carpets already. Kemper put his hand over the receiver and caught Prevadello's eye. "Give us a minute alone, will you, Marty? Thanks." Prevadello considered Kemper for a moment longer than his old partner found comfortable.

Kemper rolled his eyes in exasperation. "Marty. Please." But Prevadello was already at the door. He walked to the big Gothic window at the end of the hall and there nursed his coffee. Below, across a small square of green, an elderly woman, the eternal Swiss, trundled a barrowful of fresh-cut flowers toward Geneva's Russian church, moving between the bare trees like a wizened Puck. Someone had a sense of humor, Prevadello thought, choosing a safehouse so close to the church's gilded onion domes. Or not; he couldn't decide. On the lake, the boats docked for the winter bobbed elegantly, slender as dragonflies, means of escape in other men's lives, dreams.

* * *

"Airport security, Cointrin, sir," Kemper said, after the door closed. "They have watchers on Walsh. A bargeman on the canal heard the shot and saw Morley in the woods. Interpol didn't pick up the trail until Morley walked across the French border at Moillesulaz, just down the road from here. It's a tramcar ride to the airport."

"Alone?" Rappaport asked quietly.

"They say there's a girl with him."

"Do we know her?"

Kemper listened at length to the Swiss officer at the other end. "Says she's from a Polish steel group in town. Supposedly one of the go-fers, but she's a hood all the way. Pretty thing, apparently." Kemper grinned sardonically. He listened for what seemed a long while and then raised his eyes. "They're boarding. Shall I tell them to move on Morley now?"

Rappaport's cool façade slipped momentarily as he barked, "No!" He was pressing his fingers together and Charlie Kemper saw the fingertips were quite white. "No," Rappaport said again, this time quietly.

Kemper looked at him incredulously, then confounded even himself by shouting, "For God's sake, tell them to make the grab!"

"Shut up, Charlie. I have other fish to fry with Morley," Rappaport said, his voice almost a whisper. "Let Center babysit him, give him a spread in the Lenin Hills—Morley'd like that. Mingle with the Academicians, the upper crust."

"What the hell's going on? Sir." That was an afterthought; Kemper kicked the carpet in frustration, the phone pressed to his ear. Kemper said softly, "The Swiss say they'll bust him for murder if we don't grab him, sir."

Rappaport stretched again, like a long cat. "That'll be the day. Ask your Swiss friend if he wants an extradition tribunal with a dead Russian defector at the end of it. Ask him how it'll feel to have us, the Russians, and the French all mad as hell at a murder warrant he signed. Then ask him how that'll go down in Berne."

Kemper did as he was told, then hung up. "He says he washes his hands of it, sir."

"Exactly," was all Rappaport said. He pressed a button on the big desk.

Kemper was staring out the window again. He felt the door swing open behind him: it was May from the lobby.

"About that flight, sir. I've just confirmed takeoff from Cointrin."

"Thanks, May. Tell the drivers ten minutes. And take an early lunch, son. You deserve it."

"Thank you, sir." May flushed proudly and left.

"Charlie. Get your partner. Let's get this over with."

"Sir." Kemper opened the door and gave Prevadello a wave and watched as he made his way slowly down the rich marble hallway. Kemper took a step outside Rappaport's office and put a hand on Prevadello's forearm. "Stick around afterwards, no matter what," Charlie Kemper whispered, then conversationally, "Welcome back. Just some housekeeping. Freshen that coffee?"

"Yes, thanks," Prevadello said, his eyebrows slightly arched as Kemper took his cup. Then he muttered, *"Cui bono?"* He had stepped away from the door. There was a draft between the window seals, feeding the crackling fire. Rappaport looked at Prevadello, meticulously fitting a fresh Camel into his plastic filter stem; the crystal ashtray already held the remains of two.

"What's that, Martin? Oh, to hell." Rappaport had tipped his cup, catching it with a cuff link, spilling a crescent of coffee onto the leather blotter. He mopped the coffee with a napkin, rubbing at the morocco venomously. "Hell. Get that houseboy up here. No, wait 'til I've finished." Kemper stopped, uncertain. "Damn. Where were we?" Rappaport was stroking the leather with one hand and knocking back the last of the coffee at the same time with the other.

"Who benefits?" Prevadello asked, with more grace than he intended. "Moscow Center or the Group? Or you?"

Kemper did an opera-bouffe double take and Rappaport's eyes were instantly huge, their whites tracked with a fretwork of irritated capillary. You're saddle sore, Prevadello judged; it's been years too long for you too.

"Sure. *Somebody* had to benefit from this mess." Prevadello tossed the cold match onto the fire. "Certainly the Center didn't; they lost a beautifully placed operative in Walsh. And we lost our man to boot. Not forgetting, of course, we lose the benefit of sucking him dry, as the phrase goes." Prevadello paused, imagining Nikolai's way with the Group's interrogation people, all watery smiles and where's-the-camera, the marionette's last matinee.

Rappaport was reaching into his desk drawer; Prevadello might have been talking to the moon. "You know, I wasn't sure you were my man, Prevadello. I suspected you were losing your edge, your will. Becoming a vegetarian." Rappaport smiled winningly. "Your old partner here persuaded me otherwise. And it's time to wrap it up."

Prevadello said nothing; Kemper was rousting the fire logs. Rappaport continued, holding three envelopes in midair, like a magician. "I've made your interest-free loan an even five, there's a credit card for you, and a pair of open air tickets. Take some R and R—you deserve it. My wife tells me St. Croix is the in place this year. And *this*—" Rappaport dropped an envelope to the table top "—is a telex from NYPD, confirming your off-set money."

We own you, his smile said.

Rappaport smoothed his tie, staring at the drying stain on the desk blotter. He reached slowly for the phone, looking up only after he balanced the phone on his shoulder; he licked his lips. "Charlie, close the file. You'll want to append Ruppert's statement." His eyes drooping as he thought, Rappaport looked as if he could fall asleep. He added, "Have all Walsh's subfiles drawn under my signature. Backdate the requests, and see Quinn hasn't kept separate accounts. I don't want some hungry Finance aide getting ideas. What was his secretary's name? Walsh, I mean."

"Jane Carey," said Kemper, who was keeping up rather well, Prevadello thought.

"Have her explain Walsh's filing system and then suggest motherhood. And these binders—" Rappaport flopped the cover of the top one back and forth "—incinerate 'em. Pronto." He hung up irritably. "These Swiss phones take forever."

Prevadello didn't move. In the background, the fire crackled. "So that's all she wrote? Not going to say a few words over the corpse?"

"Pardon?" Rappaport raised his eyebrows.

"He's like this sometimes, sir," Kemper offered apologetically. "It's the Jesuit education."

"Leon, the Baptist kid," Prevadello said. "That's one corpse. Rubenshtain, the Jew Chertkov killed. Two. Chertkov. Three. Probably most of NOAH by Christmas, if I read things right. Call it a dozen, probably more. This wasn't an operation, it was a serial killing."

"You think the operation failed because the patient died, don't you?" Rappaport stood now, very calm, but two purpled spots had risen on his tanned cheeks. "You're getting sentimental. And that's against the rules."

"You want to hear about rules? I'll tell you. All my life as a cop I've had two rules. Rule number one: never, *never* trust a junkie. Rule number two: there's no junkie like a power junkie." Prevadello threw the bonus envelopes onto the big desk. "That's blood money. Give me what's mine and stay the hell out of my life. Both of you."

"That's some ego you've got there, Martin," Rappaport said, very slowly, "but you should earn your enemies. Don't make them gratuitously. I never wanted you for an enemy. Really. Now, if you will excuse me, I have a car waiting."

"Believe me, Rappaport, you're the one enemy I've earned. The hard way." Prevadello just looked at them. He turned and swept his beret from the coat hook with a single arc of the hand. He had to fumble with the unfamiliar lock mechanism for a long moment, then he was out. The other two heard the quick rubbery tweak of his thick-soled shoes on the hallway marble. Rappaport took a deep breath and felt for his pulse, the bloom of anger still on his face. "He know how to engineer a leak?"

Kemper nodded. "In his sleep."

"Think he'd do something that rash? Go to the newspapers, lick the long brown envelopes, all that?"

"I've never seen him this hot. I'll talk to him, cool him down."

"Yes. You do that." Rappaport reached for the phone.

Prevadello twisted his beret like a rag in his hands. The elevator wasn't moving. Livid, he slapped out at the buttons and the tiny elevator perversely began to rise, not fall. Prevadello ground his teeth and began slowly to curse, in Italian, rhythmically, in a careful alphabetic litany of filth dragged from his father's own catalogue of obscenities. He cursed Rappaport, then his narrow-headed ancestors, capping this by complimenting Rappaport's mother's carnal tastes; even, in a moment of Venetian invention, suggesting Rappaport mate unnaturally with the nearest *campanile*. Unperturbed, the elevator arrived at the third floor. Prevadello, cooling, chose the correct button this time.

But elevators have long memories. At the second floor, the doors opened again. There, with the three envelopes under his arm and his tie torn from his collar, was Charlie Kemper. He stared at Prevadello, then jumped aboard, like a man leaping the space between dock and ship.

"Congratulations, Charlie. All your years spent losing at bridge finally paid off."

"Thanks. Thanks very much. You make it all sound premeditated."

"Never missed a free lunch, did you?"

Kemper was sweating, his eyes rimmed with moisture and a yoke of perspiration at his collar; he was suddenly a worried man.

Prevadello pressed for the ground floor and somewhere above an ancient motor awoke. He fished for a Camel as the cage began to drop, fighting his shaking hands, calming down. "Enough's enough, Charlie. I've been peeing on Rappaport's brush fires for ten years and I can't take the body counts anymore." Kemper reached for the control panel and pressed the "stop" button sharply. The elevator hung between floors, bouncing momentarily as the cables took the strain. In the shaft below the cage a plaintive female voice was asking where the maintenance people were; there was apparently a coffee wagon requiring the elevator.

"We have only one yardstick, Marty: results. The bottom line." Kemper sprang to his toes to punctuate his anger. "Nothing else. Who benefits, he asks. Jesus." Hands on hips, Kemper had all the marks of a crossed short man—chin tilted high and eyes darting, he had reverted to the lecture. "Results get *me* through the day, I can tell you that."

In the distance a clatter of footsteps descended the main stairs. Kemper nudged Prevadello's arm. "Give me one of those cigarettes."

"You don't smoke, Charlie."

"I do now. Light it, my hands are still shaky."

A silence settled, broken only by a thump of hydraulics along the liftway. "Thanks," Kemper said. He pressed the "abwärts" button and the cage plunged for an instant before the flywheel steadied and they descended.

"Old Partner's Act, then?"

Prevadello raised his cigarette yes. Kemper raised his eyes to watch the floor indicators flash on and off: he's promised you a plum, Charlie, sure as I'm standing here. And God help you.

"O.K. Let's go for a stroll."

Then they were in the lobby and Prevadello heard an engine start and rise in tenor as Rappaport's motorcade knit together outside. Prevadello remembered Rappaport disdained elevators for the sake of his minor paunch, jogging his staff, briefcases at the ready, down the stairs with him. Through the station's front doors they watched Rappaport, alone, board his preposterous limousine, glossy even in the overcast. The crunch of departing tires rang round the alcoves of Geneva Station high above like a whisper in a skewed cathedral. Neither spoke. Prevadello muttered "sayonara" as the car doors slammed.

"Pardon?" Kemper looked up at Prevadello, baffled, but Prevadello was watching the low comedy between the protocol officer and one of Rappaport's minions as the flotilla weighed anchor. Prevadello took comfort in the omission—the protocol people had forgotten Rappaport's beloved fender flags.

Prevadello and Kemper, neither wanting to be the first to break the strained silence, followed Boulevard Dalcroze down to the quayside, where the cowled yachts hibernated for the coming winter. The first skiers had arrived, preening in posh cars sprouting racks parading up and down the street in convoys. Smoking, the two of them stared wordlessly over the water for a good five minutes while two shouting children pelted past them, trying to fly a kite in the chill Lac Leman breeze. Prevadello occupied himself with watching the water jet while Kemper stared wistfully at the boats; they stood side by side at the edge of the park near the Jardin Anglais promenade, relishing the space after the tension of Rappaport's office.

Finally the children passed. "O.K., then, let's do it." Kemper, smiling grimly, pushed a finger into Prevadello's chest. "You never heard this, get me? And don't cross me, Marty, or I'll have you back in that funny farm up in Maine with a certificate telling the quacks there you've had the biggest relapse in the history of psychiatry. Lifers, Marty. No kidding."

"Go on."

They eyed one another, warily, like two old boxers. "It was the draw play, Marty, the big one we always talked about. Rappaport pulled it off. Chertkov, Walsh, NOAH, the French false flag twist, all steppingstones. Walsh's . . ." He paused and closed his eyes. "Oh, man. What do R.C.'s call the big sin?"

"Mortal."

"Well, that's what I'm committing, believe me. I owe you one, but I have to work up to it." He pulled greedily at the Camel. "Chertkov was bargain basement stuff. Moldov was the one we wanted. Remember him, chief cook and bottle washer, Moscow Center, American desk? Shut up, I said." Kemper raised his hand in a stop sign and Prevadello closed his mouth. "No questions, even if I had the time, which I don't. So shut up and listen: Moldov was the body we wanted out of the way, and damn it, we did it. *You* did it, you were the star fullback in the biggest draw play of all time. *We've got our man running the GRU American desk, Marty.*"

"Hell, Charlie, this sounds like one of Rappaport's fantasies, like the cabana boy at Castro's villa. Remember that one?"

Kemper gripped Prevadello's arm. "Rappaport made it happen, Marty, believe me. We've got Moscow Center minutes one day off the presses to prove it."

"And Chertkov?"

"Chertkov could create one hell of a vacuum within Moscow Center when we pulled him out—and the KGB abhors a vacuum. Can't you see? A logging operation, Rappaport called it; the forest was doomed—we had to make the trees fall our way, he said." Kemper's bruised face had taken on a strange sheen, like the finish of a billiard ball. "A classic, Marty. We let the KGB knock off Moldov and our boy walks in while the chair's still warm. We've got a chance to turn Center's American Directorate, play their entire stateside game back. A wholesale, feed 'em what they eat turning, the draw play."

"I don't care if the entire Politburo's eating out of Rappaport's hand," Prevadello said quietly. "It's not what you do *for* people that counts in my book. It's what you do *to* them."

"I know what you think of me, Marty. I *am* a compromiser. I've mixed plenty of water in my wine to get where I am today. But this one was a classic. I couldn't say no. Even if it meant using you."

"Christ, Charlie, you haven't heard a word I've said. The whole scheme *sounds* great," Prevadello said, "until you figure out that if Walsh and Chertkov and all God's children were expendable, *then so was I.* Kind of takes the warm, chummy feeling out of it. And would you mind telling me how the KGB got on to us so fast? I never saw 'em coming."

"Your first call to me, from Vienna. I called Rappaport, to confirm you were taking Chertkov to Aix-les-Bains. He okayed that and then told me to call Walsh and tell him the same thing—that was the bait. Morley played his only card: the whole operation hinged on his move when I said, 'Prevadello and Chertkov are running,' " Kemper continued, listening to his own words with an expression of great seriousness. "Walsh fell in head-first. He contacted Center—in Vienna, at the airport, that we know from the watchers—and once Moldov knew, Morley was pinned; the hit team was on the way. What an amazing touch Rappaport has.''

''Listen to what you're saying, will you?'' Prevadello put a hand on Kemper's shoulder and shook him slowly for emphasis. ''Rappaport's specialty is cannibalizing people like you, Charlie, anything to keep the game going, because it's like cancer: once it stops, it's dead. Did he promise you a network? Don't answer, I don't want to know.''

''I'm in it for the duration. Rappaports come and go but the Group will always be here. What was that Zen thing you were always spouting? The leaves fall, but the tree remains. Think about it.''

''I'm thinking about Walsh. I want a front-row seat when that bastard's aired out. You make damn sure I'm there, partner.''

Kemper ground his cigarette out, then pocketed it. ''Not the place to litter, Switzerland, is it? I'll have another, Marty.''

Prevadello held the lighter, looking into Kemper's eyes. Kemper took a step back as he inhaled. ''Marty,'' he began. ''Marty, this is going to be tough. I can't explain it myself. We tracked Walsh all the way to the airport . . . but Rappaport's let Walsh go.''

It was completely instinctive, happening so fast he barely realized what he had done. Prevadello's anger crested and he hit Kemper, once, very hard, a good sound right jab square to the smaller man's face. Prevadello felt the cartilage give way and his fingers began instantly to ache. Kemper, groaning softly, staggered against a tree and the envelopes fluttered to the grass.

''You twerp, Charlie. To hell with you and your graymail. You and Rappaport should be sharing a cell next to Walsh, for mail fraud, for starters . . .'' But then Prevadello's anger was spent, draining away: the man knocked to his knees was Kemper, they were old partners, they'd seen a hell of a lot of history, as one of them, in his cups, said once.

They were both breathing hard; Prevadello wanted to shout, but instead his words came quietly. ''You bastard, you stood back and watched, sugaring Rappaport's coffee for him, knowing I was reliving Moravec the whole time, while you both left me hanging out to dry . . .'' Prevadello ran out of breath again. His stomach seemed to be leaking battery acid. ''Crap and disaster. I don't know why I waste my breath.''

Kemper was bleeding; a runnel of blood and spittle tracked down his face. Prevadello reached into his pocket and found his handkerchief, spackled with flakes of dried rubber from the seal of Chertkov's canister. Prevadello shook the rubber flakes out and handed Kemper the cloth.

Kemper moved his nose about, his eyes on Prevadello. "D'you think it's broken?" he asked, his words muffled by the handkerchief.

"I sincerely hope so." Prevadello fitted a Camel into his filter and lit it. "Told you about doing business with Venetians, Charlie."

"Finally got something right, Marty," Kemper interrupted, delicately stroking the bridge of his nose. He pulled himself to his feet. "This *is* commerce pure and simple, and you and I are a couple of door-to-door salesmen from Peoria who've just made the deal of our lives. We nailed BROKEN ARROW. And saved Rappaport's neck into the bargain. We're laughing. He *owes* us, Marty." Kemper knocked a disc of drying blood from his upper lip.

"Owes *us*? Rappaport owes NOAH and Nikolai: don't kid yourself."

"I feel rotten about writing off NOAH, but I'm not God, Marty, I can't fly twenty people out of Moscow on my back."

"We flopped, failed, blew it, botched it, Charlie. We didn't save Chertkov and we've lost Walsh forever. He could have led us to others, made it a grand slam. And writing off NOAH, a decade's work . . . that leaves me speechless." Prevadello ran a finger over his eyes, his anger dwindling to a nugget of resolve in his forebrain: *the photograph is mine.* "Speaking of debts, Ruppert wasn't at the canal, was he, Charlie?"

"No. He refused."

"Old Cal has some kind of class. I still can't believe you watched, Charlie. That was low."

Kemper dabbed his face like a debutante with Prevadello's handkerchief. "Split your own goddam hairs, Marty, but leave my head alone. I've got kids to feed." Kemper was staring now, very angry, the spoiled child. Then they weren't looking at one another anymore.

A man suddenly with things to do, Kemper had stuck out his hand. The envelopes: Kemper pushed them into Prevadello's coat pocket. "See you, Marty. Do yourself a favor and take a vacation, will you?"

Prevadello pulled the envelopes from his coat, keeping only the NYPD telex. "Keep the rest, Charlie." Prevadello pulled a stubbled piece of skin at his jaw. "I thought I knew the man, but I never thought Rappaport would let Walsh run. We made the pitch to Chertkov, we flexed him but good once we had him. We ran him, serviced him, drained him dry. And I got him killed. Chertkov trusted me and I got him killed. That's what I have to live with.'' Prevadello pulled his beret on. ''See you, Charlie. Watch your back.''

Prevadello did not offer his hand. He made his way through a crowd of Japanese tourists to the quayside walkway. He broke free of the shoal of chattering people, stopping to unwrap a newspaper at his ankles that had tumbled across the street like a dead soul. Pulled by his memories, he turned, expecting to see Kemper still standing on the park verge, but the park was empty save the sighing of the pines.

Watching the boats' reflections, Prevadello thought of Kemper, his sloop and his mortgaged life, Kemper, prince consort to a dangerous emperor. ''They also serve who stand and bait,'' Prevadello muttered, thinking of his own word-feud with Rappaport, the last shot of spite in their border war. Prcvadello laughed, knowing Rappaport, of all people, knew him for what he was and had used him, watching him knock the dominos down, one by one. Charlie was right: I wouldn't stop, couldn't stop—I'm an old boxer, an adrenalin factory. But then Rappaport knew the syndrome; he had Morley Walsh as a textbook case of the driven man. How obvious it was, really; odd, Prevadello thought, I didn't see the symmetry before. He wondered if Walsh thought the same of him.

Prevadello could see it now, in retrospect; Rappaport nudging his chessmen along the diagonals, never frontally, gently weighing lives and deaths with his actuarial eye, marking time month after patient month, two steps back, one step sideways, until the final string-pull opened the door to Moscow Center. Prevadello knew then why he hated the man: we hate best those most like us. He and Rappaport mirrored one another's relentlessness. Another symmetry? He wondered if Rappaport hated him.

Then even that thought fell away. The simple fact was that the CATALYST operation was a masterpiece. And not his.

The children had their kite airborne now, its tail diving and swinging as Prevadello watched. As he leant against the iron picket railings, he felt the round pressure in his pocket and thought, Nikolai bought this with his life. The children ran past again, trying to catch a crosswind, and Prevadello half-turned to watch, his gaze following them inland, down the rank of poplars that lined the lakeshore, until they disappeared.

Sometimes the mind refuses to run in predeterminate grooves.

Prevadello continued his walk through the antiseptic streets of Geneva, expecting an answer that would not come. The simple fact is that not until he was halfway through his second-class *pension* dinner of roast pork and frozen peas in an empty dining room did Martino Saverio Prevadello realize that neither Rappaport nor Kemper had mentioned the canister that he, star of street and squad room, had carried with him in the pocket of his grimy coat the last three hours, nor the stiff little image he had nestled at his ankle as Kemper and his men emerged from the trees at the canal side.

*Genius.*

A syllogism, then, Prevadello prompted himself peevishly, as his gravy congealed: the late Nikolai Chertkov, Rappaport's pet spy . . . *former* pet spy, Prevadello corrected himself, mindful of Kemper's latter-day news about the nameless new body in Moldov's chair. Chertkov had a message from Moscow about Morley Walsh's treachery. Half that message still resided in a milled aluminum canister two inches deep and five inches in diameter. Chertkov was dead. Therefore, the canister was a link between Walsh and Moscow—a link no one else alive knew about. Prevadello lay down his cutlery and waved away the clumsy boy who waited on him, his head suddenly full.

But try as he might, he still couldn't see the answer: Walsh had been turned in 1969, that was the received truth . . . but Chertkov had staked his life and his value as a defector upon a photograph nearly forty years old. Nineteen sixty-nine, to Prevadello's mind, looked increasingly like a shaky date.

*Finire la faccenda.*

Aroused, Prevadello climbed the stairs to his tiny room, showered, and then went out again. The night air revived him and declining a passing hack, Prevadello walked the half mile to the Geneva tourist office near the train station. It took him nearly a quarter of an hour to find the Michelin map he needed, but his walk home was five minutes shorter than the outbound leg, so spry was his new nerve.

That night, lying in his austere bed, Prevadello mulled over the mystery of the cracking photograph. And, before he fell asleep with the canister under his pillow, Prevadello wondered vaguely where Walsh was. He pictured Walsh in a hut, a military barracks off a dirt road, somewhere on the plains, in the empty quarter of Russia, five thousand miles from his stockbroker and his rich lunches. There would be a lot of wire, with guards in the towers, he guessed. And dogs. Prevadello hated dogs.

# Chapter Four

The perfunctory Monday morning funeral came back to Prevadello as he drove the B41 southeast from Geneva, into the French Alps, toward the Italian frontier, due east of the abbey where it had all begun. He remembered Chertkov's plain coffin disappearing between two naked elms as the transports rolled toward downtown Geneva on the motorway below, shivered at the memory of the cold dribble running off his beret and down his neck. Prevadello had sneezed and drawn his greatcoat collar tighter; a sleet squall had walked off the lake in gray phalanxes, lashing the hillside. He had blown his nose quietly, thinking of Dante. What was the line? *Io sono al terzo cercio della piova eterna, maldetta, fredda e greve* . . . I am in the Third Circle, that of the eternal, accursed, cold and heavy rain.

Once upon a time, Prevadello had read of a bond between pursuer and pursued, in one of those psychology magazines at the dentist's. Prevadello's memory threw him the debris of that reading as he watched the gravediggers settle the large flat stone onto the lip of the oblong vault with their crowbars. With a bang like thunder, the crowbars shot vertical and Nikolai Chertkov was entombed. And who buried Rubenshtain? Who stood in silence in his memory, who offered a word for the repose of his soul—the Moscow police? And the NOAH people, who remembered them—the bored technician at the Lubyanka crematorium, perhaps, as he signed the disposal chit and waited for his lunch?

Armed with certificates and a scroll with hard wax medallions hanging from its edge (all of which mysteriously appeared in the diplomatic bag, far too quickly for Prevadello's taste), May

260

the pallid houseboy had told the people at the prefecture that the deceased was an American war hero, an ex-POW, who, having found haven there during the war, had asked to be buried on Swiss soil. At this, local patriotism crested and overflowed, paperwork was waived and the gravediggers, paid double time, worked with gusto, their shovels clanking against the hard ground. "Nice day if it don't rain," Cal Ruppert had whispered to Prevadello, as the rain slashed under his umbrella and congealed his rough hair. Given Chertkov's debatable faith, the local judge officiated, an elderly pink man tall as a grenadier, his ankle-length robes snapping majestically under the skirt of his checked twill coat. After this choreography, the judge shook Prevadello's hand and gave him a ghastly wink; Prevadello wondered for a horrifying moment if the old fellow had been in the game and knew Walsh. But at that point, Prevadello might have seen ghosts anywhere. At the end, an oddly formal Ruppert had shaken his hand and pressed an envelope on Prevadello; he seemed to be in a hurry to get to his car. Inside was a card with a bad image of the New York City skyline, whose inside read, "No second thoughts," underlined several times, then, "See you round," both scrawled in Ruppert's big squared-off handwriting. Prevadello had scribbled several phone numbers on the envelope since, during his vigil in the pay-phone booth, sniffling and cold, trying to raise the telephone exchange of the village Chertkov's story had helped him locate on his Michelin map the night before.

Later, after crossing the Swiss-French border in another melancholy rented Renault, Prevadello was still sneezing and still cold, using coarse paper towels from a Geneva filling station on his raw nose. He had been cold during the drive over the border into the French Alps, cold passing through the first toy Alpine towns on the Autoroute Blanche. Prevadello drove warily, checking his mirror, stopping twice, and once, on a deserted curve near Findrol, crossing the highway at the top of a rise and parking.

There he stayed for half an hour, smoking and watching license plates, thinking hard. That last Friday, when Kemper had dropped a dime on him, as the saying went, calling Walsh to spring Rappaport's trap, meant in Prevadello's books his old partner was capable of anything—not to mention Moscow Center. A bread truck passed his post twice and caught Prevadello's eye, but when the truck did not return after twenty minutes, Prevadello, mollified, continued on, massaging the fan switch, in the vain hope of coaxing more heat from the duct. He left the autoroute on the N432, following the secondary road for twelve kilometers along the valley wall and finally parking against a snowdrift in the village square, below the fat-lettered sign reading PETIT-EGREMONT. After sitting for a few minutes, Prevadello slammed the car door and felt the soft new snow subside beneath his feet.

The village reminded Prevadello of the émigré neighborhoods of Queens; heavy women, clad in dark, hard-wearing cloth, impartially fondled the few children and the heaped vegetables in the store windows, as their wizened husbands whiled away the morning with talk in the café, reading the Lyon newspapers and never looking at a watch. Next door to the café was a spotless bakery, whose elderly proprietor Prevadello had seen cross the square five minutes before. A bell tinkled as Prevadello entered and smelled the warm fresh bread; behind his counter, a bright-eyed man in his sixties noisily totted a column of figures on his slate—PAS DE CREDIT said the sign over his head. After a halting conversation in Prevadello's high-school French, the baker, wondering at the thick ways of Americans, barked, ''You want a priest, you go to church''; and went back to his numbers.

Prevadello, who had respectfully heard the *oui* he needed to hear, looked out the bakery window for a moment before leaving, just to be sure. Not twenty feet away, Calvin Ruppert, Jr., his big hands in a pair of red leather mittens, sat watching the clouds pick their way through the passes from Switzerland, his long frame packed in the confines of his blue Simca. Their eyes met, and Ruppert, grinning from ear to ear, mouthed, ''No charge'' and switched on his car's wipers in a mocking salute: *You're clean.* Grinning back, Prevadello raised a single finger and pointed it at the scaffold-shrouded steeple across the square, its brass cupola rising above the peaks. Ruppert nodded and returned to his meteorological studies, a reference book on the car's dash: *nice day if it don't rain* had obviously become a hobby.

The church of Petit-Egremont was dedicated to St. Sebastian, whose haggard statue posed over the door, his blind gaze observing the second floor of the butcher's shop across the tiny square. A row of stained-glass windows stood on Sebastian's shoulders, and above the windows the scaffolding began, ringing the fragile steeple and rusting at the joints; flags of plastic groundcloth floated from the scaffolding, shredding in the wind. Major work had obviously been suspended for some time; no trucks or tool cases stood next to the little church, no rough orders shouted down from above, just the crackle of plastic.

Prevadello climbed the church steps, worn as smooth as the spiral handrails on the thick front doors by generations of pious parishioners. Continuity, Prevadello thought. That's what keeps the old ones here—the ritual is just as it was in their childhood, down to the pale statues and the after-scent of the incense. In the tiny foyer, a young priest, girdled with a carpenter's apron, stacked paint-spattered planking and hummed to himself as Prevadello opened the door.

"*Bonjour, père.* Do you speak English, please?" Prevadello inquired politely.

"*Bonjour, monsieur.* A little, yes," said the young priest. "Most of us do, what with the skiers. Can I help you?"

"I am looking for the parish priest."

"Father Joseph-Marie: I am he."

Prevadello, perplexed, replied, "Is there another . . . forgive me, but I expected someone older."

The young priest laughed and lowered the last plank neatly into place. "Oh, you're the American! You'll want old Father Duvillard, then. He's next door. You're lucky, he's just finishing his nap. Otherwise, if I may say, our curé is not quite so Christian as perhaps he should be. I'll bring him to you." And then the young priest was gone, his apron flopping against his soutane as he nimbly jumped down the stairs.

Candles flickered around the main altar, but the rest of the church was in eclipse. In the dimness, Prevadello could barely make out the expression of the Madonna, whose image never left the eyes of two old women tolling their rosaries through twists of Kleenex, their lips forming small hisses as the beads slipped through nimble fingers. The old ones had not moved, but Prevadello immediately felt recognized as a foreigner, perhaps not in faith, but in blood and tongue. He closed his eyes.

Prevadello did not know where to begin. Begin at the end, perhaps? I am here to discover what Nikolai knew: help me.

Prevadello's prayers embarrassed him. He had come to fear the silence that fell on him when the words ran out, feeling like an actor whose colleague has forgotten his lines before an expectant audience. Prevadello could see the encouraging faces beyond the footlights, frozen smiles wrapped around rigid cheeks, but still the answer did not come, and Prevadello was helpless to provoke it. He muttered a few tentative lines for the dead Rubenshtain, then Chertkov, his killer, wondering how a

God weighed the soul of a murdered murderer. I have known death and cannot comprehend the meaning of my own. Then he ran dry.

"*Quidquid habeo vel possideo,*" he mumbled, from a long-forgotten prayer, "*mihi . . . mihi . . .*" Prevadello sighed. He had forgotten the rest.

"*—largitus es id tibi totum restituo,*" said another voice, rough with age, its Latin flavored with the accent of the Haute-Savoie. " 'That which I possess through your generosity is to be returned to you totally.' That is a very beautiful prayer, the prayer of St. Ignatius. You must have been taught by the Jesuits to know that prayer."

Prevadello opened his eyes.

In the shadows of the church, he could see only the lower half of his interlocutor. The old priest's shoes were badly worn and pitched his feet out like a penguin's. His cane was outsize and he gripped it strangely, well below the crook, as if strangling the shaft, for he stood but an inch or two over five feet tall and could reach no higher without imperiling his balance. He wore an old wool sweater with the sleeves rolled and the flesh of his thin forearms was puffy and blotched, so that in the twilight of St. Sebastian's, the old priest's skin appeared camouflaged.

"Yes. Yes, I was, father."

The priest nodded a head fringed with unevenly trimmed fine white hair that trickled into his ears like artificial snow and extended his own hand, smiling slightly. The effect was magical, the luminosity of the face cleaving Prevadello's inhibitions at a stroke.

"You wished to see me? Père Armand Duvillard; you are Prevadello, from America?"

Prevadello stood and shook hands; the grip was firm and the old priest's diction was the precise English peculiar to those to whom the language comes late in life. Prevadello clasped his beret to his side and said yes.

"You have spent some time inside then?"

A flexure passed across Prevadello's face: "Inside . . ."

"Cloistered. In a monastery, I believe you Americans call them."

"Yes. Once, a long time ago. Why? How can you tell?"

"*On sait.* One knows these things, one sees. From the posture, the intensity in prayer. We French are supposed to have a feminine sense of things, aren't we?" The old priest laughed, a prim ripple of sound, like stones in a tin can. "You are out of practice, I see."

Prevadello shifted uncomfortably, the finder found out.

"We can go next door, eh? I do not like to disturb here," Father Duvillard said as he took Prevadello's arm, but Prevadello was conscious only of a sense of weightlessness at his sleeve. The two old women returned to their beads reluctantly and Prevadello knew he was marked. "—and then Father Armand *smiled*, Marie, can you imagine? Not since the steeple repairs began has he smiled like that!" Prevadello left his unproductive pew and followed the old curé down the aisle.

An immaculate whitewashed house engulfed by shrubbery huddled next to the church; flower beds of mathematical symmetry lay on either side, fingers of cut-back plants poking through the snow. The cheerful Father Joseph-Marie was shoveling the flagstone path to the door. After greeting the young priest, they walked up the path together, comfortable in the morning quiet, Duvillard worrying that Monsieur Prevadello's drive had been safe in the snow. Assuring him that indeed, the Renault was all the rental agency said it would be, Prevadello watched a fierce-looking woman pass the rectory's front windows, her arms stacked with linens. The sheets will be tight as drumheads if that one makes the beds, Prevadello thought, as Father Duvillard opened the door; a sign below the knocker read CURÉ, but there was also a handwritten greeting tacked under the front door light in a tortured French hand. Behind them, a torn plastic tarpaulin snapped from the steel tubing embracing the steeple and a spray of snow-water dappled the square.

In Duvillard's study, the housekeeper, introduced as Louise, came and went, sternly, leaving them coffee and a pair of excellent brioches. The long morning shadows of the pine shrubs mottled the walls of the parlor, casting patterns of gray-green on the white walls. In the hearth, a trio of logs burned precisely, and Prevadello guessed that was Louise's doing. A photograph of DeGaulle stood at one end of the mantelpiece in a simple steel frame. There was an awkward silence for several minutes. Duvillard sat in an enormous maroon wingback chair, still catching his breath, his cane nestled in the folds of his cassock. Prevadello rested his cup on the arm of his chair. Through the spotless window and the gaps in the hedgerow, Prevadello could see the butcher dumping the ice from his crates into the gutter as he shouted soundlessly over his shoulder at the old baker next door.

The priest fashioned a poker face. "You make good detectives, you Italians. It must be your Machiavelli, your love of secrets. You yourself are a journalist?" He peered at Prevadello with his black bird's-eyes.

"Freelance, yes. I work for myself."

Father Duvillard thought this over for a time and then his faced cleared. "Yes. I believe you do." He smiled wryly and gave a schoolmasterish wave of the fingers. "Tell me about yourself, then. What brings you here?" The old priest's face may have been smiling but his eyes were set in a shrewd stare; prove it, they said.

"I am a former policeman, from New York, retired now. I have been interested in Resistance history for some time, and I discovered, through a friend now passed away, there was an interesting war in these mountains. I thought to write a book about it."

"I would not describe any war as interesting," Father Duvillard said crossly. "They have a funny way of killing people." Father Duvillard pursed his face in distaste. "That is not a very promising topic, Prevadello. That was a very ugly time. And in France, there are still many wounds. Even in this little village. Better you leave the war alone."

"When I called your housekeeper, she mentioned you might help," Prevadello replied, equally stubbornly. "In a village this size, there are no municipal records." Prevadello paused, fixing the old priest with his eyes. "The church has everything."

"Including an unfinished steeple, Prevadello." Father Duvillard looked at Prevadello for what seemed a very long time, revolving the shaft of his walking stick expertly between his fingers. "Very well," the priest said at last. "You have come a long way. Louise said you had documents for me to see. Have you brought the documents?"

Prevadello steadied his cup and reached into his pocket for the canister photograph of the four formidable partisans. Duvillard took it slowly, like a relic, laying the stiff image in his lap. From his sweater pocket the priest retrieved a thick pair of half-spectacles.

Father Duvillard muttered something French, very fast, then caught himself, reining in his excitement. He stroked the slip on his thigh, began to speak, and then stroked the photograph again, a cautionary finger on his lips. The old priest shook his head, murmuring. He levered himself upright and moved to the window, his hands on the window ledge. The wind scratched for a moment on the rectory's thick windows and then changed course, carrying with it a cloud whose passing bared the sun and lit the white wisps of the old curé's hair.

Father Duvillard moved to the mantelpiece and reached for his breviary. He prised a small tissue-wrapped bit of color from the book's frontispiece, holding it between his fingers like an insect, as if at once fascinated and repelled. "This is my Legion d'Honneur ribbon, Monsieur Prevadello. Like the men in the photograph, I too was *maquis*. The Resistance. So you know." Father Duvillard returned the ribbon to its work as a bookmark. "Yes. I will tell you what the photograph means, monsieur, if you will tell me how you came to possess it." The priest made a teepee of his fingers, its peak at his lip, and waited.

"From my dead friend. I promised him never to tell his name." Prevadello paused. "With respect, Father, it's like guarding the secrets of the confessional."

His shoulders disappearing as he seated himself in the wingback, Duvillard shook his head. "This is an extraordinary photograph, you know that? The winter of 1943. It captures a time most men can only dream about, when every morning was a call to action, to battle. To glory. Look at this," Father Duvillard said, waving a thin hand over the photograph in his lap. "Warriors, conspirators, dreamers. The war was four years old, but this photograph was taken before the real war started." He looked down at the photograph again for a time.

"Freelance," the old priest repeated, trying the word out, oddly bemused. "It is not the same thing as the confessional at all, young man. Not at all. Let me think . . . yes. Forgive me my vice." He busied himself with preparing his pipe, which he smoked eccentrically, perpendicular to the side of his face, the bowl nearly touching his shoulder. His pipe lit, Father Duvillard then pulled his Roman collar away from his neck, clipping it like a bracelet about his arm and snuggling into the chair, his eyelids alternately rising and falling through the smoke, as eloquent as semaphore.

"You are the first, you know that? The first to ask. One of the Paris magazines called once, years ago, but no one came. And never anyone from America—there this dirty business is only a footnote." The old priest sucked surprisingly hard at his pipe. "I will be dead soon. I thought to take the story to my grave," Father Duvillard said, wistful. Dismissively waving a hand, he continued: "No matter. I cannot write and who but a fool wants to relive the war? Yes." The old priest closed his eyes and tapped his pipe against a strand of smoke, conducting his recollections, urging them out of his memory. He dug a thumbnail into the photograph over the taller, darker man's head, and then shook the photograph like a dying match.

"This one on the left is Paul Lafforgue, twenty-six when France fell in the summer of 1940. He was born in the big white house two minutes from here, next to the chemist's. He was bright, the only child of the wealthiest family in the valley, and charming, very charming. And despite his family's money—or because of it—he became a Communist." Duvillard said this flatly, biting off chunks of smoke as he spoke.

He had his hand over the bowl of his pipe, as if holding his thoughts in; Prevadello let the old priest run, content to allow the circle to close of its own accord. "In a sense, we all collaborated that first year, just to survive, to keep France going. But, in 1940, for the resistance, the Communists had a very big advantage: they were organized, they had networks, passwords, twenty years of Communist conspiracy. The rest of us, the Free French, DeGaulle's men, we were amateurs."

Making another tent with his fingers, Duvillard cleared his throat. "So Paul began a cell of the Francs-Tireurs Partisans. Here, after the Germans invaded Russia. There were four or five of the local Communists in the FTP at first, then some Spanish Communists on the run from Franco joined, and soon there were thirty-five or so, reporting to the FTP headquarters in Lyon." Duvillard sighed and moved his pipe to the other side of his mouth; he was crossing and uncrossing his legs like a restless fisherman as he spoke, trolling for faces and dates.

"I remember the time the FTP and the Free French men marched through the square here in March '43, the week the British planes came with the guns and the gold. In coins, British coins, sovereigns. With the rifles and machine guns we were *soldiers*; we were all so proud . . . a year later, Paul was dead, killed in that old truck of his. The truck burned. One of the locals pulled him out and took him on his cart to l'Abbaye de St-Etienne du Mont. There Paul died."

Father Duvillard said nothing for several minutes and for an absurd moment, Prevadello thought the old boy had fallen asleep. He tapped his cup and Duvillard opened his eyes, slowly, in mild contradiction. "There are four men in this photograph, yes? Griffon, Scorpio, and Unicorn, Igor. Scorpio was Paul's name. Unicorn was our American from London, from the OSS, parachuted in February 1943, just after Saint Valentine's day.

Our American was the only one to survive the drop. They dropped in threes. One officer fell into power cables across the valley and was killed. His other comrade landed safely, but we think he became lost in the ravines. A goat-herd found him a month later, frozen to death. They are buried in the village cemetery. When we pulled our American out of the trees up the road, we hid him in the church basement. He had broken his leg. He was very lucky to be alive." Duvillard shook his head. He delicately rubbed the photograph between his fingers. "I gave him breakfast. He spoke French well. Some of them didn't. I liked him very much. He was very brave and enthusiastic, like many of your countrymen. And strong. A big man. We called him Atlas for his size. He quite liked that.

"Igor, the blond fellow in your photograph, claimed to be a Pole, a Communist from Cracow." Duvillard lay the photograph on his side table. "Perhaps. But there were only two players in our game: London and Moscow."

Prevadello thought he had misheard. "His name was Igor?"

"I did not say that, young man. I said that is what we called him. Those of us who knew who he was. Paul, Atlas, myself. We knew." A flicker of annoyance burned in Duvillard's eyes, then died. "You mustn't jump to conclusions, or you will write a bad book. Lord knows there are enough of them about," the priest said, looking out the window. "Yes."

He continued, "Igor would come for a day at most, never leave Paul's house, then disappear. To Lyon or Clermont-Ferrand or Marseille. Very blond hair, I remember, and beautiful skin, like a woman's: he was *très fanatique*." Prevadello nearly succumbed to the temptation to interrupt but the housekeeper did it for him, shuttling in silently to take away the tray and sharing a rapid-fire bit of mountain dialect with Duvillard before leaving; she never spared Prevadello a glance.

"Forgive Louise, Monsieur Prevadello—she worries too much. Igor. Yes. Paul did not take his orders from Lyon: Igor was his link to Moscow. Paul drank too much *gnole* one night and bragged that Igor was a Red Army officer; that made a difference to Paul, to be working with a fellow officer for peace." Duvillard stretched his legs, steadying the cane with his knee.

"Our Atlas was a big man. It took four of us to get him down the stairs with his broken leg. And strong. But weak at the same time, eager to please, the way Americans sometimes are. Forgive me if I offend, young man, I mean not to." Prevadello bowed and Duvillard, lost again, stopped to pick up the thread.

"His French was not bad, but you could hear America in his laugh. At first he couldn't sit in a café like us; he looked like he belonged in New York. Wasting time, it is an art, like Louise's good brioche. But our Atlas learned very quickly, like an actor. And there was no one like him on the radio: fast, fast like the wind. At nights or when the Militia came, we hid Atlas in Madame Mercier's bakery. She was a ripe old Bolshevik, that one. Paul used to steal flour from the Germans for her."

The old priest held the thought for a moment before speaking again. "But he began to change, Atlas did. He was wearing down by the spring of '44, alone, hunted, his comrades already dead. Despite his size, he had no center, no belief, understand? Paul saw it first, the weakening. He was very good at seeing weakness, was Paul." Father Duvillard coughed and then cleared his throat. "Forgive me. I don't usually talk so much. Yes. The resistance needed money—for bribes, food, everything. London sent us gold coins in pouches, many thousands of francs. Atlas was a paymaster, sent by London to keep the peace between the Free French and the FTP, who were beginning to fight with one another. But Atlas, he was alone, and young, and naive. A simple matter to take what you want and hide it. Yes. So our American began to steal, for his own resistance purposes first, things he wanted to keep from Paul, but later went into business, buying luxuries in Lyon and Marseille—cognac, tobacco, gasoline, blankets. He needed his comforts, so Atlas trapped himself, exposed himself to Paul. Then, after New Year's, in '44, Paul found Atlas's private gold underneath the floorboards of the church, which was all wrong, because we kept the gold in the caves." Duvillard smiled. "Man is such an amusing animal: FTP also thought the floor a wonderful place to hide *their* gold. Paul must have had the surprise of his life—he called me into the church to show me." The smile disappeared.

For a single sharp moment, Prevadello thought the interview was over. But it was only Louise; the housekeeper had returned, this time with two tumblers and an open bottle.

"Ah, Louise, *merci*! You have saved the best until last," old Duvillard acknowledged, stamping his cane. "Monsieur Prevadello. You have made a friend in Louise," rejoiced Duvillard, a statement which failed to persuade Prevadello. "This is *gnole*, our mountain drink, Louise's own, for special occasions only."

Prevadello smiled dutifully. "Thank you. *Merci*, Louise."

"We will be a while yet, Louise," Prevadello heard old Duvillard tell Louise in his soft French. The housekeeper gave Prevadello a frosty smile and left as stealthily as she had come, trailing the dry scent of talcum powder.

Duvillard passed Prevadello his tumbler. "Here, enjoy yourself, relax yourself, is that correct? You intrigue me, Monsieur Prevadello. You look like a hard man, a man who dislikes compromises. A fighter. Is this a good thing in your job?"

"Mine is a difficult business," said Prevadello, inhaling the aroma of the fiery drink.

"I expected a better answer," Duvillard said, bemused, nodding to himself as he poured. Duvillard looked at Prevadello's frown and raised an amicable hand. "Prevadello, Prevadello, I understand. Far better to delight in another's mystery than to presume his simplicity. We are, none of us, simple. Not," Duvillard smiled, "even me. To your book," said the old curé and Prevadello felt a malarial chill spiral down his spine as he thought of the four men toasting one another in the photograph. The drink, far rougher than his Venetian *grappa*, brought tears to Prevadello's eyes for a moment.

Father Duvillard straightened himself, moving back into the big chair, as he nursed his own drink. "Paul knew he could do Atlas's job, not for London, but for Moscow: Paul knew he could control the resistance in the Alps *if he could control London's gold*. And if London's man was Moscow's man . . ." Duvillard opened his palms, inviting Prevadello to see the light.

"So Lafforgue turned Atlas."

"Bravo, young man! Paul did Igor's job for him. Paul was a natural actor. He was really very convincing. And he cut out the Free French, the *Gaullistes*, completely, when Atlas said yes. As he had to." Duvillard drew on his pipe. "But if you did business with Paul, you did business with Moscow. If Paul exposed the American's thefts to London . . . It would have been so easy, Paul saying, 'Work for me and all is forgiven.' London's gold—" the old priest coughed, badly, for a moment "—would have been Moscow's bankroll for their spies in France after the war. Droll, is that the word?"

"Would have been? What do you mean, father?"

"Paul's FTP cell had three purposes: first, like we Free French, to make life miserable for the Germans and the Vichy. Second, the Communists looked after their own; the FTP broke their colleagues out of jail—even one or two out of Drancy, the concentration camp outside Paris. Paul's FTP cell was part of an escape line for Communists and Jews into Switzerland. And last, the FTP apparatus was to control the Savoie after the liberation. Because of them, this was savage country after the war, Prevadello.'' Father Duvillard shook his head, skeptically eyeing his guest. ''You're not really a journalist, are you?'' he asked gently.

''There are four men in the photograph, father. You've given me three. Who was Griffon?'' Prevadello asked calmly, not looking up.

Duvillard was amused; his shoulders twitched beneath his thin cassock. ''Ah! Either you need glasses or you are not so clever as you think, Prevadello! *I* was Griffon!'' He laughed, his tired guffaws sounding like breaking sticks.

''But why didn't you tell London their gold was disappearing? You could have used couriers, the escape lines; you didn't need Unicorn's radio.''

The laughter stilled. Duvillard motioned Prevadello closer. ''Why did I not tell London?'' The old priest rolled up his sleeve and pointed to the blue numbers on his forearm. ''Because I was in concentration camp Neuengamme. The Germans came for me. Myself and twelve others. Only two of us came back.'' Duvillard pulled at his skin, watching the numbers distort as he twisted the papery flesh. ''It was a clever touch, the arrest.''

There was a silence.

''Yes. Paul made a faith of his politics. He knew no truth but Lenin, the same way some men knew no truth but DeGaulle: it is all the same illusion.'' Duvillard paused for a moment and fingered the corner of his eye. ''I told Paul this. I warned him. When we first talked of resistance.'' The life seemed to go out of the old cure. He realized his pipe had gone cold and lowered it to his lap. ''A mistake. We grew apart after that.'' Duvillard looked first into the square and then at Prevadello, or rather, through him, perhaps seeing Petit-Egremont's favorite son. ''I wake in the night; sometimes, I think about Paul. And his soul.''

A shiver passed through the old priest and he made a motion with his free hand, like a drowning man, a gesture of surrender, of the last self-control giving way. Call it crying: there were no shaking shoulders, no sobs, just tears. Father Duvillard wiped them away, but they only fell faster, falling onto the rough cloth of his cassock as his cane trembled and slipped to the floor.

''I . . . I had always trusted Paul to protect Petit-Egremont, his friends, from the worst. He wanted so badly to be sure he was on the winning side, Paul did.'' Duvillard let go his flesh. ''I suppose he was right. We French settled scores after the war, butchered our neighbors by the hundreds after the war, for the crime of being on the wrong side. *Mon Dieu*, Frenchmen were all so guilty then, shaving young girls' heads, filling the police letterboxes with denunciations, little piles of *merde* behind every house." He shook his head. "Loyalty was . . . temporary. In the truck, after the Gestapo arrested us, one of them, a big Alsatian fellow, made a joke, terrible because it is true. I had said true Frenchmen would never collaborate, no matter what. 'After it's over,' the Alsatian said, 'the judgment's easy. Either one has *supported* the winners,' the Gestapo man said, shaking his head at my stupidity. 'Or one has *collaborated* with the losers.' Then he laughed."

Prevadello could bear it no longer. He reached for his greatcoat and prised the canister from its deep pocket. "Father," he said as he unscrewed the lid, "these are bearer bonds, do you see, bonds my friend found when he was passed down Lafforgue's escape line. Take them, finish the steeple, see it done before it's too late."

Duvillard, leaning on his cane, saw the letterhead of the bonds. An extraordinary expression creased his features, half anguish, half relief. The old priest threw back his head and made a dry sound that bubbled into a deep-throated laugh. He's off his head, Prevadello thought, completely round the bend. Still Duvillard laughed.

Opening his tearing eyes, the old priest slowed his mirth and raised his cane, tapping the bonds. "I am sorry, monsieur, but you do not see? No?" He broke out laughing again. "Ask yourself a simple question, Prevadello. This money—" Duvillard waved the bonds "—where did it come from?"

"A bank. Or underwriters, I suppose."

The curé kept laughing until Prevadello's mystification brought his amusement to a halt. "Underwriters, you say . . . my dear Prevadello, how generous of you to offer these to our poor church of St. Sebastian! But if you did this in anything but good faith, you would be in the small, comfortable jail down the street."

"Father . . . I don't—"

"You don't understand, you say? You understand enough to find me in this village, with only a photograph. You will understand, Prevadello—you are a policeman, you will understand. Paul Lafforgue ran an escape line into Switzerland. The last link was an abbey near Aix-les-Bains. But Switzerland offers more than neutrality in a war, more than a haven for Jews and Com-

munists running for their lives.'' The old priest shook the tightly
folded bonds open. ''Switzerland has banks. Very honest banks.
And, unfortunately, a very well-guarded frontier. But Paul was
resourceful. Paul needed money, lots of it, for bribes, petrol,
propaganda, for his escape line. Moscow to Petit-Egremont is
a long, long way with a war on. But Paul had some money—
London's gold sovereigns—because of Atlas's foolishness. So
like a good capitalist, he decided to make more. Those bonds
are a lot of money, no?''

''With interest, over a million dollars U.S.''

''That was a tremendous sum in 1944. Even today, men rob
banks for far less. Does that amount not arouse your suspi-
cions?''

''It's a lot of money,'' was all Prevadello could think to say.

''It is not, my dear Prevadello. These bonds are absolutely
worthless.''

''Worthless? Come on, father! Men died for these!''

''That, sadly, is true. But men die for many foolish things.
There were thousands of these bonds found after the liberation,
believe me, because the Mafia, which knows a good thing when
they see it, forged millions of francs' worth of bearer bonds.
Louise's father nearly lost his farm because of them, so I know.''
Duvillard tapped his cane twice in distaste. ''After the liberation, the Corsicans found out about the FTP's smuggled gold in
our church and helped themselves one night. They took the
chalice, whatever was gold.''

''The Corsicans?''

''From Marseille. The Mafia. *Pour la héroïne*. Excuse me.
For drugs, they used the gold for drugs. They were even tougher
than the FTP, the Corsicans. Steal from a thief, it's always a
good crime.'' Duvillard showed his teeth in an acid smile. ''But
there are better. What could be safer in a Swiss bank during
war? The Banque Carrière, LeComte et Compagnie, for ex-
ample. Exclusive, discreet, a bank used by the wealthy French
aristocrats since Napoleon's day—if you check, you will find
Paul's family had numbered accounts there. Except Paul paid
his with paper, not gold. Ah, but what a nice *paradoxe, non*?
The banker paid in counterfeit.'' Duvillard's eyes focused again
and he returned from his thoughts.

''Paul bought the counterfeit bonds in Marseille from the
Mafia for twenty centimes to the franc, twenty percent of their
value. Smuggling Jews and Communists could be very good
business *if you could use the same route to cash these bonds at*

*a Swiss bank*. Bodies into Switzerland—money out. Paul's escape line ran in parallel with his business, multiplying London's money for Moscow's use. That is all your photograph means, Prevadello. A pity you came all the way from America for so little. You remind me of the other American, the one who came here again after the war, to visit. He too was disappointed."

"The other American? Not Atlas?"

"Ah, another surprise for you." The old priest knocked back the last of his *gnole*.

"This other American, what was his name?"

"During the war, we called him Le Rusé. The slim one, the crafty one."

"You can't identify him beyond that?"

Father Duvillard gave a small smile. "I like you, Prevadello. You are a man who goes after the truth. And truth is as worthless as these bonds unless you have all of it. Here, I make you a gift." Old Duvillard reopened his breviary and fingered the marbled paper of the frontispiece. "The source is not confidential," he added gently. "It was my own camera."

There, in the old priest's thin hand, was another version of Chertkov's photograph. The bottles, the playing cards, the Sten gun on the chair back, they were all there as before. So were Lafforgue, Igor the Russian officer, the younger Morley Walsh, squinting into the camera-flash in a Savoie chalet in the winter of 1943, the rawboned ancestor of the man who had once filled the lens of Prevadello's own camera—and, in Armand Duvillard's stead, on the far right of the photograph, stood a tall, thin man with an angular head and a poor beard . . . and behind the patchy beard was the face of Theodore Bradford Rappaport.

"You are surprised? We took photographs of one another that night, Prevadello, we each took a turn with my camera. The fifth man was the OSS's man in Paris, chief of all London's Resistance liaisons. He was a very good *maquis*, one of the best, Le Rusé: he really understood the French. It was he who came back here, after the war."

"To investigate the bonds?"

"You are catching on, Prevadello. Le Rusé came back alone, to investigate the affair of the bonds for your government. He was very professional, and he left as quickly as he came. Keep the photograph, Prevadello—use it for the cover of your book if you like, with my blessing. I expect somewhere in Moscow there is a copy as well." For a moment, Duvillard ran dry, and Prevadello thought the old priest might finish there. But he pressed on: "Take the photograph. I wish to be rid of it, to be rid of its memories. In the worst nights, I never think of Neuengamme camp, of my friends who died there, of the evil of the place. Do you believe that?" Duvillard did not wait for an answer, moving forward in the big chair and staring sightlessly. "I baptized him, gave him his first communion, you understand? God forgive me, but those nights I know it was Paul's idea to betray me. And that is as close as I hope to come to hell." Duvillard twice tapped his cane on the floor and then stood, unfolding his pencil body from his chair.

"Why keep this for so long, father? And Moscow? I don't understand."

The old priest unclasped his Roman collar from his arm and snapped it into place. "Memories. And," Father Duvillard said dispassionately, "because Igor demanded the negative. Come, I will walk with you to the square."

Behind him, the door latch clicked; Louise stood in the doorway, imperiously tapping her thick Japanese digital watch.

"*Merci*, Louise. See, we go, we go. Come, then, Prevadello, before she gets mad." They piled into their coats while Louise made clucking noises in French as she fussed over the old priest.

Outside the schoolchildren came parading back: lunch time was over. With the dour Louise looking on through her starched lace curtains, Duvillard, with the French instinct for the discourse of the street, led Prevadello down the rectory walk, down the sloping square, chatting as he stepped and placed his cane. From inside the church came a muted hammering. "Your assistant is a good man," Prevadello said. "A good worker."

Father Duvillard smiled. "Technically I am Father Joseph-Marie's assistant, you know. But we hide things from our bishop pretty well. Yes. So. You have your notebooks, your bonds, your photographs, Monsieur Prevadello. But you are no closer to an answer than before, are you?"

"No, father, I am not."

"Help me across the ice, *s'il vous plaît*. It is good to reflect that for some questions, there are no answers. You, Prevadello, must be careful," Duvillard said, steadying himself on the ice. "You are much like Paul, you see, both men made of two men, the man who does his duty and the thinking man. Machine and soul. Forgive me my judgments, my dear Prevadello," the old priest said gently, "but I have had thirty years to consider such things. One does not like to see the same mistake made twice. *Merci:* you may let go my arm." Together they walked slowly down the cobbled pavement off the square as the cries of the Petit-Egremont schoolchildren disappeared into the topless Alpine sky. "Let us go a little further," the old priest said thoughtfully. "I have something to show you."

The posse of schoolchildren crossed the square, their lunch time over, singing and swinging their book bags, girls with girls and boys with boys; they were all younger than twelve. The two men watched the children as they crowded down a passage off the square. "They leave now, most of them," the old priest said. "For Lyon or Marseille, for Paris, for the cities. The village is dying. I am happy for those who make new lives, but it is sad to see a generation turn its back on our village. . . ." Father Duvillard was nodding again, and it suddenly occurred to Prevadello the housekeeper had said "before the war" on the phone and Prevadello realized she meant the *other* war, that Duvillard had been Petit-Egremont's parish priest in the days of dirt roads and horsecarts: he had seen these children's parents grow up and their parents as well.

The walking was difficult—several of the stone slabs beneath their feet were buckled and heaved like ice floes by centuries of winter and thaw; Prevadello was worried for him but Father Duvillard seemed unperturbed. "I am a mountain goat. In eighty-three years, I have never fallen here, Prevadello," Duvillard said, shuffling his feet a little faster to demonstrate their sureness. "It is you city people who fall on our rough *pavé*. And, then, *mon Dieu*, the lawyers!"

Prevadello said he didn't much care for lawyers either and they laughed together, the curé jabbing his cane in the air, skewering an imaginary attorney while Prevadello tried to still his mind: Rappaport knew Walsh had been tainted all those years ago—and had waited, waited for the clock to come around again. Then long after the bonds had disappeared—except in Nikolai Chertkov's imagination, Prevadello reminded himself, slowing as Father Duvillard led them down a brief set of stairs—long after the Center had examined the calculus of Morley Walsh's loyalties and then opened its cold arms to him, Rappaport had set Walsh marching against his adopted generals. And then, mission accomplished, Rappaport had borne in mind Walsh's family, his rank and his privilege, and snuffed the scandal, letting his old friend slip away in the night to the dubious haven of a subsidized existence in Moscow, far from the prying Senate sub-committees and the telephoto cameras and the boom microphones on the courthouse steps.

Old Partner's Act, Prevadello said to himself silently: it cuts both ways.

The village was unnaturally quiet, readying itself for the afternoon business—no slap of café shutter or *quincaillerie* door disturbed the stillness, and Prevadello remembered Duvillard worrying about the children leaving; the soul of Petit-Egremont was disappearing.

"Where will you go now, Prevadello?" Father Duvillard asked.

"I'm thinking of Venice. I have family there. An uncle, some cousins. He has a taverna, a nice place. I think I'll go there and have a good think and some good food and watch the seagulls."

Father Duvillard nodded as he listened. "Yes. That is good; the sea will do you good, clear your head. You will send me a post card, no?'

Prevadello said he would and then Father Duvillard pointed with his cane. "Prevadello, we are here now." Father Duvillard had stopped at the village bridge, its graceless arches spanning an ice-fringed brook. He let go Prevadello's arm and Prevadello leaned over the stone railing, feeling the heat from the morning sun rise from the granite.

"Come, Prevadello, do keep up. This way." Father Duvillard led the walk the length of the bridge, one hand on the railing as he plodded.

Under a jarringly modern brushed steel lamppost, the old priest stopped and pointed with his stick. "Here."

Prevadello had to bend to touch it, set as it was in granite niche beneath the lamppost, had to bend to see for himself the thick brass Resistance memorial plaque, its bolt holes weeping lime, engraved A LA GLORIEUSE MEMOIRE DE *PAUL DENIS LAF-FORGUE*—MORT POUR LA PATRIE 5.12.44.

Lafforgue was Petit-Egremont's Resistance hero, Lafforgue was Moscow's man, a man who sent a friend to a concentration camp for the crime of trusting him: that was the equation. And so it is us, Prevadello thought, this old village priest and I, who know the ultimate secret, the final unacceptable truth, the arid intersection of illusions—Chertkov's, Kemper's, Walsh's, Rappaport's—mine.

At his back, a winter wind worked across the square and the trellis of scaffolding around Father Duvillard's unfinished steeple creaked; not even the birds trusted the jury-rig—a pair of sparrows hovered above the steeple, then chose safer heights. The old priest tapped Prevadello's sensible shoe with his cane.

"Send me your book, Prevadello," Father Duvillard said with infinite care, and Prevadello saw the old man's eyes were shining again as the priest considered the plaque. "I am old, so write fast, eh? Shall we go?"

Prevadello nodded yes and took the curé's arm. The air was balsam-sharp. An oddment of sound rose and blurred in the distant trees, a truck backfiring perhaps, or a snow slide triggered by the valley wind. Prevadello pressed his beret to his head as the wind gusted, and began the walk back to the square with the old priest, toward the watchful Ruppert, toward the rented car parked in the shadow of the steeple, home. The mountain forests whispered again, the echo of an echo.

## About the Author

Brendan Howley was born in 1955 in Ottawa, raised in the United States, and educated at Vassar College and the University of Western Ontario. He now lives in Stratford, Ontario, with his pianist wife and two matching cats.